Resounding praise for

PETER ROBINSON

and

COLD IS THE GRAVE

"A winner."
Houston Chronicle

"An outstanding tale of deception and murder . . .
Robinson writes eminently readable and engrossing
tales which never seem to last long enough."
Denver Rocky Mountain News

"A cohesive, seamless plot that is full
of twists and surprises . . ."
Chicago Tribune

"Fans of P.D. James and Ruth Rendell who crave more
contemporary themes than either master has provided
of late should look no further than Peter Robinson."
Washington Post Book World

Books by
Peter Robinson

PETER ROBINSON

COLD
IS THE
GRAVE

AVON BOOKS
An Imprint of HarperCollinsPublishers

This is a work of fiction. Names, characters, places, and incidents are products of the author's imagination or are used fictitiously and are not to be construed as real. Any resemblance to actual events, locales, organizations, or persons, living or dead, is entirely coincidental.

AVON BOOKS
An Imprint of HarperCollins*Publishers*
10 East 53rd Street
New York, New York 10022-5299

First Avon Books paperback printing: September 2001
First William Morrow hardcover printing: October 2000

Avon Trademark Reg. U.S. Pat. Off. and in Other Countries, Marca Registrada, Hecho en U.S.A.
HarperCollins® is a trademark of HarperCollins Publishers Inc.

Printed in the U.S.A.

10 9 8

FOR SHEILA

ACKNOWLEDGMENTS

First, many thanks to those who read and commented on the manuscript throughout its development: my wife and first reader, Sheila Halladay; my agent, Dominick Abel; my editor, Patricia Lande Grader; and my copyeditor, Erika Schmid. Also, many thanks to Robert Barnard for reading the finished manuscript and providing valuable comments.

While I frequently tweak police procedure for dramatic purposes, any accuracy I may demonstrate in the matter is owing entirely to my conversations with Area Commander Phil Gormley, Detective Inspector Alan Young and Detective Inspector Claire Stevens, all of Thames Valley Police, and Detective Sergeant Keith Wright, of Nottingham C.I.D. Any mistakes are my own.

THE WIND IT DOTH BLOW HARD
AND THE COLD RAIN DOWN DOTH RAIN
AND COLD, COLD IS THE GRAVE
WHEREIN MY LOVE IS LAIN

TRADITIONAL FOLK BALLAD

1

"**M**ummy! Mummy! Come here."
Rosalind carried on stuffing the wild mushroom, olive oil, garlic and parsley mixture between the skin and the flesh of the chicken, the way she had learned in her recent course on the art of French cuisine. "Mummy can't come right now," she shouted back. "She's busy."

"But, Mummy! You've got to come. It's our lass."

Where on earth did he learn such common language? Rosalind wondered. Every term they forked out a fortune in fees to send him to the best school Yorkshire had to offer, and still he ended up sounding like some vulgar tyke. Perhaps if they lived down south again, the situation would improve. "Benjamin," she called back. "I told you. Mummy's busy. Daddy has an important dinner tonight and Mummy has to prepare."

Rosalind didn't mind cooking—in fact, she had taken several courses and quite enjoyed them—but just for a moment, as she spoke, she wished she had been able to say that "cook" was preparing the meal and that she was busy deciding what to wear. But they had no cook, only a cleaning lady who came in once a week. It wasn't that they couldn't afford it, but simply that her husband drew the line at such extravagance. Honestly, Rosalind sometimes thought, anyone would imagine he was a born Yorkshireman himself instead of just living here.

"But it *is* her!" Benjamin persisted. "It's our lass. She's got no clothes on."

Rosalind frowned and put aside her knife. What on earth could he be talking about? Benjamin was only eight, and she knew from experience that he had a very active imagination. She even worried that it might hold him back in life. Over-imaginative types, she had found, tend toward idleness and daydreaming; they don't get on with more profitable activities.

"Mummy, hurry up!"

Rosalind felt just the slightest tingle of apprehension, as if something were about to change forever in her universe. Shaking off the feeling, she wiped her hands of the oily stuffing, took a quick sip of gin and tonic, then walked toward the study, where Benjamin had been playing on the computer. As she did so, she heard the front door open and her husband call out that he was home. Early. She frowned. Was he checking up on her?

Ignoring him for the moment, she went to see what on earth Benjamin was talking about.

"Look," the boy said as she walked into the room. "It *is* our lass." He pointed at the computer screen.

"Don't talk like that," Rosalind said. "I've told you before. It's common."

Then she looked.

At first, she was simply shocked to see the screen filled with the image of a naked woman. How had Benjamin stumbled onto such a site? He wasn't even old enough to understand what he had found.

Then, as she leaned over his shoulder and peered more closely at the screen, she gasped. He was right. She was looking at a picture of her daughter, Emily, naked as the day she was born, but with considerably more curves, a tattoo and a wispy patch of blond pubic hair between her legs. That it was her Emily, there was no mistake; the teardrop-shaped birthmark on the inside of her left thigh proved it.

Rosalind ran her hand through her hair. What was this all about? What was happening? She glanced briefly at the URL on top of the screen. She had a photographic memory, so she knew she wouldn't forget it.

"See," said Benjamin. "It is our lass, isn't it. What's she doing without any clothes on, Mummy?"

Then Rosalind panicked. My God, *he* mustn't see this. Emily's father. He mustn't be allowed to see it. It would destroy him. Quickly, she reached toward the mouse, but before her fingers could click on it, a deep voice behind her told her it was too late.

"What on earth's going on?" he asked mildly, putting a fatherly hand on his son's shoulder.

Then, after the briefest of silences, Rosalind heard the sharp intake of breath and knew that he had the answer.

His hand tightened and Benjamin flinched. "Daddy, you're hurting me."

But Chief Constable Jeremiah Riddle was oblivious to his son's pain. "My God!" he gasped, pointing at the screen. "Is that who I think it is?"

Detective Chief Inspector Alan Banks paused over his holdall, wondering whether he should take the leather jacket or the Windcheater. There wasn't room for both. He wasn't sure how cold it would be. Probably no different from Yorkshire, he guessed. At most, perhaps a couple of degrees warmer. Still, you never could tell with November. In the end, he decided he *could* take both. He folded the Windcheater and put it on top of the shirts he had already packed, then he pressed down hard on the contents before dragging the reluctant zip shut. It seemed a lot for just one weekend away from home, but it all fitted into one not-too-heavy bag. He would wear his leather jacket on the journey.

All he had to do now was choose a book and a few tapes. He probably wouldn't need them, but he didn't like to travel anywhere without something to read and something to listen to in case of delays or emergencies.

It was a lesson he had learned the hard way, having once spent four hours in the casualty department of a large London hospital on a Saturday night waiting to have six stitches sewn beside his right eye. All that time, he had held the

gauze pad to stanch the bleeding and watched the endless
supply of drug overdoses, attempted suicides, heart-attack
victims and road accidents going in before him. That their
wounds were far more serious and merited more urgent
treatment than his minor cut, Banks never had a moment's
doubt, but he wished to hell there had been something to
read in the dingy waiting area other than a copy of the previous day's *Daily Mirror*. The person who had read it before
him had even filled in the crossword. *In ink.*

But tomorrow he was going to Paris with his daughter
Tracy for a long weekend of art galleries, museums and
walks, of sumptuous dinners in small Left Bank restaurants
and idle beers at zinc-topped counters in Montmartre, looking out on the crowds passing by. They were going to take
the Eurostar, which Banks had managed to book practically
for free through a special newspaper offer. After all, it *was*
November, and most people preferred Lanzarote to a wet
weekend in Paris. He probably wouldn't need much in the
way of music or books, except when he was alone in his
room before bed, but he decided to err on the side of caution.

Banks carried the holdall downstairs and dug out a couple of extra batteries from the sideboard drawer. He slipped
them in the side pouch, along with the Walkman itself, then
picked out tapes he had made of his Cassandra Wilson,
Dawn Upshaw and Lucinda Williams CDs. Three more different women's voices and styles you probably couldn't find
anywhere on earth, but he liked them all, and between them
they covered a wide range of moods. He cast an eye over the
low bookshelf and picked out Simenon's *Maigret and the
Hundred Gibbets*. He didn't usually read crime novels, but
the title had caught his eye and someone had once told him
that he had a lot in common with Maigret. Besides, he assumed that it was set in Paris.

When Banks had finished packing, he poured himself a
couple of fingers of Laphroaig and put on Bill Evans's
Waltz for Debby CD. Then he sat in his armchair beside the
shaded reading lamp, balanced the whiskey on the arm and
put his feet up as "My Foolish Heart" made its hesitant
progress. A few lumps of peat burned in the fireplace, its

smell harmonizing with the smoky bite of the Islay malt on his tongue.

But too much smoke seemed to be drifting from the fireplace into the room. Banks wondered if he needed a chimney sweep, as a fire probably hadn't been lit in that grate for a long time. He had no idea how to find a sweep, nor did he even know if such an exotic creature still existed. He remembered being fascinated as a child when the chimney sweep came, and his mother covered everything in the room with old sheets. Banks was allowed to watch the strange, soot-faced man fit the extensions on his long thick brush as he pushed it up the tall chimney, but he had to leave the room before the real work began. Later, when he read about the Victorian practice of sending young boys naked up the chimneys, he always wondered about that chimney sweep, if he had ever done anything like that. In the end, he realized the man couldn't have been old enough to have been alive so long ago, no matter how ancient he had seemed to the awestruck young boy.

He decided that the chimney was fine, and it was probably just the wind blowing some smoke back down. He could hear it howling around the thick walls, rattling the loose window in the spare bedroom upstairs, spattering the panes with rain. Since there had been so much rain lately, Banks could also hear the rushing of Gratly Falls outside his cottage. They were nothing grand, only a series of shallow terraces, none more than four or five feet high, that ran diagonally through the village where the beck ran down the daleside to join the river Swain in Helmthorpe. But the music changed constantly and proved a great delight to Banks, especially when he was lying in bed having trouble getting to sleep.

Glad he didn't have to go out again that evening, Banks sat and sipped his single malt, listening to the familiar lyrical opening of "Waltz for Debby." His mind drifted to the problem that had been looming larger and larger ever since his last case, which had been a one-off job, designed to make him fail and look like a fool.

He hadn't failed, and consequently Chief Constable Riddle, who had hated Banks from the start, was even more pissed off at him than ever now. Banks found himself back in the career doldrums, chained to his desk and with no prospect of action in the foreseeable future. It was getting to be a bore.

And he could see only one way out.

Loath as Banks was to leave Yorkshire, especially after so recently buying the cottage, he was fast coming to admit that his days there seemed numbered. Last week, after thinking long and hard, he had put in his application to the National Crime Squad, which had been designed to target organized crime. As a DCI, Banks would hardly be involved in under-cover work, but he *would* be in a position to run operations and enjoy the adrenaline high when a big catch finally landed. The job would also involve travel, tracking British criminals who operated from headquarters in Holland, the Dordogne and Spain.

Banks knew he didn't have a good enough educational background for the job, lacking a degree, but he did have the experience, and he thought that might still count for some-thing, despite Riddle. He knew he could do the "hard sums," the language, number and management tests necessary for the job, and he thought he could count on excellent refer-ences from everyone else he had worked with in Yorkshire, including his immediate commanding officer, Detective Su-perintendent Gristhorpe, and the Director of Human Re-sources, Millicent Cummings. He only hoped that the negative report he was bound to get from Riddle would seem suspicious by its difference.

There was another reason for the change, too. Banks had thought a lot about his estranged wife Sandra over the past couple of months, and he had come to believe that their separation might be only temporary. A major change in his circumstances, such as a posting to the NCS, would certainly be of benefit. It would mean moving somewhere else, maybe back to London, and Sandra loved London. He felt there was a real chance to put things right now, put the silliness of the past year behind them. Banks had had his brief romance with Annie Cabbot, and Sandra hers with Sean. That Sandra was still living with Sean didn't weigh unduly on his mind. People often drifted along in relationships, lacking the courage or the initiative to go it alone. He was certain that she would come to see things differently when he presented her with his plan for the future.

When the telephone rang at nine o'clock, startling him out of Bill Evans's deft keyboard meanderings, he thought at first that it might be Tracy. He hoped she hadn't changed her mind about the weekend; he needed to talk to her about the future, to enlist her help in getting Sandra back.

It wasn't Tracy. It was Chief Constable Jeremiah "Jimmy" Riddle, the very reason Banks had gone so far as to contemplate selling his cottage and leaving the county.

"Banks?"

Banks gritted his teeth. "Sir?"

Riddle paused. "I'd like to ask you a favor."

Banks's jaw dropped. "A favor?"

"Yes. Do you think . . . I mean, would you mind dropping by the house? It's very important. I wouldn't ask otherwise. Not on such a wretched night as this."

Banks's mind reeled. Riddle had *never* spoken to him in such a polite manner before, with such a fragile edge to his voice. What on earth was going on? Another trick?

"It's late, sir," Banks said. "I'm tired, and I'm supposed to be—"

"Look, I'm asking you for a favor, man. My wife and I have had to cancel a very important dinner party at the last minute because of this. Can't you just for once put aside your bloody-mindedness and oblige me?"

That sounded more like the Jimmy Riddle of old. Banks was on the verge of telling him to fuck off when the CC's tone changed once again and threw him off balance. "Please, Banks," Riddle said. "There's something I need to talk to you about. Something urgent. Don't worry. This isn't a trick. I'm not out to put one over on you. I give you my word. I honestly need your help."

Surely even Riddle wouldn't stoop to pulling a stunt like this solely to humiliate him? Now Banks was curious, and he knew he would go. If he were the kind of man who could ignore a call so full of mystery, he had no business being a copper in the first place. He didn't want to go out into the foul night, didn't want to leave his Laphroaig, Bill Evans and the crackling peat fire, but he knew he had to. He put his glass aside, glad that he had drunk only the one small whiskey all day.

"All right," he said, reaching for the pencil and paper beside the telephone. "But you'd better tell me where you live and give me directions. I don't believe I've ever been invited to your home before."

Riddle lived about halfway between Eastvale and Northallerton, which meant an hour's drive for Banks in good weather, but well over that tonight. The rain was coming down in buckets; his windscreen wipers worked overtime the whole way, and there were times when he could hardly see more than a few yards ahead. It was only two days before Bonfire Night, and the piles of wood and discarded furniture were getting soaked on the village greens.

The Riddle house was a listed building, called the Old Mill because it had been built originally as a mill by Cistercian monks from the nearby abbey. Made of limestone, with a flagstone roof, it stood beside the millrace, which came rushing down through the garden. The old stone barn on the other side of the house had been converted into a garage.

As Banks drove up the short gravel drive and pulled up, he noticed that there were lights showing in two of the downstairs windows, while the rest of the place was in darkness. Almost before he could knock, the door jerked open and he found himself ushered inside a dim hallway, where Riddle took his coat without ceremony and led him through to a living room bigger than Banks's entire cottage. It was all exposed beams and whitewashed walls decked with polished hunting horns and the inevitable horse brasses. A gilt-framed mirror hung above the Adam fireplace, where a fire roared, and a baby grand piano stood by the mullioned bay window.

It was very much the kind of house Banks would associate with someone pulling in a hundred grand a year or more, but for all its rusticity, and for all the heat the fire threw out, it was a curiously cold, bleak and impersonal kind of room. There were no magazines or newspapers scattered on the low glass-topped table, and no messy piles of sheet music by the piano; the woodwork gleamed as if it had been waxed just moments ago, and everything was neat, clean and orderly. Which, come to think of it, was exactly what Banks would have expected from Riddle. This effect was heightened by the silence, broken only by the occasional howling of the wind outside and the rain spattering against the windows.

A woman walked into the room

"My wife, Rosalind," said Riddle.

Banks shook Rosalind's hand. It was soft, but her grip was firm. If this was shaping up to be a night of surprises, Rosalind Riddle was the second.

Banks had never met the chief constable's wife before—all he knew about her was that she worked with a firm of Eastvale solicitors specializing in property conveyancing—and if he had ever given a passing thought to her, he might have imagined a stout, sturdy and rather characterless figure. Why, he didn't know, but that was the image that came to mind.

The woman who stood before him, however, was elegant and tall, with a model's slim figure and long shapely legs. She was casually dressed in a gray skirt and a white silk blouse, and the two buttons open at the top revealed a V of skin as pale as her complexion. She had short blond hair—the expensive, shaggy kind of short, and the highlit sort of blond—a high forehead, prominent cheekbones and dark blue eyes. Her lips were fuller than one would expect in the kind of face she had, and the lipstick made them seem even more so, giving the impression of a pout.

Her expression revealed nothing, but Banks could tell from her brusque body language that she was distraught. She set her drink on the table and sat on the velvet-upholstered sofa, crossing her legs and leaning forward, one hand clasping the other in her lap. She reminded Banks of the kind of elegant, remote blondes that Alfred Hitchcock had cast in so many of his films.

Riddle asked Banks to sit down. He was still in uniform. A tall man, running to bulk but still fit, he sat opposite in an armchair, pulling at the sharp crease of his trouser leg, and leaned back. He was bald, and dark beetle brows arched over his hard, serious brown eyes.

Banks got the feeling that neither of them quite knew what to say now that he was there. You could cut the tension with a knife; something bad had happened, something delicate and painful. Banks needed a cigarette badly, but there was no way. He knew Riddle hated smoke, and the room had a sort of sweet lavender smell that he could tell had never been sullied by cigarettes. The silence stretched on. He was beginning to feel like Philip Marlowe at the beginning of a case. Maybe he should tell them his rates and break the ice, he thought, but before he could say anything flippant, Riddle spoke.

"Banks . . . I . . . er . . . I know we've had our differences in the past, and I'm sure this request will come as much of a surprise to you as it comes to me to be making it, but I need your help."

Differences in the past? There was an understatement if ever there was one. "Go on," he said. "I'm listening."

Riddle shifted in his chair and plucked at his creases. His wife reached forward and picked up her drink. The ring of moisture it left on the glass surface was the only thing that marred the room's sterile perfection.

"It's a personal matter," Riddle went on. "Very personal. And unofficial. Before we go any further, Banks, I want your absolute assurance that what I have to say won't be repeated outside these four walls. Can you give me that?"

Banks nodded.

"I'm sorry," Rosalind said, standing up. "You must think me a terrible hostess. You've come all this way, and I haven't even offered you a drink. Will you have something, Mr. Banks? A small whiskey, perhaps?"

"The man's driving," said Riddle.

"Surely just the one?"

Banks held his hand up. "No, thank you," he said. What he really wanted was a cup of tea, but more than that, he wanted to get this all over with and go home. If he could do without a cigarette for a while, he could do without a drink, too. He wished one of them would get to the point.

"It's about our daughter," Rosalind Riddle began, hands wriggling on her lap. "She left home when she was sixteen."

"She ran away, Ros," said Riddle, his voice tight with anger. "Let's not fool ourselves about what happened."

"How long ago was that?" Banks asked.

Riddle answered him. "Six months."

"I'm sorry to hear it," said Banks, "but I'm not sure what—"

"Our son Benjamin was playing on the computer earlier this evening," Rosalind chipped in. "By accident he stumbled across some pictures on one of those sex sites."

Banks knew that inadvertently accessing a porno site was easily enough done. Look for "Spice Girls" on some of those search engines and you might end up at "Spicy Girls."

"Some of the pictures . . ." Rosalind went on. "Well, they were of Emily, our daughter. Benjamin's only eight. He doesn't really know what any of it means. We put him to bed and told him not to say anything."

"Are you certain it was your daughter?" Banks asked. "Some of those photos can be doctored, you know. Heads and bodies rearranged."

"It was her," Rosalind answered. "Believe me. There's a distinctive birthmark."

"I'm sure this is all very upsetting," Banks said. "And you have my sympathies. But what do you want me to do?"

"I want you to find her," Riddle said.

"Why haven't you tried yourself?"

Riddle looked at his wife. The gaze that passed between them spoke volumes of discord and recrimination. "I have," said Riddle. "But I had nothing to go on. I couldn't go through official channels. I mean, it wasn't even as if there was a *crime*. She was perfectly within her legal rights. And the fewer people who knew about what happened, the better."

"You're worried about your reputation?"

Riddle's voice rose. "I know what you think, Banks, but these things *are* important. If only you realized that, you might have made something better of yourself."

"More important than your daughter's well-being?"

"Valuing reputation doesn't mean that either my husband or I care any the less about our daughter, Mr. Banks," said Rosalind. "As her mother, I resent that implication."

"Then I apologize."

Riddle spoke again. "Look, what I'm saying, Banks, is that before tonight I didn't think I had any real cause to worry about her—Emily's an intelligent and resourceful girl, if a bit too headstrong and rebellious—but now I think I do have something tangible to be concerned about. And this isn't *all* about ambition and reputation, no matter what you think."

"So why don't you try to find her yourself?"

"Be realistic, Banks. For a start, I can't be seen going off on some sort of private chase."

"And I can?"

"You're not in the public eye as much as I am. People might recognize me. I can cover for you up here, if that's what you're worried about. I *am* chief constable, after all. And I'll also cover all reasonable expenses. I don't expect you to be out of pocket over this. But you'll be on your own. You can't use police resources or anything like that. I want to keep this private. A family matter."

"You mean your career's important and mine's expendable?"

"You might try looking at it in a slightly different light. It's not that there's nothing in it for you."

"Oh?"

"Look at it this way. If you succeed, you'll have earned my gratitude. Whatever you think of me, I'm a man of honor, a man of my word, and I promise you that whatever happens, your career in Eastvale can only benefit if you do as I ask."

"And the other reason?"

Riddle sighed. "I'm afraid that if she found out it was *me* looking for her, then she'd give me the slip. She blames me for all her problems. She made that clear in the months before she left. I want you to go about this discreetly, Banks. Try to get to her before she knows anyone's looking. I'm not asking you to kidnap her or anything like that. Just find her, talk to her, make sure she's all right, tell her we'd be happy to see her again and talk things over."

"And persuade her to stop posing on Internet sex sites?"

Riddle paled. "If you can."

"Have you any idea where she went? Has she been in touch?"

"We had a postcard a couple of weeks after she'd left," Rosalind answered. "She said she was doing fine and that we weren't to worry about her. Or bother looking for her."

"Where was it postmarked?"

"London."

"That's all?"

"Apart from a card for Benjamin on his birthday, yes."

"Did she say anything else on the postcard?"

"Just that she had a job," Rosalind went on. "So we wouldn't have to worry about her living on the streets or anything like that. Not that Emily *would* live on the streets. She was always a very high-maintenance girl."

"Ros!"

"Well, it's true. And you—"

"Was there any specific reason she left?" Banks cut in. "Anything that sparked her leaving? A row or something?"

"Nothing specific," Riddle said. "It was cumulative. She just didn't come home from school."

"School?"

Rosalind answered. "A couple of years ago we sent her to a very expensive and highly reputable all-girls' boarding school outside Warwick. At the end of last term, the beginning of summer, instead of returning home, she ran off to London."

"By herself?"

"As far as we know."

"Did she usually come home for the holidays?"

"Yes."

"What stopped her this time? Were you having any problems with her?"

Riddle picked up the thread again. "When she was last home, for the spring holidays, there were the usual arguments over staying out late, drinking in pubs, hanging around with the wrong crowd, that sort of thing. But nothing out of the ordinary. She's a very bright girl. She was doing well at school, academically, but it bored her. It all seemed too easy. Especially languages. She has a way with words. Of course, we wanted her to stay on and do her A-Levels, go to university, but she didn't want to. She wanted to get out on her own. We gave her everything, Banks. She had her own horse, piano lessons, trips to America with the school, skiing holidays in Austria, a good education. We were very proud of Emily. We gave her everything she ever wanted."

Except perhaps what she needed most, thought Banks: *You*. To reach the dizzying heights of chief constable, especially by the age of forty-five, as Riddle had done, you needed to be driven, ruthless and ambitious. You also needed to be able to move around a lot, which can have a devastating effect on young children who sometimes find it hard to make friends. Add to that the hours spent on the job and on special courses, and Riddle had probably hardly set foot in the family home from one day to the next.

Banks was hardly one to take the moral high ground in raising children, he had to admit to himself. Even to reach the rank of DCI, he had been an absent father far more often than was good for Brian and Tracy. As it happened, both of them had turned out fine, on the whole, but he knew that was more a matter of good luck than good parenting on his part. Much of the task had fallen to Sandra, and she hadn't always burdened him with the children's problems. Perhaps Banks hadn't sacrificed his family to ambition the way he suspected Riddle had, but he had certainly sacrificed a lot for the sake of being a good *detective*.

"Are there any friends from around here she might have confided in?" he asked. "Anyone who might have stayed in touch with her?"

Rosalind shook her head. "I don't think so," she said. "Emily is very . . . self-sufficient. She had plenty of friends, but none that close, I don't think. It came of moving around a lot. When she moves on, she burns her bridges. And she hadn't actually spent much time in this area."

"You mentioned the 'wrong crowd.' Was there a boyfriend?"

"Nobody serious."

"His name could still be a help."

Rosalind glanced at her husband, who said, "Banks, I've told you I don't want this to be official. If you start looking up Emily's old boyfriends and asking questions around these parts, how long do you think the affair's going to remain under wraps? I told you, she's run off to London. *That*'s where you'll find her."

Banks sighed. It looked as if this was going to be an investigation carried out with his hands tied. "Does she know anyone in London, then?" he asked. "Anyone she might go to for help?"

Riddle shook his head. "It's been years since I was on the Met. She was only a little girl when we left."

"I know this might be difficult for you," Banks said, "but do you think I might have a look at this Web site?"

"Ros?"

Rosalind Riddle scowled at her husband and said, "Follow me."

Banks followed her under a beam so low that he had to duck into a book-lined study. A tangerine *iMac* sat on a desk by the window. Wind rattled the glass beyond the heavy curtains, and every once in a while it sounded as if someone sloshed a bucket of water over the windows. Rosalind sat down and flexed her fingers, but before she hit any keys or clicked the mouse, she turned in her chair and looked up at Banks. He couldn't read the expression on her face.

"You don't approve of us, do you?" she said.

"Us?"

"Our kind. People who have . . . oh, wealth, success, ambition."

"I can't say I pay you much mind, really."

"Ah, but you do. That's just where you're wrong." Her eyes narrowed. "You're envious. You've got a chip on your shoulder the size of that sideboard over there. You think you're better than us—purer, somehow—don't you?"

"Mrs. Riddle," said Banks, with a sigh, "I don't need this kind of crap. I've driven all the way out here on a miserable night when I'd far rather be at home listening to music and reading a good book. So if we're going to do this, let's just get on with it, shall we, or shall I just go home and go to bed?"

She studied him coolly. "Hit a nerve, did I?"

"Mrs. Riddle, what do you want from me?"

"He's thinking of going into politics, you know."

"So I've heard."

"Any hint of a family scandal would ruin everything we've worked so hard for all these years."

"I imagine it probably would. It's best to get into office first, *then* have the scandal."

"That's cynical."

"But true. Read the papers."

"He says you have a tendency to make waves."

"I like to get at the truth of things. Sometimes that means rocking a few boats. The more expensive the boat, the more noise it seems to make when it rocks."

Rosalind smiled. "I wish we could all afford to be so high-minded. This job will require the utmost discretion."

"I'll bear that in mind. *If* I decide to take it on." Banks held her stare until she blinked and swiveled her chair back to face the screen.

"I just thought we'd get that clear before you get to look at nude pictures of my daughter," she said without looking at him.

He watched over her shoulder as she started to work at the keyboard and mouse. Finally, a black screen with a series of thumbnail photographs appeared. Rosalind clicked on one of them and another screen, with about five more thumbnail images, began to load. At the top of the screen, the script announced that the model's name was Louisa Gamine, and that she was an eighteen-year-old biology student. Looking at the pictures, Banks could believe it.

"Why Louisa Gamine?" he asked.

"I've no idea. Louisa's her middle name. Louise, actually. Emily Louise Riddle. I suppose she thinks Louisa sounds more exotic. Maybe when she left she decided she needed a new identity?"

Banks understood that. When he was younger he had always regretted that his parents hadn't given him a middle name. So much so that he made one up for himself: Davy, after Davy Crockett, one of his heroes at the time. That lasted a couple of months, then he finally accepted his own name: Alan.

Rosalind clicked on one of the images, and it began to fill the screen, loading from top to bottom. Banks was looking at an amateur photograph, taken in a bedroom with poor lighting, which showed a pretty young girl sitting naked and cross-legged on a pale blue duvet. The smile on her face looked a little forced, and her eyes didn't seem quite focused.

The resemblance between Louisa and her mother was astonishing. They both had the same long-legged grace, the same pale, almost translucent, complexion, the same generous mouth. The only real difference, apart from their ages, was that Louisa's blond hair hung over her shoulders. Otherwise, Banks felt he could easily have been looking at a photograph of Rosalind taken maybe twenty-five years ago, and that embarrassed him. He noticed a discoloration the shape of a teardrop on the inside of Louisa's left thigh: the birthmark. She also had a small ring of some sort in her navel, and below it, what looked like a black tattoo of a spider. Banks thought of Annie Cabbot's rose tattoo above her left breast, how long ago it was since he had last seen it, and how he would probably never see it again, especially if he managed to reconcile with Sandra.

The other photos were much the same, all taken in the same location, with the same poor lighting. Only the poses were different. Her new surname was certainly apt, Banks thought, as there was definitely something of the *gamine* about her, a young girl with mischievous charm. There was something else that nagged him about the surname she had chosen, too, but he couldn't think what it was at the moment. If he put it to the back of his mind, it would probably come eventually. Those things usually did.

Banks examined the pictures more closely, aware of Rosalind's subtle perfume as he leaned over her shoulder. He could make out a few details of the room—the corner of a pop-star poster, a row of books—but they were all too blurred to be of any use.

"Seen enough?" asked Rosalind, tilting her head toward him and hinting that perhaps he was lingering too long, enjoying himself too much.

"She looks as if she knows what she's doing," said Banks.

Rosalind paused, then said, "Emily's been sexually active since she was fourteen. At least, as far as we know. She was thirteen when she started becoming . . . wayward, so it might have been earlier. That's partly why we sent her away to school in the first place."

"That's not unusual," said Banks, thinking with alarm of Tracy. He was sure she hadn't been active quite that young, but it was hardly something he could ask her about. He didn't even know whether she was active now, come to think of it, and he didn't think he wanted to know. Tracy was nineteen, so she had a few years on Emily, but she was still Banks's little girl. "Do you think the school helped?" he asked.

"Obviously not. She didn't come back, did she?"

"Have you spoken with the principal, or with any of her classmates?"

"No. Jerry's too worried about indiscretion."

"Of course. Print that one." Banks pointed to a photograph where Louisa sat on the edge of the bed staring expressionlessly into the camera, wearing a red T-shirt and nothing else. "Head and shoulders will do. We can trim off the bottom part."

Rosalind looked over her shoulder at him, and he thought he could sense a little gratitude in her expression. At least she didn't seem so openly hostile as she had been earlier. "You'll do it?" she asked. "You'll try to find Emily?"

"I'll try."

"You don't need to make her come home. She won't want to come. I can guarantee you that."

"You don't sound as if you want her to."

Rosalind frowned, then said, "Perhaps you're right. I did

suggest to Jerry that we simply let her go her own way. She's old enough, and certainly she's smart enough to take care of herself. And she's a troublemaker. I know she's my daughter, and I don't mean to sound uncaring, but . . . Well, you can see for yourself what's happened after only six months, can't you? That tattoo, those pictures. . . . She never considers anyone else's feelings. I can just imagine what chaos life would be like here if we had all her problems to deal with as well."

"As well?"

"Nothing. It doesn't matter."

"Is there anything else you think I should know?"

"I don't know what you mean."

"Anything you're not telling me."

"No. Why should there be?"

But there was, Banks sensed by the way Rosalind glanced away from him as she spoke. There may have been family problems that neither she nor her husband wanted to discuss. And maybe they were right not to. Perhaps he should hold his curiosity in check for once and not rip open cans of worms the way he usually did. Just find the girl, he told himself, make sure she isn't in any danger, and leave the rest well alone. Lord knows, the last thing he wanted to do was get caught up in the Riddle family dysfunctions.

He scribbled down as much information as he could get from the Web site, which was run by an organization called GlamourPuss Ltd., based in Soho. It shouldn't be too difficult to track them down, he thought, and they should be able to point him toward Emily, or Louisa, as she now preferred to be called. He just hoped she wasn't on the game, as so many teenagers who appeared on porno Web sites were. She didn't sound like the type who would turn to prostitution for gain, but it sounded as if she might try anything for kicks. He would have to cross that bridge when, and if, he got to it.

Rosalind printed the photo, took some scissors from the desk drawer and trimmed it from the navel ring down before she handed it to him. Banks followed her back into the living room, where Riddle sat staring into space. "All done?" he said.

Banks nodded. He didn't bother sitting. "Tell me something," he said. "Why me? You know damn well how things stand between us."

Riddle seemed to flinch slightly, and Banks was surprised at the venom in his own voice. Then Riddle paused and looked him in the eye. "Two reasons," he said. "First, because you're the best detective in the county. I'm not saying I approve of your methods or your attitude, but you get results. And in an unorthodox business like this, well, let's just say that some of your maverick qualities might actually be of real value for a change."

Even being damned with faint praise by Jimmy Riddle was a new experience for Banks. "And second?" he asked.

"You've got a teenage daughter yourself, haven't you? Tracy's her name. Am I right?"

"Yes."

Riddle spread his hands, palms out. "Then you know what I'm getting at. I think you can imagine something of how I feel."

And to his surprise, Banks could. "I can't start till next week," he said.

Riddle leaned forward. "You've nothing pressing on right now."

"I was planning a weekend away with Tracy. In Paris."

"Please start now. Tomorrow. In the morning. I need to know." There was a sense of desperation in Riddle's voice that Banks had never heard from him before.

"Why so urgent?"

Riddle stared into the huge fireplace, as if addressing his words to the flames. "I'm afraid for her, Banks. She's so young and vulnerable. I want her back. At the very least I need to know how she is, what she's doing. Imagine how you'd feel if it happened to you. Imagine what you'd do if it was *your* daughter in trouble."

Damn it, thought Banks, seeing his weekend in Paris with Tracy start to slip beyond his grasp. *Daughters.* Who'd have them? Nothing but trouble. But Riddle had touched a nerve all right. Now there was no getting away from it, no declining; Banks knew he *had* to head off to London to find Emily Louise Riddle.

"Oh, Dad! You *can't* mean it! You woke me up in the middle of the night to tell me we can't go to Paris after all?"

"I'm sorry, love. We'll just have to postpone it for a while."

"I don't *believe* this. I've been looking forward to this weekend for *ages*."

"Me, too, sweetheart. What can I say?"

"And you won't even tell me why?"

"I can't. I promised."

"You promised *me* a weekend in Paris. It was easy enough to break *that* one."

Touché. "I know. I'm sorry."

"Don't you trust me to keep my mouth shut?"

"Of course I do. It's not that."

"What, then?"

"I just can't tell you yet. That's all. Maybe next week, if things work out."

"Oh, don't bother." Tracy fell into one of her sulky silences for a while, the way her mother did, then said, "It's not dangerous, is it?"

"Of course not. It's a private matter. I'm helping out a—" Banks almost said "friend" but managed to stop himself in time. "I'm helping someone out. Someone in trouble. Believe me, love, if you knew the details, you'd see it's the right thing to do. Look, when it's over, I'll make it up to you. I promise."

"Heard that before. Been there. Got the T-shirt."

"Give me a little leeway here, Tracy. This isn't easy for me, you know. It's not just you who's upset. I was looking forward to Paris, too."

"Okay, I know. I'm sorry. But what about the tickets. The hotel?"

"The hotel's easily canceled. I'll see if I can get the tickets changed."

"You'll be lucky." She paused again. "Wait a minute! I've just had an idea."

"What?"

"Well, I know *you* can't go, but there's no reason I shouldn't go, is there?"

"Not that I know of. Except, would you really want to be in Paris all by yourself? And it's not safe, especially for a young woman alone."

Tracy laughed. "I can take care of myself, Dad. I'm a big girl now."

Yes, Banks thought, all of nineteen. "I'm sure you can," he said. "But I'd be worried."

"You're *always* worried. It's what fathers do best for their daughters: worry about them. Besides, I wasn't necessarily thinking of going by myself."

"What do you mean?"

"I'll bet Damon would like to go. He doesn't have any lectures tomorrow, either. I could ask him."

"Wait a minute," said Banks. "Damon? Who on earth is Damon?"

"My boyfriend. I bet he'd jump at the chance of a weekend in Paris with me."

I'll bet he would, Banks thought, with that sinking feeling. This wasn't going at all the way he had expected it to. He had expected recriminations, yes; anger, yes; but this . . . ? "I'm not so sure that's a good idea," he said weakly.

"Of course it is. You know it is. We'd save money, too."

"How?"

"Well, you'll only have to cancel one of the hotel rooms, for a start."

"Tracy!"

She laughed. "Oh, Dad. Parents are so silly, you know. If kids want to sleep together, it doesn't have to be in a foreign city at night. They can do it in the student residence in the daytime, you know."

Banks swallowed. Now he had an answer to a question he had avoided asking. In for a penny, in for a pound. "Are you and Damon . . . I mean . . . ?"

"Don't worry. I'm a very careful girl. Now, the only problem is getting the tickets to us before tomorrow morning. I don't suppose you'd like to drive over tonight, would you?"

"No, I wouldn't," said Banks. Then he weakened. After all, she was right; there was no reason to spoil her weekend just because his own was spoiled, Damon notwithstanding. "But as a matter of fact, I have to go down to London tomorrow anyway, so I can go that far on the train with you." And check Damon out, too, while I'm at it, he thought. "I'll give you the tickets then."

"That's great!"

Banks felt depressed; Tracy sounded far more thrilled at going off with Damon than with him. But she would; she was young. "I'll see you in the morning," he said. "At the station. Same time as we arranged."

"Cool, Dad. Thanks a lot."

When he hung up the telephone, Banks fell back into his armchair and reached for his cigarettes. He had to go to London, of that there was no doubt. In the first place, he had promised, and in the second, there was something Riddle didn't know. Tracy herself had almost run away from home once, around her thirteenth birthday, and the thought of what might have happened if she had gone through with it haunted him.

It had happened just before they left London for Eastvale. Tracy had been upset for days about leaving her friends behind, and one night, when Banks actually happened to be home, he heard a noise downstairs. Going to investigate, he found Tracy at the door with a suitcase in her hand. In the end, he managed to persuade her to stay without forcing her, but it had been touch and go. One part of their bargain was that he had agreed not to tell her mother, and he never had. Sandra had slept through the whole thing. Remembering that night, he could imagine something of how the Riddles must feel.

Even so, was this what he got for doing his enemy a favor? He got to go hunting for a runaway teen while his own daughter got a dirty weekend in Paris with her boyfriend. Where was the justice in that? he asked. All the answer he got was the howling of the wind and the relentless music of the water flowing over Gratly Falls.

2

On Friday afternoon, Banks was walking along Old Compton Street in the chilly November sunshine, having traveled down to London with Tracy and Damon that morning. After a grunted "Hi," Damon had hardly spoken a word. The train was almost full, and the three of them couldn't sit together, which seemed a relief to Tracy and Damon. Banks had to sit half the carriage away next to a fresh-faced young businessman wearing too much after-shave and playing FreeCell on his laptop computer.

Most of the journey he spent listening to Lucinda Williams's *Car Wheels on a Gravel Road* and reading *The Big Sleep*, which he had substituted for *Maigret and the Hundred Gibbets* when he realized he wasn't going to Paris. He had seen the Bogart film version a few weeks ago and enjoyed it so much it had made him want to read the book. Besides, Raymond Chandler seemed more suitable reading for the kind of job he was doing: *Banks, PI*.

Shortly before King's Cross, his thoughts had returned to Tracy's boyfriend.

Banks wasn't at all certain what to think of Damon. The grunt was no more than he would have expected from any of his daughter's friends, and he didn't read anything into it, except perhaps that the lad was a bit embarrassed at coming face-to-face with the father of the girl he was sleeping with. Even the thought of that made Banks's chest tighten, though he told himself not to get upset, not to interfere. The last thing he wanted to do was alienate his daughter, especially as he was hoping to get back together with her mother. It wouldn't do any good, anyway. Tracy had her own life to lead now, and she was no fool. He hoped.

He had left the young lovers at King's Cross and first gone to check in at the small Bloomsbury hotel he had telephoned the previous evening. Called simply Hotel Fifty-Five, after the street number, it was the place he favored whenever he visited London: quiet, discreet, well-located and relatively inexpensive. Riddle might have said he would pay any expenses, but Banks wouldn't want to see the CC's face if he got a bill from the Dorchester.

The morning's rain had dispersed during the journey, and the day had turned out windy and cool under the kind of piercingly clear blue sky you only get in November. Maybe the bonfires would dry out in time for Guy Fawkes Night after all, Banks thought, as he zipped his leather jacket a bit higher. He tapped his briefcase against his thigh to the rhythm of some hip-hop music that drifted out of a sex shop.

Banks had strong feelings and memories associated with Soho ever since he used to walk the beat or drive the panda cars there out of Vine Street Station, after it had been re-opened in the early seventies. Certainly the area had been cleaned up since then, but Soho could never be *really* clean. Cleanliness wasn't in its nature.

He loved the whiff of villainy he got whenever he walked Old Compton Street or Dean Street, where a fiddle had been simply a hair's breadth away from a legitimate business deal. He remembered the cold dawns at Berwick Street Market, a cigarette and mug of hot sweet tea in his hands, chatting with Sam, whose old brown collie Fetchit used to sit under the stall all day and watch the world go by with sad eyes. As the other stallholders set up their displays—fruit, crockery, knives and forks, knickers and socks, watches, egg slicers, you name it—Sam used to give Banks a running commentary on what was hot and what wasn't. Probably dead now, along with Fetchit. They'd been old enough back then, when Banks was new to the job.

Not that Soho was ever without its dark side. Banks had found his first murder victim there in an alley off Frith Street: a seventeen-year-old prostitute who had been stabbed and mutilated, her breasts cut off and several of her inner organs removed. "Homage to Jack the Ripper," as the newspaper headlines had screamed. Banks had been sick on the spot, and he still had nightmares about the long minutes he spent alone with the disemboweled body just before dawn in a garbage-strewn Soho alley.

As with all the dead in his life, he had put a name to her: Dawn Wadley. Being junior at the time, Banks was given the job of telling her parents. He would never forget the choking smell of urine, rotten meat and unwashed nappies in the cramped flat on the tenth floor of an East End tower block, or Dawn's washed-out junkie mother, apparently unconcerned about the fate of the daughter she gave up on years ago. To her, Dawn's murder was just another in the endless succession of life's cruel blows, as if it had happened solely in order to do her down.

Banks turned into Wardour Street. Soho had changed, like the rest of the city. The old bookshops and video booths were still around, as was the Raymond Revue Bar, but cheap sex was definitely on the wane. In its place came a younger crowd, many of them gay, who chatted on their mobiles while sipping cappuccinos at chic outdoor cafés. Young men with shaved heads and earrings flirted on street corners with clean-cut boys from Palmer's Green or Sudbury Hill. Gay bars had sprung up all over the place, and the party never stopped.

Banks checked the address for GlamourPuss Ltd. he had got from the first place he tried: the phone book. Sometimes things really are that easy.

From the outside, it looked like any number of other businesses operating in Soho. The building was run-down, paint flaking from the doors, the lino on the creaky corridors cracked and worn, but inside, through the second set of doors, it was all high-tech glam and potted plants, and he could still smell the fresh paint on the walls.

"Can I help you, sir?"

To Banks's surprise, there was a female receptionist sitting behind a chest-high semicircle of black Plexiglas. Written on it, in florid pink script scattered with some sort of glitter, at about waist height, was the logo "GlamourPuss Ltd.: Erotica and More!" Banks had the idea, somehow, that women—right-thinking women, anyway—didn't want anything to do with the porn business, that they wanted, in fact, to outlaw it if they could. Maybe this was a wrong-thinking woman? Or was she the respectable face of porn? If so, it was about nineteen, with short henna hair, a ghostly complexion and a stud through its left nostril. A little badge over her flat chest read "Tamara: Client Interface Officer." Banks's mind boggled. *Can we interface, Tamara?*

"I'd like to see the person in charge," he said.

"Do you have an appointment, sir?"

"No."

"What is the purpose of your visit?"

She was starting to sound like an immigration official, Banks thought, getting irritated. In the old days he would probably have just tweaked her nose-stud and walked right on in. Even these days he might do the same under normal circumstances, but he had to remember he was acting privately; he wasn't here officially as a policeman. "Let's call it a business proposition," he said.

"I see. Please take a seat for a moment, sir. I'll see if Mr. Aitcheson is free." She gestured to the orange plastic chairs behind him. An array of magazines lay spread out on the coffee table in front of them. Banks lifted a couple up. Computer stuff, mostly. Not a *Playboy* or a *Penthouse* in sight. He looked up at Tamara, who had been carrying on a hushed conversation by telephone. She smiled. "He'll be with you in a moment, sir." Did she think he was looking for a job, or something? As what?

Banks was beginning to feel more as if he were in a dentist's waiting room than a porn emporium, and that thought didn't give him any comfort. Clearly, things had changed a lot since he had walked the Soho beat; enough to make him feel like an old fogy when he was only in his mid-forties. In the old days, at least you knew where you were: people like

GlamourPuss Ltd., as befit their name and business, used to operate out of seedy offices in seedy basements; they didn't run Internet Web sites; they didn't have client-interface officers; and they certainly didn't come out from under their stones to meet strangers offering vague business propositions the way this young man was doing right now, smiling, hand outstretched, wearing a suit, no less.

"Aitcheson," he said. "Terry Aitcheson. And you are?"

"Banks. Alan Banks."

"Pleased to meet you, Mr. Banks. Follow me. We'll go to the office. Far more private in there."

Banks followed him past Tamara, who gave a little wave and a nose twitch that looked painful. They crossed an open-space area filled with state-of-the-art computer equipment and went into a small office which looked out over Wardour Street. There was nothing either on the desk or the walls to indicate that GlamourPuss Ltd. dealt in pornography.

Aitcheson sat down and clasped his hands behind the back of his neck, still smiling. Up close, he looked older than Banks had first guessed—maybe late thirties—balding, with yellowing front teeth that were rather long and lupine. A few specks of dandruff speckled the shoulders of his suit. It was hardly fair, Banks thought, that even when you're going bald you *still* get dandruff. "Okay, Mr. Banks," said Aitcheson, "what can I do for you? You mentioned a business proposition."

Banks felt a little more at home now. Smarmy smile and suit aside, he had dealt with pillocks like Aitcheson before, even if their offices weren't as pretty and they didn't bother to offer up a smug facade of decency. He took the truncated picture of Emily Riddle from his briefcase and put it on the desk, turning it so that Aitcheson could see the image the right way up. "I'd like you to tell me where I can find this girl," he said.

Aitcheson studied the photo. His smile faltered a moment, then returned full force as he pushed the photograph back toward Banks. "I'm afraid we don't give out that sort of information about our models, sir. For their own protection, you understand. We get some . . . well, some rather strange people in this business, as I'm sure you can understand."

"So she *is* one of your models?"

"I was speaking generally, sir. Even if she were, I couldn't give you the information you want."

"Do you recognize her?"

"No."

"What if I told you this came from a Web site run by your company?"

"We operate several Web sites, sir. They act as a major part of our interface with the public." He smiled. "You have to be on the Web these days if you want to stay in business."

Interface. That word again. It seemed to be a sort of buzzword around GlamourPuss Ltd. "Are escort services part of your business?"

"We have an escort agency as one of our subsidiary companies, yes, but you can't just bring in a girl's picture from one of our Web sites and place an order for her. That would be tantamount to pimping on our part."

"And you don't do that?"

"We do not."

"What exactly *is* your business?"

"I should have thought that was obvious. Erotica in all its forms. Sex aids, videos, magazines, erotic encasement equipment and services, Web-site design and hosting, CD-ROMS, travel arrangements."

"Erotic encasement equipment and services?"

Aitcheson smiled. "It's a variation on bondage. Mummification's the most popular. Some people liken it to an erotic meditative state, a sort of sexual nirvana. But there are those who simply prefer to be wrapped in cling film with rose thorns pressed against their flesh. It's all a matter of taste."

"I suppose it is," said Banks, who was still trying to get his head around mummification. "And travel arrangements? What travel arrangements?"

Aitcheson graced Banks with a condescending smile. "Let's say you're gay and you want a cruise down the Nile with like-minded people. We can arrange it. Or a weekend in Amsterdam. A sex-tour of Bangkok."

"Discount vouchers for brothels? Fifty pee off your next dildo? That sort of thing?"

Aitcheson moved to stand up, his smile gone. "I think that's about all the time I can spare you at the moment, sir."

Banks stood up, leaned over the desk and pushed him back down into his chair. It wheeled back a couple of inches and hit the wall, taking out a small chunk of plaster.

"Just a minute!" Aitcheson said.

Banks shook his head. "You don't understand. That picture came from *your* Web site. Even if you don't remember putting it up there yourself, you can find out who did and where it came from."

"What's this got to do with you anyway? Wait a minute. Are you a copper?"

Banks paused and glanced down at the photo again. The younger version of Rosalind Riddle's features—pale skin, pouting lips, high cheekbones, blue eyes—looked up at him from under her fringe with a sort of mocking, come-hither sexuality. "It's my daughter," he said. "I'm trying to find her."

"Well, I'm sorry, but we don't run a location service for missing kids. There are organizations—"

"Pity, that," Banks cut in. "Her being so young, and all."

"What do you mean?"

Banks tapped the photo. "She can't have been more than fifteen when this was taken."

"Look, I'm not responsible for—"

"I think you'll discover that the law says otherwise. Believe me, I've read up on it." Banks leaned forward and rested his hands on the desk. "Mr. Aitcheson," he said, "here's my business proposition. There are two parts to it, actually, in case one of them alone doesn't appeal. I must admit, I'm not always certain justice is done when you bring in the police and the lawyers. Are you? I mean, you could probably beat the charges of distribution and publication of indecent photographs of minors. *Probably.* But it could be an expensive business. And I don't think you'd like the sort of *interface* it would create with your public. Do you follow? *Child pornography* is such an emotive term, isn't it?"

Aitcheson's smile had vanished completely now. "You sure you're not a copper?" he whispered. "Or a lawyer?"

"Me? I'm just a simple working man."

"Two parts. You said two parts."

"Ah, yes," said Banks. "As I said, I'm a simple working man, and I wouldn't want to get tangled up with the law myself. Besides, it would be bad for young Louisa, wouldn't it—all that limelight, giving evidence in court and all that. Embarrassing. Now, I work on a building site up north, and my fellow workers tend to be a conservative, even rather prudish lot when it comes to this sort of thing. It's not that they mind looking at a pair of tits on a *Playboy* centerfold or anything like that, mind you, but, believe me, I've heard them talking about child pornography, and I wouldn't want to be on the receiving end of some of the actions they propose to deal with the people who spread it, if you know what I mean."

"Is this a threat?"

"Why not? Yes, let's call it that: a threat. Suits me. Now, you tell me what I want to know, and I won't tell the lads at the building site about GlamourPuss exploiting young Louisa. Some of them have known her since she was a little baby, you know. They're very protective. As a matter of fact, most of them will be down here next week to see Leeds play Arsenal. I'm sure they'd be happy to find the time to drop by your offices, maybe do a bit of remodeling. Does that sound like a good deal to you?"

Aitcheson swallowed and stared at Banks, who held his gaze. Finally, he brought out his smile again, a bit weaker now. "It really *is* a threat, isn't it?"

"I thought I'd already made that clear. Do we have a deal?"

Aitcheson waved his arm. "All right, all right. I'll see what I can do. Can you come back on Monday? We're shut over the weekend."

"I'd rather we got it over with now."

"It might take a while."

"I can wait."

Banks waited. It took all of twenty minutes, then Aitcheson came back into the office looking worried. "I'm sorry," he said, "but we just don't have the information you require."

"Come again?"

"We don't have it. The model's address. She's not on our books, not part of our . . . I mean, it was an amateur shoot. I seem to remember she was the photographer's girlfriend. He used to do some work for us now and then, and apparently he took those photos as a bit of a lark. I'm sure he didn't know the model's true age. She looks much older."

"She's always looked older than her years," Banks said. "It's got a lot of boys into trouble. Well, I'm relieved to hear she's not on your books, but I don't think we're a lot further forward than when I first arrived, do you? Is there anything you can do to make amends?"

Aitcheson paused, then said, "I shouldn't, but I can give you the photographer's name and address. Craig Newton. As I said, he used to do a spot of work for us now and then, and we've still got him on file. We just got a change-of-address notice from him a short while ago, as a matter of fact."

Banks nodded. "It'll have to do." Aitcheson scribbled down an address for him. It was in Stony Stratford, commuter country. Banks stood up to leave. "One more thing," he said.

"Yes?"

"Those photos of Louisa on your Web site. Get rid of them."

Aitcheson allowed himself a self-satisfied smile. "Actually," he said, "I've done that already. While you were waiting."

Banks smiled back and tapped the side of his nose with his forefinger. "Good lad," he said. "You're learning."

Back at his hotel, Banks picked up the telephone and did what he had been putting off doing ever since he discovered he was bound for London the previous day. Not because it was something he didn't want to do, but because he was nervous and uncertain of the outcome. And there was so much at stake.

She answered on the fourth ring. Banks's heart pounded. "Sandra?"

"Yes. Who is this? Alan?"

"Yes."

"What do you want? I'm in a bit of a hurry right now. I was just on my way out."

"Off somewhere with Sean?"

"There's no need to make it sound like that. And as a matter of fact, no, I'm not. Sean's away photographing flood damage in Wales."

Let's hope the flood water carries him away with it, Banks thought, but bit his tongue. "I'm in town," he said. "In London. I was wondering if, maybe, tomorrow night you might be free for a meal. Or we could just have a drink. Lunch, even."

"What are you doing down here? Working?"

"In a manner of speaking. Are you free?"

He could almost hear Sandra thinking across the wires. Finally, she said, "Yes. Actually. Yes, I am. Sean won't be back until Sunday."

"So will you have dinner with me tomorrow night?"

"Yes. All right. That's a good idea. There's a few things we have to talk about." She named a restaurant on Camden High Street, not far from where she lived. "Seven-thirty?"

"Can you make it eight, just to be on the safe side?"

"Eight, then."

"Fine. See you there."

"See you."

Sandra hung up and Banks was left with the dead line buzzing in his ear. Maybe she hadn't exactly welcomed him with open arms, but she hadn't cut him off, either. More importantly, she had agreed to see him tomorrow And dinner was far more intimate than lunch or a quick drink in the afternoon. It was a good sign.

It was already dark by late afternoon when Banks took the train out of Euston. The Virgin InterCity sped through Hemel Hempstead so fast he could hardly read the station nameplate, then it slowed down near Berkhamsted for no reason Banks was aware of except that trains did that every now and then—something to do with leaves on the tracks, or a cow in a tunnel.

Berkhamsted was where Graham Greene came from, Banks remembered from *A Sort of Life*, which he had read a year or two ago. Greene had been one of his favorite writers ever since he first saw *The Third Man* on television back in the old Met days. After that, in his usual obsessive fashion, he collected and read everything he could get his hands on, from the "entertainments" to the serious novels, films on video, essays and short stories.

He was particularly taken by the story of the nineteen- or twenty-year-old Greene going out to Ashbridge Park in Berkhamsted with a loaded revolver to play Russian roulette. It was eerie now to imagine the awkward, gangly young man, destined to become one of the century's most famous writers, clicking on an empty chamber that autumn over seventy-five years ago, not far from where the train had just stopped.

Banks had also been impressed by Greene's writings on childhood, about how we are all "emigrants from a country we remember too little of," how important to us are the fragments we do remember clearly and how we spend our time trying to reconstruct ourselves from these.

For most of his life, Banks hadn't dwelled much on his past, but since Sandra had left him a year ago, he had found himself returning over and over again to certain incidents, the heightened moments of joy and fear and guilt, along with the objects, sights, sounds and smells that brought them back, like Proust's madelaines, as if he were looking for clues to his future. He remembered reading that Greene, as a child, had had a number of confrontations with death, and these had helped shape his life. Banks had experienced the same thing, and he thought that in some obscure, symbolic way, they partly explained why he had become a policeman.

He remembered, for example, the hot summer day when Phil Simpkins wrapped his rope around the high tree in the churchyard and spiraled down, yelling like Tarzan, right onto the spiked railings. Banks knew he would never forget the squishy thud that the body made as it hit. There had been no adults around. Banks and two others had pulled their writhing, screaming friend off the railings and stood there wondering what to do while he bled to death, soaking them in the blood that gushed from a pierced artery in his thigh. Someone later said they should have tied a tourniquet and sent for help. But they had panicked, frozen. Would Phil have lived if they hadn't? Banks thought not, but it was a possibility, and a mistake, he had lived with all his life.

Then there was Jem, a neighbor in his Notting Hill days, who had died of a heroin overdose; and Graham Marshall, a shy, quiet classmate who had gone missing and never been found. In his own way, Banks felt he was responsible for them, too. So many deaths for one so young. Sometimes Banks felt as if he had blood on his hands, that he had let so many people down.

The train stopped in Milton Keynes. Banks got off, walked up the stairs and along the overpass to the station exit.

He had never been to Milton Keynes before, though he had heard plenty of jokes about the place. One of the new towns, built in the late sixties, it was constructed on a grid system, with planned social centers, hidden pedestrian paths, rather than pavements, and hundreds of roundabouts. It sounded like the sort of design that would go down well in America, but the British sneered at it. Still, at not much over half an hour by train from London, and a much cheaper place to live, it was ideal commuting territory.

As it was, it was too dark to see much of the place. The taxi seemed to circle roundabout after roundabout, all of them with numbers, like V5 and H6. Banks didn't see any pavements or people out walking. He hadn't a clue where he was.

Finally, when the taxi turned into Stony Stratford, he found himself on a typical old village High Street, with ancient pubs and shop facades. For a moment, he wondered if it was all fake, just a faux finish to give the illusion of a real English village in the midst of all that concrete-and-glass modernity. It *seemed* real enough, though, and when the taxi pulled into a street of tall, narrow prewar terrace houses, he guessed that it probably was real.

The youth who answered the door looked to be in his mid- to late twenties; he wore black jeans and a gray sweatshirt advertising an American football team. He was about Banks's height, around five feet eight or nine, with curly dark hair and finely chiseled features. His nose had a little bump at the bridge, as if it had been broken and not properly set, and he was holding something that looked like a squat vacuum flask, which he kept tipping gently from side to side. Banks recognized it as a developing tank.

Craig Newton, if that indeed was who it was, looked both puzzled and annoyed to find a stranger on his doorstep early on a Friday evening. Banks didn't look like an insurance salesman—besides, how many salesmen still called at houses in these days of direct mail and electronic advertising? He also didn't look like a religious type, or a copper.

"What are you collecting for?" Newton asked. "I'm busy."

"Mr. Newton? Craig Newton?"

"Yes. What do you want?"

"Mind if I come in for a moment?"

"Yes, I do. Tell me what you want."

"It's about Louisa."

Craig Newton stepped back a couple of inches, clearly startled. "Louisa? What about her?"

"You *do* know her, then?"

"Of course I do. If it's the same person we're talking about. Louisa. Louisa Gamine." He pronounced it in Italian fashion, with a stress on the final *e*. "What's wrong? Has something happened to Louisa?"

"Can I come in?"

He stood back and gave Banks enough room to enter. "Yes, I'm sorry. Please."

Banks followed him down a narrow hallway into the front room. These old terrace houses weren't very wide, but they made up for it in length, with both kitchen and bathroom tacked on at the back like afterthoughts. Comfortably messy, the first thing the room told Banks was that Newton probably lived alone. A number of magazines, mostly to do with photography or movies, littered the coffee table, along with a few empty lager cans. A TV set stood at the far end. "The Simpsons" was showing. There was also a faint whiff of marijuana in the air, though Newton didn't appear stoned at all.

"Has something happened to Louisa?" he asked again. "Is that why you're here? Are you a policeman?"

"Nothing's happened to her as far as I know," said Banks. "And no, I'm not a policeman. I'm looking for her."

He frowned. "Looking for Louisa? Why? I don't follow."

"I'm her father." The lies were starting to come rather more easily now, after just a little practice, and Banks wasn't sure how he felt about that. Something to do with the end justifying the means crossed his mind and made him feel even more uneasy. Still, it wasn't as if he hadn't told plenty of lies in the course of his work, so why worry about it now he was doing the same thing as a private citizen? All in a good cause, if it could help a teenage runaway get herself sorted *and* get Jimmy Riddle off his back for good.

Craig raised his eyebrows. "Her *father* . . . ?" Then he seemed suddenly to notice the developing tank he was shaking. "Shit. Look, I've got to finish this off properly or it's a week's work down the tubes. Come up if you like."

Banks followed him upstairs, where Craig had turned his spare room into a makeshift darkroom. He didn't need complete darkness for this stage of the process, so a dim light glowed on the wall. With expert, economic gestures, Craig emptied the tank of developer, poured in the stop bath and shook the tank again for a while. After that, he emptied it out again and poured in the fixer.

Banks noticed a number of photographs of Emily Riddle tacked to a corkboard. Not nude shots, but professional-looking folio stuff. In some she wore a strapless black evening gown and had her hair pinned up. In another she was wearing a vest and baggy jeans, showing her bare midriff with its spider tattoo, trying to look like Kate Moss or Amber Valletta.

"These are good," he said to Craig.

Craig glanced over at them. "She could be a model," he said sadly. "She's a natural."

The harsh chemical smells transported Banks back not to his life with Sandra, who was a keen amateur photographer, but to his childhood, when he used to go up to the attic darkroom with his Uncle Ted and watch him processing and printing. He liked the printing best, when the blank piece of paper went in the developing tray and you could watch the image slowly forming. It seemed like magic. Every time they went over, he pestered his Uncle Ted to take him up. There was a safe light on the wall, too, he remembered, just enough to see by, and it gave an eerie glow in the small room. But mostly it was the sharp, chemical smells he remembered, and the way constant exposure to the chemicals made his Uncle Ted's fingernails brown, the same way nicotine stained Banks's fingers when he started smoking. He used to scrub it off with pumice stone so his mother wouldn't notice.

Then the visits to Uncle Ted's stopped abruptly and nobody ever said why. It was years before Banks thought about those days again and managed to work it out for himself. He remembered his uncle's hand on the small of his back, perhaps rubbing just a little, or the arm draped casually across his shoulders in an avuncular way. Nothing more. Never anything more. But there was some kind of scandal—not involving Banks, but someone else. Uncle Ted suddenly broke off his connection with the local Youth Club and no longer acted as a Boys' Brigade leader. Nothing was said, no police were involved, but he was suddenly a pariah in the community. That was how things like that were dealt with back then in that sort of close working-class community. No doubt one or two of the local fathers lay in wait one night and gave him a beating, too, but Banks heard nothing about that. Uncle Ted was simply never mentioned again, and if Banks ever asked to go visit or mentioned the name, his mother's mouth formed into a tight white line—a definite warning sign to shut up or else. Eventually, he stopped mentioning it and moved on to discovering girls.

"Okay," said Craig, emptying out the fixer and inserting

a hose attached to the cold water tap. "We're all right for half an hour now."

Banks followed him downstairs, still half-lost in memories of Uncle Ted, slowly moving to memories of Sandra, and how they made love in the red glow of her darkroom once.

Back in the living room, "The Simpsons" had given way to a documentary on Hollywood narrated in a plummy, superior accent. Craig turned the TV off and they sat down opposite one another in the narrow room.

Banks reached for his cigarettes; he'd been a long time without. "Mind if I smoke?"

"No, not at all." Craig passed him a small ashtray from the mantelpiece. "I don't indulge, myself, but it doesn't bother me."

"Not cigarettes, anyway."

Craig blushed. "Well, a bit of weed never did anyone any harm, did it?"

"I suppose not."

He continued to study Banks, his look wary and suspicious. "So, you're Louisa's father," he said. "Funny, you don't look Italian. She said her father was Italian. Mèt her mother in Tuscany or somewhere like that on holiday."

"What did she say about me?"

"Not much. Just that you were a boring, tight-arsed old fart."

Well, Banks thought, if you will go around assuming other people's identities, you have to be prepared for the occasional unflattering remark—especially if that identity is Jimmy Riddle's. On that score, Emily Riddle probably wasn't far wrong. "Do you know where Louisa is?" he asked.

"Haven't seen her for a couple of months," said Craig. "Not since I moved out here."

Banks showed him the photo. "This *is* the person we're talking about, isn't it?"

Craig looked at the photo and gasped. "You've seen them, then?"

"Yes. Is it the same girl we're talking about?"

"Yeah. That's her. Louisa."

"My daughter. What happened? The photos on the Web site?"

"Look, I'm sorry. It was just a lark, really. It was her as much as me. *More,* really. Though I don't expect you to believe me."

"You took the photos?"

"Yes. We were living together at the time. Three months ago."

"Here?"

"No. I was still in London then. Had a little flat in Dulwich."

Emily Riddle was a fast worker, Banks thought. Only away from home three months and she was living with someone. "How did they get onto the GlamourPuss Web site?"

Craig looked away, into the empty fireplace. "I'm not proud of it," he said. "I used to do some work for them. I went to school with one of the blokes who run the site, and I met him in a pub when I was a bit down on my luck, just after college. I'd studied photography, got my diploma, but it was hard to get started in the business. Anyway, he offered me a bit of paying work every now and then. Models. It didn't seem that much different from life studies in college."

It probably didn't, really, Banks thought. Sandra was a photographer, too, and Banks had seen plenty of life studies she had taken at the camera club, male *and* female. He pointed to the cropped photo of Louisa. "You got paid for this?"

"No. Good Lord, no. This wasn't paid work. Like I said, it was a lark. A bit of fun. We were . . . well, we'd been smoking a bit of weed, if you must know. After I'd taken them, Louisa said I should put them on the Web with some of the other stuff I'd done—the professional stuff. She said it would be really cool. Rick said he liked them, so we put them up in the amateurs gallery. But that's all. I mean Louisa doesn't have any connection with the rest of the Glamour-Puss business."

Just what Aitcheson had said at the office. Maybe it was true. "I'm glad to hear that. Are you sure?"

"Certain. She never did. The photos were just a one-off. A joke. I was trying out a new digital camera and . . . well, one thing led to another."

"Okay," said Banks, waving his hand. "Let's put that behind us. I'd really like to find Louisa, just to talk to her. I'm sure you understand. Can you tell me where she is?"

"I wasn't lying. I don't know where she is. I haven't seen her in two months."

"What happened?"

"She met another bloke."

"And left you?"

"Like a shot."

"Who is he?"

"I don't know his name . . . I . . ." Craig turned away again.

"Craig? Is something wrong?"

"No. Maybe. I don't know."

"Talk to me, Craig."

Craig stood up. "How about a drink?"

"If it'll help loosen your tongue."

"Lager okay?"

"Lager's fine."

Craig brought a couple of cans from the fridge and offered one to Banks. He took it and popped the tab, watching the foam well up and subside. He took a sip and leaned back in the chair. "I'm waiting."

"You *sure* you're not a copper?"

"I told you. I'm Louisa's father. Why?"

"I don't know. Just something . . . Never mind. Besides, you don't really look old enough to be her father. Not like I imagined, anyway. I would've expected some bald wrinkly in a suit, to be honest. With a funny accent, waving his arms around a lot."

"I'm flattered," said Banks, "but how old did you think she was?"

"Louisa? Nineteen. When I met her, that is."

"How long ago was that?"

"About three or four months. Why?"

"Because she'd just turned sixteen, that's why."

Craig spluttered on his beer. "She never! I mean, for crying out loud. I wouldn't've touched . . . You've seen the photos. You're her *father,* for Christ's sake!"

"Calm down," said Banks. "Louisa always did look older than her age, even if she didn't always act it."

"She had that . . . I don't know . . . she seemed young but mature, worldly and innocent at the same time. That was one of the attractive things about her. To me, anyway. She was a walking mass of contradictions. I swear, if you were me, and she told you she was nineteen, twenty-one, even, you'd believe her."

"How old are you?"

"Twenty-seven. Look, I'm sorry. I really am. About everything. But she told me she was nineteen and I believed her. What can I say? Yes, I was attracted to her. But I'm no cradle snatcher. That wasn't it at all. Most of my girlfriends have been older than me, as a matter of fact. She just had this aura, like she knew what it was all about, but when it got right down to it she was vulnerable, too, and you felt like you wanted to protect her. It's hard to explain."

Banks felt sad and angry, as if this really *were* his own daughter he was discussing. Stupid. "What happened? You say you don't know where she is, that she found another boyfriend. Who?"

"I told you I don't know his name. I'd tell you if I did. I don't know who he is. All I know is the last time I saw her she was with him. They were coming out of a pub in Soho, not far from the GlamourPuss offices. I'd been there having a pint with that old schoolfriend, Rick, and trying to shake a bit more business out of him. I'd been taking a few candids out in the street. I was upset about her leaving me without a word, so I went up to her and tried to talk to her."

"What happened?"

"A couple of goons attacked me." He pointed to his nose. "That's how I got this." Then he pointed to his head. "And I had to have seven stitches where my head hit the pavement."

"Two goons?"

"That's what they looked like. Bodyguards. Minders. Nobody said a word. It all happened so quickly."

"When did this happen?"

"About a month ago."

"What was Louisa doing at the time?"

"She was hanging on this bloke's arm, not doing anything really. She looked high. I mean *really* high, not just like a couple of drinks and a spliff high. I heard her giggling when I went down."

"And the man she was with? What did he look like?"

"Stone-faced. All sharp angles, like it was carved from granite. Hard eyes, too. Didn't blink. Didn't smile. Not a word. When I was on the ground, one of the goons kicked me, then they all just disappeared. Someone came out of the pub and helped me up, and that was that. I was lucky they didn't break my camera. It was a Minolta. An expensive one."

Banks thought for a moment. He didn't like what he was hearing at all. "Can you tell me anything more about this man?"

Craig shrugged. "Don't know, really. I didn't get a really good look at him. Tall. Maybe about six two or three. Looked older."

"Than who?"

"More your age than mine."

Banks felt his stomach rumbling and realized he hadn't eaten all day, except for a slice of toast with his morning coffee. He hadn't finished with Newton yet, though; there were still things he needed to know. "Is there anywhere decent to eat around here?" he asked.

"Couple of good Indian places down the High Street, if that's your sort of thing."

"Fancy a meal? On me."

Craig looked surprised. "Sure. Why not? Just let me hang up the negs to dry. Won't be a minute." He left the room. Banks stayed where he was, finishing his lager, and thought a bit more about darkrooms, Uncle Ted, and Sandra naked in the infrared light. Dinner. Tomorrow.

They walked down to the narrow High Street. The wind had dropped, but it was a chilly evening and there weren't many people out. Banks was glad of his warm leather jacket. They passed a sign on the wall of one of the buildings that made some reference to Richard III. Historical too, then, Stony Stratford.

"It's supposed to be where he picked up the princes in the tower," said Craig. "Before they were in the tower, like. You know, the ones he killed."

Craig picked a relatively inexpensive Indian restaurant. It was comfortably warm inside, and the exotic smells made Banks's mouth water the minute they got in the door. When they had ordered beers and were nibbling on poppadams in anticipation of their main courses, Banks picked up the subject of Louisa again. "Did she ever mention this boyfriend to you before?"

"No. One day everything seemed fine, the next she packed her stuff—what little she had—and she was gone before I got home. I had a wedding to shoot that day. My first, and it was a big deal. When I got home, all I found was a note. I remember it word for word." He closed his eyes. " 'Sorry, Craig, it's just not working out. You're a sweet lad. Maybe see you around. Hugs and Kisses, Louisa.' That was it."

"You had no idea at all what was going on? That she'd met someone else?"

"Not at the time, no. But the bloke's often the last to find out, isn't he?"

"Had you been arguing?"

"Yeah, but that was par for the course with Louisa."

"You argued a lot?"

"A fair bit."

"What about?"

"Oh, the usual stuff. She was bored. Our life lacked glamour and excitement. She wanted to go places more. She said I wasn't paying enough attention to her, that I was taking her for granted."

"Was it true?"

"Maybe. Some of it. I was working a lot, getting paying jobs, like that wedding. I suppose I was probably spending more time in the darkroom than I was with her. And I didn't know where she was half the time. I mean, we'd only been living together a month or so. It wasn't as if we were an old married couple, or something."

"She went out alone a lot?"

"She said she was out with her mates. Sometimes she didn't come back till two or three in the morning. Said she'd been clubbing. Well, you don't hold on to a girl like Louisa by clipping her wings, so there wasn't a lot I could do about it. It got me down a bit, though."

"Did you know any of her friends?"

"Only Ruth. She introduced us."

"Ruth?"

"Yeah. Ruth Walker."

"How did she know Louisa?"

"Dunno. But Ruth's always taking in strays. Heart of gold, she's got. Do anything for you. Louisa was staying with her when we met. I've known Ruth since I was at college. She was doing a computer course at the university, and she helped me out with some digital photography software. We got to be friends. I'd go see her once in a while, you know, take her down to the pub or out to see a movie or a band or something—she's really into the live-music scene—and one time I went, there was Louisa, sitting on her sofa. I won't say it was love at first sight, but it was definitely *something*."

Lust, no doubt, thought Banks. "Were you and Ruth lovers?"

"Ruth and me? Nah. Nothing like that. We were just friends."

The food came—balti prawns for Craig and lamb korma for Banks, along with pullao rice, mango chutney and naans—and they paused as they shared out the dishes. The ubiquitous sitar music droned in the background.

"Okay," said Banks after a few bites to stay the rumbling of his stomach. "What happened next?"

"Well, Ruth had got Louisa a job at the same company she worked for out Canary Wharf way. Nothing much, just fetching and carrying, really. Louisa didn't have any great job skills. But it brought in a quid or two, helped get her on her feet."

"Did Louisa talk much about her past?"

"Only to put it down. Sounds as if you gave her a pretty rough time. Sorry, but you asked."

"I suppose I did." Banks tasted the lamb. It was a bit too greasy, but it would do. He soaked up some sauce with his naan.

"Anyway," Craig went on, "she didn't last long there. Didn't seem to take to office work at all, as a matter of fact. Or any work, for that matter."

"Why was that?"

"I think it was mostly her attitude. Louisa thinks other people are there to work for her, not the other way around. And she's got attitude with a capital *A*."

"How did she survive after that?"

"She had a few quid of her own in the bank. She never said how much, but she never seemed to go short. Sometimes she borrowed off Ruth or me. She could go through money like nobody's business, could Louisa."

"And the new boyfriend?"

Craig nodded. "If he's the sort of bloke who can afford minders, then he's probably not short of a few quid, is he? Gone up in the world, she has, young Louisa."

That's right, Banks thought. And if he's the sort of bloke who *needs* minders, then the odds are that he makes his money in a dodgy way, a way that could make him enemies who want to do him physical harm, a way that could also put Emily in jeopardy. The more Banks heard, the more worried about her he became. "Are you sure you've got no idea who he is, where I can find them?"

"Sorry. If I knew, I'd tell you. Believe me."

"Do you think Ruth Walker might know?"

"It's possible. She wouldn't tell me when I asked her, but I think Louisa must have told her I was obsessed with her, stalking her or something."

"Were you?"

"Course not."

"Then what makes you think that?"

"Just the way she looked at me. We haven't been quite the same since that whole thing with Louisa, Ruth and me. But she might tell you."

Banks shrugged. "It's worth a try."

Craig gave him the address of Ruth's flat in Kenning-

ton. "You know, I really liked Louisa," he mused. "Maybe
I loved her . . . I don't know. She was pretty wild, and her
mood swings . . . well . . . all I can say is she could make
one of those divas look stable. But I liked her. Still, maybe
I'm better off without her. At least I can concentrate on my
work now, and I need to do that. Lord knows, she ran me
ragged. But for a while there, when she'd first gone, there
was a big hole in my life. I know it sounds corny, but I'd
no energy, no real will to go on. The world didn't look the
same. Not as bright. Not as interesting. Gray."

Welcome to reality, thought Banks. He had come prepared to be hard on Craig Newton—after all, Craig *had*
taken the nude photographs of Emily that had ended up on
the GlamourPuss Web site for every pervert to drool over—
but the lad was actually turning out to be quite likable. If
Craig was to be believed, he had genuinely thought that
Emily was nineteen—and who wouldn't, going by the evidence Banks had seen and heard so far—and the Web photos had simply been a foolish lark. Craig also seemed to care
about Emily—he hadn't only been with her for the sex, or
whatever else a sixteen-year-old girl had to offer a twenty-
seven-year-old man—and that went a long way in Banks's
estimation.

On the other hand, this new boyfriend sounded like trouble, and Emily Louise Riddle herself sounded like a royal
pain in the arse.

"Why did you move out here?" Banks asked. "Because of
Louisa?"

"Partly. It was around that time. It's funny, but I'd mentioned getting out of London a couple of times and Louisa
went all cold on me, the way she did when she wasn't getting her own way or heard something she didn't like. Anyway, I got the chance of a partnership in a small studio here
with a bloke I went to college with. A straight-up, legit
business this time—portraits and weddings, mostly. No
porn. I was fed up of London by then, anyway. Not just the
thing with Louisa, but other things. Too expensive. Too
hard to make a living. Too much competition. The hours I
was putting in. You've really got to hustle hard there, and I

was discovering I'm not much of a hustler at heart. I began to think I'd be better off as a bigger fish in a smaller pond."

"And?"

He looked up from his prawns and smiled. "It seems to be working out." Then he paused. "This is weird, though. I never thought I'd be sitting down having a curry with Louisa's dad, chatting in a civilized manner. I've got to say, you're not at all what I imagined."

"So you said. A boring old fart."

"Yeah, well, that's what *she* said. Wouldn't let her do anything, go anywhere. Kept her a virtual prisoner in the house."

"Lock up your daughters?"

"Yeah. Did you?"

"You know what she's like. What do you think I should have done?"

"With Louisa? I used to think I knew what she was like. Now I'm not so sure. From what you say, she told me a pack of lies right from the start. How can I believe anything about her? What do you do with someone like her?"

Indeed, thought Banks, feeling just a little guilty over his deception. What *do* you do? The thing was, that the more he found himself pretending to be Louisa's father, the more he found himself slipping into the role. So much so that on the slow train back to Euston later that evening, after Craig had kindly given him a lift to the station, when he thought about what his own daughter might be up to in Paris with Damon, he wasn't sure whether he was angry at Tracy or at Emily Riddle.

And the more he thought about the situation, the more he realized that it had never been *finding* Emily Riddle that concerned him; it was what he was going to do *after* he'd found her that really bothered him.

3

Saturday morning dawned cool and overcast, but the wind was quickly tearing a few holes in the ragged clouds. "Enough blue sky to make baby a new bonnet," as Banks's mother would say. Banks lingered over coffee and a toasted tea cake in a café on Tottenham Court Road, not far from his hotel, reading the morning papers and watching people checking out the electronics shops across the road.

He had slept well. Surprisingly so, since the hotel was the same one that he and Detective Sergeant Annie Cabbot had stayed in during his last case. Not the same room, thank God, but the same floor. Memories of her skin warm and moist against his kept him awake longer than he would have liked and made him feel vaguely guilty, but in the end he drifted into a deep and dreamless sleep, from which he awoke feeling unusually refreshed.

According to his *A to Z,* Ruth Walker lived quite close to the cramped flat off Clapham Road that Banks and Sandra had lived in for a few years in the early eighties, when the kids were little. Not exactly the "good old days," but happy for the most part, before the Job started taking too much of a toll on him. Simpler, maybe. Sandra worked part-time as a dental receptionist on Kennington Park Road, he remembered, and Banks was usually too busy out playing cops and robbers to take his wife to the theater or help the kids with their homework.

It wasn't much more than a couple of miles from the West End, as the crow flies, and he decided the walk would do him good. He had always loved walking in cities, and London was a great place for it. He had been cheated out of Paris, so he would have to make the best of where he was. If he set off now, he realized, he would probably arrive around lunchtime. If he got Louisa's address from Ruth, he would go there in the early evening, between six or seven, which he had always found was a good time to catch people in. That should also leave him plenty of time to meet Sandra at eight in Camden Town.

A cool wind skipped off the murky river and whistled around his ears as he crossed Lambeth Bridge. He glanced back. Shafts of light lanced through the clouds and lit on the Houses of Parliament. It was odd, Banks thought, but when you visit a place you used to live in for a long time, you see it differently; you become more like a tourist in your own land. He would probably never have even noticed Big Ben or the Houses of Parliament in the days when he had lived there. Even now, his copper's eye was more tuned to the two shifty-looking skinheads across the road, who seemed to be following a couple of Japanese tourists, than it was to the beauty of the London architecture.

It was pushing twelve-thirty when Banks got to Ruth's street just off Kennington Road. The brick terrace houses were four stories high and so narrow they seemed pressed together like a mouthful of bad teeth. Here and there someone had added a lick of bright paint to a window frame, or put out a few potted plants in the bay window.

The name "R. A. Walker" appeared by the third-floor bell, a dead giveaway that the occupant was a woman. Banks pressed and heard it ring way up in the distance. He waited, but nobody came. Then he tried again. Still nothing. After standing on the doorstep for a few minutes, he gave up. He hadn't wanted to phone ahead and tip her off that he was coming—finding that surprise often worked best in situations like this—so he had been prepared to wait.

Banks decided to have his lunch and call back in an hour or so. If she wasn't in then, he'd think of a new plan. He found a serviceable pub on the Main Street and enjoyed a pint as he finished reading the newspaper. A few regulars stood at the bar, and a younger crowd was gathered around the video machines. One man, wearing a tartan cap, kept nipping around the corner to the betting shop and coming back to tell everyone in a loud voice how much he'd lost and how the horse he'd backed belonged in the glue factory. Everyone laughed indulgently. Nobody paid Banks any mind, which was just the way he liked it. He glanced over the menu and settled finally on a chicken pot pie. It would have suited Annie Cabbot just fine, Banks thought as he searched in vain among peas and carrots for the meat; Annie was a vegetarian.

A short while later, he stood on Ruth Walker's doorstep again and gave her bell a long push. This time, he was rewarded by a wary voice over the intercom.

"Who is it?"

"I've come about Louisa," Banks said. "Louisa Gamine."

"Louisa? What about her? She's not here."

"I need to talk to you."

There was a long pause—so long that Banks thought Ruth had hung up the intercom on him—then the voice said, "Come up. Top floor." A buzzer went off and Banks pushed the front door open.

The stairs were carpeted, though the fabric had worn thin in places and the pattern was hard to make out. A variety of cooking smells assailed Banks as he climbed the narrow staircase: a hint of curry, garlic, tomato sauce. When he got to the top, there was only one door. It opened almost immediately when he knocked, and a young woman looked at him through narrowed eyes. After she had studied him for a while, she opened the door and let him in.

The best Banks could say of Ruth Walker was that she was plain. It was a cruel and unfair description, he knew, but it was true. Ruth was the kind of girl who, in his adolescence, always went around with an attractive friend, the one you really wanted. The Ruths of this world you usually tried to palm off on *your* friend. There was nothing distinguishing about her except, perhaps, the intelligence perceptible in her disconcerting and restless gray eyes. Already she seemed to have a permanent frown etched in her forehead.

She was dressed simply in baggy jeans and a T-shirt commemorating an old Oasis tour. Her hair, dyed black, gelled and cut spiky, didn't suit her round face at all. Nor did the collection of rings and studs through the crescent edges of her ears. Her complexion looked dry as parchment, and she still suffered the ravages of acne.

The flat was spacious, with a high ceiling and one of those Chinese-style globe lampshades over the bulb. Bookshelves stood propped on bricks against one wall, not much on them, apart from tattered paperbacks and a few software manuals, and a computer stood on the desk under the window. A sheepskin rug covered part of the hardwood floor, and various quilts and patterned coverlets hung over the secondhand three-piece suite. It was a comfortable room; Ruth Walker, Banks had to admit, had made a nice home for herself.

"I don't usually let strangers in," she said.

"A good policy."

"But you mentioned Louisa. You're not one of her new friends, are you?"

"No, I'm not. You don't like them?"

"I can take them or leave them." Ruth sniffed and reached for a packet of Embassy Regal resting on the coffee table. "Bad habit I picked up in university. Want a cup of tea?"

"Please." It would set them at ease, Banks thought, create the right atmosphere for the sort of informal chat he wanted. Ruth put the cigarettes down without lighting one and walked into the kitchen. She had a slight limp. Not enough to slow her down, but noticeable if you looked closely enough. Banks looked at the book titles: Maeve Binchy, Rosamunde Pilcher, Catherine Cookson. A few CDs lay scattered beside the stereo, but Banks hadn't heard of most of the groups, except for the Manic Street Preachers, Sheryl Crow, Beth Orton, Radiohead and P.J. Harvey. Still, Ruth probably hadn't heard of Arnold Bax or Gerald Finzi, either.

When Ruth came back with the tea and sat opposite him, she still seemed to be checking him out, probing him with those suspicious gray eyes of hers. "Louisa," she said, when she had finally lit her cigarette. "What about her?"

"I'm looking for her. Do you know where she is?"

"Why?"

"Does it matter?"

"It might. You could be out to do her harm."

"I'm not."

"What do you want with her, then?"

Banks paused. Might as well do it again; after all, he'd got this far on a lie, and it was beginning to fit so well he almost believed it himself, even though he had never met Emily Riddle. "I'm her father," he said. "I just want to talk to her."

Ruth just stared at him a moment, her eyes narrowing. "I don't think so." She shook her head.

"You don't think what?"

"That you're Louisa's father."

"Why not?"

"He wouldn't come looking for her, for a start."

"I love my daughter," Banks said, which at least was true.

"No. You don't understand. I saw a photo. A family photo she had with the rest of her things. There's no point lying. I *know* it wasn't you."

Banks paused, stunned as much by Emily's taking a family photo as by Ruth's immediate uncovering of his little deception. Time for a change of tack. "Okay," he said. "I'm not her father. But he asked me to look for her, to try to find her and ask her if she'd talk to him."

"Why didn't he come himself?"

"He's afraid that if she knows he's looking for her she'll make herself even more scarce."

"He's got that one right," said Ruth. "Look, why should I tell you anything? Louisa left home of her own free will, and she was of legal age. She came down here to live her own life away from her parents. Why should I mess things up for her?"

"I'm not here to force her to do anything she doesn't want," said Banks. "She can stay down here if she likes. All her father wants is to know what she's doing, where she lives, if she's all right. And if she'll talk to him, great, if not—"

"Why should I trust you? You've already lied to me."

"Is she in any trouble, Ruth?" Banks asked. "Does she need help?"

"Help? Louisa? You must be joking. She's the kind who always lands on her feet, no matter what. After she's landed on her back first, that is."

"I thought she was a friend of yours?"

"She was. Is." Ruth made an impatient gesture. "She just annoys me sometimes, that's all. Most people do. Don't your friends piss you off from time to time?"

"But *is* there any real reason for concern?"

"I'm sure I don't know."

Banks sipped some tea; it tasted bitter. "Where did you meet her?"

"Down near King's Cross. She came up to me in the street and asked me the way to the nearest youth hostel. We got talking. I could tell she'd just arrived and she wasn't quite sure what to do or where to go." Ruth shrugged. "I know how lonely and friendless London can be, especially when you're new to it all."

"So you took her in?"

"I felt sorry for her."

"And she lived with you here?"

Ruth's cheeks reddened. "Look, I'm not a lezzy, if that's what you're thinking. I offered her my spare room till she got on her feet. That's all. Can't a person do someone a good turn anymore without it being turned into some sort of sex thing?"

"I didn't mean to suggest that," said Banks. "I'm sorry if it upset you."

"Yeah . . . well. Just be careful what you go around saying to people, that's all."

"You and Louisa *are* friends, though, you said?"

"Yeah. She stayed here for a while. I helped get her a job, but it didn't take. Then she met Craig, a bloke I knew from college, and she went off to live with him."

Ruth spoke in a curiously dispassionate way, but Banks

got the impression there was a lot beneath the surface she wasn't saying. He also got the sense that she was constantly assessing, evaluating, calculating, and that being found out in his little lie had put him somehow in thrall to her. "I've talked to Craig Newton," he said, "and he told me she left him for a new boyfriend. Sounds like a nasty piece of work. Know who he is?"

"Just some bloke she met at a party."

"Were you there? Did you meet him?"

"Yes."

"Have you seen them since?"

"They came round here once. I think Louisa was showing him off. *He* certainly didn't seem impressed by what he saw."

"Do you know his name?"

"Barry Clough."

"Do you know the address?"

Ruth fumbled for another cigarette, and when she had lit it and breathed out her first lungful of smoke, she nodded. "Yeah. They live in one of those fancy villa-style places out Little Venice way. Louisa had me over to a dinner party there once—catered, of course. I think she was trying to impress *me* that time."

"Did it work?"

"It takes more than a big house and a couple of has-been rock stars. And maybe a back-bencher and a bent copper or two."

Banks smiled. "What does he do for a living?"

"Some sort of businessman. He's got connections with the music business. If you ask me, he's a drug dealer."

"What makes you say that?"

"Fancy house. Always lots of coke around. Rock stars. Stands to reason, doesn't it?"

"Does Louisa take drugs?"

"Is the Pope Polish?"

"How long ago did they meet?"

"Bit over two months."

"Have you seen much of her since that time?"

"Not much. You're beginning to sound like a copper, you know."

Banks didn't like the way she was looking at him, as if she *knew*. "I'm just worried, that's all," he said.

"Why? She's not *your* daughter."

Banks didn't want to explain about his own daughter, at this moment no doubt walking around Paris hand in hand with Damon, or perhaps not even bothering with the sights, deciding instead to spend the weekend in bed. "Her father's a good mate of mine," he said instead, the words almost sticking in his throat as he uttered them. "I'd hate to see any harm come to her."

"Bit late for that, isn't it? I mean, it was nearly six months ago when she first came down here. He should have put a bit more effort into finding her back then, if you ask me." She paused, narrowed her eyes again, then said, "I'm not sure about you. There's something you're not telling me. You weren't screwing her, were you? I wouldn't put it past her. She was no innocent from the provinces, even when she first came here. She knew what was what."

"She's a bit young for me," Banks said.

Ruth gave a harsh laugh. "At your age I should think it's often a matter of the younger the better. Why do you think they have prostitutes as young as thirteen, fourteen? 'Cos the girls like it?"

Banks felt the sting of her remark, but he couldn't think of an appropriate response. "We're getting off track here."

"Not if you want me to give you Louisa's address, we're not. I've got to satisfy myself you're not a pervert, not some creep, haven't I? And don't come the age bit. She could coax a ninety-year-old bishop out of his cassock, could Louisa."

"All I can do is repeat what I've already told you. There was nothing like that. I've got a daughter her age, myself."

"You do?"

"Yes."

"What's her name?"

Surprised, Banks answered, "Tracy."

Ruth evaluated him some more. "You don't look old enough."

"Want to see my birth certificate?"

"No, that's not necessary. Besides, I don't suppose you actually carry it around with you, do you?"

"It was a . . . never mind," said Banks, feeling he had had just about as much of Ruth Walker and her sharp edges as he could take. No wonder Emily had run off with Craig Newton at the first opportunity.

Ruth got up and walked to the window. "Would you believe that sad pillock over there?" she said a few moments later, almost muttering to herself. "He works security, on the night shift. Hasn't a clue the bloke from number fifty-three is shagging the arse off his wife every night. Dirty bastard. Maybe I should tell him?"

Before Banks could make any comment, Ruth turned sharply, arms folded, a smug smile on her face. "All right," she said. "I'll tell you where they live. But you're wasting your time. She's had it with the lot of you. She won't listen to a word you've got to say."

"It's worth a try. At least I'll find out whether she's all right, what she's up to."

Ruth gave him a pitying look. "Maybe you will," she said. "And maybe you won't."

Shortly after six o'clock that evening, Banks got off the tube at Warwick Avenue and walked toward the address Ruth had given him. Had it been a lovely summer evening, he might have walked down the steps to the canal and admired the brightly colored houseboats, but it had turned dark by late afternoon, as usual, and it was a chilly evening, with the smell of rain in the wind.

The address turned out to be a villa-style building, square and detached within a high enclosing wall. In the wall stood an iron gate. A locked gate.

Banks could have kicked himself for not expecting something like this. If Louisa's boyfriend was the type to go around with minders, he was also the type to live in a bloody fortress. Getting to see Emily Riddle wouldn't be quite so easy as knocking on the door or ringing the bell.

At the front, two of the downstairs windows and one upstairs were lit behind dark curtains, and a light shone over
the front door. Banks tried to think of the best approach. He
could simply call through on the intercom and announce
himself, see if that gained him admission. Alternatively, he
could climb the gate and go knock on the door. Then what?
Rescue the damsel in distress? Climb to the upstairs window
on her hair? Flee with her over his shoulder? As far as he
knew, though, Emily Riddle wasn't in distress, nor was she
held captive in a tower. In fact, she might well be having the
time of her life.

He stood in front of the gate and stared through the bars,
cheeks so close he could feel the cold from the iron. There
was nothing else for it, really; he would have to use the intercom and just hope he could gain admittance. He obviously couldn't pass himself off as Emily's father this time,
but if he said he came with an important message from her
family, that ought to get him inside. It might just work.

Before he could press the buzzer, he felt a strong hand
grasp the back of his neck and push his face toward the bars,
so the cold iron chafed against his cheeks. "What the fuck
are you doing here?" the voice asked him.

Banks's first impulse was to kick back hard at the man's
shins with his heel, or tread down sharply on his instep, then
slip free, swivel around and lash out. But he had to hold
himself in check, remember why he was here, who he was
supposed to be. If he beat up his assailant, where would that
get him? Nowhere, most likely. On the other hand, maybe
this was his best way in.

"I'm looking for Louisa," he said.

The grip loosened. Banks turned and found himself facing a man in a tight-fitting suit who looked as if he might
have been one of Mike Tyson's sparring partners. Probably
just as well he *hadn't* tried to fight back, he thought.

"Louisa? What do you want with Louisa?" the man said.

"I want to talk to her, that's all," he said. "Her father sent
me."

"Fuck a duck," said the minder.

"I was going to ring the bell," Banks went on. "I was just

looking to see if there were any lights on, if there was anyone home."

"You were?"

"Yes."

"I think you'd better come with me, mate," the minder
said, which was exactly what Banks had hoped for. "We'll
see what Mr. Clough has to say about that."

The minder slipped a credit-card style key into the mechanism at the side of the intercom, punched in a seven-digit
number which Banks was amazed he had the brains to remember, and the gate slid open on oiled hinges. The minder
was holding Banks by the arm now, but only hard enough to
break a few small bones, as he led him down the short path
to the front door, which he opened with a simple Yale key.
Sometimes security, like beauty, is only skin-deep.

They stood in a bright corridor, which ran all the way
through to a gleaming modern kitchen at the back of the
house. Several doors led off the corridor, all closed, and immediately to their right, a thickly carpeted staircase led to
the upper levels. It was a hell of a lot fancier than Ruth's flat,
Banks thought, and grander than anything Craig Newton
could afford, too. *Always landed on her feet.* The Riddles
said they had given Emily all the advantages that money
could afford—the horse, piano lessons, holidays, expensive
schooling—and they had certainly raised a high-maintenance
daughter by the looks of this place.

Muffled music came from one of the rooms. A pop song
Banks didn't recognize. As soon as the front door shut behind them, the minder called out, "Boss?"

One of the doors opened and a tall man walked out. He
wasn't fat, or even overly muscular like the minder, but he
certainly looked as if he lifted a few weights at the gym once
or twice a week. As Craig Newton had pointed out, his face
was all angles, as if it had been carved from stone, and he
was handsome, if you liked that sort of thing, rather like a
younger Nick Nolte.

He was wearing a cream Armani suit over a red T-shirt,
had a deep suntan and a gray ponytail about six inches long
hanging over his back collar. Around his neck he wore a

thick gold chain, which matched the one on his wrist and the chunky signet ring over the hairy knuckle on his right hand. Banks pegged him at early to mid-forties, which wasn't much younger than Jimmy Riddle. Or Banks himself, for that matter.

The hard glint in his eyes and the cocky confidence with which he moved showed that he was someone to watch out for. Banks had seen that look before in the eyes of hardened criminals, people to whom the world and its contents are there for the taking, and for whom any impediments are simply to be brushed aside as easily as dandruff off the collar.

"What's this?" he asked, eyes on Banks.

"Found him lurking by the gate, boss. Just standing there. Says he wants to see Louisa."

Barry Clough raised an eyebrow, but the hardness in his eyes didn't ease a jot. "Did he now? What might you be wanting with Louisa, little man?"

"Her father asked me to look for her," Banks said. "He wants me to deliver a message."

"Private investigator?"

"Just a friend of the family."

Clough studied Banks closely for what seemed like minutes, then a glint of humor flashed into his eyes the way a shark flashes through the water. "No problem," he said, ushering Banks into the room. "A girl should stay in touch with her family, I always say, though I can't say as she's ever offered to take me home to meet Mummy and Daddy yet. I don't even know where they live."

Banks said nothing. The minder shifted from foot to foot.

"You're lucky to find us in," said Clough. "Louisa and I just got back from Florida a couple of days ago. Can't stand the bloody weather here in winter. We take off as often as we can. I'll call her down for you. In the meantime, take a load off. Drink?"

"No, thanks. I won't take long."

Clough looked at his watch. An expensive one. "You've got twenty minutes," he said. "Then we've got a Bonfire Night party to go to. Sure you won't have that drink?"

"No, thanks."

Banks sat down as Clough left the room. He heard muffled footsteps on the staircase. The minder had disappeared into the kitchen. The room Banks found himself in had that old-fashioned wainscoted look he wouldn't have expected judging by what he had seen of the bright hall and the modern kitchen at the back. Paintings hung on the walls, mostly English landscapes. A couple of them looked old and genuine. Not Constables or anything, but they probably cost a bob or two. On one wall stood a locked, barred glass case full of guns. Deactivated collector's models, Banks guessed. Nobody would be stupid enough to put real guns on display like that.

Logs crackled and spit out sparks from the large stone hearth. The music was coming from an expensive stereo set up at the far end of the room. Now he was closer to the source, Banks realized he *did* recognize it; it was an old Joy Division album. "Heart and Soul" was playing.

He heard voices upstairs, but he couldn't make out what they were saying. At one point, a woman's voice raised almost to the point where he could hear the defiance in her tone, then, at a barked order from the man, it stopped. A few seconds later, the door opened and in she walked. He hadn't heard her come down the stairs, and nor did he hear her float across the Turkish carpet.

Craig Newton was right. Talk about a mix of innocence and experience. She could have been sixteen, which she was, but she could have been twenty-six just as easily, and in some ways she reminded Banks even more of her mother in the flesh than in the photographs he had seen: blue eyes, cherry lips. What he hadn't been able to tell from those photos, though, was that she had a smattering of freckles across her small nose and high cheekbones, and that her eyes were a much paler blue than Rosalind's. The Florida sun didn't seem to have done much for her skin, which was as pale as her mother's. Perhaps she had stayed indoors or walked around under a parasol like a Southern belle.

Rosalind was a little shorter and fuller-figured than her daughter, and of course her hairstyle was different. Emily had a ragged fringe, and her fine, natural-blond hair fell straight to her shoulders and brushed against them as she moved. Tall and long-legged, she also had that anorexic, thoroughbred look of a professional model. Heroin-chic. She was wearing denim capris that came halfway up her calves, and a loose cable-knit sweater. She walked barefoot, he noticed, showing off her shapely ankles and slim feet, the toenails painted crimson. For some reason, Coleridge's line from "Christabel" flashed through Banks's mind: ". . . her blue-veined feet unsandalled were." It had always seemed an improbably erotic image to him, ever since he first came across the poem at school, and now he knew why.

Though Emily walked with style and self-possession, there was a list to her progress, and when he looked closely, Banks noticed a few tiny grains of white powder in the soft indentation between her nose and her upper lip. Even as he looked, her pointed pink tongue slipped out of her mouth and swept it away. She smiled at him. Her eyes were slightly unfocused and the pupils dilated, little random chips of light dancing in them like feldspar catching the sun.

"I don't believe I've had the pleasure," she said, stretching out her hand to him. It came at the end of an impossibly long arm. Banks stood up and shook. Her cool, soft fingers grasped his loosely for a second, then disengaged. He introduced himself. Emily sat in an armchair by the fire, legs curled under her, and toyed with a loose thread at the end of one sleeve.

"So you're Banks?" she said. "I've heard of you. Detective Chief Inspector Banks. Am I right?"

"You're right. All good, I hope?"

She smiled. "Intriguing, at least." Then her expression turned to one of boredom. "What does Daddy want after all this time? Oh, Christ, what *is* this dreadfully dull music? Sometimes Barry plays the most depressing things."

"Joy Division," said Banks. "He committed suicide. The lead singer."

"I'm not bloody surprised. I'd commit suicide if I sounded like him." She got up, shut off the CD and replaced it with Alanis Morissette's *Jagged Little Pill*. Alanis sang about all she really wanted. She didn't sound a lot more cheerful than

Joy Division, Banks thought, but the music was more upbeat, more modern. "He's still an old punk at heart, is Barry. Did you know he used to be a roadie for a punk band?"

"What does he do now?" Banks asked casually.

"He's a businessman. Bit of this, bit of that. You know the sort of thing." She laughed. It sounded like a crystal glass shattering. "Come to think of it, I don't really know what he does. He's away a lot. He doesn't talk about it much." She put a finger to her lips. "It's all terribly hush-hush."

I'll bet it is, thought Banks. As she had been speaking, he found himself trying to place her accent. He couldn't. Riddle had probably moved counties more times than he'd had hot dinners to make chief constable by his mid-forties, so Emily had ended up with a kind of characterless, nowhere accent, not especially posh, but certainly without any of the rough edges a regional bias gives. Banks knew that his own accent was hard to place, too, as he had grown up in Peterborough, lived in London for over twenty years and in North Yorkshire for about seven.

As Emily talked now, she walked around the room touching objects, occasionally picking up an ornament, such as a heavy glass paperweight with a rose design trapped inside, and putting it back, or moving it somewhere else. She ended up standing by the fireplace, elbow leaning on the mantelpiece, fist to her cheek, one hip cocked. "Did you tell me what you'd come for?" she asked. "I don't remember."

"You haven't given me a chance yet."

She put her hand to her mouth and stifled a giggle. "Ooh, I'm sorry. That's me, that is. Talk, talk, talk."

Banks saw an ashtray on the table with a couple of butts crushed out in it. He reached for his cigarettes, offered Emily one, which she took, and lit one for himself. Then he leaned forward a little in his armchair and said, "I was talking to your father a couple of days ago, Emily. He's worried about you. He wants you to get in touch with him."

"My name's Louisa. And I'm not going home."

"Nobody said you were. But it wouldn't do you any harm to get in touch with him and let him know how you're doing, where you are, would it?"

"He'd only get angry." She pouted, then moved away from the fireplace. "How did you find me? I didn't tell *anyone* where I'm from. I didn't even use my real name."

"I know," said Banks. "But, really: Louisa *Gamine*. You're a clever girl, you've had an expensive education. It took me a little while to work it out, but I got there in the end. *Gamine* means a girl with mischievous charm, but 'gamine' is an anagram of 'enigma,' which means puzzle, or, in this case, Riddle. Your father said you were very good with language."

She clapped her hands together. "Clever man. You got it. What a brilliant detective. But that still doesn't answer my question."

"Your little brother saw your photo on the Internet."

Emily's jaw dropped and she fell back onto the chair. It was hard to tell, but Banks thought her reaction was genuine. "Ben? Ben saw that?"

Banks nodded.

"Oh, shit." She flicked her half-smoked cigarette into the fire. "That wasn't supposed to happen."

"I don't imagine it was."

"And he told Mum?"

"That's right."

"She'd never have told Dad. Not in a million years. She knows what he's like as well as I do."

"I don't know how he found out," said Banks, "but he did."

Emily laughed. "I'd love to have seen his face."

"No, you wouldn't."

"And he sent you to look for me?"

"That's about it."

"Why?"

"Why did he send me?"

"Well, I'm damn sure he wouldn't bother coming himself, but why you? He doesn't even *like* you."

"But he knows I'm good at my job."

"Let me guess. He's promised you he'll leave you alone if you do as he asks? Don't trust him."

"I can't honestly say as I do, but I've got . . ."

"What?"

"Never mind. It doesn't matter."

"Tell me what you were going to say."

"No." Banks didn't want to tell her about Tracy, that in an odd sort of way he was doing this for her, making up for his own absences and shortcomings as a father.

Emily sulked for a few moments, then she stood up again and paced in front of him, counting off imaginary points on her fingers. "Let me see . . . the pictures took you to Glamour-Puss . . . right? That took you to Craig . . . ? But he doesn't know where I am. I told . . . Ah, Ruth! Ruth told you?"

Banks said nothing.

"Well, she would. She's a jealous cow. She'd just love to cause trouble for me, the ugly bitch, just because I've met someone like Barry and she's still stuck in her poky little flat in Kennington. Do you know . . ."

"What?"

"Nothing. Never mind."

"What were you going to say?"

Emily smiled. "No. Now it's my turn to tease. I'm not telling you." Before Banks could frame a response, she stopped pacing and knelt in front of him, looking up into his face with her sparkling blue eyes. "So you saw them, too, did you? The photos."

Banks swallowed. "Yes."

"Did you like them? Did they excite you?"

"Not particularly."

"Liar." She jumped up again, a smile of triumph on her face. "Besides, they were just a joke. A laugh. Daddy's got nothing to worry about from them. It's not as if I've taken up a career in the porno business or anything."

"I'm glad to hear it," said Banks.

"He's just worried about me ruining his spotless reputation, isn't he?"

"That's part of it." Banks didn't feel he necessarily had to paint an idealized picture of Riddle, especially to his runaway daughter. She probably knew him better than anyone. "But he did also seem genuinely concerned about you."

"I'm sure he did." Emily had sat down again now and

seemed thoughtful. "Chief Constable Jeremiah Riddle, champion of family values, quality time, the caring, concerned copper. 'My daughter the slut' wouldn't fit at all with that image, would it?"

"It wouldn't do any harm if you just gave him a call and reassured him everything's okay, would it?" Banks said. "And what about your mother? She's worried sick, too."

Her eyes flashed. "You don't know anything. What do you know about it?" She fingered the collar of her sweater and seemed to draw in on herself. "It was like being in prison up there. You can't go here. You can't do that. You can't see him. You can't talk to her. Don't forget your piano lessons. Have you done your homework? Be in before eight o'clock. I'd no room to breathe. It was stifling me. I couldn't be free, couldn't be myself."

"Are you now?"

"Of course I am." She stood up again. Red patches glowed on her cheeks. "Tell Daddy to fuck off. Tell the old man to just fuck off. Let him wonder. Let him worry. I'm not going to set his mind at rest. Because . . . you know what?"

"What?"

"Because he was never fucking there anyway. He used to make all these rules and you know what . . . he was never even there to enforce them. Mummy had to do that. And she didn't even care enough. *He was never even there to enforce his own stupid rules*. Isn't that a laugh?" She went to lean against the fireplace again. Alanis Morissette was singing about seeing right through someone, and Banks knew what she meant. Still, he'd done his job, done as he'd been asked. He could give Jimmy Riddle Emily's London address, tell him about Barry Clough. If Riddle wanted to send in the locals to check out Clough's gun collection, set the forensic accountants on his business interests and put in a call to the drugs squad, that was his business. Banks's job was over. It was up to Riddle to take it from there. He tore a page from his notebook and wrote on it. "If you change your mind, or if there's anything else you want to tell me, any message you want me to deliver, this is where I'm staying. You can phone and leave a message if I'm not there."

For a moment, he thought she wasn't going to take it, but she did. Then she glanced at it once, crumpled it up and threw it in the fire. The door opened and Barry Clough strode in, smile on his face. He tapped his wristwatch. "Better get ready, love," he said to Emily. "We're due at Rod's place in half an hour." He looked at Banks, the smile gone. "And your time's up, mate," he said, jerking his thumb toward the front door. "On your bike."

4

Banks was running about five minutes late for his dinner with Sandra when he got off the tube at Camden Town. The drizzle had turned into a steady downpour now, and puddles in the gutter were smeared with the gaudy reflections of shop signs and traffic lights. Luckily, the restaurant wasn't far from the underground.

Banks turned up his jacket collar, but he was still soaked by the time he dashed into the restaurant. At first he didn't recognize the woman who smiled and waved him over to her table by the window. Though he had seen Sandra briefly just a couple of months ago, she had changed her appearance completely since then. For a start, she had had her blond hair cut short and layered. If anything, the style emphasized her dark eyebrows more than ever, and Banks had always found Sandra's eyebrows one of her sexiest features. She was also wearing a pair of round gold-rimmed glasses, not much bigger than the "granny glasses" that were so popular in the sixties. He had never seen her in glasses before, hadn't known she needed them. From what he could make out, her clothes looked artsy, all different layers: a black shawl, a red silk scarf, a red-and-black-patterned jumper.

Banks edged into the chair opposite her. He was starving. It seemed ages since that dismal chicken pot pie in Kennington. "Sorry I'm a bit late," he said, drying off his hair with a serviette. "I'd forgotten what a pain the bloody tube can be."

Sandra smiled. "It's all right. Remember, I'm used to your being late."

Banks let that one go by. He looked around. The restaurant was busy, bustling with waiters and parties coming and going. It was one of those places that Banks thought trendy in its lack of trendiness, all scratched wood tables and partitions, pork chops, steaks and mashed potatoes. But the mashed potatoes had garlic and sun-dried tomatoes in them and cost about three quid a side order.

"I've already ordered some wine," Sandra said. "A half-liter of the house claret. I know you prefer red. Okay with you?"

"Fine." Banks had turned down a drink at Clough's house because he hadn't wanted to be beholden to the bastard in any way, but he wanted one now. "You're looking good," he said. "You've changed. I don't mean that you didn't always look good. You know what I mean."

Sandra laughed, blushed a little and turned away. "Thank you," she said.

"What's with the glasses?"

"They come with age," she said. "Anytime after your fortieth birthday."

"Then I'm really living on borrowed time."

A waiter brought the wine and left it for them to pour themselves. *Pretentious in its unpretentiousness.* Sandra paused as Banks filled their glasses, then lifted hers for a toast. "How are you, Alan?" she asked.

"Fine," said Banks. "Just fine. Couldn't be better."

"Working?"

"Aren't I always?"

"I thought Jimmy Riddle had shuffled you off to the hinterlands?"

"Even Riddle needs my particular skills every now and then." Banks sipped some wine. Perfectly quaffable. He looked around and saw it was okay to light a cigarette. "May I cadge one?" Sandra asked.

"Of course. Still can't give them up completely?"

"Not completely. Oh, Sean doesn't like it. He keeps going on at me to stop. But I don't think one or two a month is really bad for your health."

Good sign, that, Banks thought: Sean the nag. "Probably not," he said. "I keep waiting for them to announce they were wrong all along and cigarettes are really *good* for you, and it's all the raw vegetables and fruit that do the damage."

Sandra laughed. "You'll have a long wait." She clinked glasses. "Cheers."

"Cheers. I was out where we used to live this lunchtime. Kennington."

"Really? Why? A sentimental journey?"

"Work."

"It was a pretty cramped flat, as I remember. Much too small with the kids. And that dentist I worked for was a groper."

"You never told me that."

"There's lots of things I never told you. You usually seemed to have enough on your plate as it was."

They studied the menu for a couple of minutes. Banks saw that he was right about the mashed potatoes. And the garlic and sun-dried tomatoes. And the price. He ordered venison sausage with braised red cabbage and garlic mashed potatoes. No sun-dried tomatoes. It seemed the perfect comfort meal for a night like this. Sandra went for steak and frites. Their orders given to the waiter, they smoked and drank in silence awhile longer. Now he was here with her, Banks didn't know how to approach what he wanted to say. He felt curiously tongue-tied, like a teenager on his first date.

If Sandra would put this silliness with Sean aside and come back, he wanted to tell her, it was still possible that they could rebuild their relationship and move on. True, they had sold the Eastvale semi and Banks's cottage would be a bit small for two, but they could manage there for a while at least. If Banks went through with his transfer to the National Crime Squad—*if* they offered him it—then who knew where they might end up living. And with Riddle owing him now, he would be all right for a glowing recommendation.

"I saw Brian last week," Sandra said.

"He told me when I phoned him the other evening. I wanted to drop by and see him while I was here, but he said they were off to play some gigs in Scotland."

Sandra nodded. "That's right. Aberdeen. He's really excited about their prospects, you know. They've already almost finished their first CD."

"I know." Their son Brian played in a rock band. They had just cut their first record with an indie label and were on the verge of getting a deal with a major record company. Banks had heard the band play the last time he was in London and had been knocked out by his son's singing, playing and songwriting talent, had come to see him in a whole new light, a person unto himself, not just an extension of the family. He had almost written Brian off as an idler and a layabout after he nearly failed his degree, but Brian was his own person in Banks's mind now. Independent, talented, free. The same feeling had happened with Tracy, when he had seen her with her new friends in a pub shortly after she started university. He knew he'd lost her, then—at least lost the daughter of his imagination—but in her place he had found a young woman he liked and admired, even if she was off in Paris with the monosyllabic Damon. Letting go can be painful, Banks had learned over the years, but sometimes it hurts more if you try to hold on.

"I thought you were taking Tracy to Paris this weekend?"

"She told you?"

"Of course. Why shouldn't she? I am her mother, after all."

Banks sipped some wine. "Something came up," he said. "She's gone with a friend."

Sandra raised an eyebrow. "Male or female?"

"Male. Bloke called Damon. Seems all right. Tracy can take care of herself."

"I know that, Alan. It's just . . . just *difficult*, that's all."

"What is?"

"Trying to bring up two kids this way."

"Apart?"

"You know what I mean."

"Even if we were still together, it would be like this. We're not bringing them up anymore. They're grown up now, Sandra. They live away from home. The sooner you accept that, the better."

"Do you think I don't know that? I'm just saying it's hard, that's all. They both seem so distant now."

"They are. But as I said, it would be like that anyway."

"Maybe."

Their food arrived and they both tucked in. The sausage was good, more meat than fat for a change, and so were the garlic mashed potatoes. Sandra pronounced her positive verdict on the steak. A few minutes into the meal, she said, "Remember when I dropped by to see you up at Gratly?"

"How could I forget?"

"I want to apologize. I'm sorry. I shouldn't have done that. Not unannounced. It was unfair of me."

"Never mind."

"How is she?"

"Who?"

"You know who I mean. Your pretty young girlfriend. What was her name?"

"Annie. Annie Cabbot. Detective Sergeant Annie Cabbot."

"That's right." Sandra smiled. "I can't believe you tried to con me into thinking the two of you were working. Her barefoot in those tight shorts. It was plain as the nose on your face. Anyway, how is she?"

"I haven't seen much of her lately."

"Don't tell me I scared her off?"

"Sort of."

"Well, she can't have much staying power if she let a little thing like that scare her away."

"I suppose not."

"I'm sorry, Alan. Really I am. I don't want to spoil anything for you. I *want* you to find someone. I want you to be happy."

Banks ate more food and washed it down with wine. Soon, the carafe was empty. "Another?" he suggested.

"Fine," said Sandra. "I'll probably only have one glass, though. If you think you can manage the rest by yourself . . ."

"I'm not driving." Banks ordered more wine and filled their glasses when it came.

"Was there anything . . . I mean, was there any particular reason you wanted to see me?" Sandra asked.

"Do I need a reason to have dinner with my own wife?"

Sandra flinched. "I didn't mean you *needed* one, I just . . . For crying out loud, Alan, we've been separated for a year now. We've hardly spoken so much as a few words to one another in that time. And that mostly over the telephone. You can't expect me not to wonder if you've got some sort of hidden agenda."

"I just thought it was time we buried the hatchet, that's all."

Sandra studied him. "Sure?"

"Yes, I'm sure."

"All right, then. Consider it buried." They clinked glasses again. "How's Jenny Fuller?"

Jenny was a mutual acquaintance; she was also a clinical psychologist and Banks had sought her help on a number of cases. "I haven't seen a lot of her. She's pretty busy now she's back teaching at York."

"You know," Sandra said, toying with her few remaining frites and looking at him sideways, "there was a time when I thought you and Jenny . . . I mean, she's a very attractive woman."

"It just never worked out that way," said Banks, who had often wondered why it hadn't, even when it seemed that both of them wanted it to. Fate, he supposed. "She's got poor taste in men," he said, then laughed. "That wasn't meant to sound that way. I didn't mean to imply that I'd be a particularly good choice for her, just that she seems destined to end up with men who treat her badly, as if she's constantly reliving some sort of relationship, trying to get it right and failing every time. She can't break the cycle."

"I know what you mean," said Sandra. "She told me once that despite everything she's done she doesn't have a lot of confidence in herself, much self-esteem. I don't know."

They finished their meals, put their plates aside and Banks lit another cigarette. Sandra declined his offer of one. While she was at the ladies', he poured himself more wine and debated how to broach the subject that was on his mind. As she walked back across the restaurant he noticed she was wearing jeans under her various flowing layers of clothing, and her figure still looked good. His heart gave a little lurch, and another part of him stirred, unbidden.

Sandra looked at her watch after she sat down. "I can't stay very much longer," she said. "I promised to meet some friends at half ten."

"Party?"

"Mmm. Something like that."

"You never did that up in Eastvale."

"Things have changed since then. Besides, Eastvale closes down at nine o'clock. This is London."

"Maybe we never should have left," Banks said. "It seemed like a good idea at the time. I mean, let's be honest, I was getting pretty burned out. I thought a quieter life might bring us closer together. Shows how much I know."

"It was nothing to do with that, Alan. It wouldn't have mattered where we were. Even when you were there you were always somewhere else."

"What do you mean?"

"Think about it. Most of the time you were out working; the rest of the time you were thinking about work. You just weren't at home. The damnedest thing is, you never even realized it; you thought everything was just hunky-dory."

"It was, wasn't it? Until you met Sean."

"Sean has nothing to do with this. Leave him out of it."

"Nothing would suit me better."

They fell silent. Sandra seemed restless, as if she wanted to get something off her chest before she left. "Stay for a coffee, at least," Banks said. "And we'll leave Sean out of it."

She managed a thin smile. "All right. I'll have a cappuccino. And please don't tell me I didn't drink that in Eastvale either. You can't get a bloody cappuccino in Eastvale."

"You can now. That new fancy coffee place opposite the community center. It wasn't open when you left. Sells latte, too."

"So the North's getting sophisticated, after all, is it?"

"Oh, yes. People come from miles around."

"To sell their sheep. I remember."

"Yorkshire never really suited you, did it?"

Sandra shook her head. "I tried, Alan. Honestly I did. For your sake. For mine. For Brian and Tracy's. I tried. But in the end I suppose you're right. I'm a big-city girl. Take it or leave it."

Banks filled his wineglass as Sandra's cappuccino arrived. "I've applied for another job," he told her finally.

She paused with the frothing cup halfway to her lips. "You're not leaving the force?"

"No, not that." Banks laughed. "I suppose the force will always be with me."

Sandra groaned.

"But I'll most likely be leaving Yorkshire. In fact there's a good chance I could be based down here. I've applied for the National Crime Squad."

Sandra frowned and sipped some coffee. "I read about that in the papers a while ago. Sort of an English FBI, they said. What brought all this about? I thought at least *you* were happy up to your knees in sheep droppings. Was it Jimmy Riddle?"

Banks scraped his cigarette around the rim of the ashtray. "A lot of reasons," he said, "and Jimmy Riddle was a big one. I'm not so sure about that now. But maybe I've run my natural course up there, too. I'm just a bit behind you; that's all. I don't know. I think I need something new. A challenge. And maybe I'm a big-city boy at heart, too."

Sandra laughed. "Well, good luck. I hope you get what you want."

"It could mean travel, too. Europe. Hunting down dangerous criminals in the Dordogne."

"Good for you."

Banks paused to stub out his cigarette and take another sip of wine. Here goes nothing, he thought. "We've been apart about a year now, right?"

Sandra frowned. "That's right."

"It's not that long, is it, when you think about it? People give up things for a while, then go back to them. Like smoking."

"What on earth are you talking about?"

"Maybe that wasn't a good analogy. I was never much

good at this sort of thing. What I'm saying is that people sometimes separate for a year or more, do other things, live in other places, then . . . you know, they get back together. Once they've got it out of their system. People can be an addiction, like cigarettes, but better for you. You find you can't give them up."

"Back together?"

"Yes. Not like before, of course. It never could be like before. We've both changed too much for that. But better. It could be better. It might mean you coming up to Yorkshire for a little while, just until things get sorted, but I promise—and I mean this—that even if the NCS doesn't work out, I'll get a transfer. I've still got contacts at the Met. There's bound to be something for a copper with my experience."

"Wait a minute, Alan. Let me get this straight. You're suggesting that I come up and live with you in that tiny cottage until you can get a job down here?"

"Yes. Of course, if you don't want to, if you'd rather just wait until I get something—whatever—then I can understand that. I know it's too small for two, really. I mean, you could come for the occasional weekend. We could see each other. Have dates, like when we were first together."

Sandra shook her head slowly.

"What? You don't like my idea?"

"Alan, you haven't heard a word I've said, have you?"

"I know things got bad. I know you had to leave. I don't blame you for that now. What I'm saying is that we can make a go of it again. It could be different this time."

"No."

"What do you mean?"

"No means no."

"Okay." Banks emptied his glass and poured some more. There wasn't much left in the second carafe by now. "I suppose it must have been a shock coming out of the blue like that. Why don't you at least take some time to think about it? About us. I apologize for springing it on you like this. You take the opportunities where and when you find them."

"Can't you hear what I'm saying, Alan? N O. No. We're not moving back in together, neither up in Yorkshire nor down here in London. When I first moved out, I'll admit I didn't know what would become of us, how I would feel in a year's time."

"And you know now?"

"Yes."

"So? What is it?"

"I'm sorry, Alan. Jesus, you have to go and make this so bloody difficult, don't you?" She took her glasses off and wiped her eyes with the backs of her hands.

"I don't understand."

"Alan, we're not getting back together. Not now. Not next month. Not ever. What I want to tell you is that I want a divorce. Sean and I want to get married."

Banks looked in the large tilted mirror and saw short black hair still wet with beads of rain, which also glistened on the shoulders of his black leather jacket. Beyond the array of whiskey bottles, he saw a face that was perhaps too lean and sharply angled to be called handsome, and two bright, slightly out-of-focus blue eyes looking into themselves. He saw the kind of bloke you gave a wide berth unless you were looking for trouble.

Around him, life went on. The couple beside him argued in low, tense voices; a drunk rambled on to himself about Manchester United; noisy kids fed the machines with money, and the machines beeped and honked with gratitude. The air was dense with cigarette smoke and tinged with the smell of hops and barley. Barmen dashed about filling shouted orders, standing impatiently as the Optics dispensed their miserly measures of rum or vodka. One of them, shaking drops of Rose's lime juice from a nozzled bottle into a pint of lager, muttered, "Jesus Christ, hurry up. I could piss faster than this."

Banks took a long swig of beer and lit another cigarette, marveling for the umpteenth time in the last hour or so at how calm he felt. He hadn't felt this calm in ages. Certainly not in his last few months with Sandra. After she had dropped her bombshell earlier in the evening, she had dashed out of the restaurant in tears, leaving Banks alone with his wine and the bill. The whole place had seemed to fall silent as the pressure mounted in his ears, and he felt pins and needles prickle over his entire body. *Divorce. Marry Sean*. Had she really said that?

She had, he realized after he had paid up and wobbled down the rain-lashed streets of Camden Town into the first pub he saw. And now here he was at the bar, on his second pint, wondering where were the anger, the pain, the rage he was supposed to feel? He was stunned, gob-smacked, knocked for six, as anyone would be after hearing such news. But he didn't feel as if the bottom had fallen out of his world. Why?

The answer, when it came, was so simple he could have kicked himself. It was because Sandra was *right*. They weren't going to get back together. He'd been deluding himself for long enough, and reality had finally broken through. He had simply been going through the motions he thought he was supposed to go through. When it really came down to it, neither of them really *wanted* to get back together. It was over. And this was one sure way of bringing about closure. Divorce. Marriage to Sean.

Sure, Banks knew, you can't write off twenty years of marriage completely, and there would always be a residue of affection, even of love and, perhaps, of pain. But—and this was the important thing—it was finally *over*. There would be no more ambiguity, no more vain hope, no more childish illusions that some external change—a new place to live, a new job—would make everything all right again. Now they could both walk away from the dead thing that was their marriage and get on with their lives.

There would be sadness, yes. They'd have regrets, perhaps a few, as the song went. They would also always be tied together by Brian and Tracy. But he realized as he looked in the pub mirror at his own reflection that if he was to be *really* honest with himself right now—and this was the moment for it—then he should be celebrating rather than drowning his sorrows. Tomorrow he would phone Sandra and tell her to go ahead with the divorce, to marry Sean, that it was fine. But tonight he would celebrate freedom. What he really felt was *relief*. The scales had fallen from his eyes. Because there was no hope, there was hope.

And so he raised the rest of his pint in celebration and drew one or two curious looks when he toasted the face in the mirror.

Rain had smudged the neon and car lights all over the road like a finger painting as Banks walked a little unsteadily looking for the next pub. He could hear the sound of distant fireworks and see rockets flash across the sky. He didn't want to go back to the lonely hotel room just yet, didn't feel tired enough, despite what felt like a long day.

The next pub he found was less crowded, and he managed to find a seat in the corner, next to a table of pensioners well into their cups. He knew he was a bit drunk, but he also knew he was well within the limits of reason in his thoughts. And so he found himself thinking about what had transpired that day, how uneasy he felt about it all. Especially about his meeting with Emily Riddle at Barry Clough's villa. The more he thought about that, the more out of kilter everything seemed.

Emily had been high; that much was obvious. Whether she was on coke or heroin, he couldn't be certain, but the white powder on her upper lip certainly indicated one or the other. Coke, he would guess, given her jerkiness and her mood swings. She had probably been smoking marijuana, too. Craig Newton had also said she was really high when he saw her in the street, the time Clough's minders beat him up. So was she a junkie or an occasional user? Sometimes the one shaded right into the other.

Then there was Barry Clough himself: the expensive villa, the gold, the furnishings, the Armani suit, the guns. That he was a "businessman" was all anyone would say about him, and that was a term that covered a multitude of sins. What did he really have to do with the music business? What sort of party had he met Emily at? That he was a crook of some kind, Banks had no doubt, but as to what kind of criminal activity or activities were his bent, he didn't know. How did he make his money? Drugs, perhaps. Porn? Possibly. Either way, he was bad news for Emily, no matter how much of a ball she thought she was having now, and he was even worse news for Jimmy Riddle's career prospects.

Banks hadn't felt good about walking away from Clough's house like that. Just as he hadn't felt good about not taking on the minder at the gate. Under normal circumstances, he would have gone in there with authority, with teeth, but he was acting as a private citizen, so he had to take whatever they dished out. He was also committed to acting discreetly, and who knew what damaging revelations might come out into the light of day if he upset Clough? Part of him, perhaps due to the overstimulation of alcohol, wanted to go back there and ruffle Clough's feathers, antagonize him into making some sort of move. But he knew enough not to give in to the desire. Not tonight, at any rate.

Instead, he called upon the gods of common sense, finished his pint and hurried out into the street to find a taxi. A good night's sleep was what he needed now, and tomorrow would bring what it would.

Tomorrow came too early. It was 3:18 A.M. by the digital clock on Banks's bedside table when the telephone rang. Groaning and rubbing the sleep from his eyes, he groped for it in the dark and finally grasped the handset.

"Banks," he grunted.

"I'm sorry to bother you at this hour, sir," said the desk clerk, "but there's a young lady in the lobby. She seems very distraught. She says she's your daughter and she insists on seeing you."

In Banks's half-asleep, alcohol-sodden consciousness, the only thought that came clear out of all that was that Tracy was there and she was in trouble. Perhaps she had been talking to Sandra and was upset about the impending divorce. "Send her up," he said, then he got out of bed, turned on the table lamp and pulled on his clothes. His head ached and his mouth was dry. Figuring it would take Tracy a minute or so to get up to his third-floor room, he nipped into the bathroom and swallowed a few Paracetamols from his traveling medicine kit, along with a couple of glasses of water. When he had done that, he filled and plugged in the little kettle and put a teabag in the pot.

By the time the soft knock came at his door, Banks was beginning to realize there was something wrong with the picture he had envisaged. Tracy knew where he would be, of course; he had given her the name of the hotel before she left for Paris with Damon. But it was still only Saturday night, or Sunday morning, so shouldn't they both still be in Paris?

When he opened the door, Emily Riddle stood there. "Can I come in?" she said.

Banks stepped aside and locked the door behind her. Emily was wearing a black evening gown, loose-fitting, cut low over her small breasts and slit up one side to her thigh. Her bare arms were covered with goose pimples. Her blond hair was messily piled on her head, the remains of the so-phisticated style disarrayed by the wind and rain. She looked like a naughty debutante. A twenty-five-year-old naughty debutante at that. But more remarkable than all that were the tear down the right shoulder of her dress and the question mark of dried blood at the corner of her mouth. There was also a weal on her cheek that looked as if it might turn into a bruise. Her eyes looked heavy, half-closed.

"I'm so tired," she said, then she tossed her handbag on the bed and flopped into the armchair.

The kettle came to a boil and Banks made some tea. Emily took the hot cup from him and held it to herself as if she needed the heat. Her eyes opened a little more.

Suddenly, it seemed like a very small room. Banks perched on the edge of the bed. "What is it?" he asked. "What happened, Emily? Who did this to you?"

Emily started crying.

Banks found her a tissue from the bathroom, and she wiped her eyes with it. They were bloodshot and pink around the rims. "I must look a sight," she said. "Have you got a cigarette, please?"

Banks gave her one and took one himself. After she had

taken a few drags and sipped some tea, she seemed to compose herself a bit more.

"What happened?" Banks asked again. "Did Clough do this?"

"I want to go home. Will you take me home? Please?"

"In the morning. Tell me what happened to you."

Her eyes started to close and she leaned back in the chair with her legs stretched out and ankles crossed. Banks worried that she would slide right onto the floor, but she managed to stay put. She looked at Banks through narrowed eyes and blew some smoke out of her nose. It made her cough, which spoiled the sophisticated effect she had probably been aiming for.

"Tell me what happened," he asked her again.

"I don't want to talk about it. I ran . . . in the rain . . . found a taxi and came here."

"But you threw the address away."

"I can remember things like that. I only have to look once. Like my mother." She finished her cigarette and seemed to doze off for a moment.

"Did Clough do this to you? Was it him?"

She pretended to sleep.

"Emily?"

"Uh-huh?" she said, without opening her eyes.

"Was it Clough?"

"I don't want to go back there. I can't go back there. Will you take me home?"

"Tomorrow. I'll take you home tomorrow."

"Can I stay here tonight?"

"Yes." Banks stood up. "I can get a room for you. I don't think they're full."

"No." Her eyes opened wide and she jerked forward so quickly she spilled tea over the front of her dress. If it burned her, she didn't seem to feel it. "No," she said again. "I don't want to be by myself. I'm scared. Let me stay here with you. Please?"

Christ Almighty, thought Banks. If anyone found out about this, his career wouldn't be worth twopence. But what else could he do? She was upset and she was scared. Something bad had happened to her. He couldn't simply abandon her.

"Okay," he said. "Take the bed, and I'll sleep in the chair. Come on."

He leaned forward to help her up. She seemed listless. When she finally got out of the chair, she stumbled forward against his chest and put her arms around his neck. "Have you got anything to smoke?" she said. "I'm coming down. I need something to soften the edges. I think somebody put something in my drink." He could feel her warm body touching his under the thin material of the dress, and he remembered the images he had seen of her naked. He felt ashamed of his erection and hoped she didn't notice, but as he disentangled her arms and moved away, she gave him a cockeyed, mischievous smile and said, "I told you before you were a liar."

She did something with the straps of her dress, and it slipped off her shoulders over her waist to the floor. She was wearing white bikini panties and nothing more. Her nipples stood out dark and hard on her small white breasts. The black spider tattoo between her navel ring and the elastic of her panties seemed to be moving, as if it were spinning a web.

"For crying out loud," said Banks, picking up the bedspread and swathing it around her. She giggled and fell on the bed. "Of course you don't have anything to smoke," she said. "You're a copper. Detective Chief Inspector Bonks. No, he doesn't. Yes, he does. No, he doesn't." She giggled again, then turned on her side and put her thumb in her mouth, drawing up her legs in the fetal position. "Hold me," she said, taking her thumb out for a moment. "Please come and hold me."

Banks shook his head and whispered, "No." There was no way he was getting in that bed with her, no matter how much she said she was in need of comfort. If he thought about it, he should probably throw her out and tear up the sheets, but he couldn't do that. Instead, he managed to pull some more blankets over her, and she offered no resistance. For a while, she seemed to be muttering and murmuring as best she could with her thumb back in her mouth, then he heard her start snoring softly.

Banks knew there would be no more sleep for him tonight. In the morning, he would go to Oxford Street when the shops opened and buy her some clothes, then they would take the first train back to Eastvale. He would drive her to her father's house and there he would leave her, leave them all to sort it out. His job would be over.

But as he sat in the chair and smoked another cigarette, listening to the wind and rain rattling the window, and to Emily's ragged snoring, he couldn't help but mull the situation over. It was all wrong. He was a copper; a serious offense had been committed; the law had been broken; he should be *doing* something, not sitting in the armchair smoking as his chief constable's sixteen-year-old daughter slept in his bed practically starkers with her thumb in her mouth, to all intents and purposes nothing but a child in a woman's body.

Three fifty-two. A long wait until dawn. He glanced through the curtains and saw a flash of white moon through the gray wisps of cloud. Emily stirred, turned over, farted once and started snoring again. Banks reached for his Walkman on the table beside him and put in the Dawn Upshaw tape. Songs about sleep.

Come, Sleep, and with
Thy sweet deceiving
Lock me in delight awhile.

Not much hope of that, Banks thought, not after the day he had just been through.

5

The Charlie Courage murder occurred in early December, about a month after Banks had delivered Emily Riddle to her father's house, a little battered and shop-soiled, but not too much the worse for wear. Judging by her silence on the train journey back to Yorkshire, he imagined she might lie low for a while before taking on the world again. In the meantime, Banks had been preoccupied with major changes at Eastvale Divisional Headquarters.

The county force had been reorganized from seven divisions into just three, and Eastvale was the new headquarters of the large Western Division, which took in just about the entire county west of the A1 to the Lancashire border, and from the Durham border in the north to the border with West Yorkshire in the south. There were vast areas of wilderness and moorland, including most of the Yorkshire Dales National Park, and the main occupations were the service industry, tourism, agriculture and a smattering of light industry. There were no major urban areas, but a number of big towns such as Harrogate, Ripon, Richmond, Skipton and Eastvale itself.

There was, of course, plenty of crime, and in keeping with its new status, the Eastvale station had been extended into the adjoining building, where Vic Manson's fingerprints unit, scenes-of-crime, computers and photography departments had all set up shop. Renovations were still going on, and the place was filled with noise and dust.

While the section stations would continue to police their areas as before—indeed, they were to be given even more autonomy—Eastvale was now to be responsible for most of the criminal investigation within the new Western Division. Nobody was sure yet how many CID officers—or Crime Management Personnel, as some now liked to call them—they would end up with, or where they would all be put, but staffing increases had already begun.

One of the first moves that the Director of Human Resources, Millicent Cummings, had made was to transfer Detective Sergeant Annie Cabbot to the new team. Millie told Banks that she thought Annie had worked well with him on their previous case, no matter what Chief Constable Riddle thought of its messy outcome, and that as Annie was going for her inspector's boards as soon as she could, the experience would be good for her.

Millie, of course, along with Riddle and everyone else, didn't know about Banks's affair with Annie, and Banks could hardly say anything now. This was a good opportunity for her to get back in the swing of things, and he certainly wasn't going to stand in her way. Annie *was* a good detective, and if she could handle working with Banks, he could at least try to accommodate her.

The county also had a new Assistant Chief Constable (Crime) in the shape of Ron McLaughlin, known jokingly as "Red Ron" because he leaned more to the left than most senior policemen. ACC McLaughlin was known to be a hard but fair man, one who believed in using his officers' abilities to the fullest, and he was also rumored to enjoy a wee dram of malt every now and then.

It was a misty, drizzling day—what the locals called "mizzling"—when Riddle got the chance to make good on his promise to Banks. Over the last year or so, all serious crimes in the division that couldn't be handled by Detective Superintendent Gristhorpe, Detective Sergeant Hatchley and whichever DCs happened to be assigned to Eastvale Divisional Headquarters at the time, had been passed on to other divisions, or to the Regional Crime Squad, leaving Banks free to devote all his duty hours to paperwork and administration.

Since he had done Riddle the big favor of bringing Emily back home, since the big changes around the station, and since things had finally come to an end with Sandra, the thought of moving from his Gratly cottage and starting a new job with the NCS had begun to lose its appeal, and Banks had withdrawn his application. Eastvale was starting to seem like a good bet again, and it was where he wanted to be.

Despite the drizzle and the filthy gray sky, Banks felt in a buoyant, optimistic mood. He was reading a report on the sudden increase of car theft in rural areas, and in need of a break, he went to stand by the window to smoke a pro-scribed cigarette and look down on the market square in the late afternoon.

The renovators were mercifully silent, no doubt planning their next major assault, and Banks's radio played quietly in the background: Prokofiev's Piano Concerto No. 3. The Eastvale Christmas lights, turned on in the middle of No-vember by some third-rate television personality Banks had never heard of, made a pretty sight outside his window, hanging across Market Street and over the square like a bright lattice of jewels. Soon they'd be putting up the huge Christmas tree by the market cross, and the church choir would be out singing carols at lunchtime and early evening, collecting for charity.

Brian thought he would be busy with the band over the holidays, but Tracy had phoned the previous day and prom-ised to spend Christmas with her father before heading down to London to see her mother on Boxing Day. Banks had never been much of a fan of Christmas—far too many holiday seasons spent working and witnessing the gaudy excess of suicides and domestic murders that peaked around that time of year had taken care of that—but this called for celebration; this year he would make an effort, buy a small tree, presents, put up some decorations, cook Christmas dinner.

Last year had been a complete washout. He had turned down all offers of meals, drinks and parties from friends and colleagues and spent the entire holiday alone in the Eastvale semi he had once shared with Sandra, wallowing in his own misery and keeping up his maintenance buzz with liberal tots of whisky. Brian and Tracy had both phoned, of course, and he had managed to bluff his way past any worries they might have had about him, but there was no denying it had been a grim time. This year would be different. Delia Smith had a book about cooking for Christmas, he remembered; perhaps he would go to Waterstone's and buy it before going home.

The telephone brought him back to his desk. "Banks here."

"Chief Inspector Banks? My name's Collaton, Detective Inspector Mike Collaton. I'm calling from Market Harborough, Leicestershire Constabulary. I just called your county headquarters and they put me on to you."

"What can I do for you?"

"Earlier today a motorist stopped by the roadside near here and nipped down a lane into the woods for a piss. He found a body."

"Go on," said Banks, tapping his pen on the desk, still wondering what the connection was.

"It's one of yours. Thought you might be interested."

"One of my what?"

"Local villains. Bloke by the name of Charles Courage. Same as the brewery. Lived at number seventeen Cutpurse Lane, Eastvale." He laughed. "Sounds like it could hardly be a more appropriate address, going by his record."

Jesus Christ, Charlie Courage! *Dutch,* as his cronies jokingly called him on account of that was about the only courage he ever exhibited. Charlie Courage had been a thorn in the side of Eastvale Division for years. In truth, he was a petty villain, a minor player, but around Eastvale he was still a big fish in a small pond. Charlie Courage had done a little bit of everything—except anything that involved violence or sex—from handling stolen goods to sheep-stealing, when it was worth stealing them. You had to give Charlie his due; he was a character. Two or three years ago, he used to have a stall in Eastvale market, Banks remembered, right in front of the police station, where he blithely sold videos and CDs that in all likelihood had "fallen off the back of a lorry." While questioning him about a local break-in once, Banks had even bought the Academy of Ancient Music's CD of Mozart's C Minor Mass for $3.99. A bargain at twice the price. He didn't ask where it had come from. To his credit, Charlie had also acted as police informer on a number of occasions. Rumor had it that he had been going straight lately.

"You've heard of him?" DI Collaton went on.

"I've heard of him. What happened?"

"Shot. Looks like the weapon used was a shotgun. Made a real mess, anyway."

"Any chance it was accidental, or self-inflicted?"

"Not unless he shot himself in the chest, then got up after he was dead and hid the weapon. We can't find any sign of it."

"Are you sure it's Charlie? What on earth was he doing all the way down there? It's not like Charlie to leave his parish."

"I'm afraid we can't shine any light on that just yet, either. But it's definitely him. I got the ID from fingerprints. Seems he did two years once for something involving sheep. I've heard about you lot up there and your sheep. Some sort of unspeakable deed, was it?"

Banks laughed. "Stealing them, actually. They used to be worth a bit. You might remember. As for the other, I can't say I've any idea what Charlie got up to in his spare time. Far as I know, he was single, so he could please himself. Anything more you can tell me?"

"Not much. I've checked around, and it seems he doesn't have any living relatives."

"Sounds like Charlie. I don't think he ever did."

"Anyway, I thought I'd ask you to have a look around his house, if you would, see if there's anything there. Save my lads some legwork. We're a bit short-staffed down here."

"Aren't we all? Sure. I'll have a look. What about his car?"

"No sign of any car. Maybe you'd like to come down here tomorrow morning, see the scene, toss a few ideas around, that sort of thing? I've a feeling that if there are any answers to be found, they're probably at your end. The postmortem's tomorrow afternoon, by the way."

"Okay," said Banks. "In the meantime I'll go have a quick poke around Charlie's place right now and see about organizing a thorough search later. If he's dead, I won't have to worry about a warrant. I'll drive down tomorrow morning."

Banks took Collaton's directions to the Fairfield Road police station in Market Harborough, then hung up and went into the main CID office. Since the reorganization began, they had been assigned three new DCs and were promised three more. DC Gavin Rickerd was a spotty, nondescript sort of lad given to anoraks and parkas. Banks couldn't help feeling he must have been a train-spotter in a previous lifetime, if not in this one. Kevin Templeton was more flash, a bit of a jack-the-lad, but he got things done, and he was surprisingly good with people, especially kids.

The third addition was DC Winsome Jackman, who hailed from a village in the Cockpit Mountains, high above Montego Bay, Jamaica. Why she had wanted to leave there for the unpredictable summers and miserable winters of North Yorkshire was beyond Banks's ken. At least superficially. When it came right down to it, though, he imagined that a village in the Jamaican mountains was probably no place for a bright and beautiful woman like Winsome to forge ahead in a career.

Why she hadn't become a model instead of joining the police was also beyond Banks. She had the figure for it, and her face showed traces of her Maroon heritage in the high cheekbones and dark ebony coloring. She could certainly give Naomi Campbell a run for her money, and from what Banks had read about the supermodel in the papers, Winsome was a far nicer person. Some of the lads called her "Lose-Some" because of the time, back in uniform, when she had chased and caught a mugger in a shopping center, only to have him then slip out of her grasp and escape. She took it good-naturedly and gave as good as she got. You had to when you were the only black woman in the division.

As it turned out, everyone was out of the office except Kevin Templeton and Annie, who looked up from her computer monitor as Banks entered.

"Afternoon," she said, flashing him a quick smile. Annie had a hell of a smile. Though not much more than a twitch of the right corner of her mouth, near the small mole, accompanied by a quick blaze of light from her almond eyes, it was dazzling. Banks felt his heart lurch just a little. God, he hoped this working together wasn't going to be too difficult.

"See what you can dig up on a local villain called Charlie Courage," he said. Then, more or less on impulse, he added, "Fancy a ride down to Market Harborough tomorrow?" He found himself holding his breath after the words were out, almost wishing he could take them back.

"Why not?" she said, after a short pause. "It'll make a nice break."

"Much on?"

"Nothing the lads can't handle on their own."

Kevin Templeton grunted from his corner.

"Okay. I'll pick you up here around nine."

Back in his office, Banks found himself hoping that things worked out with Annie on the job. He liked working with female detectives, and he still missed his old DC, Susan Gay, with all her uncertainties and sharp edges. When he had worked with Annie before, he had come to value her near-telepathic communication skills and the way she could mix logic and intuition in her unique style of thinking. He had also cherished her touch and her laughter, but that was another matter, one he couldn't let himself dwell on anymore. Or could he?

He left the office in a good mood. For the moment, Riddle had proved true to his word, and Banks finally had a case he might be able to get his teeth into. It was DI Collaton's call, of course, but Collaton had asked for help right off the bat, which led Banks to think that he probably didn't want to spend too long away from hearth and home tracking the roots of the crime up in dreary Yorkshire, especially with Christmas being so close. Well, good for him, Banks thought. Cooperation between the forces and all that. His loss was Banks's gain.

It was after five when Banks pulled up behind a blue Metro in front of Charlie Courage's one-up-one-down. Cutpurse Lane was a cramped ragbag of terraced cottages behind the community center. Dating from the eighteenth century for the most part, the mean little hovels had privies out back and no front gardens. During the yuppie craze for "bijou" a few years ago, a number of young couples had bought cottages on Cutpurse Lane and installed bathrooms and dormer windows.

As far as Banks knew, Charlie Courage had lived there for years. Whatever Charlie had done with his ill-gotten gains, he certainly hadn't invested them in improving his living conditions. It was a syndrome Banks had seen before in even more successful petty crooks than Charlie. He had even known one big-time criminal who must have brought in seven figures a year easily, yet still lived hardly a notch above squalor in the East End. He wondered what on earth they used the money they stole for, except in some cases to support mammoth drug habits. Did they give it to charity? Use it to buy their parents that dream house they had always yearned for? People had odd priorities. Charlie Courage, though, had not been a drug addict, was not known for his charity, and he didn't have any living relatives. A mystery, then.

First, Banks knocked on the neighbor's door, which was opened by a short, stocky man in a wrinkled faun V-necked pullover, who looked unnervingly like Hitler, even down to the little mustache and the mad gleam in his eyes. He stood in the doorway, the sound of the television coming from the room behind him.

Banks showed his identification. "Knightley," the man said. "Kenneth Knightley. Please come in out of the rain." Banks accepted his invitation. The drizzle was the kind that immediately seemed to get right through your raincoat and your skin, all the way to your bones.

Banks followed him into a small, neat living room with rose-patterned wallpaper and a couple of framed local landscapes hanging above the tile mantelpiece. Banks recognized Gratly Falls, just outside his own cottage, and a romantic watercolor of the ruins of Devraulx Abbey, up Lyndgarth way. A fire blazed in the hearth, making the room a bit too hot and stuffy for Banks's liking. He could already smell the steam rising from his raincoat.

"It's about your neighbor, Charles Courage," he said. "When did you last see him?"

"I don't have much to do with him," said Knightley. "Except to say hello to, like. He always keeps to himself, and I've not been the most sociable of fellows since Edie died, if truth be told." He smiled. "Edie didn't like him, though. Thought he was a wrong 'un. Why? What's happened?"

"I'm afraid Mr. Courage is dead. It looks as if he's been murdered."

Knightley paled. "Murdered. Where? I mean, not . . . "

"No. Not next door. Some distance away, actually. Down Leicester way."

"Leicester? But he never went *anywhere*. One time I did talk to him, I remember him telling me you'd never catch him going to Torremolinos or Alicante for his holidays. Yorkshire was good enough for him. Charlie didn't like foreign places or foreigners, and they began at Ripon as far as he was concerned."

Banks smiled. "I've met a few people like that, myself. But one way or another, he did end up in Leicestershire. Dead."

"That's probably what killed him then. Finding himself in Leicestershire." Knightley paused and ran his hand across his brow. "Sorry, I shouldn't be so flippant. A man's dead, after all. I don't see how I can help you, though."

"You said you saw him last a couple of days ago. Can you be more precise?"

"Let me think. It was early Sunday afternoon. It must have been then because I was just coming back from The Oak. I always go there on a Sunday lunchtime for a game of dominoes."

"About what time would this be?"

"Just after two. I can't be doing with all these new hours, all-day opening and whatnot. I stick to the old times."

"How did he seem?"

"Same as usual: a bit shifty. Said hello and that was that."

"Shifty?"

"He always looked shifty. As if he'd just that minute done something illegal and wasn't quite sure he'd got away with it yet."

"I know what you mean," said Banks. Charlie Courage usually *had* just done something illegal. "So there was nothing odd or different about his behavior at all?"

"Nothing."

"Was he alone?"

"Far as I could tell."

"Coming or going?"

"Come again?"

"Was he just arriving home or leaving?"

"Oh, I see. He was going out."

"Car?"

"Aye. He's got a blue Metro. It's usually . . . just a minute . . ." Knightley stood up and went to the curtain, which he pulled back a few inches. "Aye, there it is," he said, pointing. "Parked right outside." Banks saw the car in front of his and made a mental note to have it searched.

"Did you see or hear anyone with him in the house over the last few days?"

"No. I'm sorry I can't be much help. Like I said, there was nothing unusual at all. He went off to work, then he came home. Quiet as a mouse."

"*Work?* Charlie?"

"Oh, aye. Didn't you know? He'd got a job as a night watchman at that new business park down Ripon Road. Daleview, I think it's called."

"I know the one."

Business park. Another to add to Banks's long list of oxymorons, along with military intelligence. That was an interesting piece of news, anyway: Charlie Courage with a job. A night watchman, no less. Banks wondered if his employers knew of his past. It was worth looking into.

"Is there anything else you can help me with, Mr. Knightley?"

"I don't think there is. And it's no use asking Mrs. Ford on the other side. She's deaf as a post."

"I don't suppose you have a key to Mr. Courage's house, do you?" he asked.

"Key? No. Like I said, we didn't do much more than pass the time of day together out of politeness's sake."

Banks stood up. "I'm going to have to have a good look around the place. If there's no key, I'll have to break in somehow, so don't be alarmed if you hear a few strange noises next door."

Knightley nodded. "Right. Right, you are. Charlie Courage. Murdered. Bloody hell, who'd credit it?"

Banks walked around the back of the terrace block to see if he could find an easy way into Charlie's place. A narrow cobbled alley ran past Charlie's backyard. Each house had a high wall and a tall wooden gate. Some of the walls were topped with broken glass, and some of the gates swung loose on their hinges. Banks lifted the catch and pushed at Charlie's gate. It had scratched and faded green paint and one of the rusty hinges had broken, making it grate against the flagstone path as he opened it. It wasn't much of a backyard, and most of it was taken up by a murky puddle that immediately found its way through his shoes. First, out of habit, Banks tried the doorknob.

The door opened.

Perhaps Charlie hadn't had time to lock up properly before being abducted, Banks thought, as he made his way inside the dark house. He found a light switch on the wall to his right and clicked it on. He was in the kitchen. Nothing much there except for a pile of dirty dishes waiting to be washed. They never would be now.

He walked through to the living room, which was tidy and showed no signs of a struggle. Noting the new-looking television and DVD setup, not what you could afford on a night watchman's salary, Banks got some idea of what Charlie had done with his money. He went upstairs.

There were two small bedrooms, a bathroom with a stained tub and a tiny WC with a ten-year-old *Playboy* magazine on the floor and a copy of Harold Robbins's *The Carpetbaggers* resting on the roll of toilet paper. One bedroom was empty except for a few cardboard boxes filled with magazines—mostly soft porn—and secondhand paperbacks, and the other, Charlie's, revealed only an unmade bed and a few clothes.

Downstairs, in one of the sideboard drawers, Banks found the only items of interest: the title deed to the house, Charlie's driving license, a checkbook, and a bankbook that indicated Charlie had made five cash deposits of £200 each over the past month, in addition to what seemed to be his regular paycheck. A thousand quid. Interesting, Banks thought. That would at least account for the new TV and DVD setup. What had the crooked little devil been up to? And had it got him killed?

Wednesday morning dawned every bit as dismal as Tuesday. It was still dark when Banks drove into Eastvale, sipping hot black coffee from a specially designed carrying mug on the way. The other CID officers were already in the office when he got there, and DS Hatchley, in particular, looked downhearted that he had missed the opportunity of a day trip to Leicestershire. Or perhaps he was jealous that Banks had Annie's company. He gave Banks the kind of bitter, defeated look that said rank pulled the birds every time, and what was a poor sergeant to do? If only he knew.

"You'll be driving, I suppose?" Annie said when they got out back to the car park.

That was another thing Banks appreciated about Annie: she was a quick learner with a good memory. It *was* unusual for a DCI to drive his own car. Having a driver was one of the perks of his position, but Banks *liked* to drive, even in this weather. He liked to be in control. Every time he let someone else drive him, no matter how good they were, he felt restless and irritated by any minor mistakes they made, constantly wanting to get his own foot on the clutch or the brake. It seemed much simpler to do the driving himself, so that was what he did. Annie understood that and didn't question his idiosyncrasy.

Banks slipped a tape of Mozart wind quintets in the Cavalier's sound system as he turned out of the car park. "Mmm, that's nice," said Annie. "I like a bit of Mozart." Then she settled back into the seat and lapsed into silence. It was another thing Banks liked about her, he remembered, the way she seemed so centered and self-contained, the way she could appear comfortable and relaxed in the most awkward positions, at ease with silence. It had also taken him a while to get used to her complete lack of deference to senior ranks, especially *his,* as well as to her rather free and easy style of dress, learned from growing up in an artists' commune surrounded by bearded artistic types such as her painter father, Ray Cabbot. Today she was wearing red winkle-picker boots that came up just above her ankles, black jeans and a Fair Isle sweater under her loose suede jacket. Rather conservative for Annie.

"How are you liking it at Eastvale?" Banks asked as they joined the stream of traffic on the A1.

"Hard to say yet. I've hardly got my feet under the desk."

"What about the traveling?"

"Takes me about three-quarters of an hour each way. That's not bad." She glanced sideways at him. "It's about the same for you, as I remember."

"True. Have you thought of selling the Harkside house?"

"I've thought of it, but I don't think I will. Not just yet. Wait and see what happens."

Banks remembered Annie's tiny cramped cottage at the center of a labyrinth of narrow, winding streets in the village of Harkside. He remembered his first visit there, when she had asked him on impulse for dinner and cooked a vegetarian pasta dish as they drank wine and listened to Emmylou Harris, remembered standing in the backyard for an after-dinner smoke, putting his arm around her shoulders and feeling the thin bra strap. Despite all the warning signs . . . he also remembered kissing the little rose tattoo just above her breast, their bodies, sweaty and tired, the unfamiliar street sounds the following morning.

He negotiated his way from the A1 to the M1. Lorries churned up oily rain that coated his windscreen before the wipers could get through it; there were more long delays at roadwork signs where nobody was working; a maniac in a red BMW flashed his lights about a foot from Banks's rear end and then, when Banks changed lanes to accommodate him, zoomed off at well over a ton.

"What did you find out about Charlie?" he asked Annie when he had got into the rhythm of motorway driving.

Annie's eyes were closed. She didn't open them. "Not much. Probably not more than you know already."

"Tell me anyway."

"He was born Charles Douglas Courage in February 1946—"

"You don't have to go that far back."

"I find it helps. It makes him one of the generation born immediately after the war, when the men came home randy and ready to get on with their lives. He'd have been ten in 1956, too young for Elvis, perhaps, but twenty in 1966, and probably just raring for all the sex, drugs and rock and roll you lot enjoyed in your youth. Maybe that was where he got his start in crime."

Banks risked a glance away from the road at her. She still had her eyes closed, but there was a little smile on her face. "Charlie wasn't into dealing drugs," he said.

"Maybe it was the rock and roll, then. He was first arrested for distribution of stolen goods in August 1968—to wit, long-playing records. *Sergeant Pepper's Lonely Hearts Club Band*, to be exact, stolen directly from a factory just outside Manchester."

"A music lover, our Charlie," he said. "Carry on."

"After that comes a string of minor offenses—shoplifting, theft of a car stereo—then, in 1988, he was arrested for theft of livestock. To be exact, seventeen sheep from a farm out Relton way. Did eighteen months."

"Conclusion?"

"He's a thief. He'll steal anything, even if it walks on four legs."

"And since then?"

"He appears to have gone straight. Helped Eastvale police out on a number of occasions, mostly minor stuff he found out about through his old contacts."

"Got a list?"

"DC Templeton's working on it."

"Okay," said Banks. "What next?"

"A number of odd jobs, most recently working as a night watchman at the Daleview Business Park. Been there since September."

"Hmm. They must be a trusting lot at Daleview," said Banks. "I think one of us might pay them a visit tomorrow. Anything else?"

"That's about it. Single. Never married. Mother and father deceased. No brothers or sisters. Funny, isn't it?"

"What is?"

Annie stirred in the car seat to face him. "A small-time villain like Charlie Courage getting murdered so far from home."

"We don't know where he was murdered yet."

"An inspired guess. You don't shoot someone in the chest with a shotgun and then drive him around bleeding in a car for three hours, do you?"

"Not without making a mess, you don't. You know, it strikes me that Charlie might have been taken on the long ride."

"The long ride?"

Banks glanced at her. She looked puzzled. "Never heard of the long ride?"

Annie shook her head. "Can't say as I have."

"Just a minute . . ." A slow-moving local delivery van in front of them was sending up so much spray that the windscreen wipers couldn't keep up with it. Carefully, Banks changed lanes and overtook it. "The long ride," he said, once he could see again. "Let's say you've upset someone nasty—you've had your fingers in the till, or you've been telling tales out of school—and he's decided he has to do away with you, right?"

"Okay."

"He's got a number of options, all with their own pros and cons, and this is one of them. What he does—or rather, what his hired hands do—is they pick you up and take you for a ride. A long ride. It's got two main functions. The first is that it confuses the local police by taking the crime away from the patch that gave rise to it. Follow?"

"And the second? Let me guess."

"Go on."

"To scare the shit out of him."

"Right. Let's say you're driven from Eastvale to Market Harborough. You know exactly what's going to happen at the end of the journey. They make sure you have no doubt about that whatsoever, that there's going to be no reprieve, no commuting of the death sentence, so you've got three hours or thereabouts to contemplate your life and its imminent and inevitable end. An end you can also expect to be painful and brutal."

"Cruel bastards."

"It's a cruel world," said Banks. "Anyway, from their perspective, it acts as a deterrent to other would-be thieves or snitches. And, remember, it's not as if we're dealing with lily-whites here. The victim is usually a small-time villain who's done something to upset a more powerful villain."

"Charlie Courage, small-time villain. Fits him to a tee."

"Exactly."

"Except that he was supposed to be going straight, and there aren't any major crime bosses in Eastvale."

"Maybe he wasn't going as straight as we thought. Maybe he was just avoiding drawing our attention. And they don't have to be that big. I'm not talking about the Mafia or the Triads here. There are plenty of minor villains who think life is pretty cheap. Maybe Charlie fell afoul of one of them. Think about it. Charlie worked as a night watchman. He put a thousand quid in the bank—above and beyond his wages—over the past month. What does that tell you, Annie?"

"That he was either selling information, blackmailing someone or he was being paid off to look the other way."

"Right. And he must have been playing way out of his league. Maybe we'll get a better idea when we talk to the manager up there tomorrow. Nearly there now."

Banks negotiated his way around Leicester toward Market Harborough, about thirteen miles south. When they got to the High Street there, it was almost noon, and it took Banks another ten minutes to find the police station.

Before they got out of the car, Banks turned to Annie. "Are we going to be okay?" he asked.

"What do you mean?"

"You know what I mean. This. Working together."

She flashed him a smile. "Well, we seem to be doing all right so far, don't we?" she said, and slipped out of the car.

DI Collaton turned out to be a big bear of a man with thinning gray hair, a red face and a slow, country manner. A year or so away from retirement, Banks guessed. No wonder he didn't want to get involved in a murder inquiry. He looked at his watch and said, "Have you two eaten at all?"

They shook their heads.

He grabbed his raincoat from the stand in the corner of his office. "I know a place."

They followed him to a small pub about two streets away. Judging by the smiles and hellos exchanged, Collaton was well-known there. He led them to a corner table, which gave a little privacy, then offered the first round of drinks. Annie asked for a tomato juice, though Banks knew she enjoyed beer. He ordered a pint of the local best bitter. A fire burned in the hearth and Christmas decorations festooned the walls and ceiling. Apart from the buzz of conversation around the bar, the place was quiet, which was the way Banks liked his pubs, and all too rare these days. As was Annie's habit in pubs, she seemed to mold herself to the hard chair and stretch her legs out, crossing them at the ankles. DI Collaton raised his eyebrows at her red winkle-pickers, but said nothing.

After Banks had ordered game pie, on Collaton's recommendation, and Annie, being a vegetarian, went for the Ploughman's Lunch, he lit what he realized with some surprise was his first cigarette of the day.

"We don't get a lot of murders down here," said Collaton after his first sip.

That didn't surprise Banks. From what he had seen, he supposed Market Harborough to be a bit smaller than Eastvale—maybe seventeen or eighteen thousand people—and Charlie Courage was Eastvale's first murder victim of the entire year so far. In December, no less. "Any idea why they might have chosen your patch?" he asked.

Collaton shook his head. "Not really. It's handy for the M1," he said, "but a bit off the beaten track. If they were taking him somewhere, and he got troublesome . . . "

"Any witnesses?"

"Nobody saw or heard a thing. It's out Husbands Bosworth way, toward the motorway, and at this time of year there's nobody around. More in summer, tourist season, like."

Banks nodded. Same as Eastvale. "Any physical evidence?"

"Tire tracks. That's about all."

"Anything interesting or unusual on his person?"

"Just the usual. Except his wallet was missing."

"I doubt robbery was the motive," Banks mused. "Maybe a London mugger might blow away someone with a shotgun, but not in some leafy Midlands lane."

"My thoughts exactly," said Collaton. "I thought maybe they'd taken it to help keep his identity unknown a bit longer. Maybe they didn't know he'd got form and we'd find out that way."

"Possibly."

"Had he been up to anything lately?"

"We don't know yet," said Banks. "Rumor has it he's been going straight. Had a job as a night watchman. We know he made five cash deposits of two hundred quid each over the past month, though, and I doubt that he came by the money honestly."

Their food arrived. Collaton was right about the game pie. Annie nibbled at her cheese and pickled onion. Collaton kept looking at her out of the corner of his eye, when he thought no one noticed. At first Banks thought he was simply puzzled by her, as people often were, then he realized the dirty old bugger fancied her. And him old enough to be her father.

Suddenly, Banks felt himself struck almost as physically as by a blow by the memory of Emily Riddle in his hotel room. Not so much by her white and slender nakedness, the spider tattoo or the feel of her body pressing against his as by her torn dress, her fear, the little question mark of blood, and Barry Clough. Why on earth hadn't he followed up on that? The next morning he had simply gone out to Oxford Street as soon as the shops opened and, not being skilled at shopping for women's clothing, bought her a tracksuit because it seemed easiest. Though he had questioned her about the previous night, she had given away nothing, maintaining a surly silence all the way home. Did she even remember how she got to his hotel room and her awkward attempt at seducing him?

When he had driven her home from the station and left her with her parents, she had given him a look he found hard to interpret. Sad, yes, partly, and perhaps also a little let-down; defeated, a little hurt, but not completely without affection, a sort of complicit recognition that they had shared something together, been through an adventure. Banks had decided on the way that he had no reason to tell Riddle what happened down there. If Emily wanted to do so, that was fine, but his part of the bargain was over; she was Riddle's problem now.

Still, it had gnawed at him over the past few weeks—Clough especially. Perhaps, if he had time over the next couple of days, he could make a few discreet inquiries of old friends on the Met, see if Clough had form, find out what his particular line of work was. Dirty Dick Burgess ought to know; he had been working with one of the top-level criminal intelligence departments for a while now. But Riddle had asked Banks to be discreet, and sometimes, when you set things in motion, you couldn't always stop them as easily as you wanted to, and you didn't know in which direction they would spin. That was Banks's problem, as Riddle had told him more than once: he had never learned when to leave well enough alone.

"Sir?"

Banks snapped back from a long distance when he felt Annie's elbow in his ribs. "Sorry. Miles away."

"DI Collaton asked if we wanted to have a look at the scene after lunch."

Banks looked at Collaton, who showed concern in his eyes, whether for Banks's health or the lapse in attention wasn't clear. "Yes," he said, pushing his empty plate aside. "Yes, by all means let's go have a look at poor old Charlie's final resting place."

After viewing the spot where Charlie Courage's body had been discovered, just off a muddy track in some woods near Husbands Bosworth, they attended the postmortem in Market Harborough Hospital.

Courage's body had already been photographed, fingerprinted, weighed, measured and X-rayed the previous day. Now, the Home Office pathologist, Dr. Lindsey, and his assistants, worked methodically and patiently through a routine they must have carried out many times. Lindsey began with a close external examination, paying special attention to the gunshot pattern.

"Definitely a shotgun wound," he said. "Twelve-bore, by the looks of it. Range about two or three yards." He pointed out the central entrance opening over the heart and the numerous single small holes around it from the scattered shot. "Any closer and it would have been practically circular. Much farther away and the shot would have spread out more into smaller groups. There's still some wadding embedded in the wounds, too. Look." He held up a piece. "Depends whether they used a sawn-off, of course, as the shot patterns don't hold as far. Even so, it was pretty close range. And judging by the angle of the main wounds, it looks as if either his killer was very tall or the victim was on his knees at the time."

Banks guessed that if he was right in assuming Charlie had been taken for the long ride, then his killer would have used a sawn-off shotgun. The legal length for shotgun barrels was twenty-four inches, not including the stock, and no villain is going to walk or drive around with something that big.

"Then there's this bruising," Dr. Lindsey went on, pointing out the discoloration around Courage's stomach and kidneys. "It looks as if he was beaten either with fists or some hard object before he was killed. Enough to make him piss blood for a week at least."

"Perhaps somebody wanted him to tell them something?" Collaton said.

"From what I knew of Charlie, he'd give up his grandmother if you so much as waved your fist in his face. They might have wanted him to tell them something, but my bet is that he did, and then they carried on beating him up just for the fun of it."

Next, Dr. Lindsey began his dissection with the Y-incision. He took blood samples, then removed and inspected the inner organs, working from the trachea, esophagus and what was left of the heart, down to the bladder and spleen.

As all this was going on, Banks kept a close eye on Annie. He didn't know how good she was at postmortems on fairly fresh corpses, as the last one they had been to was of a skeleton disinterred after fifty years. Though she paled a little when Dr. Lindsey opened up the body cavity and swallowed rather loudly as he squished out the various organs as if he were shucking oysters, she stood her ground.

Until, that is, the power saw started ripping into the front quadrant of the skull. At that, Annie swayed, put her hand to her mouth and, making a gurgling sound, dashed out of the room. Dr. Lindsey rolled his eyes and Collaton glanced at Banks, who just shrugged.

Dr. Lindsey pulled out the brain, looked it over, tossed it from hand to hand as if it were a grapefruit, then put it aside for weighing and sectioning.

"Well," he said, "until we get the tests back on the blood and tissue samples, we won't know whether he was poisoned before he was shot. I doubt it, myself. Judging by the blood, I'd say the gunshot wound was the cause of death. It blew his heart open. And going by the lividity, I'd also say he was killed at the same spot he was found."

"Did you determine time of death?" Banks asked, though he knew it was the question all pathologists hated the most.

Dr. Lindsey frowned and searched through a pile of notes on the lab bench. "I made some rough calculations at the scene. Only rough, of course. I've got them somewhere. Now, where . . . ah here it is. Rigor, temperature . . . allowing for the chilly weather and the rain . . . he was found on Tuesday, that's yesterday, at about four P.M., and I surmised he'd been dead at least twenty-four hours, perhaps longer."

Charlie had been seen by his neighbor on Sunday afternoon at around two o'clock, and if he had been killed sometime Monday afternoon, that left over twenty-four hours, the last twenty-four hours of his life, unaccounted for. When they got back to Eastvale, Banks would have to initiate some house-to-house inquiries in the neighborhood, find out if anyone had seen Charlie later than Sunday lunchtime, and if anyone had seen him *with* anyone. He hadn't got to the lane near Husbands Bosworth in his own car, and he certainly hadn't walked there. The fresh tire tracks that Collaton's men had found most likely belonged to the car that had taken him there, as the lane was an out-of-the-way place. Depending on how good the impressions were, it might be possible to match them up with a particular car—if, of course, they found the car, and if the tires hadn't been changed.

They had learned just about all they could from Dr. Lindsey for the moment, and Banks thanked him for his prompt postmortem and left with Collaton, looking out for Annie as he walked along the corridors.

They found her standing out in the misty, gray afternoon taking deep breaths. When she saw them, she looked away and ran her hand over her chestnut hair. "Christ, I'm sorry. I feel such an idiot."

"It's all right," said Banks. "Don't worry about it."

"It's not that I haven't been to one before." She pulled a face. "I was okay, honest I was, until . . . It was the smell, the saw burning the bone, and the noise it made. I couldn't . . . I'm sorry. I feel like such a fool."

It was the first time Banks had seen any real break in Annie's on-the-job composure. "I told you," he said. "Don't worry about it. Are you up to going home?"

She nodded. He imagined it would be a quiet journey. Annie was clearly pissed off at herself for showing signs of weakness.

Banks looked at Collaton. The indulgent expression on his face indicated he would probably have forgiven Annie *anything*.

It was late when Banks finally got home, after calling in at the station to issue some actions for the following morning. The traffic on the M1 was murder, especially around Sheffield, and patches of dense fog on the A1 meant they had to move at a crawl, keeping in view the rear lights of the lorry in front of them. Banks was reminded of the time when he was lost in the fog, heading for a friend's house, and had blindly followed the car in front right into a private drive. He had been damned embarrassed when the irate driver came to ask him what the hell he thought he was doing.

Annie recovered from her little spell of embarrassment a lot quicker than Banks expected. He had to remind himself that this wasn't Susan Gay, and that Annie didn't worry so much about appearing weak or incompetent; she simply got on with her work and her life.

The fog in the dale slowed him down most on the last leg of his journey. Wraiths of gray mist nuzzled up the daleside and swirled on the road before him. The road ran several feet up the hillside from the valley bottom, where the River Swain meandered through The Leas, and most of the fog had settled low. Banks knew the road well enough not to take too many foolish risks.

Back at the cottage, he found two messages waiting. The first was from Tracy, asking him for ideas about what she should buy her mother for Christmas. A wedding dress, perhaps? Banks thought. But he wouldn't say that to Tracy.

The next caller didn't identify herself, but he knew immediately who she was: "Hello, it's me. Look, I'm sorry I haven't been in touch . . . it was probably very rude of me . . . I mean, I never really thanked you and all, did I, you know,

for what you did for me? I suppose I was pretty fucked up."
There, she broke off and Banks could hear her suck on a cigarette and blow out the smoke. He thought he could hear
background noise, too. "Anyway, you must let me buy you
lunch at least. Hey, look, I'll be over in Eastvale tomorrow,
so why don't you meet me at the Black Bull on York Road
over from Castle Hill, say about one o'clock? Is that all
right?" There was a silence on the line, as if she were actually expecting an answer. Then she sighed. "Okay, then,
hope to see you tomorrow. And I'm sorry. Really, I am.
Ciao."

Banks remembered the last time he had seen Emily at the
door of the old mill house, in the pink tracksuit he had
bought for her on Oxford Street, an outfit she obviously
loathed, giving him that enigmatic look as he delivered her
to her parents. He remembered Jimmy Riddle's clipped
thanks and Rosalind's cool silence. It was all unspoken, but
he had sensed Riddle's awkward, hidden love for his daughter and Rosalind's distance.

So Emily Riddle wanted to thank him. Should he go?
Yes, he thought, reaching for the bottle of Laphroaig; hell,
yes, he would go.

6

The Black Bull was a young people's pub at night, with live music and a steady supply of illegal drugs, mostly Ecstasy and crystal meth. It had been targeted by the Eastvale police's "Operation Pubwatch" on more than one occasion, never without a few arrests being made. At lunchtime, though, it had a totally different character, and most of the customers worked in the various offices and shops along York Road. The only music issued quietly from the jukebox, and the only drugs being consumed were nicotine and alcohol, with perhaps a little caffeine for those who preferred tea or coffee with their pie and chips.

When Banks arrived spot on one o'clock, Emily was nowhere in sight. He bought himself a pint and found a table near the window. The road outside was busy, and the traffic splashed up dirty water from the roadside puddles.

As he was studying the blackboard and trying to decide between Bar BQ Chicken and Thai Red Curry, Emily breezed in, out of breath, the way Jenny Fuller always seemed to do, as if it had been a great effort getting there only fifteen minutes late. She plonked her bulging handbag on the chair beside Banks, gave him an impish grin and made for the bar. When she came back she was carrying one of those strange cocktails that young drinkers, especially female, seem to think are really interesting: in this case, Kahlua and Coke. She must have charmed the landlord into believing she was old enough to drink, Banks thought, though in all honesty she did look well over eighteen. She had a cigarette in her mouth almost before she sat down, a maneuver Banks was surprised she could make, given that her slightly flared blue jeans looked painted on. Still, it was a testament to Emily's natural style that she didn't look in the least bit tarty, and she had chosen to wear no makeup at all. Not that she needed any. Once she had lit her cigarette and had taken a sip of her drink, she shucked her mid-length jacket to reveal a black silk blouse. After she had tidied her hair, she seemed ready to talk, but she kept on fidgeting.

There were moments when Banks looked at her and saw a sophisticated young woman looking back, wise enough in the ways of the world to exploit them for her own ends. Other times, he saw the gauche, nervous teenager, unable to look an adult in the eye. She was still too close to her childhood to recognize its value. When you were Emily's age, Banks remembered, all you wanted to do was enter that magical world of privilege and freedom you saw all around you—adulthood. Hence the smoking, the drinking, the sex. You didn't realize until much, much later—too late, some might say—that the privileges and freedoms you coveted came with a very high price tag indeed.

"Have you decided yet?" she asked.

"Decided what?"

"What you're having for lunch. It's my treat. I told you on the phone."

"You don't have to do that."

"I know. Daddy probably paid you well already for bringing me home. But I want to."

"I'll have the Thai Red Curry, then." Banks didn't usually go for more exotic food in pubs, but the Bull had a good lunchtime reputation. "And he didn't pay me anything."

She raised a neatly plucked eyebrow.

"Just so you know."

Emily paused, then said, "All right." She gestured for the woman delivering food at the next table to come over and started to give her order. The woman frowned, told her to go and order it herself at the bar, then stalked off.

"Get her," said Emily, pulling a face. Kid again.

Banks scraped his chair against the stone floor. "I'll go." He didn't want her to have to go through the agony of getting up and sitting down again; wearing those jeans, she might rupture her spleen or her bladder.

"No." She jumped to her feet with surprising agility. "I told you I'd get it."

Banks watched her walk to the bar, taller than ever in her platform heels, and noticed all the men's eyes were on her body. There wasn't one of them who wouldn't do *anything* for her. Or to her. The women, however, turned up their noses in distaste and cast disapproving frowns in Banks's direction. What the hell, Banks asked himself, was he doing sitting in a pub with the chief constable's daughter, who was definitely breaking one law by drinking under age—even if you could hardly call Kahlua and Coke a real drink—and God knows how many other laws simply by the way she looked? It was fortunate that none of the men could be arrested for their fantasies. Not yet.

"Done." Emily sat again and plucked her cigarette out of the ashtray. "At least they'll bring it to the bloody table. You don't have to get up and fetch it yourself. Honestly, the service industry in this country."

Banks wondered how many other countries she had experienced and realized it was probably more than his own daughter had. Chief constables were always getting junkets to America, Belgium, South Africa or Peru. He wondered if the service in Peru was better than that in Yorkshire. Probably.

"What are you having?" he asked.

"Me? Nothing. I don't eat lunch."

"Nor dinner, either, by the looks of you."

"Now, now. Remember, you didn't disapprove of 'the looks of me' too much in that hotel room."

So she did remember. Banks felt himself blush, and it got all the worse when he saw Emily was laughing at him. "Look—" he said, but she waved him down.

"Don't worry. I haven't told Daddy." She pouted and wiggled her shoulders. "Besides, it's the waiflike look. Most older men like it. Don't you?"

"What about boys your own age?"

She snorted. "They're so immature. Oh, they're all right for dancing and buying you drinks and stuff, but that's about all. All most of them can talk about is football and sex." She licked her cherry lips. "I prefer older men."

Banks swallowed. He could see where that came from: a father who was never there, someone she desperately wanted to love and be loved by. "Like Barry Clough?" he said.

A shadow crossed her fine porcelain features. "That's one of the things I wanted to talk to you about," she said. Then her face brightened into a smile. "But first I really do want to thank you. I mean it. I know I wasn't very nice at the time, but I appreciate what you did, taking care of me like that. I was really fucked up. Big-time."

"Do you remember much about it?"

"In the hotel room? Yes. Until I fell asleep. You were the perfect gentleman. And the next morning you went and bought me a tracksuit. A pink one. It was ugly, but that was sweet of you. I'm sorry I wasn't very friendly on the way home, but I was really down."

"Thai curry?"

The woman held out a dish of steaming curry. Banks admitted to ownership, and she set it down, narrowly avoiding spilling it on the table, gave Emily a hard glare and walked off.

"What *is* her problem?" Emily said. "I mean, *really!* The stupid cow."

"She doesn't like you," said Banks. "She doesn't like the way you treated her, and I'd guess she doesn't like your looks much, either."

"What the fuck do I care if she likes my looks?"

"You asked. I'm simply telling you."

"Anyway, what's she supposed to be here for if not to serve people food? It's not as if she's not getting paid or anything."

"Look," said Banks. "I'm not going to argue. It's not her job to take orders, and you've got a pretty snotty attitude, when it comes right down to it." Banks dipped into his curry. It was good and hot.

Emily glared at him for a few seconds, sulking, then started fidgeting with the large ring on her right index finger. "Stupid old bitch," she muttered.

Banks ignored her and tucked in, easing the heat with an occasional swig of beer. He finished the pint quicker than he had intended to and, before he could stop her, Emily had jumped to her feet and bought him another one. It was the barmaid who served her this time, not the landlord, and Banks noticed them talking, Emily taking something out of her handbag and showing it to her.

"What was all that about?" he asked when she came back.

"Nothing," she said, putting her drink down. "Christ, this place is in the fucking dark ages."

"What do you mean?"

"I only asked for a TVR, didn't I, and do you think the sad bitch behind the bar had any idea what I was talking about?"

"I can't say I have any idea what you're talking about, either."

Emily looked at him as if he came from another planet. "Well, I had to explain it to *her*, too. It's tequila, vodka and Red Bull. Great stuff, gives you a real alcohol high without all that slurring and stumbling. Me and . . . well, you know who . . . we used to drink it in the Cicada Dust in Clerkenwell."

"And?"

She pulled a face. "What do *you* think?"

"They didn't have it?"

"Of course they didn't."

"So what did you settle for?"

"A Snowball."

Banks had heard of that one: Advocaat and lemonade. He had thought it long out of fashion. He remembered that his mother sometimes used to drink a Snowball at Christmas when he was a kid. Just the one, usually, as she was never much of a drinker. "Mmm, it's good." Emily held out the glass. "Want a sip?"

"No, thanks. Have you been in touch with any of the crowd down there? Craig? Ruth?"

Emily shook her head. "Not much."

"Craig said Barry's minders beat him up outside a pub in Soho while you looked on laughing."

"The lying bastard."

"It didn't happen?"

"Oh, it happened, but not the way he told it."

"You tell me, then."

"It was in Clerkenwell, outside Barry's club. Craig found out about the place and he started hanging around there, pretending to be taking photographs. He was obsessed. He just wouldn't let go. I told him to stay away, but he wouldn't listen. He even started coming in, but Barry had him barred. When he came up to me, it was the last straw. I wouldn't have let them hit him like that if I could have stopped them, but it all happened so quickly. It was his own fault, really."

"He said he didn't know where you lived."

"He didn't. I told Ruth to make sure she didn't tell him. He knew about the club from before, though, from the party."

"Which party?"

"The one where I met Barry. At some promoter's house. Ruth took us. She knows people in the music scene and all that."

"Craig was there, too?"

"Yes. That's how he knew Barry owned a club in Clerkenwell. I started seeing Barry after that night and a week or so later I left Craig. He was just getting to be too much."

"I see. And were you laughing when they beat him up?"

"I wasn't laughing. I was crying. The fool."

"Why would he lie to me?"

"The truth would hardly make him look good, would it? Craig might seem so nice and well-balanced on the surface, but he's got a mean streak, too, you know."

"Did he ever hit you?"

"No. He knew I wouldn't stand for that. It was just . . . oh, you know, if I came home late or something, he'd always be waiting up and go on at me, calling me a slut and a whore and stuff. It was mean. Nasty. Then he was all pathetic the next morning, telling me he loved me and buying me presents and all that when all he really wanted was to get into my knickers."

"I still don't understand why he would lie to me. He believed I was your father. Surely he must know I'd find out the truth when I found you?"

Emily laughed. "Silly. It's the last thing I'd tell my father. Think about it."

Banks did. She was right. "But you're telling *me*."

"That's different. You're not my father. You're not like him at all. You're . . ."

"I'm what?"

"Well, you're more like a friend. Cute, too."

"I'm flattered, Emily, but you'd better not tell your father that."

She giggled and put her hand to her mouth, as if embarrassed to catch herself out in a juvenile act. "You're right about that."

"Have you heard from Craig at all since you've been back in Yorkshire?"

"No. I've not seen or heard from him since that night outside the club."

"What about Ruth?"

"I've talked to her a couple of times on the phone. But I didn't give her much cause to like me, did I? I think she fancied Craig and I took him away from her."

"It was as much his choice. Besides, she'll get over it."

"Yeah . . . well . . . Ruth's got enough problems without me adding to them."

"What do you mean?"

"Nothing. She's just a bit fucked up. Couldn't you tell?"

"She did seem strange." Not much stranger than Emily herself, though, Banks thought. He pushed his empty plate aside and lit a cigarette. It wasn't as if there was anything to be gained by trying to act as a positive, nonsmoking role model to Emily. "Are you going to tell me what happened in London that night?" he asked. "Before you arrived at the hotel."

Emily licked at the rim of her glass. "I've been thinking about it."

"And?"

She looked around, then leaned forward conspiratorially. "I've decided I will."

Banks could smell the Advocaat on her breath. He leaned back. "I'm all ears."

Annie had not been completely honest with Banks, she admitted to herself the next afternoon as she drove out to the Daleview Business Park to meet Charlie Courage's boss at SecuTec, Ian Bennett. As usual, when she found it difficult to talk about something, she had been flip, all style and no substance. Working out of Eastvale, with Banks, bothered her more than she had been able to tell him. It wasn't that she couldn't separate her job from her personal life—she felt she could do the job perfectly well, no matter with whom she worked—but so much proximity to Banks might weaken her resolve to end their relationship. After all, she had given him up not because she didn't feel anything for him, but because she found herself feeling too much too soon, and because he brought too many complications from his previous relationship with him, a marriage of over twenty years. Working with him again, she had to admit to herself that she still fancied him.

To hell with it, she told herself, sneaking a quick glance at the map on the car seat beside her. Almost there. She would just do her bloody job and let the rest take care of itself. One thing her brief romance with Banks *had* done was renew her faith in the Job, make her think about *why* she had become a policewoman in the first place. Now she had a better sense of herself, more confidence, and she was damn well going for inspector. Not that the Job was everything, mind you—she wasn't going to make *that* mistake and end up a dried-up old spinster with no life other than work—but she *was* willing to commit herself as much as it took. And because her work life was going to be hard, she wanted to keep her personal life simple. With Banks in her bed, it wouldn't be.

The black wrought-iron railings to her left bore a large painted sign saying DALEVIEW BUSINESS PARK, along with a list of businesses located there. Annie turned through the gates, which were probably intended more for decoration than security, she thought, and looked for the SecuTec office.

The business park consisted of a large, one-story red brick building, built in the shape of a pentagon and divided into a number of different units, each with its own logo, and some with showcase windows and parking spots for two or three cars out front. Though it wasn't a shopping precinct as such, the pottery shop and the needlecraft center had outlets there, along with a stair-lift company, a furniture workshop and an Aga center. The other units were taken up by offices: a company that rented holiday cottages, for example, and a mail-order exercise-video distribution company, Annie noticed. She wondered if that was some sort of euphemism for what they *really* sold. If it was a front for a porn operation, then it might be connected with Charlie Courage's murder.

Ian Bennett opened the office door for her before she even reached it.

"DS Cabbot," she said, fishing for her warrant card.

"It's all right," said Bennett, smiling. "I believe you. Come on in."

She followed him into the small office.

"So this is what the well-dressed young policewoman is wearing these days," he said, looking her up and down.

Under her navy-blue raincoat, which hung open, she was wearing boots, black tights, a short denim skirt and a white sweater, none of which she felt was particularly weird. What did he expect? A uniform? A twinset and pearls?

Bennett was younger than she had expected from the voice on the telephone, probably about her age, early thirties, with thick curly dark hair and more of a tan than you can get hanging around Yorkshire in winter. He looked as if he played sports to keep in shape, something that involved a lot of running around, such as tennis or squash, and while his salary probably didn't stretch as far as Armani, he was wearing high-end designer casuals that must have set him back a bob or two. A mobile phone bulged ostentatiously from the pocket of his zip-up suede jacket. Annie guessed that the BMW she had parked next to was probably his.

"So this is what the well-dressed young yuppie-on-the-go is wearing to impress the girls these days," she countered, aware as soon as she had done so that it wasn't the best way to start an interview. Big problem, Annie: You've never been able to suffer fools gladly, which gives you at least one thing in common with Alan Banks. *Stop thinking about him.*

SecuTec had only a small office at Daleview, where Charlie Courage had spent his nights on guard duty. Annie glanced around and saw that he'd had a small television for company, along with facilities for making tea and a microwave oven for heating up his midnight snack. The office was too small for the two of them, and it smelled of warm plastic. Annie sat on what would have been Charlie's desk and Ian Bennett leaned against the opposite wall by a company calendar. Like so many of those things, it showed a buxom, skinny-waisted smiling blonde in a bikini. She was holding a spanner.

Bennett flushed at her insult. "I suppose I deserved that," he said, running his hand over his hair. "I always say something silly when I meet an attractive woman. Sorry. Can we start again?"

Annie gave him a low-wattage smile, the kind she reserved for the masses. "Best all round," she said.

Bennett cleared his throat. "I'm afraid I can't tell you very much," he began. "I didn't know Mr. Courage well."

"When did he last work?"

"Sunday night. He was on the four-to-midnight shift."

"Are you certain? Did you see him?"

"No, but he logged in. I mean, he has to log in with us so we know someone's there."

"How does he do this?"

Bennett pointed at the desk beside her. "Computer."

"Could someone else have done it? Pretended to be him?"

"I suppose it's possible. But they'd have to know his user name and his password."

"I see. Was this the shift he always worked?"

"No. Other days he worked from midnight till eight in the morning."

"Was he the only night watchman?"

"No. It works like this. Every day the units are open, we have the other security guard, Colin Finch, work four to midnight and Mr. Courage work midnight till eight, when the units start opening in the morning. Then, when we get to Sunday, they alternate. Colin does four to midnight Saturday, Charlie does midnight to eight. Then Colin does eight to four, and so on."

"I see," said Annie, who remembered the horrors of shift work very well indeed. Most of the time she hadn't known whether she was coming or going. "So Colin Finch would have seen Mr. Courage when they changed shifts at four on Sunday?"

"Yes. I should think so."

"Can you give me his address?"

"Of course." Bennett fiddled with the computer and gave Annie a Ripon address. "He'll be in at four today, though, if you're still around."

Annie looked at her watch. It was half past two. "Did you know that Mr. Courage had a criminal record?"

The question seemed to embarrass Bennett. "He had? Er, actually, no, we didn't know."

"Surely a security firm like yours runs checks on potential employees?"

"Normally we do. Yes, of course. But this one . . . well . . . it seems he slipped between the cracks."

" 'Slipped between the cracks'?"

"Yes."

"I see." Annie made a note in her brand-new notebook. What she actually wrote was, "Don't forget to pick up something for dinner at Marks & Sparks," but Bennett wasn't to know that. "Have there been any incidents at the park over the past few months, since Mr. Courage started working here?"

"No. Nothing at all. As far as SecuTec is concerned, Mr. Courage seemed to be doing his job well."

"Nothing gone missing?"

"Nothing."

"The other tenants, are they all satisfied?"

"Yes. As I said, we've had no problems, no complaints at all. I don't suppose it's something you police ever consider, but have you thought at all that Mr. Courage might indeed have gone straight, as they say? I mean, just because a man makes a couple of mistakes, it doesn't mean he's marked forever, does it?"

Annie sighed. This wasn't going to work, she could tell. "Mr. Bennett," she said, "why don't you leave the recidivism-versus-rehabilitation argument to people who know what they're talking about and just answer my questions?"

He smiled. "I thought that's what I was doing. I mean, I've told you there were no problems. I was only suggesting that it might indicate Mr. Courage had changed his ways. You do believe that criminals can change their ways, don't you, Detective Constable Cabbot?"

"It's detective *sergeant*," Annie corrected him, adding a silent "pillock" under her breath. "And I'm merely suggesting that we'll get you back in your Beemer and on your way to your next meeting much faster if you simply answer my questions."

Bennett fiddled with his mobile, as if hoping it would ring. "Carry on," he said, with a drawn-out, long-suffering sigh.

Annie smiled to herself. He would no doubt tell his guests at tonight's dinner party or whatever about his brush with police brutality. "What exactly were his duties?" she asked.

"He was supposed to walk around the park, check doors and everything once an hour. To be honest, though, it wasn't much of a job; there wasn't a lot for him to do."

"I shouldn't think so with all these modern security gizmos. Why bother hiring a night watchman at all, then?"

"It was a matter of appearances, really. The tenants like it. Believe it or not, no matter how many sophisticated alarm systems you put in place, people always feel a bit more confident if there's a human being around."

"That's comforting," said Annie. "I don't suppose I need to worry about Robocop much anymore."

"Sorry?"

"A joke. Never mind. Carry on."

"Oh, I see. A copper with a sense of humor. Anyway, having someone on the premises discourages vandals, too."

"What about a dog?"

"They can be effective, but you can't just leave them alone. Besides, there's the whole problem of lawsuits if they actually bite anyone."

"How did Mr. Courage get the job?"

"He applied through normal channels. I must say, he *seemed* credible enough."

"The mark of a master criminal."

"You're joking again?" Bennett smiled.

Annie didn't smile back. "Mr. Courage was paid by check, am I correct?"

"Actually, no. His wages were paid directly into his bank account."

"Were there ever any cash bonuses?"

Bennett frowned. "Cash bonuses? I don't know what you mean."

"Cash in hand."

"Certainly not. That's not SecuTec's policy."

"And no money has ever been reported missing by any of the businesses operating out of this park during the period of Mr. Courage's employment as night watchman?"

"No."

Annie closed her notebook. "Very well, Mr. Bennett," she said. "You can go now. We might need to get in touch again later."

"Fine. Feel free to do whatever you need here, but please remember to lock up when you leave."

Bennett practically ran out of the office. Annie stood in the doorway and watched him reverse the BMW, then take off in what would have been a cloud of dust, had the ground not been so wet. As it was, one of the puddles he hit sent a sheet of water over a woman just walking into the needlework-center shop a few units down. She looked down at her soaked raincoat and tights and glared after the car, shaking her fist.

She shouldn't have been quite so sharp with Bennett,

Annie thought, as she watched him clear the gates and turn right onto the main road. He was a smug pillock, true enough, but she'd had to deal with plenty of those in her time, and she hadn't usually resorted to bullying. He looked like the kind who'd put in a complaint, too. Would that have any effect on her attempt to make inspector? She doubted it. But she also made a mental note to watch herself and be a lot more compassionate toward fools and pillocks.

Now, she thought, it was simply a matter of deciding whether to go right or left and spend an hour or so talking to the people who operated the businesses at Daleview. They would probably know a lot more about its day-to-day operations than Mr. Ian bloody Bennett. After that, with any luck, Colin Finch would have reported for duty.

"Barry was very angry after you left," Emily said, toying with, rather than smoking, another cigarette. "I've never seen him so angry. When he gets angry, he goes all cold. He doesn't go red in the face and shout or anything, like Dad, he just gets this fixed sort of smile and does everything in a very slow, careful sort of way, like straightening the cushions on the settee or lighting a cigarette. And he talks very quietly. It's frightening."

"Do you know why he was angry?"

"Because you came asking questions. He doesn't like anyone asking questions, especially strangers."

"What did he do to you?"

"Barry? He didn't do anything. I'm telling you. He was angry in that cold way he had. He just told me to get ready for the party, then we did another couple of lines of coke and off we went."

"What kind of party was it?"

"The usual sort. Music-business people, a few minor bands, groupies, along with a few young entrepreneurs, other club owners. The kind of people Barry collects. There was a bonfire and fireworks outside, but mostly we stayed indoors."

"Drugs?"

She laughed. "Oh, yes. Of course. Always drugs."

"Does Barry deal?"

"No. He just buys."

"Go on."

Emily paused. For all her bravado, Banks could tell she had difficulty talking about it. "Barry was weird all evening. I tried to just . . . you know . . . stay away from him until his mood had passed, keep my distance, talk to some of the guys in the bands and stuff, but he kept appearing, smiling in that cold way of his, putting his arm around me, touching me . . . sometimes even squeezing . . . hurting me . . ." She drank some of her Snowball, grimaced and said, "I don't think I like this, after all. Would you get me a lager and lime or something like that? I'm thirsty."

"I'm not buying you an alcoholic drink, Emily. You're under age."

"Don't be a spoilsport. I'm already drinking one, aren't I?"

"You're right. I probably shouldn't even be sitting with you. But I am. If you want me to get you a drink you'll get a lemonade or a Coke."

"I won't tell you the rest of my story."

"Doesn't matter."

"Bastard. And I thought you were supposed to be my friend."

Banks said nothing. Emily sashayed to the bar, drawing all the male eyes again. Banks sipped some beer and lit his second cigarette. He was definitely going to make some inquiries into Mr. Barry Clough and his "business" activities over the next few days.

Emily came back with a pint of lager and lime and spilled some as she set it triumphantly on the table. For a while, she didn't say anything, then she took a long swig, paused and said, "It was pretty late. I don't know. Two or three in the morning. Everyone was really wasted. I was feeling weird, like someone had put something in my drink. It might have been one of those date-rape drugs I've read about, but I'd had so much other stuff I didn't fall asleep. I just felt strange.

Floating. Anyway, Barry took me aside and said there was something he wanted me to do for him." As she spoke, she looked into her drink and the fingers of her right hand rubbed at the table's surface. Banks noticed the chewed nails. "He took me upstairs toward one of the bedrooms. I thought he wanted a blow job or something. He sometimes did. I didn't really want to, I was feeling so spaced out, but . . . if it would get him off my back for a while . . . Anyway, it wasn't that. He opened the bedroom door and there was Andy inside. Anyway, he was stark naked and he . . . I mean, we'd all been taking V & E, so he was, you know, it was . . ."

"V and E?"

She looked at him as if he were an idiot. "Viagra and Ecstasy. Anyway, like I said, he was . . . like he had a lamppost between his legs. Barry just gave me a push forward and told me to be nice to him, then I heard the door shut. Anyway, when Barry pushed me I fell on the bed and Andy started pulling at my clothes, rubbing against me. It was gross. I might have been stoned, and I'll admit I've not always been a good girl, but this was seriously out of line. I mean, it ought to be *my* choice who I have sex with, not someone else's, oughtn't it? And it wasn't even him so much. I mean, he was a pathetic creep, but the thought that Barry had *given* me to him as a sort of punishment for you coming and asking questions . . . I don't know. It just made me sick, that's all."

She paused to drink some lager and lime. Banks felt his anger rise along with the guilt; it was his arrival that had caused the problems for Emily. He told himself that, no matter what, with someone like Clough she would have got to that point eventually anyway, but it didn't help right then. He also remembered the night, not so long ago, in a London bistro, when Annie Cabbot had told him about her sexual humiliation at the hands of some CID colleagues. "Who was this Andy? Did you know him?"

"Like I said, I'd seen him around. He's one of Barry's gofers. At least I've heard Barry telling him off and ordering him to do stuff sometimes. Takes the piss out of him something terrible, too. Andy has a stutter, see. I mean, that was one of the most humiliating things about it. Like, Barry had *given me to one of his employees*. To someone he thought was a bit of a joke. It made me feel worthless. Like shit."

"What was his full name?"

"Andrew Handley. But everyone calls him Andy Pandy. Anyway, you know the rest. Or most of it."

"How did you get away?"

"We struggled. He wasn't really expecting any resistance, so I just kneed him in the balls and he hit me and let go. The door wasn't locked. I ran out, downstairs and out of the house without looking back. I was only worried that Barry might be lurking around at the bottom of the stairs or something and that he'd stop me, but I didn't see him. I was lucky. We were near Victoria Station, so I ran to the taxi rank and the only place I could think of to go was your hotel. And that's it. The sad story of Barry and Emily. Or Barry and Louisa."

"Did he ever mistreat you before that?"

"No. But I never gave him cause to."

"What do you mean?"

Emily thought for a moment, then said, "With Craig, it was easy. He was jealous, maybe a bit too much, and it made him a bit crazy. With Barry, it's different. He's possessive, not jealous. He expects loyalty. You know that there are certain lines you're not supposed to cross. I'm not a fool. I might not know exactly what he's into, but I know it's probably illegal. And I know he hurts people. I saw him hurt Craig."

"Was that part of the appeal?"

"What? That he hurts people?"

"That he's a criminal, whereas your father's a policeman. After all, they're about the same age."

Emily snorted. "That sounds just like something my father would say. Do you all take the same course in pop psychology?"

"There is a kind of logic in it."

"It's not that at all. Barry's appeal is that he's exciting to be with, he gives great parties, has great drugs and people respect him."

"Fear him, you mean."

"Whatever. If fear's the only way you can get respect, what's wrong with that? Nobody disses Barry."

"Why aren't you still with him, then?"

She started rubbing at the table again. "I told you."

A confused kid. Banks had to stop himself from leaning forward and putting his hand over hers. It would have simply been a paternal gesture on his part, though he was aware that neither Emily nor the others in the pub would view it that way. He also noted that in her entire list of Barry Clough's attributes, Emily had not mentioned sex, that he was great in bed. Sex was probably a matter of power for Clough. Banks didn't doubt for a moment that Clough used Emily sexually—she had already said as much—but to her, he guessed, it was more a matter of the price to be paid for the high life than a joy to be shared. And the fact that she priced herself so low was a matter for concern.

"Are you afraid of him, Emily?"

"Course not. It's just . . ."

"What?"

She frowned. "He's very possessive, like I said. Barry doesn't like to lose his prized possessions."

An hour later, Annie was wet and miserable and none the wiser. She had walked between each of the units on the estate, talked to managers and workers and discovered absolutely nothing. If anything dodgy had been going on at the Daleview Business Park, it had been kept a very close secret.

It was with a great sense of relief, then, that she approached the last but one listed business. Banks had called for a late-afternoon meeting to pool their findings, and after that Annie had visions of a long hot bath, some microwavable Marks and Sparks concoction, and an evening alone to do as much or as little as she wished.

The needlework center was warm and dry, smelling of scented candles, predominantly rose and lemon. It was the kind of place that seemed made of nooks and crannies, all filled with such essentials as pin boxes, thread, etuis, stitch-layers, needle threaders, working frames, stitch-count converters and a thousand other more esoteric items. Finished tapestries hung on the walls. More of a showroom than a shop, it had no counter, but there was a comfortable-looking three-piece suite where clients could sit and discuss their requirements.

A young woman came out of an office at the back, the same woman Bennett had splashed in his hasty getaway. Annie introduced herself and said that she had been visiting all the units clockwise from the SecuTec office.

The woman held out her hand. "My name's Natalie," she said. "Welcome to my empire, for what it's worth. I can't tell you anything, but I've just put the kettle on, if you want to stay out of the rain for a few moments."

"Please," said Annie. "I could murder a cuppa right now." If accepting free cups of tea counted as corruption, there wouldn't be a copper in the whole of England not up on charges.

"Won't be a minute." Natalie walked back into the office.

Annie was examining the needlecraft kits and wondered if they would be relaxing or frustrating to do. She had a sudden memory of her mother sitting cross-legged on the floor, her long hair all over the place, wearing one of her flowing velvety creations covered in beadwork and embroidery. She was working on a sampler of a local village scene. It was an odd image, as Annie had never thought of her mother doing needlecraft before, though she knew she made her own clothes, and they were always beautifully embroidered. She would have to phone and ask Ray, her father. Maybe some of the samplers were down at the commune near St. Ives, and she could take one as a memento. Her mother had died when she was only five. As Annie watched, in her imagination, her mother looked up and smiled at her. Annie felt suddenly sad when Natalie returned with the tea.

It must have shown.

"What is it?" Natalie asked. "You look as if you've seen a ghost, love."

"Oh, nothing. Memories, that's all."

Natalie looked around her showroom as if trying to search for the offending object. Annie decided it was time to get on track. "Thanks for the tea," she said, taking a sip. "I know you said you couldn't tell me anything, but I suppose you've heard what happened to Mr. Courage?"

"Oh, yes. Word gets around here pretty quickly. After all, most of us have been here since the place opened, so we're used to each other. Shall we sit down?" She gestured to the three-piece suite and Annie sat in the armchair. She felt so weary she wondered whether she would ever be able to get out of it again.

"Did you know him at all?" she asked.

"No. But I know he hadn't been here very long."

"Since September."

"Was it? If you say so. Anyway, Mr. Bennett brought him around and introduced him to everyone just before he started, so we'd recognize him, know who to call if there were any problems, but other than that I never even saw him again. You see, I'm usually gone by five o'clock most days, except Thursday and Friday, when I stay open till seven. At least I will until after Christmas, then there's not much point until the weather starts getting better. You'd be surprised how many tourists we get just dropping by in spring and summer, but most of my trade comes from regular customers. This is a very specialized business. They know what they want and they know I have it for them. They usually telephone first, of course. Oh, listen to me rattling on. But I did warn you I didn't know anything."

Annie smiled and sipped some more tea. "It's all right," she said. "Gives me a chance to warm up and drink my tea. So far everyone I've spoken to says there have been no incidents at the park, not even petty theft. Is that right?"

"Well, I can't speak for everyone, but I've had a bit of shoplifting here once in a while. Nothing serious, you understand, but irritating, petty stuff. Thread, packets of needles, that sort of thing."

"Kids?"

"I doubt it. We don't get a lot of kids here. Needlecraft's hardly the in thing with the younger generation these days."

"I doubt that it ever was."

"Still, it's a living. Anyway, I suppose shoplifting's the kind of thing you have to expect in a place like this, but as I said, it's nothing serious."

"There are some pretty organized gangs of shoplifters. Keep your eyes open. If it gets serious, let us know."

Natalie nodded.

Annie shifted in her chair. "Much as I'd love to, I'm afraid I can't sit here all day," she said, with a quick glance through the window. It was still pouring down outside. She looked at the list Ian Bennett had given her and got to her feet. "One more to go."

Natalie frowned. "Not if you went clockwise from the SecuTec office, there isn't anyone else."

Annie glanced at the list. "What do you mean? I've got something called PKF Computer Systems listed here, right next door to you."

"The computer people? They're gone."

"When did they move out?"

"Over the weekend. I don't suppose Mr. Bennett got around to updating the list yet."

"How many people worked there?"

"Only two regulars, as far as I could tell. It's one of the smaller units."

"Do you know their names?"

"Sorry. I hardly saw them. They weren't the most sociable types."

"What about people coming and going?"

"Just delivery vans. The usual stuff."

"Okay. Thank you very much for your time, Natalie. And for the tea."

"My pleasure. It livens up a dull afternoon."

Annie left the needlecraft center and walked to the next unit. If there had been a sign over the door, none hung there now. Instead of a plate-glass window, as on some of the showrooms, the old PKF unit had three smaller windows at the front. Annie peeped through one of them, and as far as she could make out the inside was empty, completely cleared out. That was all it took to trigger the little alarm bell in her copper's mind. Charlie Courage, last seen alive by a neighbor on Sunday afternoon, apparently worked the four-to-midnight shift that evening and was found dead Tuesday nearly two hundred miles away. He had received five cash payments of two hundred quid each over the past month. And now this computer company had done a bunk over the weekend.

It certainly ought to be worth a quick look around their deserted premises, and by the time she had finished, Annie thought, Colin Finch would probably be in the SecuTec office. She should just have time to talk to him before heading back to the station for the meeting.

"Don't think I want you acting like some sort of avenging angel," Emily said. "You've already done your knight-in-shining-armor bit, thank you very much."

"Why are you telling me all this, then?"

"Because you asked. And because I owe you an explanation. That's all."

"You admitted you're frightened of Clough."

"That was silly of me." She gave a slight shudder. "It was just, you know, talking about it, remembering how he was that night. And I . . ."

"What?"

"It's nothing."

"Go on."

"Oh, just that I thought I saw Jamie in the Swainsdale Centre." She laughed, put her forefinger to her head and twisted it back and forth. "Me being crazy again. Paranoid Emily, that's what they'll be calling me." Her nail was chewed almost to the quick, Banks noticed.

"Jamie who?"

"Jamie Gilbert. He's one of Barry's closest employees. Barry talks and Jamie jumps. I don't like him. He's good-looking, but he's mean. He gives me the creeps."

"When was this?"

"A couple of days ago. Monday, I think. But it can't have been him. I must have been seeing things. Barry doesn't even know who I really am or where I live, does he? Remember Louisa Gamine?"

"How could I forget?" Banks wasn't certain that a man like Barry Clough lacked the resources to find out what he wanted about anyone. "Be careful, though. If you think you see him or Clough around here again, make sure you tell me. Okay?"

"I can take care of myself."

"Emily, promise you'll tell me if you think you see either of them again."

Emily waved her hand. "All right. All right. Don't get your underpants in a twist about it."

"You never did tell me what business Clough's in."

"That's because I don't know."

"Are you certain he's not a drug dealer?"

"No. I mean, I don't think so. Like I said, he's always got drugs around. He knows people, does people favors and things, maybe gets them some stuff, but he's not a dealer. I'm sure of that."

"How does he make his money?"

"I told you, I don't know. He never talked about it to me. As far as Barry is concerned, women are purely for recreation, not business. There's the club, I suppose, for a start. That takes up a fair bit of his time. And I think maybe he manages some bands and does some concert promotion. He's got business interests all over the country. He was always off here and there. Leeds. Dover. Manchester. Bristol. Sometimes he took me with him, but to be honest it was pretty boring waiting for him in some hotel room or walking the streets of some dingy little dump in the rain. Once he even asked me if I wanted to come here with him."

"Here? The Black Bull?"

"Eastvale, silly. Can you imagine it? Me and Barry walking around Eastvale? I mean, my mother *works* here." She slapped the table and made the glasses wobble. "I don't want to talk about him anymore. It's over. Barry will move on to his next little girl and I'll get on with my life."

"How are things at home?"

She pulled a face. "Just what you'd expect."

"What's that?"

"Boring. They just want me to keep quiet and stay out of the way. Mother pretty much ignores me. Dad has his political cronies over most of the time. You should see the way some of them look at me. But he doesn't notice. He's too busy planning his future."

"And what about you? What do you want to do?"

Emily brightened and took a long swig of her lager and lime. "I've been thinking I might like to go to university after all."

"Don't you have to do your A-Levels first?"

"Of course. But I can do that at a sixth-form college. I could even do them at home if I want to. It's not as if they're hard or anything."

"Ah," said Banks, who had found even his O-Levels hard. "And where would you go to university?"

"Oxford or Cambridge, of course."

"Of course."

Her eyes narrowed. "Are you taking the piss?"

"Farthest thing from my mind."

"Right. Yeah . . . well . . . anyway, I also thought I wouldn't mind going to university in America. Harvard or Stanford or somewhere like that. Not Bryn Mawr. It sounds like that nasty little Welsh town we lived in for a while when I was a kid. And not that one in Poughkeepsie, either. That sounds like somewhere you keep pigs."

"What would you study?"

"I'm not sure yet. Maybe languages. Or acting. I was always good in school plays. But there's plenty of time to think about all that."

"Yes, there is." Banks paused and fiddled for another cigarette. Emily lit it for him with a gold lighter. "I don't want to sound like your father," he went on, "but this drugs thing . . ."

"I can take them or leave them."

"You sure?"

"Sure. I never did much anyway. Just a bit of coke, crystal meth, V & E."

"Viagra and Ecstasy?"

"You remember."

"You took that?"

"Sure."

"But Viagra's . . . I mean, what does it do? For a woman?"

She came up with a wicked grin and tapped his arm. "Well, it doesn't exactly give me a hard-on, but it does make fucking really good. Mostly, it gives you a real rush, sort of like speed."

"I see. And you've had no problems giving up all this stuff?"

"I'm not an *addict,* if that's what you're getting at. I can stop anytime I want."

"I'm not suggesting that you're an addict, just that it can be difficult without outside help."

"I'm not going on one of those stupid programs with all those losers, if that's what you mean. No way." She pouted and looked away.

Banks held his hands up. "Fine. Fine. All I'm saying is that if you find you *need* any help . . . Well, I know you can hardly go to your father. That's all."

Emily stared at him for a while, as if digesting and translating what he had said. "Thanks," she said finally, not meeting his eyes, and managed a small smile. "You know why my dad hates you?"

Startled, Banks almost choked on his drink. When he had regained some of his composure, he suggested, "Personality clash?"

"Because he envies you. That's why."

"Envies me?"

"It's true. I can tell. I've heard him going on to Mother. Do you know, he thinks you've been having it off with some Pakistani tart in Leeds?"

"She's not Pakistani, she's from Bangladesh. She's not a tart. And we've never had it off."

"Whatever. And the music. That drives him crazy."

"But why?"

"Don't you know?"

"I wouldn't be asking if I did."

"It's because you've got a life. You have a woman on the side, you listen to opera or whatever, *and* you get the job done, you get results. You also do it the way you want. Dad's by the book. Always has been."

"But he's one of the youngest chief constables we've ever had. Why on earth should *he* be jealous of *my* achievements?"

"You still don't get it, do you?"

"Obviously not."

"He's envious. You're everything he'd like to be, but he can't. He's locked himself on a course he couldn't change even if he wanted to. He's sacrificed everything to get where he's got. Believe me, I should know. I'm one of the things he's sacrificed. All he's got is his ambition. He doesn't have time to listen to music, be with his family, have another woman, read a book. It's like he's made a pact with the devil and he's handed over all his time in exchange for earthly power and position. And there's something else. He can handle the politics, pass exams and courses by the cartload, manage, administrate better than just about anyone else on the force, but there's one thing he could never do worth a damn."

"What's that?"

"He couldn't detect his way out of a paper bag."

"Why should that matter?"

"Because that's why he joined up in the first place."

"How do you know?"

"I don't. I'm only guessing. But I've seen his old books once, when we were staying at my grandparents' house in Worthing. They're all, like, sixties paperback editions and stuff, with his name written inside them, all very neatly. A lot of those Penguins with the green covers. Detective stories. Sherlock Holmes. Agatha Christie. Ngaio Marsh. All that boring old crap. And I looked in some of them. Do you know what he's done? He's made his own notes in the margins, about who he thinks did it, what the clues mean. I even read one of them while we were there. He couldn't have been more wrong."

Banks felt queasy. There was something obscene about this intimate look into Riddle's childhood dreams that made him uncomfortable. "Where did *you* learn the pop psychology?" he said, trying to brush the whole thing off.

Emily smiled. "There is a kind of logic to it. Think about it. Look, it's been great seeing you, but I really have to be going. I have to meet someone at three. Then I'm off clubbing tonight." She gathered her handbag, more the size of a small rucksack, really, patted her hair and stood up. "Maybe we can do this again?"

"I'd like that," Banks said. "But it's on my terms next time, or not at all."

"Your terms?"

"No booze."

She stuck her tongue out at him. "Spoilsport. Bye." Then she picked up her jacket, turned with a flourish and strutted out of the pub. The men all watched her go with hangdog expressions, some of them brought crudely back to reality by harsh remarks from their wives sitting next to them. One woman gave Banks a particularly malevolent look, the kind she probably reserved for child molesters.

After Emily had gone, Banks spent a few moments thinking over what she had said. Self-analysis had not been a habit of his, and it was something he had only really indulged in since the split with Sandra, since his move to the cottage, even. There he had spent many a late evening watching the sunset over the flagstone roofs of Helmthorpe as shadows gathered on the distant valley sides, and probing himself, his motives, what made him the man he was, why he had made the mistakes he had made. There he was, a man in his forties taking stock of his life and finding out it wasn't at all what he thought it had been.

So Riddle hated him because he was a natural detective and because he appeared to have a life, including this illusory mistress. Some of Riddle's envy, then, if that was what it was, was based on error. What could be more pathetic than envying a man the life you only *imagine* he has? It was just a precocious teenager's analysis, of course, but perhaps it wasn't too far from the mark. After all, it wasn't as if Riddle had ever given Banks a chance, right from the start. Still, he thought, knocking back the last of his pint, that wasn't his problem anymore. With Riddle in his corner, things were bound to change for the better. As he pulled up his collar and left the pub, he was aware of the women's eyes burning holes in the back of his raincoat.

7

DS Jim Hatchley was the last to arrive at the scheduled meeting that Thursday afternoon, rolling in a little after quarter past five smelling of ale and tobacco and looking as if he'd been dragged through a hedge backwards. Banks, Annie Cabbot and DCs Rickerd, Jackman and Templeton were already gathered in the "boardroom," so called because of its panels, wainscoting and oil portraits of dead mill owners. A thin patina of dust from the renovations had even reached as far as the long banquet table, usually so highly polished you could see your reflection in it.

"Sorry, sir," muttered Hatchley, taking his seat.

Banks turned to Annie Cabbot, who had just started an account of her afternoon at the Daleview Business Park. "Go on, DS Cabbot," he said. "Now that we're all here."

"Well, sir, there's not a great deal to add. Charlie turned up for work on Sunday afternoon, as usual, logged in, and he went home at midnight. His replacement for the midnight-to-eight shift, Colin Finch, says he actually saw him at four and midnight, so we know he was still alive when he left the park."

"Did this Finch have anything more to tell us?" Banks asked.

"Said he hardly knew Charlie. They were ships that passed in the night. His words, not mine. And he'd no sense of anything dodgy going on at Daleview. Nobody else I spoke to there admits to knowing Charlie, either—not surprising, when you consider he was usually at work when the rest had gone home—and there had been no incidents reported at the park, so he didn't even have very much to do."

"Could his death be unrelated to his work, then?" Banks asked.

"It's possible," Annie said, glancing at Hatchley. "After all, he did have form. Mixed with some pretty rough company in his time. But there *was* one odd thing."

"Yes?"

She took an envelope out of her briefcase and set it on the table. "One of the companies operating out of Daleview—PKF Computer Systems—cleared out lock, stock and barrel on Sunday evening."

"Moonlight flit?"

"No, sir. All aboveboard, according to Colin Finch. Just very short notice. They were gone by midnight, when he started his shift."

"Couldn't pay their bills?"

"They weren't owing when they left, but I should imagine a cash-flow problem might be at the back of it all."

"Likely," said Banks. "But they did nothing wrong?"

"No. Interesting timing, though, wouldn't you say?"

"I would." PKF had cleared off during Charlie Courage's final evening shift. Banks didn't like coincidences any more than any other copper worth his salt. "Go on."

"Anyway, Ian Bennett had given me carte blanche and the keys were all there in Mr. Courage's old office, so I had a quick shufti around the PKF unit."

"Find anything?"

"Clean as a whistle. They'd obviously taken care to make sure they left nothing behind. Except this. I found it lodged behind the radiator. It must have fallen there." She held the envelope and tipped it. A cracked plastic case about five-by-five-and-a-half inches fell onto the polished table's surface.

"A CD case," said Banks. "I suppose you'd expect to find something like that if they were in the computer business. Software and all that."

"Yes," said Annie. "It probably means nothing. In fact,

the whole PKF thing's probably nothing, but I handled it carefully just in case. We might want to check with fingerprints."

"You think there's something dodgy about PKF?"

Annie leaned back in her chair. She even looked comfortable in the notoriously hard and bum-unfriendly boardroom chair, thought Banks. "I don't know, sir. It's just the timing, them leaving the same weekend Courage disappeared. It might be worth looking into the company, see who they are, what they do. It might help explain Charlie's sudden riches."

Banks nodded. "Right you are. You can get stuck into that tomorrow. And it wouldn't do any harm to get in touch with Vic Manson about those prints, either. If someone working at PKF turns up in our records, as well as Charlie . . ." He glanced over at the three DCs at the far end of the table. They had been on a house-to-house to find out if anyone had seen Charlie Courage after Sunday lunchtime. "Anything on the victim's movements?"

Winsome Jackman spoke first. "A neighbor saw him going to work late Sunday afternoon, sir, and the man across the street saw him taking his milk in at about eight o'clock on Monday morning."

"Anyone else?"

Winsome shook her head. Kevin Templeton said, "The woman at number forty-two, Mrs. Finlay, noticed something. She says she thought she saw Charlie get in a car with a couple of men later on Monday morning."

"Description?"

"Nothing very useful, sir." Templeton doodled in the dust on the table as he spoke. "One was medium height, the other was a bit taller. They wore jeans and leather jackets—brown or black. The taller one, he was going bald; the other had short fair hair. She said she didn't get a good look and wasn't really paying attention. I asked her if she thought Mr. Courage was being forced in the car in any way, and she told me she didn't get that impression, but she could have been wrong."

Banks sighed. It was typical of most witness statements.

Of course, if you didn't know you were witnessing anything momentous, such as a man's final journey, you didn't pay that much attention. Most people don't see much on the peripheries; they're more concerned about where they're going, what they're doing and thinking. "What about the car?"

"Light-colored. Maybe white. That was the best she could say. Nothing fancy, but new-looking, with a nice shiny finish."

"Okay," said Banks. "Time? Did we fare any better there?"

"A little bit, sir," said Templeton. "She said it must not have been long after ten o'clock, because she had just started listening to 'Woman's Hour,' and that starts at ten o'clock."

"Interesting."

"Maybe the trip was prearranged?" Annie suggested. "It could have been something he was looking forward to. Maybe he thought he was going somewhere nice, getting some more money?"

"Could be." Banks turned to Hatchley. "What did your afternoon in the fleshpots of Eastvale turn up, Jim?"

Hatchley scratched the side of his bulbous nose. "Charlie was up to something dodgy, I can tell you that much."

"Go on."

Hatchley got his notebook out. Workmen started hammering somewhere in the extension. Hatchley raised his voice. "According to Len Jackson, one of his old colleagues, Charlie was on to a nice little earner, and it wasn't his job at Daleview, either."

"Was it connected with that?"

"Charlie didn't say. He was pretty vague about it all. What he did say, though, was that he was already bringing in a bit of extra and pretty soon he'd be in for a much larger slice of the pie. What he was getting now was peanuts to what he'd have soon."

"Interesting. But he didn't say what pie?"

"No, sir. Charlie was pretty cagey about it, apparently. He wanted his old mates to know he was doing well, but not how he was doing it. Scared of the competition, I suppose."

"Okay," said Banks. "Well, at least that tells us we're on the right track. All we need to know now is what he was into and who was running it. Makes it sound easy, doesn't it?" He shook his head. "Charlie, Charlie, you should've stayed on the straight and narrow this time."

"He never was big-time, wasn't Charlie," added Hatchley. "He must have got in way over his head, not known who he was dealing with."

Banks nodded. "Okay, that's it for now," he said.

Back in his office, with his door tightly shut to keep the noise out, Banks phoned DI Collaton down in Market Harborough to give him an update, more out of professional courtesy than anything else, as there wasn't much to report. After that, he decided to call it a day. He tidied his desk and locked up, then headed for the door. Annie Cabbot was a flight ahead of him on her way down the stairs. She turned at the sound of his footsteps. "Oh, it's you. Off home?"

"Unless you'd like to go for a quick drink or something?"

"I don't think so," she said. "That bloody rain's soaked right into my bones. All I want is to pick up something for dinner, then a long hot bath and a good book to curl up with."

"Some other time?"

She smiled and pushed open the door. "Yes. Some other time."

Maybe she should have accepted Banks's offer of a drink, Annie thought, as she crossed the market square. It wouldn't have done any harm, just a quick drink and a chat. She didn't want to seem to be always giving him the brush-off, and it wasn't as if the men were exactly queuing up to take her out. But things were still a little sensitive, and her inner voice told her to back off, so she did. Not that she always did what her inner voice told her to; if she had done that she would never have got in trouble in her life, and what a boring old time that would have been. But this time, she listened; at least for now.

Though she could still smell it in the air, the rain had stopped and the evening had turned quite mild. Colored lights hung across Market Street and around the cross, and the shoppers were out in force. She was lucky that most of the shops were staying open late until Christmas, or she'd have nothing but a couple of moldy old carrots and potatoes for dinner. There was the Indian shop on Gallows View that was always open, but they didn't have much selection; besides, that was too far away in the wrong direction. What she wanted was something easy, something she could boil in the bag or stick in the oven for half an hour, no fuss.

In the end, it was a toss-up between vegetarian lasagna and Indonesian curry. The lasagna won, mostly because she had a bottle of Sainsbury's Chianti at home that would complement it nicely. She also needed eggs, milk, cereal and bread for breakfast.

As she wandered the busy aisles casting her eyes over the myriad varieties of meals specially prepared for those who dined alone, she remembered a book she had read many years ago—something her father had given her—that explained the underhand strategies supermarkets use to make you buy things you don't want. The lighting, for a start, and the soft, hypnotic music. At this time of year, of course, it was all Christmas music played in a cheery, sugary sort of style. Annie sometimes thought that if she heard one more "fa-la-la-la-la" she would scream. The manufacturers also used certain colors in packaging their products, and there was something about bright things being placed at eye level that just made you reach out and grab them. She couldn't remember all the details, but the book had made an impression on her, and she always felt manipulated when she left a supermarket with more than she had intended to buy. Which she always did. It was the chocolate ice cream this time; it had hardly been at eye level, nor was the package of a color that made you reach for it, but even stuck away in the freezer it had seemed to be screaming, "Buy me! Buy me!" and now it nestled in her basket as she waited in the queue to pay.

Maybe if she had been at Eastvale a couple of months, she thought, then she might have taken Banks up on his offer. It was just too soon: too soon after their affair, and too soon after her transfer. If truth be told, she still didn't trust herself with him, either. A couple of drinks might loosen her inhibitions a bit too much, as they almost had the last time she'd been out with him. Then where would she be? It had been all right sleeping with Banks when she worked out of Harkside and he worked out of Eastvale, but if they were both in the same station, it could be awkward.

Suddenly, as she was queuing up to pay, Annie saw someone she knew, someone she had never expected to see again, not here, not anywhere. And someone she had never wanted to set eyes on again. He was walking into the wines and spirits section. As far as she could tell, he hadn't seen her. What the hell was he doing here? Annie felt her skin turn clammy and her heart start to pound.

"That'll be five pounds seventy-two pee, please, love," said the plump, smiling woman at the checkout desk. Annie fiddled around in her purse and found a five-pound note and four twenty-pee pieces, which she promptly dropped from her shaking hands all over the floor. She picked them up and handed them to the woman.

"What's up, love? You look as if you've seen a ghost."

"Something like that," Annie muttered, hurriedly putting away her purse and heading out with her groceries. She risked one quick glance over her shoulder. He was standing by the bargain reds section scanning the labels and prices. She was still certain that he hadn't seen her.

She burst out onto York Road and took a gulp of fresh air. Her heart was still beating fast and she felt herself shaking inside. It was Wayne Dalton; she was sure of it. Detective Inspector Wayne Dalton. One of the two men who had held her down while a third had raped her over two years ago.

Banks knew he shouldn't have asked Annie out like that, on impulse, and he hoped he hadn't put her off for good. He didn't want to appear to be pestering her, especially as they worked together and he was, technically, her boss. Not that Annie would ever accuse him of sexual harassment, but . . .

As it happened, his evening turned out to be just what he needed. He made a cheese-and-onion sandwich for tea and ate it while he read the paper in the kitchen. His son, Brian, phoned at about nine o'clock, excited about the CD. On a whim, Banks asked if he had ever heard of Barry Clough. He hadn't, but said he'd ask around among his colleagues in the business. He also reminded Banks that punk had been a long time ago, as if Banks needed reminding of that.

After lunch with Emily Riddle, Banks also felt the need to talk to Tracy. It would help balance his sanity. After listening to Emily for over an hour, he had come away with a very warped idea about teenage girls. He needed to know they weren't all like her, especially his own daughter.

Amidst all the craziness, though, and after all she'd been through, Emily still seemed to have a cool head on her shoulders, if her talk about getting her A-Levels and going to university was to be believed. Like Banks, Tracy had had to work hard to get where she was. She was a bright girl, but not one of those who don't have to apply themselves. The harder she worked, the higher her marks. Emily seemed to think her progress in the world was simply a matter of choice, of deciding what to do and then having it fall into her lap. Perhaps it was for her. Now that he had got a little beyond first impressions, Banks couldn't help but like Emily, but she was the kind of girl he fretted about, and the kind who constantly exasperated him. He almost felt sorry for Jimmy Riddle.

Tracy didn't answer. Out with Damon, no doubt. He left her a message, nothing urgent, just to call if she didn't get in too late.

For a change from peat, Banks lit a log fire in the hearth, though it wasn't a particularly cold evening, and sat down in the old armchair he had picked up at a local estate auction. The blue walls that he had worried might feel cold in winter had turned out just fine, he thought, as he watched the shadows cast by the flames flicker over them. Knotty wood spat and crackled in the fireplace, taking Banks back to his childhood, when the coal they used sometimes hissed and spat. There was no other source of heat in the house, so it was his father's job in winter to get up while it was still dark and light the fire. Usually, when Banks came down for his jam and bread before school, there was a good blaze going, and it had taken most of the chill off the cool damp night air. The years in between, in various London flats and the Eastvale semi, he hadn't had a coal or log fire, only gas or electric, so it was a luxury he was availing himself of a lot this winter.

He put the first CD of Miles Davis's Carnegie Hall concert on, the one with Gil Evans and his orchestra, picked up the latest Kate Atkinson novel, which lay facedown on the chair arm, about half read, and lit a cigarette. Though he had intended an early night, he found himself enjoying both the music and the book so much that he put another log on the fire and slipped in the second CD. It was a quarter past eleven, and he had set the book aside for a few moments to listen to the live version of the adagio from Rodrigo's *Concierto de Aranjuez,* when the telephone rang.

Thinking it might be Tracy, he turned down the stereo and snatched up the phone. The first thing that assaulted his ears was loud music in the background. He couldn't make out exactly what it was, but it sounded like some sort of post-rave-techno-dance mix. The next thing to assail him was the squeaky voice of DC Rickerd shouting over the music.

"Sir?"

"Yes," sighed Banks. "What is it?"

"Sorry to bother you, sir, but I'm on duty tonight."

"I know that. What is it? Will you get to the point? And do you have to shout so loud?"

"Well, I'm at the Bar None, sir. It's pretty noisy here."

The Bar None was one of Eastvale's most popular night-clubs for the young crowd. Situated under the shops across the market square from the police station, it usually opened up an hour or so before pub closing time and attracted those kids who were too pissed to drive to Leeds or Manchester, where there were far better clubs. "Look," said Banks, "if there's been a fight or something, I don't want to know."

"No, sir, it's nothing like that."

"Well?" Banks lost Rickerd's next words to a surge in the background noise. "Can you get them to turn the music down?" he yelled.

"It's a suspicious death," Rickerd said.

"How suspicious?"

"Well, she's dead, sir. I'm pretty sure of that. Inspector Jessup agrees with me, sir. And the blokes from the ambulance. It looks as if somebody beat her up pretty badly."

If Chris Jessup, inspector in the uniformed branch, thought it was serious enough to call Banks in, then it probably was. "Who is the victim?" he asked.

"You'd better get down here, sir . . ." Here he became inaudible again. ". . . can't handle . . . myself."

"How many of you are there?"

"Inspector Jessup and me and three PCs, sir."

"That should be enough. I'm sure Inspector Jessup knows exactly what to do. Help him make sure no one leaves and secure the scene. We don't want anyone else tramping about near the body until I get there, including the ambulance crew. Understand?"

"Yes, sir."

"Better put a call through to Dr. Burns, too. It'll take him a while to get there." Banks was about to ask Rickerd to send for the SOCO unit, but decided to wait until he could assess the scene himself. No sense spending the taxpayers' money until he knew exactly what he was dealing with. "Have you got the victim's name?"

"Yes, sir. She had a driving license and one of those proof-of-age cards some of the clubs give out to kids. It's got her photo on it."

"Good work. What's her name, Rickerd?"

"It's Walker, sir. Ruth Walker."

"Shit," said Banks. "I'll be right there."

Could it be the same Ruth Walker Banks had talked to in London? If so, what the hell was she doing in an Eastvale nightclub, unless she had come up from London to go clubbing with Emily Riddle? And if Ruth was dead, then Banks wouldn't be at all surprised if Emily was in trouble, too.

Banks picked up his cigarettes and grabbed his leather jacket off the hook at the back of the door. Before he left, he went back to the phone. It was a snap decision between Jim Hatchley, who lived in Eastvale, and Annie Cabbot, who had as long a drive as Banks. Annie won, hands down. He would have been a liar if he had denied any personal preference for

Annie's charms over Jim Hatchley's ugly mug, but he didn't do it from entirely selfish motives. Annie was new to Eastvale, and she needed all the experience she could get; she was ambitious, whereas Hatchley was content to remain a DS for the rest of his days; Annie would welcome the opportunity, whereas Hatchley would grumble at being dragged out of bed in the middle of the night; Hatchley had his wife and baby to consider, while Annie lived alone.

There you go rationalizing, Banks thought, as he dialed her number. He could justify calling her until the cows came home if he had to, but what it came down to was that he still fancied her and he thought, with Sandra announcing she wanted to divorce and remarry, that he might be able to get over the stumbling blocks that had derailed him and Annie in the first place and rekindle what they once had.

But even that desire took second place to his concern about Ruth Walker and Emily Riddle.

Annie drove home like a bat out of hell, and when she got to her tiny terrace cottage, she locked, bolted and chained the door, then checked the back and all the windows. Only when she was certain that everything was as secure as it could be did she pour herself a large glass of wine and sit down.

Her hand was still shaking, she noticed, as she took a gulp. And she'd thought she'd got over her experience. The counseling had helped at first, but when the counselor said she could do no more, it had been Annie's own inner strength that pulled her through. Through meditation, yoga and diet, she had slowly healed herself. The country seclusion had helped, too: leaving a big city force for a peaceful backwater like Harkside.

She still had dreams in which she experienced the fear, claustrophobia and powerlessness she had felt during the assault and woke up sweating and screaming, and she still had dark moods in which she felt worthless and tainted. But not so often. And she could handle them now; she knew where they came from and could almost stand outside looking down on them, separating herself from the bad feelings, isolating them as you would a tumor. She had even got so far, after two years, as allowing herself that romantic and sexual involvement with Banks, which had been extremely satisfying, not least because it pleased her to find she was still capable of it. What had ended that was nothing at all to do with her rape experience; it was plain, old-fashioned fear of involvement, of emotional entanglement, something that had always been a part of her.

What the hell was Wayne Dalton doing in Eastvale? That was what she wanted to know. Was he on a case? Had he been reassigned to Western Divisional Headquarters? She didn't think she could handle working with him, not after what happened. The last she had heard he had transferred to the Met. Surely he couldn't be seeking her out? Coming to torment her? True, she had complained to their chief super the following morning, but there was no evidence; it was simply her word against the three of them. The chief super knew that something had gone on, and he also knew it was something he didn't want aired in *his* station, thank you very much, so Annie got shipped out sharpish and the three men, after being rapped on the knuckles, were encouraged to transfer at their leisure.

Later, in her bath, Annie remembered Wayne Dalton's flushed and sweating face as he held her, the little ginger hairs up his nose as he stood over her, waiting his turn. A turn that never came. She remembered walking the streets for hours after her escape, languishing in her bath, just like now, listening to the radio, the sounds of normal life, and scrubbing their filth from her body. Something she shouldn't have done. Something she, in her turn, had advised rape victims *not* to do. But it was far easier to say "Do as I say, not as I do." At the time, she hadn't thought, had only wanted an escape, a way of undoing what had been done, of going back in time to a day when it had never happened. Foolish, perhaps, but perfectly reasonable, she thought.

And she was still in her bath, on her third glass of wine when, close to twenty past eleven, her telephone rang.

*   *   *

It was five to twelve when Banks, who had driven well over the speed limit the whole way, parked in the market square next to the ambulance and headed for the club door. DC Rickerd had got a uniformed constable to guard the entrance, Banks was pleased to see, and had even put blue-and-white police tape across the doorway. As he headed down the stone steps, he was also pleased to hear that the music had been silenced and the only sounds drifting up were the murmured conversations of detained clubbers grumbling at the tables.

"Over here, sir."

The only lights on were the colored disco lights that whirled over the dance floor, eerie without the accompaniment of music and gyrating bodies. Banks could make out Rickerd and Jessup standing by the door to the ladies' toilet with the ambulance crew, a couple of uniformed officers and a young man. Before he could get there, someone tugged at his sleeve.

"Excuse me, are you in authority?"

"Looks that way," said Banks. The speaker, wearing jeans and a white shirt, was probably in his early twenties, skinny, with bright eyes and dilated pupils. It wasn't particularly hot in the Bar None, but a sheen of sweat covered his face.

"Why are you keeping us here? It's been nearly an hour now. You can't just keep us here."

"It's my understanding that there's been a serious crime, sir," said Banks. "Until we get things sorted, I'm afraid none of you is going anywhere." He noticed the boy was still holding his sleeve and plucked it away.

"But this is outrageous. I want to go home."

Banks leaned forward, close enough to smell the beer and fish and chips on his breath. "Look, sonny," he whispered, "go sit down with your mates and be quiet. One more word out of you and I'll have the Drugs Squad down on you like a ton of bricks. Understand?"

The boy looked as if he was going to protest further, but thought better of it and swayed over to the table where his friends sat. Banks continued on his way to meet Rickerd and Jessup. One of the ambulance crew looked at him and shook his head slowly. Annie Cabbot hadn't arrived yet. She had sounded edgy when he'd called and he had wondered if he had woken her. She said not.

"In here, sir," said a whey-faced Rickerd, pointing into the ladies'. "It's not very pretty." Someone had placed more tape at the entrance, effectively creating an inner crime scene. That was often useful, as you could afford to let some people in the first scene and lead them to think they were privileged, but you kept the real crime scene uncontaminated.

"Who's he?" Banks gestured toward the young man beside Rickerd.

"He found her, sir."

"Okay. Keep an eye on him. I'll talk to him later. Did you call Dr. Burns?"

"Yes, sir. He said he'd get here as soon as he could."

Banks turned to Inspector Jessup. "What happened, Chris?"

"Call came it at six minutes past eleven. That lad you just noticed. Name's Darren Hirst. It seems he was with the victim. She went to the toilet and didn't come out. He got worried, went in for a butcher's and called us."

Banks slipped on his latex gloves and stepped under the tape.

The ladies' toilet was small, given the size of the club. White tile, three stalls, two sinks under a long mirror. The ubiquitous condom machine hung on the wall, the kind that sells all sorts of flavors and colors—Lager & Lime, Rhubarb & Custard, Curry & Chips. The stalls had flimsy wooden doors. "Cindy Sucks Black Cock" was scrawled in lipstick across the front of one of them.

"It's this one, sir," said Rickerd, pointing to the end stall.

"Was it locked?"

"Yes, sir."

"How did you open it?"

Rickerd took off his glasses and wiped them with a white handkerchief. It was a habit Banks had noticed in him before. "From the next stall, sir. I stood on the toilet seat, leaned over with a stick and slipped the bolt. It was easy enough. We're bloody lucky the door opens outwards."

"A locked-toilet mystery, then," Banks muttered, thinking

Rickerd had shown more initiative than he would have expected.

"I didn't disturb anything any more than necessary, sir. Just to establish who she was and that she was dead. Inspector Jessup supervised, and the others made sure no one left."

"That's all right. You did well." He pulled the door slowly toward him with his fingertips, anxious not to mess up an already messy scene.

"You won't believe this, sir," Rickerd said. "I've never seen anything like it."

Neither had Banks.

The girl's body was wedged crabwise from wall to wall, her back arched about two feet over the toilet, knees jammed against one wall and her shoulders pushed up hard against the other, her neck bent at an awkward angle. A trickle of blood had run from her nose and there were contusions on her face and head. Broken mirror glass and white powder lay scattered on the floor amid the spilled contents of her handbag. Banks knew that the eyes of the dead have no expression, but hers seemed full of terror and agony, as if she had looked the Grim Reaper right in the eye. Her face was dark, suffused with blood, and the corners of her mouth were turned up in a parody of a grin.

But the worst thing about it all, the thing that caused Banks's blood to scream in his ears and his knees to turn watery and bring him so close to falling down that he had to grab on to the doorjamb to stay on his feet, was that the body wasn't Ruth Walker's at all; it was Emily Riddle's.

8

"Alan?" The voice seemed to reach Banks's ears from a great distance. "Alan? So now you're hanging around ladies' toilets, eh?"

Banks felt someone touch his sleeve, and he turned to see Annie Cabbot standing in the doorway. Never had he seen a more welcome sight. He wanted to fall forward into her arms, have her stroke his head and kiss his face and tell him everything was all right, he'd just had a bad dream, that's all, and it would all be gone in the morning.

"Alan, you're pale as ashes. Are you all right?"

Banks moved away from the doorway to let Annie have a look. "I've got a daughter not much older than her," he said.

Annie frowned and edged forward. Banks watched her and noticed the way her eyeballs flicked around, taking in all the details: the body's unusual position, the broken mirror, the white powder, the spilled cosmetics, the contusions. Some of the buttons on Emily's black silk blouse had popped, and the dark spider tattoo was visible against the pale skin below her navel ring. Annie touched nothing but seemed to absorb everything. And when she had finished, even *she* was pale.

"I see what you mean," she said when they had both gone to stand outside the toilet again. "Poor cow. What do you think happened?"

"It *looks* as if someone got in there with her and beat the living shit out of her, but that doesn't make sense."

"No," said Annie. "There's hardly enough room for one, let alone space to swing a few punches."

"And the stall was locked," Banks added. "I suppose she could have been beaten elsewhere, then crawled inside and locked it herself before she died, maybe in a vain attempt to keep her attacker out . . ." He shrugged. It seemed a pretty thin thesis. Even if she had locked herself in there to escape a beating, how had she ended up arched crabwise over the toilet? It was the most unusual body position Banks had ever seen, and though he had a glimmer of an idea about what might have caused it, he needed the expert knowledge of a doctor. "We'll have to wait for the doc. Ah, speak of the devil."

Dr. Burns walked across the dance floor and greeted them. "Where is she?" he asked.

Banks pointed toward the ladies'. "Try not to disturb things too much. We haven't got photographs yet."

"I'll do my best." Burns passed under the tape.

"Call the SOCOs and the photographer," Banks said to Annie. He gestured toward Rickerd and lowered his voice. "DC Rickerd phoned me, and I wanted to be certain we really had a crime on our hands before making a hue and cry."

"What about the people in the club?"

"Nobody leaves. Including the bar staff. Chris Jessup's lads have instructions to keep them all where they are. There's no telling how many left between the boyfriend's phone call and Jessup's arrival, though."

"It's still early for this kind of place," said Annie. "People would be more likely to be arriving than leaving."

"Unless they'd just killed someone. Ask one of the uniforms to take everyone's name and address."

Annie turned to go.

Banks called after her. "And, Annie?"

"Yes?"

"Be prepared for one of the biggest shitstorms that's ever come your way as a copper."

"Why?"

"Because the victim's Emily Riddle, the chief constable's daughter."

"Jesus Christ," said Annie.

"Exactly."

Annie went off to attend to her duties while Banks collared Darren Hirst, the boy who had found the body. He seemed still in shock, trembling, tears in his eyes. Banks could understand that, having seen Emily's body himself. He had seen many forms of death in his years as a policeman, and though he never quite got inured to it, he certainly had an advantage over the boy. Leaving a uniformed constable guarding the entrance to the toilet, Banks led Darren to an empty table. The club's manager hovered nearby, clearly wanting to know what was going on but not daring to ask. Banks waved him over.

"What time did you open tonight?" he asked.

"Ten o'clock. It starts slow. We don't usually get much of a crowd until after eleven."

"Has this place got surveillance cameras?"

"On order."

"Great. Bar still open?"

"The other policeman said I shouldn't serve any more drinks," he said.

"Quite right, too," said Banks, "but this lad's had a bit of a shock and I can't say I've had a pleasant surprise, either, so bring us a couple of double brandies, will you?"

"I thought you weren't supposed to drink on duty."

"Just bring the drinks."

"All right, mate. No need to get shirty." The bartender strode off. When he came back, he plonked the drinks down on the table. The measures looked small, but Banks paid him anyway.

"When can I go home?" the man asked. "Only, if we're not serving drinks, we're not making any money, see, and there's not a lot of point staying open."

"You're not open," said Banks. "And if I get much more of that crap out of you, you won't be opening again in the foreseeable future. There's a dead girl in your toilets, in case you hadn't heard."

"Fucking drug addicts," the bartender muttered as he stalked away.

"All right, Darren," said Banks when the bartender was out of earshot. "Like to tell me what happened?" He lit a cigarette. Darren refused his offer of one. The brandy was poor quality, but its bite put a bit of warmth back in Banks's veins.

"She said she wasn't feeling well," Darren began, after a sip of brandy. A little color crept back into his cheeks.

"Back up a bit," said Banks. "How well did you know her? Was she your girlfriend?"

"No, nothing like that. I mean, I know her, like, in the group. We were just friends, that's all. We all hang out together. She's a bit weird and wild, is Emily, but she can be a lot of fun. We started in the Cross Keys, down Castle Hill."

"I know it."

"After that we just walked around town a bit and dropped in for a quick drink at the Queen's Arms. Then we came here." He pointed to a group of shell-shocked kids at a table across the room. "The others are over there."

"What time did you meet in the Cross Keys?"

"About half past six, seven o'clock."

"Do you remember what time Emily got there?"

"She was the last to arrive. Must've been about seven, maybe a few minutes later."

So that left Emily four hours unaccounted for between the three-o'clock appointment she had mentioned to Banks and meeting her friends in the Cross Keys.

"How did she seem?"

"Fine."

"Normal?"

"For Emily."

"And what time did you come here?"

"About half ten. It was pretty quiet. Like the barman says, it doesn't usually get going till half past eleven or so. But they serve drinks, and there's music, so you can dance."

"How many people would you say were here?"

"Not a lot. They kept coming in, like, but it wasn't that busy."

"More than now?"

Darren looked around. "No, about this many."

"What happened next?"

"We got some drinks in, then Emily went to the toilet. We were dancing after that, I remember, then she said she wasn't feeling very well."

"What did she say was wrong with her?"

Darren shook his head. "Just that she didn't feel well. She said she was getting a stiff neck." He rubbed his own neck and looked at Banks. "Was it drugs? It was drugs, wasn't it?"

"Why do you ask that?"

"Just the way she was behaving. You know, like she was flying up there in her own world. Like I said, she's pretty wild."

"How well did you know Emily, Darren?"

"I told you, hardly at all. When she was home from school for the holidays she'd hang out with me and Rick and Jackie and Tina over there. That's all. I was never her boyfriend or anything. She wasn't interested in me like that. We just danced sometimes, went out with the gang. Had fun." He ran his hand over his greasy dark hair.

"Did you ever supply her with drugs, Darren?"

"Me? Never. I don't touch them."

There was something in his tone that made Banks believe him. For the moment. "Okay. So she felt poorly. What happened next?"

"She said she thought she might need some more medicine."

"What did she mean by that?"

"More drugs, I assumed. Whatever she was taking."

"Go on."

"So she went back to the toilet."

"How long after her first visit?"

"Dunno. Fifteen, twenty minutes, maybe."

Banks looked up and saw Peter Darby, the photographer, come in with his battered Pentax hanging around his neck. Banks pointed toward the toilets, where the uniformed policeman still stood on guard, and Darby nodded as he headed toward the tape. Annie dropped by the table and told him the SOCOs were on their way. Banks asked her to take statements from Darren and Emily's friends across the room. He drank down the rest of his brandy and asked, "What happened next?"

"She was a long time. I started to get worried, especially with her saying she wasn't feeling well."

"When you say a long time, just how long do you mean?"

"I don't know. Ten minutes. Quarter of an hour. Maybe longer. You don't expect someone to stay in the toilet that long if they're all right. I thought maybe she was being sick. She'd been drinking steadily most of the evening, a really weird mix of stuff, and she didn't eat anything in the Cross Keys."

Or at lunchtime in the Black Bull, Banks remembered, where she had also been drinking some odd concoctions. "Were many people going in and out of the ladies' toilet during that time?"

"I never really looked. But the place wasn't that busy, so maybe not."

"You didn't ask anyone to check on her? Jackie or Tina?"

"Tina went in after about five minutes and came right back out. She said Emily was making funny sounds, as if she was being sick or something, and she wouldn't open the door of the stall."

"Wouldn't or couldn't?"

Darren shrugged.

"What did you do then?"

"I thought about it for a bit, then I decided to go in and see what was up."

"When was this?"

"Must've been about five or ten minutes later, when she still hadn't come out."

"Had others been in and out in the meantime?"

"Like I said, I didn't keep an eye on the place all the time, but I saw a couple of girls come and go."

"Are they still here?"

Darren pointed out two of the girls at separate tables. "Okay," said Banks, "we'll talk to them later. They didn't say if anything was wrong, though?"

"No. Just Tina thought she was being sick."

"So you went in the ladies' yourself?"

"Eventually, yes. I was worried. I mean, I'd been dancing with her. I felt she was sort of . . ."

"Your responsibility?"

"In a way. Yes."

"Even though she wasn't your girlfriend?"

"She was still a friend."

"What did you find in there?"

Darren looked away and turned pale again. "You know. You've seen it. God, it was horrible. It's like she wasn't even human."

"I'm sorry to put you through it, Darren, but it could be important. Describe to me what you found. Was anyone else in there at the time?"

"No."

"Was the stall door locked?"

"Yes."

"So how did you know there was something wrong?"

"First I called her name and she didn't answer. Then I just, like, listened at the door and I couldn't hear anything. No sounds of her being sick or even breathing. I got really scared then."

"So what did you do?"

"I went into the next stall and climbed on the toilet. The walls don't come right up to the ceiling, so you can lean over and look down. That's when I saw her. She was looking up at me . . . all bruised and twisted . . . and her eyes . . ." He put his head in his hands and started to sob.

Banks touched his shoulder. "It's all right, Darren. Go ahead and cry."

Darren let his tears run their course, then wiped his eyes with his sleeve and looked up. "Who could *do* something like that?"

"We don't know. We don't know *how,* either. Apart from the two girls you mentioned, did you see anyone else go in the toilet while Emily was in there sick?"

"No. But I told you I wasn't looking all the time."

"You must have been looking quite often, though, if you were worried. You must have been keeping an eye on the door to see if Emily came out again."

"I suppose so. But I didn't notice anyone else, no."

"See any men go in?"

"No."

"Did anyone come in and out while you were there checking on her?"

"No. Look, *I* didn't do this. You're not—"

"Nobody's suggesting that, Darren. I'm just trying to get everything clear, that's all. When you saw her, did you know that she was dead?"

"I couldn't *know*. I mean, I didn't take her pulse or anything. I didn't touch her. But her eyes were open, staring, and her neck was in a weird position, as if someone had broken it or something. And I couldn't see any signs of life."

"What did you do?"

"I went to the manager and he phoned the police."

"Did anyone else enter the toilet before Inspector Jessup and DC Rickerd arrived?"

"I don't think so. The manager had a quick look—I was with him the whole time—then he phoned the police and the ambulance. He stayed by the door until the policemen arrived, and he wouldn't let anyone in the ladies'. He made a couple of girls use the men's toilet. They complained. I remember that. But the police were quick."

"They didn't have far to come. Did anyone leave the club?"

"A couple of people might have left. But mostly people were arriving. It was still early. And I wasn't really paying attention. I was just worried about Emily, and afterwards I was sort of in shock. The music kept going for quite a long time after . . . after I found her. People were still dancing. Even after the police came. They didn't really know anything serious had happened."

"Okay, Darren, nearly finished. You're doing really well. Did anything at all odd happen during the evening, either here or when you were at the Cross Keys or the Queen's Arms, that gave you cause for concern about Emily?"

"No. Nothing I can think of."

"She seemed in good spirits?"

"Yeah."

"She didn't get into an argument with anyone?"

"No."

"Did she make any telephone calls?"

"Not that I remember. Everything was fine."

"Did she mention drugs at all?"

"No."

"Did you get the impression she was on drugs before you got here?"

"She might have been a bit high when she arrived at the Cross Keys."

"At seven?"

"Yes. I mean, she wasn't out of it or anything, just a bit giddy. But it wore off."

That was probably when she got the drugs, Banks thought: between leaving him in the Black Bull and arriving at the Cross Keys four hours later. She'd been smoking grass or snorting coke with someone in the meantime. Christ, *why* hadn't he asked her where she was going? Would she have told him, anyway? "Did you see her talking to anyone in here before she went to the toilet?" he asked.

"Only us. I mean, we got a table together. We didn't know anyone else here. I went to get the drinks in."

"Could she have bought the drugs from someone here?"

"I suppose she could've done, but I didn't see her."

"Inside the toilets, maybe?"

"It's possible."

"What about the Cross Keys?" The Cross Keys wasn't exactly the mecca of drugs in the way the Black Bull was, but it wasn't an innocent either. "Did you see her talking to any strangers there?"

"No. I don't think so."

"Did she disappear for any length of time?"

"No."

"Okay, Darren. You'll have to give a formal statement later, but it's nothing to worry about."

"Can I go now?"

"I'm afraid not."

"Can I sit with my friends?"

"Of course."

"Is it okay if I use my mobile? I'd like to call my mum and dad, tell them . . . you know, I might be late."

"Sorry, Darren," said Banks. "Not yet. If you really need to let them know, just tell one of the uniformed officers and he'll see to it for you. Go sit with your friends now."

Darren slouched off to the table and Banks got up and turned to see Dr. Burns coming out of the toilet. Peter Darby's camera flashed in the open door behind him.

"So what is it?" Banks asked Dr. Burns when they found a table at which they couldn't be overheard. He had his own suspicions, though he had never seen an actual case before, but he wanted Dr. Burns to get there first. It was partly a matter of not wanting to look like an idiot, not jumping to conclusions. After all, she *could* have been beaten to death.

"I'm not certain yet," said Burns, shaking his head.

"But your immediate impression. I'll bet you've got a pretty good idea."

Burns grimaced. "We doctors don't like giving our immediate impressions."

"Was she beaten up?"

"I very much doubt it."

"The bruising?"

"At a guess I'd say that happened from her head banging into the walls during the convulsions. Hang on a minute; are you all right?"

"I'm fine." Banks fumbled for another cigarette to take the taste of bile out of his mouth. "What do you mean, convulsions?"

"As I said, I don't think anyone attacked her. She was alone in there. You noticed the white powder and the broken mirror."

Banks nodded.

"Cocaine, most likely."

"Are you saying she died of a cocaine overdose?"

"Hold on a minute. I never said that."

"But it's possible?"

Burns paused. "Hmm. Possible. A cocaine overdose *can* cause spasms and convulsions in extreme cases."

"But?"

"It would have to be extremely pure. As I said, it's possible, but it's not the most likely explanation."

"What is, then?"

"How long has she been dead?"

"They called the police at six minutes after eleven, so it must have happened a bit before then. I got here at ten to twelve."

Burns looked at his watch. "And it's twenty past now. That means she can't have been dead much more than, say, an hour and a half. Yet rigor's complete. That's highly unusual. I assume you also noticed the stiffness?"

"Yes. So what do you think killed her?"

"At a guess, and it's just a guess until we get toxicology results, I'd say it was strychnine poisoning."

"It crossed my mind, too, though I'm far from being an expert. I've never actually seen a case before. I've only read about it in textbooks."

"Me, too. It's really quite rare these days. But that would cause the convulsions. She'd have been thrashing herself about the tiny stall quite enough to cause the bruises and contusions you saw on her body. Her back was also arched in a way indicative of final strychnine spasms—it's called *opisthotonos*—and you must have noticed the way the facial muscles were twisted in a sort of extreme grimace, or grin—*risus sardonicus*—and the darkness of the face, the wild, staring eyes?"

The images were impossible to forget, and Banks knew he would have nightmares about them for years, the way he still had about the disemboweled Soho prostitute, Dawn Wadley.

"I'm hesitant to commit myself without a full tox check, but that won't take long. It's one of the easiest poisonous substances to test for. I've never investigated a death by strychnine before, but that's what it looks like to me. Only my immediate impressions, mind you. I also touched a little of the powder to my tongue. Along with the numbness caused by the cocaine, there's a bitter taste, associated with strychnine."

"What killed her? Heart?"

"She'd have died of asphyxiation, most likely, or maybe

just sheer exhaustion from the convulsions. Her neck may be broken too, but you'll have to wait for the postmortem to confirm that. Not pretty, whichever way you look at it."

"No. Deliberate, though?"

"Oh, I would think so, wouldn't you? And I'd pretty much rule out suicide, for a start. Even if she did want to kill herself, strychnine is hardly the drug of choice. I've never heard of a case. Besides, from what I can tell, it was mixed with cocaine. That means she was looking for a good time, not for death."

"Any chance it could just be a bad batch?"

"There's always a chance of that. Dealers use all kinds of weird substances to step on the drugs they sell, including strychnine. But not usually enough to kill a person."

"How much would that be?"

"It varies. Doses as low as five milligrams can kill, especially if they're absorbed directly into the bloodstream and bypass the digestive system. We'll soon find out if it was a bad batch, anyway."

"You mean we'll have a whole spate of them?"

"It's possible."

"God forbid," said Banks.

"It depends on a number of factors. As I said, a fatal dose can vary widely. What killed this girl might not kill just anyone. She was pretty thin, and it doesn't look as if she ate much. Somebody with more body weight, someone more solid, more robust . . . who can say? But we'll hear about it if it happens."

Banks remembered how Emily hadn't eaten lunch. Darren said she hadn't eaten dinner, either. "But if she inhaled it, the stomach contents wouldn't matter."

"Not as much as if she'd ingested it, no. But general health and stomach contents are all factors we have to take into account."

"And if it's not a bad batch, then someone had it in for her specifically."

"That just about sums it up. Either way you look at it, somebody killed her. But that's your realm, isn't it? Ah, here come the cosmonauts."

Banks looked up and saw the SOCOs entering in their white protective overalls.

"I'll arrange for the mortuary wagon," said Dr. Burns. "I'd better tell them they'll probably need a crowbar to prize her out of there. And I'll get in touch with Dr. Glendenning first thing in the morning. Knowing him, he'll have her opened up by lunchtime." He stood, but paused a moment before leaving. "Did you know her, Alan? You seem to be taking this very much to heart."

"I knew her slightly," said Banks. "I might as well tell you now. You'll find out soon enough. She's the chief constable's daughter."

Dr. Burns's reaction was exactly the same as Annie's.

"And, Doc?"

"Yes?"

"Let's keep this under our hats for the time being, shall we? The strychnine."

"My lips are sealed." Dr. Burns turned and left.

For a moment, Banks stood alone watching the spinning disco lights and listening to mumbled conversations around him. Peter Darby came out of the toilet and said he'd got what he wanted. The SOCOs were in there taking the place apart, collecting samples for analysis. Banks didn't envy them the task of working in a toilet; you never knew what you might catch. Vic Manson would soon be dusting for prints, of which he'd probably find as many as the SOCOs would pubic hairs, and before long the mortuary wagon would come and whisk Emily Riddle's body off to the basement of Eastvale Infirmary.

All so bloody predictable. Routines Banks had been part of time and time again. But this time he wanted to cry. Cry and get rat-arsed. He couldn't help but remember Emily's excited talk about her future that lunchtime, about how she didn't fancy Poughkeepsie or Bryn Mawr because of the sound of their names. He remembered the time she turned up at the hotel in London, passing herself off as his daughter, how her dress slid to the ground and he saw her white and naked. Remembered her stoned, adolescent attempt at seducing him. God, if only she knew how close she'd come.

Then the way she curled up in the fetal position like a little child on the bed, her thumb in her mouth, the blanket covering her, while he sat in the armchair smoking and listening to Dawn Upshaw sing about sleep and the windows rattled and the winter sun rose and tried to claw its way through the gray, greasy clouds.

Dead.

And perhaps because of him, because he had respected his vow of discretion and done nothing, despite all his misgivings.

Annie came over from the table where she had been talking to Emily's friends. Banks told her what Dr. Burns had said about strychnine. Annie whistled. "Learn anything over there?" he asked.

"Not a lot. They say she seemed a bit high when she arrived at the Cross Keys, and they're certain she took something here the first time she went to the toilet."

"Same as Darren says. Can't have been the same batch, though, can it?"

"I suppose not. Do you believe them?"

"For the most part. Maybe we'll lean on them a bit harder tomorrow. What it looks like is that the first time she snorted made her feel ill shortly afterwards, so she went back for more and the convulsions hit."

"So what now?"

"We can start by searching everyone on the premises. They're all suspects at the moment, including the bar staff. Can you get that organized?"

"Of course. I very much doubt we'd have any problems arguing reasonable suspicion, do you?"

"I doubt it." PACE rules stated that you had to have "reasonable suspicion" before searching people, and if you searched them somewhere other than at the police station without first arresting them, you had to have reasonable grounds for assuming they might be a danger to themselves or others. With the chief constable's daughter lying dead of possible strychnine poisoning only a few yards away, Banks didn't think they'd have much trouble arguing their case. "Take it easy, though. If anyone kicks up a fuss, take him over to the station and have the custody officer deal with him. I want this done by the book. You'd better let Detective Superintendent Gristhorpe know, too."

"Will do."

"I also want all the known coke dealers in the area brought in for questioning. And we'll need to activate the incident room over at the station." He looked at his watch. "We might not be able to get everything in order until morning—especially as far as the civilian staff are concerned—but in the meantime we'll need an office manager."

"DC Rickerd?"

Banks looked at Rickerd, who was taking a statement at the other side of the club. "Good idea," he said. "Let him show his mettle."

While Rickerd demonstrated only minimal detective skills, he had an almost obsessive interest in details and the minutiae of organization: exactly what a good office manager needed, as it was his job to supervise the recording and tracking of all information retrieved both from a crime scene and during an investigation.

If truth be told, you needed more than a skill for organization, but Rickerd would do. Maybe he would find his true métier. Banks knew that having a train-spotter in the department would come in useful one day. Rickerd was just the kind to carry around that little book full of printed train numbers and draw a neat line with pen and ruler through each one he actually saw. He was too young for the steam trains, though. When Banks was a kid, there were still a few of them in service, many with exotic names like The Flying Scotsman, sleek, streamlined beauties. Many of Banks's friends had been train-spotters, but standing on a windy station platform all day and noting down numbers to cross off later in a little book had never appealed to him. These days, with all the diesels looking like clones of one another, didn't seem to be much point in train-spotting anymore.

Banks called Rickerd over and explained what he wanted him to do. Rickerd went off looking pleased with himself to be given such responsibility. Then Banks lit a cigarette and leaned against a pillar. "I'd better go tell her parents," he sighed.

"One of the uniforms can do that." Annie put her hand on his arm in a curiously intimate gesture. "To be quite honest, Alan, you look all in. Maybe you should let me take you home."

Wouldn't that be nice? Banks thought. Home. Annie. Maybe even bed. The adagio from *Concierto de Aranjuez* drifting up from downstairs. The clock put back so that none of this had ever happened. "No," he said. "I've got to tell them myself. I owe them that much."

Annie frowned. "I don't understand. What do you owe them?"

Banks smiled. "I'll tell you all about it later." Then he walked up the stairs to the deserted market square.

Banks felt sick and heavy with dread as he approached Riddle's house close to one-thirty that morning. The Old Mill stood in almost complete darkness behind the privet hedge, but a glimmer of light showed through the curtains of one of the ground-floor rooms, and Banks wondered if it had been left on as a means of discouraging burglars. He knew it hadn't when he saw the curtain twitch at the sound of his car on the gravel drive. He should have known Jimmy Riddle would be up working well after midnight. Hard work and long hours were what had got him where he was in the first place.

When he turned the engine off, he could hear the old millrace running down the garden. It reminded him of Gratly Falls outside his own modest cottage. He hardly had time to knock before a hall light came on and the door opened. Riddle stood there in an Oxford shirt and gray chinos; it was the first time Banks had seen him in casual dress.

"Banks? I thought that was your car. What on earth . . . ?"

But his voice trailed off as recognition that something was seriously wrong crept into his features. Whether he'd been a good one or not, Riddle had been a copper for long enough to know that the call in the middle of the night was hardly a social one; he knew enough to read the expression on Banks's face.

"Maybe we could sit down, have a drink," Banks said, as Riddle stood aside to let him in.

"Tell me first," said Riddle, leaning back on the door after he closed it.

Banks couldn't look him in the eye. "I'm sorry, sir," he said. The honorific sounded odd even as he spoke the word; he had never called Riddle "sir" before, except in a sarcastic tone.

"It's Emily, isn't it?"

Banks nodded.

"My God."

"Sir." Banks took Riddle's elbow and guided him into the living room. Riddle collapsed into an armchair and Banks found the cocktail cabinet. He poured them both a stiff whiskey; he was beyond worrying about drink driving at that point. Riddle held the glass but didn't drink from it right away.

"She's dead, isn't she?" he said.

"I'm afraid so."

"What happened? How?"

"We're not sure yet, sir."

"Was there an accident? A car crash?"

"No. It was nothing like that."

"Out with it, man. This is my daughter we're talking about."

"I know that, sir. That's why I'm trying to tread softly."

"Too late for that, Banks. What was it? Drugs?"

"Partly."

"What do you mean, 'partly'? Either it was or it wasn't. Tell me what happened to her!"

Banks paused. It was a terrible thing to tell a dead girl's father how painfully she had died, but he reminded himself that Riddle was also chief constable, a professional, and he would find out soon enough, anyway. Best he find out now. "We're keeping this strictly confidential for the time being, but Dr. Burns thinks it might have been cocaine spiked with strychnine."

Riddle jerked forward and spilled some whiskey on his trousers. He didn't even bother to wipe it off. "*Strychnine!* My God, how . . . ? I don't understand."

"She was taking cocaine at a nightclub in Eastvale," Banks said. "The Bar None. You might have heard of it?"

Riddle shook his head.

"Anyway, if the doctor is right, somebody must have put strychnine in her cocaine."

"Christ, Banks, do you realize what you're saying?"

"I do, sir. I'm saying that, in all likelihood, your daughter was murdered."

"Is this some sort of sick joke?"

"Believe me, I wish it were."

Riddle ran his hand over his shiny bald skull, a gesture Banks had often thought ridiculous in the past; now it reeked of despair. He drank some of his whiskey before asking the hopeless question everyone asks in his situation: "You're sure there's no mistake?"

"No mistake, sir. I saw her myself. I know it's no consolation, but it must have been very fast," Banks lied. "She can't have suffered very much."

"Rubbish. I'm not an idiot, Banks. I've studied the textbook. I *know* what strychnine does. She'd have gone into convulsions, bent her spine. She'd have—"

"Don't," Banks said. "There's no sense torturing yourself."

"Who?" Riddle asked. "Who would want to do something like that to Emily?"

"Have you noticed anything strange while she's been here?"

"No."

"What about today, the last few days? Any changes in her behavior?"

"No. Look, you went to London, Banks. You found her. What about the people she was hanging around with down there? This Clough character. Do you think he could have had something to do with it?"

Banks paused. Barry Clough had been the first to come to his mind when Dr. Burns had told him about the poisoned cocaine. He also remembered how Emily had told him that Clough hated to lose his prize possessions. "That's a distinct possibility," he said.

Riddle plucked at the creases of his trousers, then he let out a long sigh. "You'll do what you have to do, Banks. I know that. Wherever it leads you."

"Yes, sir. Is there . . . ?"

"What?"

"Anything you want to tell me?"

Riddle paused. He seemed to think hard for a few moments, then he shook his head. "I'm sorry. I can't help you. It's out of my hands now." He knocked back the rest of the whiskey. "I'll go to the mortuary and identify her."

"It'll wait till morning."

Riddle got up and started pacing the room. "But I must do *something*. I can't just . . . I mean, Christ, man, you've just told me my daughter's been murdered. *Poisoned*. What do you expect me to do! Sit down and cry? Take a bloody sleeping pill? I'm a policeman, Banks. I have to do something."

"Everything possible is being done," said Banks. "I think you'd be best off spending the time with your wife and son."

"Don't soft-soap me, Banks. My God, just wait till the press gets hold of this."

Here we go again, thought Banks: his bloody *reputation*. It was only out of respect for Riddle's bereavement that Banks said mildly, "They hadn't got a whiff when I left the scene, but I don't suppose it'll take them long. The place will be swarming with them come morning. We want to try and keep the strychnine aspect quiet."

Riddle seemed to collapse in on himself, all his energy gone. He looked tired. "I'll wake up Ros and tell her. I appreciate your coming, Banks. I mean personally, you know, not sending someone else. The best thing you can do is get back to the scene and stay on top of things. I'll be depending on you, and for once I don't care how many bloody corners you cut or whose feet you tread on."

"Yes, sir." Riddle was right; probably the best thing Banks could do right now was throw himself into the investigation. Besides, people need to be alone with their grief. "I'll need to talk to you both at some point," he said. "Tomorrow?"

"Of course." They heard a sound from the doorway and turned. Benjamin Riddle stood there in his pajamas clutching a battered teddy bear. He rubbed his eyes. "I heard voices, Daddy. I was scared. What is it? Is something wrong?"

9

It was still dark when Banks drove to Eastvale the following morning, and a thin mist nuzzled in the dips and hollows of the road and clung to the buildings, the cobbles and the ancient cross in the market square. It was that time of morning when lights were coming on in the small offices above the shops, some of which were already open, and the mist diffused their light like thin gauze. The air was mild and clammy.

Across the square, the Bar None was still taped off, and a uniformed officer stood on guard. After leaving Riddle's house the previous night, Banks had returned to the club to find the SOCOs still at work and Annie taking statements. Detective Superintendent Gristhorpe had also driven in all the way from Lyndgarth.

Banks had hung around for a while, talking the scene over with Gristhorpe, but there was nothing more he could do there. When the media people started pestering him for comments, he drove home and spent a couple of sleepless hours on the sofa thinking about Emily Riddle's terrible death before heading right back to the station. He tried to keep at bay the feelings of guilt that were crowding at the edge of his mind like circling sharks. He succeeded only partially, and that was because he had a job to do, something to focus on and exclude the rest. The problem was that the bad feelings would continue to accumulate even when he wasn't looking, and the day would come when there were so many of them he could no longer ignore them. By then, he knew from experience, it was usually too late to end up feeling good about himself. For the time being, though, he couldn't afford the self-indulgence of guilt.

The renovators hadn't turned up yet, so things were quiet in the extension. Banks went to his office, read his copies of last night's reports and made some notes on his own impressions. He did this, as most good coppers did, for himself, not for the files; they were very personal impressions, and sometimes they could lead somewhere, often not. Whatever else they were, they were no substitute for facts or evidence. He included in his notes, for example, his sense that Darren Hirst was telling the truth and a gut feeling that Emily had got the drugs somewhere other than the Cross Keys or the Bar None. Already, he noted from the reports, a couple of very sleepy local dealers were cooling their heels in the detention cells in the basement of the station. More would soon follow.

By the time the sun was sniffing its nose at the cloudy horizon, the station was humming with activity. The incident room was quickly taking on form and function, and DC Rickerd had been up all night getting it organized. Computer links had been set up, phone lines activated and civilian staff were drifting in for data-input, logging and recording duties. By the time Banks felt the need for his breakfast coffee, ACC McLaughlin had arrived from county headquarters at Newby Wiske, outside Northallerton. He set up camp in the boardroom, and fifteen or twenty minutes later, Banks was summoned in.

McLaughlin, Annie Cabbot and Detective Superintendent Gristhorpe were waiting for him. Banks greeted them and sat down. Annie looked tired, and he imagined she had got as little sleep as he had. She also seemed nervous, which was unusual for her.

"Red Ron" McLaughlin was about fifty, tall and slim, with short, thinning gray hair combed forward, and a small gray mustache. He wore silver-rimmed glasses, which balanced on the tip of his nose, and he had a habit of peering over them at whomever he was speaking to. His eyes were the same shade of gray as his hair.

"Ah, DCI Banks," he said, then he shuffled some papers and looked over his glasses. "Right. I'll get straight down to brass tacks. I met with Chief Constable Riddle this morning—in fact, he came to see me—and he was most emphatic that he wanted you to head the investigation into his daughter's death. What do you think of that?"

"I *had* hoped for the case," said Banks, "but in all honesty I never expected to be given it."

"Why not?"

"Because I knew the deceased, sir. Only vaguely, but I knew her. And her family. I assumed we'd have to bring in someone from outside."

"That would be normal procedure." McLaughlin scratched his earlobe. "The chief constable did explain your involvement," he went on. "Apparently, he asked you to go to London and find his daughter, which you did. Is that correct?"

"Yes, sir."

"And you then accompanied her back home?"

"Yes, sir." Banks felt Annie staring at him but didn't turn to meet her look.

"I hardly think that disqualifies you from acting as senior investigating officer. Do you?"

Banks thought for a moment. He would have to tell Red Ron about the lunch. Someone was bound to come forward about that, and it wouldn't take long now that Emily's murder had featured on the breakfast news. Enough people in the Black Bull had noticed them, and probably at least one or two of them knew who Banks was.

On the other hand, if he told McLaughlin *everything*, he'd be off the case for certain, no matter what Riddle wanted. It was a delicate balancing act. There was also a risk that someone from the Hotel Fifty-Five in London would see Emily's photo in the papers and come forward, although Banks thought that had been long enough ago, and Emily had looked sufficiently different that night, dressed up for the party, her hair piled on top of her head, that it was probably very unlikely.

Still, if Banks accepted the post as SIO, he would be in the best position possible to head off any trouble at the pass. He also knew far more about Emily's life in London than anyone else up there, which gave him an advantage when it came to tracking down possible leads. It was bloody unethical, he knew that, probably more unethical than anything he'd done before. After all, one of Riddle's bugbears had been that Banks too often acted as a maverick. But, Banks guessed, that was why Riddle had asked him to go to London, and that was why he now wanted him to head the investigation. Riddle had said as much last night.

"No, sir," Banks answered finally. "I'd like to take the case." He was aware as he spoke the words that he might well be digging his own grave. The last thing he needed to do was give the new ACC a reason for hating his guts right off the bat. But it couldn't be helped. Emily came first here; he owed her that much at least. He had said he only knew her vaguely. It wasn't a lie, but like many unsatisfactory truths, it left too much out. How could Banks describe the bond he had felt with Emily? It wasn't entirely paternal, but it wasn't simple friendship either.

"As you all know, I'm new to this job and this region," McLaughlin explained. "I've done my homework, studied the turf, but I can't hope to be up to scratch this soon. According to Mr. Riddle, you're the best man for the job. Detective Superintendent Gristhorpe here agrees, and nothing I've seen in your file contradicts that."

That was a surprise to Banks; he thought Riddle had weighed his file down with negative reports. But McLaughlin frowned and continued, "I'm not saying there aren't a few black marks against you, Banks. You've made some mistakes I'd like you to avoid making under my command, but your case results speak for themselves. There's going to be a lot of changes around here, with the new organization, and I'm hoping you can play a big part in them. Is that clear?"

"Yes, sir."

"That's settled then," said McLaughlin. "You'll act as SIO on the Emily Riddle case. I take it you'll have no objection to acting as deputy investigating officer, DS Cabbot?"

"No, sir," said Annie. "Thank you."

McLaughlin turned to Gristhorpe. "And you'll liaise with me at Regional Headquarters, Superintendent. Okay?"

Gristhorpe nodded.

"What about HOLMES?" McLaughlin asked.

HOLMES, acronym of the Home Office Large Major Enquiry System, was a computer database system developed since the Yorkshire Ripper investigation. Everything would be entered there, from witness statements to SOCO reports. It would all be indexed and cross-indexed so that nothing got lost in the mass of disparate paperwork the way the Ripper's identification had. "I think we should activate it now," said Banks. "Given the seriousness of the case. I'll put DC Jackman on it. She's a trained operator."

"Very well." McLaughlin looked from Banks to Annie. "By the way, Dr. Glendenning has offered to conduct the postmortem early this afternoon, so don't eat a heavy lunch. I think you should both be there. I'll also get some more DCs assigned as soon as possible," McLaughlin went on. "There'll probably be a lot of legwork on this. I understand you already have a murder investigation on the go. Can you handle this one, too?"

"I think so, sir." Banks remembered often having several serious cases on the go when he worked for the Met. "Officially, the Charlie Courage murder is still DI Collaton's case. Leicestershire Constabulary. DS Cabbot did some of the preliminary interviews, but I can put DS Hatchley on it."

McLaughlin paused and made a steeple of his hands and looked over his glasses. "We don't want to appear as if we're playing favorites, ladies and gentlemen," he said, "but there's no denying we're giving this case a very high priority indeed. Have you any thoughts so far, DCI Banks?"

"It's too early to say, sir. I'd like to have another talk with the family, maybe later today."

"Chief Constable Riddle said something about her hanging around with some unsavory types in London. Anything in that?"

"It's possible," said Banks. "There was one in particular, name of Barry Clough. I'll be having a very close look at him."

"Any other developments? DS Cabbot?"

"We searched the people in the club last night, sir," Annie said, "but we didn't find anything except a few tabs of Ecstasy, a bit of marijuana and the odd amphetamine pill or two."

"All according to PACE, I hope?"

"Yes, sir. Two people resisted and I had them taken over to the station. They were cautioned by the custody officer before being strip-searched. They were both carrying drugs in sufficient quantities for resale. One had crystal meth, the other what appears to be cocaine."

"Any connection with Ms. Riddle's death?"

"As far as we could tell, sir, it wasn't cut with strychnine, but we're holding him while it goes to the lab for tox testing."

McLaughlin jotted something on his pad. "What about CCTV?" he asked. "Was the club covered?"

"Unfortunately," said Banks, "the Bar None hasn't had any cameras installed yet, but we might get something from ours."

The installation of closed-circuit television cameras in the market square had been a thorny issue around the division that summer, when Eastvale had experienced a public-order problem caused by drunken louts gathering around the market cross after closing time. Fights broke out between rival gangs, often in town from villages in the Dale, or between locals and squaddies from the nearby army base. In one case an elderly female tourist was hit by flying glass and had to have sixteen stitches in her face.

Knaresborough, Ripon, Harrogate and Leeds had installed CCTV in their city centers and upped their arrest rates considerably, but at first the town council had poohpoohed the idea of doing the same in Eastvale, arguing that it would take them over-budget and that it wasn't necessary because the police station itself was located on one side of the market square, and all any officer had to do was look out of the window.

After considerable debate, and mostly because they were impressed by the rise in Ripon's arrest rate, the council had relented and four cameras were installed on an experimental basis. They fed directly into a small communications room set up on the ground floor of Eastvale Divisional Headquarters, where the tapes were routinely scanned for the faces of familiar troublemakers and any signs of criminal activity. Banks thought it all smacked a bit too much of Big Brother, but was willing to admit that in a case like this the tapes might be of some value.

"They'll at least tell us if anyone left after Emily and her friends arrived at the club," he went on. "Darren Hirst was too upset and confused to be certain last night."

"Good idea," McLaughlin said. "Any point staging a reconstruction?"

Banks took a deep breath. Now was the time. "I don't think so, sir. I had a brief lunch with Emily yesterday. She wanted to thank me for persuading her to return home, and she also expressed some concern about this Clough character."

"Go on," said McLaughlin, without expression.

Banks felt Annie's eyes boring into the side of his head again. Even Gristhorpe was frowning. "She left the Black Bull to meet someone, or so she said, at three o'clock. We don't know where she was between then and when she met her friends in the Cross Keys around seven. Darren said he thought she was a little high when she arrived at the Cross Keys, so I would guess that she'd been taking drugs with someone, perhaps the person who gave her the poisoned cocaine. After that, they were together as a group all evening. I think we'd have more to gain from a concentrated media campaign. Posters, television, newspapers."

"I'm concerned about this lunch you had with the victim," said McLaughlin.

"There was nothing to it, sir. We were in public view the entire time, and I remained there after Emily left. I think she was genuinely worried about Clough. She didn't feel she could talk to her father, but she wanted me to know."

"Why you?"

"Because I'd met him when I was searching for her. She knew I'd understand what she was talking about."

"Nasty piece of work, then?"

"Very, sir."

"Did she give you any idea of where she was going or who she was meeting?"

"No, sir. I wish she had." Banks wished he had even *asked* her.

"What did she talk about?"

"As I said, she was grateful to me for persuading her to go home. She talked about her future. She wanted to take her A-Levels and go to university in America."

"And she expressed concern about Clough?"

"Yes, sir."

"Did she say he'd been in touch with her, threatened her or anything like that?"

"She said he hadn't contacted her, but she seemed worried. She said he didn't like to lose his prize possessions. And she thought she saw one of his employees in the Swainsdale Centre."

"Do you think she knew something was going to happen to her, that she was in fear for her life?"

"I wouldn't push it that far, sir."

"Even so," said McLaughlin, "she was a member of the public expressing concern over a dangerous situation she had got herself into and asking for police help. Wasn't she?"

"Yes, sir," said Banks, relieved that McLaughlin had seen fit to throw him a life belt. Banks didn't see any point in telling him that Emily had been drinking underage in his presence, or that they had spent half a night alone together in a London hotel room.

"Good. I'll leave you to fill out the appropriate paperwork to that effect, then, so we can put it on file in case of any problems. I should imagine you were busy at the time and simply postponed the paperwork?"

"Yes, sir."

"Perfectly understandable. And you don't need me to tell you that quick, positive results on this would be beneficial all around."

"No, sir."

With that, ACC Ron McLaughlin left the boardroom.

"You may leave, too, DS Cabbot," said Gristhorpe. "Alan, I'd like a word."

Annie left, flashing Banks a tight, pissed-off look. Banks and Gristhorpe looked at one another. "Terrible business," said Gristhorpe. "No matter what you thought of Jimmy Riddle."

"It is, sir."

"This lunch, Alan? It only happened the once, just the way you say it did?"

"Yes, sir."

Gristhorpe grunted. He was looking old, Banks thought— his unruly hair, if anything, grayer lately, dark bags under his eyes, his normally ruddy, pockmarked complexion paler than usual. He also seemed to have lost weight; his tweed jacket looked baggy on him. Still, Banks reminded himself, Gristhorpe had been up pretty much all night, and he wasn't getting any younger.

"She was a good lass," Banks said. Then he shook his head. "No. What am I saying? That's not true. She was what you'd call a wild child. She was exasperating, a pain in the arse, and she no doubt ran Jimmy Riddle ragged."

"But you liked her?"

"Couldn't help but. She was confused, a bit crazy maybe, rebellious."

"A bit like you when you were a lad?" said Gristhorpe with a smile.

"Perish the thought. No. She was exactly the sort of girl I hoped Tracy wouldn't turn into, and thank the Lord she didn't. Maybe it was easy to admire the spirit in her because I wasn't her father, and she wasn't really my problem. But she was more confused than bad, and I think she'd have turned out all right, given the chance. She was just too advanced for her years. I want the bastard who did this to her, sir. Maybe more than I've ever wanted any bastard before in my career."

"Be careful, Alan." Gristhorpe leaned forward and rested his arms on the table. "You know as well as I do that you wouldn't be anywhere near this case if it weren't for Jimmy Riddle. But if you screw up just once because it's too personal for you, I'll be down on you like the proverbial ton of bricks. Which is probably nothing to what ACC McLaughlin will do. Got it?"

"Got it," said Banks. "Don't worry. I'll play it by the book."

Gristhorpe leaned back and smiled at him. "Nay, Alan," he said. "You wouldn't want to do that. What'd be the point of having you on the case, then? All I'm saying is don't let anger and a desire for revenge cloud your judgment. Look clearly at the evidence, the facts, before you make any moves. Don't go off half-cocked the way you've done in the past."

"I'll try not to," said Banks.

"You do that."

Someone knocked at the door and Gristhorpe called out for him to come in. It was one of the uniformed officers from downstairs. "A DI Wayne Dalton, Northumbria CID, to see DCI Banks, sir."

Banks raised his eyebrows and looked at Gristhorpe. "Okay," he said, glancing at his watch. "Give him a cup of coffee and sit him in my office. I can spare him a few minutes."

Banks wasn't the only one who had spent a restless night; Annie Cabbot had also lain awake during the hour or two she had spent in bed shortly before dawn, her nerve ends jumping at every little sound. She had tried to tell herself not to be so weak. After all, she had prevented Dalton and his crony from raping her two years ago, so why should she be worried about him now? Her martial arts training might be a bit rusty, but she could defend herself well enough if it came to that.

The problem was that reason has no foothold at four or five in the morning; at those hours, reason sleeps and the mind breeds monsters: monsters of fear, of paranoia. And so she had tossed and turned, her mind's eye flashing on images of Dalton's sweat-glossed face and hate-filled eyes, and of Emily Riddle dead, her skinny frame wedged in a toilet cubicle at the Bar None nightclub, her eyes wide open in terror and facial muscles contorted into a grimace.

Now, however, as she came out of the meeting and headed for her office in what little light of day there was, she realized that she wasn't physically afraid of Dalton. She had always known he was the type who could only act violently as part of a gang. His appearance had shaken her, that was all, stirred up memories of that night she would rather forget. The only problem was that she didn't know quite what to do, if anything, about him.

She thought of telling Banks but dismissed the idea quickly. If truth be told, she was pissed off at him. Why hadn't he told her about his relationship with the victim last night? There had been plenty of time. It would have made her feel more like a DIO and less like a bloody idiot this morning when the ACC brought the matter up.

In a way, she regretted now that she had even told Banks about the rape in the first place, but such intimacy as they had had breeds foolish confessions; she had certainly never told anyone else, not even her father. And now that she was actually working with Banks, even though she still fancied him, she was going to try to keep things on a professional footing. Her career was moving in the right direction again, and she didn't want to mess things up. ACC McLaughlin had given her a great chance for kudos in making her DIO. The last thing she wanted to do was go crying to the boss. No, Dalton was *her* problem, and she would deal with him one way or another.

Banks found DI Dalton standing in his office facing the wall, Styrofoam cup of coffee in his hand, looking at the Dalesman calendar. December showed a snow- and ice-covered Goredale Scar, near Malham. Dalton turned as Banks entered. He was about six feet tall and skinny as a rake, with pale, watery blue eyes and a long, thin face with a rather hangdog expression under his head of sparse ginger hair. Banks put his age at around forty. He was wearing a lightweight brown suit, white shirt and tie. A little blood from a shaving cut had dried near the cleft of his chin.

He stuck his hand out. "DI Wayne Dalton. I seem to have come in the middle of a flap."

"Haven't you heard?"

"Heard what?"

"The chief constable's daughter was killed last night."

Dalton rolled his eyes and whistled. "I'd hate to be the bastard who did that, when you catch him."

"We will. Sit down. What brings you this far south?"

"It's probably a waste of time," said Dalton, sitting opposite Banks, "but it looks like one of our cases stretches down to your turf."

"Wouldn't be the first time. We've quickly become a very small island indeed."

"You can say that again. Anyway, late Sunday night—actually, early Monday morning—about twelve-thirty, to be as precise as we can be at this point—a white van was hijacked on the B6348 between the A1 and the village of Chatton. The contents were stolen and the driver's still in a coma."

"What's his name?"

"Jonathan Fearn."

Banks tapped his pencil on his desk. "Never heard of him."

"No reason you should have. He lived here, though." Dalton consulted his notebook. "Twenty-six Darlington Road."

"I know it," said Banks, making a note. "We'll look into him. Any form?"

"No. What's interesting, though, is that it turns out this white van was leased by a company called PKF Computer Systems, and—"

"Hang on a minute. Did you say PKF?"

"That's right. Starting to make sense?"

"Not much, but go on."

"Anyway, we ran a check on PKF and, to cut a long story, it doesn't exist."

"What do you mean?"

"Exactly what I say. PKF Computer Systems is not registered as an operating business."

"That means someone made up the name . . ."

". . . printed some letterhead paper, got a phone line installed, opened a bank account . . . exactly. A dummy company."

"Any idea who?"

"That's where I was hoping you might be able to help. We traced PKF to the Daleview Business Park, just outside Eastvale, and we confirmed that the van must have been on its way to a new trading estate near Wooler. At least PKF had rented premises there starting that Monday morning."

"Let me get this straight," said Banks. "PKF, which doesn't exist, moves lock, stock and barrel from the Daleview Business Park, where they haven't been operating more than two or three months, on Sunday night and heads up the A1 toward another business park near Tyneside, where they've also rented premises. A few miles short of their destination, the van's hijacked and its contents removed. Right?"

"So far."

"On Tuesday," Banks continued, "the night watchman of the Daleview Business Park was found dead in some woods near Market Harborough, Leicestershire. Shotgun wound."

"Execution?"

"Looks that way. We think he was killed Monday afternoon."

"Connection?"

"I'd say so, wouldn't you? Especially when it turns out our night watchman had been putting away another two hundred quid a week over and above his wages."

"And PKF is a phony."

"Exactly."

"Any idea what that van might have been carrying?" Dalton asked.

"The only thing my DS found when she checked out the PKF unit at Daleview was an empty jewel case for a compact disc."

"Compact discs? First time I've ever heard of a CD hijack."

"We don't know that that's the reason. All I'm saying is that we found a jewel case at PKF, which fits with their working in the computer business. Maybe it was computer equipment the thieves were after?"

"Could be. That stuff can be valuable."

"Any leads at all?"

Dalton shook his head. "We've been keeping an eye on the unit they rented near Wooler, but no one's shown up yet. Given what's happened, we don't expect them to now. It was late, on a quiet road, so there were no witnesses. They left the van in a lay-by. As I said, the driver's still in a coma and fingerprints will be working to sort out their findings till kingdom come. You and I both know that anyone doing a professional job like this would be wearing gloves, anyway. This was the only lead we got—PKF and the Daleview Business Park."

"Okay," said Banks, standing. "We'll keep in touch on this one."

"Mind if I stick around a day or two, have a look at the business park, poke about?"

"Be my guest." Banks pulled his pad toward him. "The way things are right now we can use all the help we can get. You could also get in touch with DI Collaton at Market Harborough. It looks as if this is all connected. Where are you staying?"

"Fox and Hounds, on North Market Street. Got in yesterday evening. Nice little en suite."

"I know the place," said Banks. "Let us know if you find anything."

"Will do." Dalton touched the tips of his fingers in a friendly salute, then left the office.

Banks walked over to the window and looked out on the cobbled market square. The gold hands against the blue front of the church clock stood at quarter past ten. The morning mist had disappeared and it was as light now as it was likely to be all day. He saw DI Dalton walk across the square, pause and linger a moment at the taped-off, guarded entrance of the Bar None, then turn left on York Road toward the bus station and the Swainsdale Centre.

It was difficult for Banks to drum up much enthusiasm for the Charlie Courage investigation since Emily's murder, but he knew he had to keep on top of it. He also knew that they should have checked into PKF the way Dalton had. Any further signs that he was dragging his feet, and Red Ron would, quite rightly, have him on the carpet. Emily was a priority, yes, but that didn't mean poor Charlie counted for nothing. Maybe Dalton would come up with something useful. Banks would put him in touch with Hatchley, and with Annie, so she could share what she'd discovered at Daleview.

Looking at the weak gray light that seemed to cling to everything, bleeding the townscape of all color, Banks wished he could escape to somewhere warm and sunny for a couple of weeks, find a nice spot on the beach and read novels and biographies and listen to the waves all day. Normally he didn't like that kind of holiday, preferring to explore a foreign city on foot, but there was something about the long, dark Yorkshire winters that made him yearn for the Canaries or the Azores. Or Montego Bay. If he could afford it, though, he thought he would like to go to Mexico for a while, see some Mayan ruins. But that was out of the question, especially with the mortgage on the cottage and Tracy at university.

Besides, Banks thought, opening the window a few inches and lighting a cigarette, he couldn't desert Emily now. He was responsible for what happened to her, at least in part. There was no escaping that. If he hadn't gone down to London and stirred things up with Clough, then it was unlikely that she would have come back home and ended up dead in a crummy Eastvale nightclub. She had gone the way of Graham Marshall, of Jem and of Phil Simpkins, and he couldn't, wouldn't, just let it go; he *had* to do something.

"Let it roll, Ned," said Banks. He was in the CCTV viewing room downstairs along with DCs Winsome Jackman and Kevin Templeton, Annie Cabbot and their civilian video technician, Ned Parker.

The screen showed the market square from the police station, including the edge of the Queen's Arms to the right, the church front to the left and all the shops, pubs and offices directly opposite, including the entrance to the Bar None. The picture was a grainy black and white, with a slight fish-eye effect, and the glare of the Christmas lights caused one or two problems with the contrast, but it was still possible to make out figures coming and going. Whether they would be able to identify someone coming out of the Bar None from this tape alone, Banks was doubtful.

The time appeared in an on-screen display at the bottom right-hand side, and, starting at 10:00, Parker advanced it quickly so that the people crossing the market square looked like extras in a Keystone Cops chase. Somewhere around twenty-five past, Banks noticed a group of people enter the screen from the right, the exit of the Queen's Arms, and told Parker to slow down to normal speed. He then watched Emily walk across the market square. She seemed a little unsteady on the cobbles as she crossed the square, which didn't surprise him considering the platform heels she was wearing and the amount she had had to drink that day.

When she got to the market cross, she turned to face the police station and did a little dance, and when she finished, she bowed with a flourish to the camera, but before walking away she gave it the finger, just one, in the American style, then she turned and swung her hips exaggeratedly as she walked on to the nightclub. The others laughed. Banks himself smiled as he watched her, almost forgetting for a moment that this was a little cheeky gesture that would never be repeated.

Banks watched them enter the club and asked Parker to keep it running at normal speed as he watched others follow. As far as he could make out, there was no suspicious activity in the market square. No little packages of white powder exchanging hands. As he watched, he realized how much he wanted to be watching what was happening *inside* the club, but there were no cameras there.

At 10:47, two people walked out of the club and headed down York Road. Banks couldn't make out their features, but it looked like a boy in jeans and a short leather jacket and a girl in a long overcoat and a floppy hat. He asked Parker to freeze the frame, but it didn't help much.

After that, another three couples went in, but no one came out. When DC Rickerd and Inspector Jessup entered the frame, Banks told Parker to turn the machine off.

It was beginning to look very much as if Emily had scored her coke long before she went to the Bar None, as Banks had guessed, and that would make it all the more difficult to find out who had supplied her with the lethal concoction.

"Okay," Banks said, standing up and stretching. "That's all your entertainment for today. Winsome, bring in Darren Hirst, would you? Maybe he can help us with the two who left."

"Friendly, sir?"

"Friendly. He's not a suspect, just helping us with our inquiries."

Winsome smiled at the hackneyed phrase. "Will do, sir."

"Kevin, I'd like you to work with Ned here and see if you can pull a decent image of those two who left. Something we can show around."

"Okay, Guv."

"And, Kevin?"

"Guv?"

"Please don't call me 'Guv.' It makes me feel as if I'm on television."

Templeton grinned. "Right you are, *sir*."

Then Banks looked at his watch and turned to Annie. "We'd better go," he said. "We've got an appointment with Dr. Glendenning in a few minutes."

Banks drove out to the Old Mill after Emily Riddle's postmortem, Fauré's Requiem playing on the stereo. He still felt angry and nauseated at what he had just seen. It wasn't the first young girl he had watched Dr. Glendenning open up on the slab, but it was the first whose vitality he had known, whose fears and dreams had been shared with him, and watching Dr. Glendenning calmly bisecting the black spider tattoo with his scalpel as he made his "Y" incision had almost sent Banks the way Annie went down in Market Harborough. Annie had been fine this time, though. Quiet and tense, but fine, even when the saw ripped into the bone of Emily's skull.

Dr. Glendenning had confirmed Dr. Burns's original determination that strychnine, mixed in a high ratio with pharmaceutical cocaine, had caused Emily's death. Glendenning had performed the simple toxicology test for strychnine himself, dissolving some of the suspect crystals in sulfuric acid and touching the edge of the solution with a crystal of potassium chromate. It turned purple, then crimson, then all color faded. Proof positive. Further tox tests would be done at Wetherby, but for now, this was enough. So far, all the media knew was that she had died of a suspected drug overdose, but it wouldn't be long before some bright spark of a reporter sniffed out the truth. Sometimes the press seemed even more resourceful than the police.

As it turned out, Emily's neck wasn't broken; she had died of asphyxiation. Other than the fact that she was dead, Glendenning had also told Banks, she was in extremely good health. The drugs and drink and cigarettes clearly hadn't had time to take their toll on her.

The Old Mill stood at the end of a cul-de-sac, like Banks's more humble abode, so the uniformed officers on guard could stand well over a hundred yards away, where it turned off from the main road, and keep reporters away without even being seen by the Riddles. Banks showed his warrant card and the officer on duty waved him through. Rosalind answered the door and led him through to the same room where he had given Riddle the news. She was dressed in black and her eyes looked dark with lack of sleep. Banks guessed that Riddle must have awoken her as soon as he had left last night. They wouldn't have had any sleep since then.

"Banks." Riddle got slowly to his feet when Banks entered the room. He was dressed in the same clothes he had been wearing last night, a little more the worse for wear. He looked haggard, and there was a listlessness and a defeated air about his movements that Banks had never seen him exhibit before. He had always been energetic and abrupt. Perhaps he had taken a tranquilizer, or perhaps this was the toll that recent events had taken on his system. Whichever it was, the man looked as if he could use a doctor as well as a good night's sleep. "Any news?" he asked, without much hope in his voice.

"Nothing yet, I'm afraid." Banks didn't want to mention the postmortem, though he knew Riddle would be aware that it had been conducted. He only hoped the CC had enough common sense not to bring something like that up in front of his wife.

"Confirmed cause of death?" he asked.

"It's what we thought."

Rosalind put her hand to her throat. "Strychnine. I've read about that."

Banks glanced at Riddle. "You've told her . . . ?"

"Ros understands she's to talk to no one about the cause of death. I don't suppose it'll be a secret for long, though?"

"I doubt it," said Banks. "Not now the postmortem's over. Glendenning's sound as a bell, but there's always someone there who lets the cat out of the bag. Mrs. Riddle," he said, perching at the edge of his armchair, "I need to ask you some questions. I'll try to make it as painless for you as possible."

"I understand. Jerry explained it to me."

"Good. Emily had been back from London about a month. During that time, had she given you any cause for concern?"

"No," said Rosalind. "In fact, she'd been extremely well-behaved. For Emily."

"Meaning?"

"Meaning, Chief Inspector, that if she wanted to stay out all night at a rave, she would. Emily always was a willful child, as I'm sure you're aware, difficult to control. But I saw no evidence of drug use, and she was generally polite and good-natured in her dealings with me."

"I gather that wasn't always the case?"

"It was not."

"Had she been out a lot since her return?"

"Not much. Last night was only the second or third time."

"When was the last time?"

"The night before. Wednesday. She went to the pictures with some friends. That new cinema complex in Eastvale, and a week or so ago she went to a friend's birthday party in Richmond. She was home shortly after midnight both times."

"What did she do with her time?"

"Believe it or not, she stayed in and read a lot. Watched videos. She also made inquiries about getting into a sixth-form college. I think she was finally deciding to take life a bit more seriously."

"Did she ever confide in you about any problems she might be having? Boys, or anything like that?"

"That wasn't Emily's way," said Rosalind. "She was always secretive, even when she was little. She liked a sense of mystery."

"What about boyfriends?"

"I don't think there was anyone special. She hung around with a group of people."

"It must have been difficult for her to make friends locally, with being off at school down south so much of the time."

"It was. And you probably know yourself, the locals aren't always that welcoming of southerners, even these days. But when she was home for the holidays she'd meet people. I don't know. She didn't seem to have any real trouble making friends. She was outgoing enough. And of course, she still knew people from when she was at Saint Mary's School here. That was only two years ago."

"What about Darren Hirst? Did she ever mention him?"

"Yes. In fact, it was *his* birthday party she went to last week. But he wasn't her boyfriend; he was just part of the group she hung out with. The lad with the car. They came to the house to pick her up on Wednesday—Darren and a girl, Nina or Tina or something—and they certainly seemed pleasant enough, although I didn't approve of her hanging around with people who were, for the most part, three or four years older than she was. I knew she went to pubs and could get served easily enough, and I didn't like it. I told her often enough, but she just accused me of going on at her, and in the end I gave up."

"Did she ever mention someone called Andrew Handley?"

"No."

"Andy Pandy?"

"Is this some sort of joke? Who's he?"

"It's not a joke. That's his nickname. He's a colleague of the man Emily was living with in London."

"Never heard of him," said Rosalind. She reached forward, grabbed a tissue from the box on the table and sniffled into it. "I'm sorry," she mumbled. "Please excuse me."

Riddle moved over to her and touched her shoulder hesitantly, without much warmth, it seemed. In response, Rosalind's body stiffened, and she turned away. Banks thought he glimpsed something in her eyes as she turned—fear or confusion, perhaps. Did she suspect her husband of being involved in Emily's death? Or was he protecting her? Whatever it was, there was something desperately out of kilter with the Riddle family.

"Did Emily speak to you of her plans for the future, Mrs. Riddle?" Banks asked, switching the direction of the interview to something he thought might be a little easier for her to deal with.

"Only that she wanted to do her A-Levels and go to university," said Rosalind, still dabbing her eyes with the tissue. "Preferably in America. I think she wanted to get as far away from here and from us as she could."

Out of sight, out of mind, thought Banks. And less likely to damage Riddle's fledgling political career, if that wasn't already damaged beyond repair. He remembered on his first visit, when the Riddles asked him to go to London and find Emily, how he had got the impression that Rosalind hadn't particularly wanted her to come back home. He got the same impression now. "And you approved?"

"Of course I did. It's better than her running off to London and living with some . . . I don't know . . . some drug dealer."

"We don't know that he was a drug dealer," said Banks. "In fact, Emily swore he wasn't, and I'm inclined to believe her."

"Well, Emily always could twist men around her little finger."

"Not Clough. She met her match there."

"Do you really think he could be responsible?" asked Riddle.

"Oh, yes. The impression I got is that he's a dangerous man and he doesn't like to be crossed."

"But why would he want to harm her? He had no real motive."

"I don't know," said Banks. "All I can say is that I've met him and I'm convinced he's into something. Perhaps he did it out of sheer maliciousness, because he didn't like to be crossed. Or perhaps he thought she knew too much about his business interests. Did she ever talk about him to you?"

"No. What are you doing about him?" Riddle asked.

"I'm going to London first thing tomorrow. Before that, I just want to find out if there are any more leads I should be following up here." Banks paused. "Look, I had lunch with Emily the day she died and—"

"You did what?"

"She phoned and asked me to lunch, said she'd be in Eastvale. She wanted to thank me."

"She never told us," said Riddle, looking at Rosalind, who frowned.

"Well, your wife did say she was secretive. And given that, my next question is probably a waste of time, but when she left, she said she was going to meet someone else. Did she say anything to either of you about meeting someone in Eastvale that afternoon?"

They both shook their heads. "What did she say to you?" Rosalind asked. "Did she tell you anything?"

"About what?"

"I don't know. Anything that might help explain what happened."

"Only that she thought she'd seen one of Clough's men in Eastvale. I gather she didn't mention that to you?"

"No," said Rosalind.

"When did you last see her yesterday?"

"We didn't," Riddle answered. "Both Ros and I had gone to work long before she got up that morning, and when we got back she was out."

"So the last time you saw her was Wednesday?"

"Yes."

"Did she phone anyone or get any phone calls?"

"Not that I know of," said Riddle. "Ros?"

Rosalind shook her head.

"Did she spend much time on the telephone while she was up here?"

"Not a lot, no."

"Do I have your permission to ask British Telecom for a record of your telephone calls since Emily came home?"

"Of course," said Riddle. "I'll see to it myself."

"That's all right, sir. I'll put DC Templeton on it. Did she have any visitors from London, make any trips back down there?"

"Not that we know of, no," said Riddle.

"Are you both sure there's no one else you can think of who I should be looking closely at for this?"

"No," said Riddle, after a moment's pause for thought. "Not up here. As Ros said, she hung around with a group. They were probably with her at the club. You can talk to them and ascertain whether you think any of them had anything to do with it."

"We've already talked to them, but we'll follow up on that. I must say, on first impressions I don't think any of them are responsible. Do you know where she got her drugs?"

It was Rosalind who answered. "I told you that I don't think she was taking drugs since she came back."

"Are you certain?"

"Not completely. But . . . I . . ." She glanced at her husband and blushed before she went on. "I searched her room once. And once or twice, I looked in her handbag. I found nothing."

"Well, she was definitely taking cocaine the night she died," said Banks.

"Maybe it was her first time since London?"

"When you searched her handbag, Mrs. Riddle, did you come across a driving license and an age-verification card?"

Rosalind looked puzzled. "A driving license? Good Lord, no. Emily was too young to drive. Besides, I didn't look in her purse."

"I'm not saying she did actually drive a car, but when she was found, the officer at the scene found a driving license in her handbag and thought it was hers. He also found one of those cards the clubs issue as proof of age, though they're nothing of the kind. That's why there was some confusion over the identity at first."

"It doesn't mean anything to me," said Rosalind. "I don't understand."

"What about the name Ruth Walker?"

Banks saw a strange look flash in across Rosalind's eyes, perhaps the surprise of recognition, but it was gone so fast that he didn't trust his own judgment. She pressed her lips tight together. "No."

"She was another friend of Emily's in London. Apparently this Ruth met her in the street and took her in when she first arrived. You didn't know about that?"

"No."

"What about Craig Newton? Ring any bells?"

"Who was he?"

"Her first boyfriend in London. There was a bit of trouble between him and Clough. He seemed a decent enough lad when I talked to him, but he might have been jealous, and he might have held a grudge against Emily for ditching him. She told me he'd been following her around and pestering her." Banks stood up. "Clearly I'm going to find more answers down there. For the moment, though, are you certain neither of you can think of anyone who would want to harm Emily?"

They both shook their heads.

Banks looked at Riddle. "You're a policeman, sir," he said. "Can you think of anyone who might have a grudge against you?"

"Oh, come on, Banks. You know I've hardly been fighting in the trenches for years. That's not a chief constable's job."

"Even so . . . ?"

"No, I can't think of anyone offhand."

"Would you check through your previous arrests, no matter how old? Just for form's sake."

"Of course." Riddle saw Banks to the door. "You'll keep in touch, won't you?" he said, grasping Banks's arm tightly. "I've been advised to stay away from the office for the time being, so I'm taking a leave of absence. But I'm sure I could be more effective there. Anyway, the moment you know, I want to know. Understand? The moment."

Banks nodded and Riddle released his grip.

Back at the incident room, Banks discovered that Darren Hirst had been and gone. DC Jackman had interviewed him and said he had been unable to shed any light on the couple who had left the Bar None at ten forty-seven. He hadn't even remembered seeing them in the first place. Now it was a matter of getting the rather blurred and grainy image that Ned Parker had pulled from the CCTV video copied up and shown around. It was possible that someone might have re-membered seeing them in the pubs around the market square. It would probably come to nothing, but then most police work did.

He also found out that three people who had been in the Black Bull yesterday at lunchtime had phoned in and said they had seen the victim with an older man. One person had positively identified the man as "that detective who was on telly about that there reservoir business in t'summer." Just as well he'd told the ACC and the Riddles.

Banks walked into the detectives' office. Down the corri-dor, it sounded as if someone was going at the floor with a pneumatic drill. He shut the door behind him and leaned against the wall. Hatchley and Annie Cabbot were at their desks. Annie gave him a dirty look, and Hatchley said he had been out investigating an alien abduction.

Banks smiled. "Come again? Since when have you been working on the 'X Files,' Jim?"

"It's true," said Hatchley. "Honest to God." He chuckled; it sounded as if he was coughing up a big one. "Toy shop down on Elmet Street," he went on. "They put out an inflat-able little green man to advertise a new line of toys and somebody nicked it. Some kid, probably. Still, it's an alien abduction."

Banks laughed. "There's one for the books. Ever hear of a fellow called Jonathan Fearn?" he asked.

"Rings a bell." Hatchley scratched his ear. "If I'm thinking of the right one, he's an unemployed yobbo, not above a bit dodgy dealing every now and then. We've had our eyes on him as driver on a couple of warehouse robberies over the years."

"But he's got no form?"

Hatchley shrugged. "Just lucky. Some are. It won't last."

"His luck's already run out. He's in hospital in Newcastle, in a coma."

Hatchley whistled. "Bloody hell. What happened?"

Banks told him as much as he knew. "Do you know of any connection between this Fearn character and Charlie Courage?"

"Could be," Hatchley said. "I mean, they hung out in the same pubs and neither of them was beyond a bit of thievery every now and then. Sound like two peas from the same pod to me."

"Thanks, Jim," said Banks. "Poke around a bit, will you? See if you can find a connection."

Hatchley, always happy to be sent off to do his work in pubs, beamed. "My pleasure."

"There's a DI Dalton around the place somewhere. Down from Northumbria, staying at the Fox and Hounds. He might be able to help. Liaise with him on this one."

"Will do."

Annie followed Banks out of the office and caught up with him in the corridor. "A word?"

"Of course," said Banks. "Not here, though. This noise is driving me crazy. Queen's Arms?"

"Fine with me."

Banks and Annie walked across Market Street to the Queen's Arms.

"I want to know just what the hell you think you've been

playing at," Annie said when they had got drinks and sat down in a quiet corner. She spoke softly, but there was anger in her voice, and she sat stiffly in the chair.

"What do you mean?"

"You know damn well what I mean. What went on between you and the victim?"

"Emily Riddle?"

"Who else?"

Banks sighed. "I'm sorry it happened the way it did, Annie, sorry if I embarrassed you in any way. I would have told you, honestly. I just hadn't found the right time."

"You could have told me last night at the scene."

"No, I couldn't. There was too much else going on, too much to do, too much to organize. And I was bloody upset by what I saw—all right?"

"No, it's not all right. You made me feel like a complete idiot this morning. I've been working on the case as long as you had, and here are you coming up with a suspect I've never even heard of. Not to mention having lunch with the victim on the day she died."

"Look, I've said I'm sorry. What else can I say?"

Annie shook her head. "It's not on, Alan. If I'm supposed to be your DIO, I'm not supposed to be the last bloody person on earth who hears about important developments."

"It wasn't an important development. It had already happened."

"Stop splitting hairs. You named a suspect. You had a prior relationship with the victim. You should have told me. It could have a bearing on the investigation."

"It *does* have a bearing on the investigation. And I *will* tell you if you'll let me."

"Better late than never."

Banks told her about London, about GlamourPuss, Clough, Ruth Walker and Craig Newton—everything except the night in the hotel room—and about what he and Emily had discussed over lunch the previous day. When he had finished, Annie seemed to relax in her chair the way she normally did.

"I wasn't keeping it from you, Annie," he said. "It was just bad timing, that's all. Honestly."

"And that's all there is to it?"

"That's all. Scout's honor."

Annie managed a smile. "Next time anything like that happens, tell me up front, okay?"

"Okay. Forgive me?"

"I'm working on it. What next?"

"I'm going down to London tomorrow to do a bit of checking up."

"And me?"

"I want you to take care of things at this end. I'll only be gone for the weekend, most likely, but there's a lot to do. Get posters made up, contact the local TV news people and see if you can get an appeal for information on. Anyone who saw her between the time she left the Black Bull just before three and the time she met her friends in the Cross Keys at seven. And stress the fact that even though she was technically only sixteen, she looked older. Men will certainly remember if they saw her. Check local buses and taxis. Get DC Templeton to organize a house-to-house of the area around the Black Bull. Maybe we'll even get reinforcements. Who knows? We might get lucky. Maybe someone saw Clough handing over a gram of coke to her."

"Sure."

"And there's another thing."

"What's that?"

"I had a visit from a DI Dalton this morning. Northumbria CID. It's about the Charlie Courage business. Seems there's some connection with a hijacked van up north. Seeing as you did the preliminary interviews at Daleview, I'd like you to have a quick chat with him before you hand over the file to DS Hatchley. He might be able to help us. He's staying at the Fox and Hounds. You never know. Maybe if you're lucky he'll even buy you a pint."

That evening at home, Banks tossed a few clothes into his overnight bag, followed by Evelyn Waugh's *The Ordeal of Gilbert Pinfold* and his Renee Fleming and Captain Beefheart tapes. He would have to buy a portable CD player, he decided; it was becoming too time-consuming and expensive to tape everything, and CD timings were getting more difficult to match with the basic ninety- or one-hundred-minute tape format.

When he had finished packing, he phoned Brian, who answered on the third ring.

"Hi, Dad. How's it going?"

"Fine. Look, I'm going to be down your way again this weekend. Any chance of your being around? I'll be pretty busy, but I'm sure we can fit in a lunch or something."

"Sorry," said Brian. "We've got some gigs in Southampton."

"Ah, well, you can't blame a father for trying. One of these days, maybe. Take care, and I hope you're a big success."

"Thanks. Oh, Dad?"

"Yes?"

"You remember that bloke you were asking about a while back, the ex-roadie?"

"Barry Clough?"

"That's him."

"What about him?"

"Nothing, really, but I was talking to one of the producers at the recording studio, name of Terry King. Old geezer like you, been around a long time, since punk. You know: The Sex Pistols, The Clash, that sort of thing? Surely you must remember those days?"

"Brian," said Banks, smiling to himself, "I even remember Elvis. Now cut the ageism and get to the point."

"It's nothing, really. Just that he remembered Clough. Called himself something else, then, one of those silly punk names like Sid Vicious—Terry couldn't remember exactly what it was—but it was him, all right. Apparently he got fired from his roadie job."

"What for?"

"Bootlegging live concerts. Not just the band he worked with, but all the big names."

"I see." Banks remembered the booming business in

bootleg LPs in the seventies. First Bob Dylan, Jimi Hendrix, The Doors and other popular bands were all bootlegged, and none of them made a penny from the illegal sales. The same thing also happened later with some of the punk bands. Not that any of them needed the money, and most of them were too stoned to notice, but that wasn't the point. Clough's employers *had* noticed and given him the push.

"Like I said, it's not much. But he says he's heard this Clough bloke is a gangster now. A tough guy. Be careful, Dad."

"I will. I'm not exactly a five-stone weakling myself, you know."

"Right. Oh, and there's one more thing."

"Yes?"

"There's this car a mate of mine's selling. Only three years old, got its MOT and everything. I got another—"

"Brian, what do you want?"

"Well, I've got the asking price down a couple of hundred from what it was, but I was wondering, you know, if you could see your way to helping me out?"

"What? Me help out my rich and famous rock-star son?" Brian laughed. "Give us a break."

"How much do you need?"

"Three hundred quid would do nicely. I'll let you have it back when I *am* rich and famous."

"All right."

"You're sure?"

"That's what I said, isn't it?"

"That's great! Thanks, Dad. Thanks a lot. I mean it."

"You're welcome. Talk to you later."

Banks hung up. Three hundred quid he could ill afford. Still, he would come up with it somehow. After all, he had saved a bundle by missing out on Paris, and he had given Tracy a bit of spending money that weekend. He remembered how much he had wanted a car when he was young; the kids with cars seemed to get all the girls. He had finally bought a rusty old VW Beetle when he was at college in London. It lasted him the length of his course there, then clapped out on the North Circular one cold, rainy Sunday in

January, and he hadn't got another one until he and Sandra were married. Yes, he'd find a way to help Brian out.

Next, Banks tried Tracy's number and was surprised when she answered right away: "Dad! I've been wanting to talk to you. I just heard about Mr. Riddle's daughter on the news. Are you all right? I know you didn't get along with him, but . . . Did you know her?"

"Yes," said Banks. Then he told Tracy the bare details about going to London to find Emily instead of going with her to Paris that weekend.

"Oh, Dad. Don't feel guilty for doing someone a favor. I was disappointed at first, but Damon and I had the most wonderful time."

I'll bet you did, thought Banks, biting his tongue.

Tracy went on. "All I heard was that she died after taking an overdose of cocaine in the Bar None, and they're all saying she lived a pretty wild life. Is it something to do with what happened in London?"

"I don't know," said Banks. "Maybe."

"That's terrible. Was it deliberate?"

"Could have been."

"Do you have any idea who . . . ? No, I know I shouldn't ask."

"It's all right, love. We don't at the moment. A few leads to follow, that's all. I'm going back to London tomorrow. I just wanted to talk to you first, see if you were still on for Christmas."

"Of course. I wouldn't miss it for the world."

"Good."

"She was only sixteen, wasn't she?"

"That's right."

Tracy paused. "Look, Dad . . . I just want you to know . . . I mean, I know you worry about me sometimes. I know you and Mum worried about me when we were all together, but you didn't really need to. I'm . . . I mean, I never did anything like that."

"I know you didn't."

"No, Dad. You don't *know*. You can't *know*. Even if you knew what signs to look for, you weren't there. I don't mean to be nasty about it. I know about the demands of your job and all, and I know you loved us, but you just *weren't there*. Anyway, I'm telling you the truth. I know you think I've always been little Miss Goody Two-shoes, but it's not true. I did try smoking some marijuana once, but I didn't like the way it made me feel. And once a girl gave me some Ecstasy at a dance. I didn't like that, either. It made my heart beat too fast and all I did was sweat and feel frightened. I suppose you could say I'm a failure as far as drugs are concerned."

"I'm glad to hear it." Banks wanted to ask if she'd been sexually active at fourteen, too, but he didn't think it would be a fair question to put to his daughter. She would tell him what she wanted when she wanted to.

"Anyway," Tracy went on, "I'm sure you're very busy. And I'm sure if anyone's going to catch him, it'll be you."

Banks laughed. "I appreciate your confidence in me. Take care, love. Talk to you soon."

"Bye, Dad."

Banks hung up the phone gently and let the silence enfold him again. He always had that same empty, lonely feeling after he'd spoken to someone he loved over the telephone, as if the silence had somehow become charged with that person's absence. He shook it off. It was a mild enough night outside and he still had time to go to his little balcony by the falls for a cigarette and a finger or two of Laphroaig.

10

"**B**arry Clough," said Detective Superintendent Richard "Dirty Dick" Burgess, chewing on a piece of particularly tough steak. "Now there's an interesting bloke."

It was Saturday lunchtime, and Banks and Burgess were sitting in a pub just off Oxford Street, the air around them laced with smoke and conversation. It was a mild day, much warmer than the last time Banks had been to London in early November. The pub was crowded with Christmas shoppers taking a break, and one brave couple actually sat at a table outside. Burgess was drinking lager and lime, but Banks had only coffee with his chicken in a basket. He had a busy day ahead and needed to stay alert.

He had phoned Burgess before leaving Eastvale that morning. If anyone could uncover information on Clough, it was Dirty Dick Burgess. He had recently got himself into a bit of trouble for dragging his feet over the investigation into the murder of a black youth. As a result, he'd been shunted off to the National Criminal Intelligence Service, where he couldn't do so much harm. It didn't seem to bother Burgess that he had been identified as a racist; he took it all in his stride with his usual lack of concern.

The two had known each other for years, and while they had tentatively come to enjoy each other's company, their relationship remained mostly confrontational. Banks especially didn't share Burgess's strong right-wing leanings, nor did he concur with his racist and sexist opinions. In his turn, Burgess had called Banks a "pinko." About the only thing they had in common was that both were from working-class backgrounds. Burgess, though, unlike Banks, was the Margaret Thatcher kind of working-class lad who had come to the fore in the eighties; someone who had triumphed over a deprived background, then devoted himself to the pursuit of material benefits and felt no sympathy or solidarity with any of his class who couldn't or wouldn't follow suit.

Banks, or so he hoped, retained some compassion for his fellowman, especially the downtrodden, and occasionally even the criminal. It was difficult to maintain such a view, being a copper all those years, but he had sworn to himself not long after finding Dawn Wadley's dismembered body in the Soho alley that as soon as he stopped caring, he would quit. He had thought that his move from the Met to the softer patch of Eastvale would have made life easier, but somehow, without the sheer volume of human misery that had been his lot in the city, every case seemed to take more of a toll on him. It was similar to the way people found it hard to respond to the deaths of millions of foreigners in a flood or an earthquake, but fell to pieces when a kindly old neighbor was run over.

"Any man's death diminishes me, because I am involved in Mankind," as John Donne had said, and Banks knew exactly what he meant.

The odd thing about working day-in, day-out against murderers, pimps, drug dealers, muggers and the rest was that you could distance yourself. Partly you did it by developing a dark sense of humor, telling tasteless jokes at crime scenes, getting pissed with the lads after attending a postmortem, and partly you just built a wall around your feelings. But in Eastvale, where he had more time to devote himself to important cases—especially murders—his defenses had been slowly eroded until he was nothing but a bundle of raw nerve ends. Each case took a little bit more of his soul, or so he felt.

Banks remembered some of the victims, especially the young ones—Deborah Harrison, Sally Lumb, Caroline

Hartley. He had come to know and care about all these victims. Even Gloria Shackleton, murdered long before Banks had been born, had come to obsess him only a few months ago. And now Emily Riddle. It didn't matter what anyone said about not becoming personally involved with cases, Banks thought. You *had* to be personally involved; there had to be something more at stake than mere crime statistics.

"Problem is," Burgess went on, "we don't really know enough about him."

"Any form?"

Burgess sniffed. "Minor drug bust in '74. Half a pound of Nepalese black. Said it was for his own consumption. Well, I believed him—I could go through that much in a week easily—but the magistrates didn't. They gave him eighteen months, out in nine."

"Is he still dealing?"

"Not that we know of. If he is, he's not in the premier league." Burgess pushed his plate away. "Too bloody tough for my teeth," he said. Apart from his crooked and stained teeth, Banks noticed, Burgess seemed in better shape than the last time they had met. He had even lost a little weight. He still had his graying hair tied in a ponytail, which irritated Banks, who thought that middle-aged men with ponytails looked like prize wankers, and his gray eyes were as sharp, as cynical and as world-weary as ever.

The last time they had met, Banks remembered, was in Amsterdam over a year ago, when Burgess had got pissed and fallen in a canal. Banks had helped him out and taken him back to the hotel, and the last he had seen of him, Burgess was trailing dirty canal water across the lobby, his shoes squelching as he went, head held high, trying to walk in a straight line, with dignity. He had been wearing the same scuffed leather jacket he was wearing today.

"How does he pay for that bloody great villa of his?" Banks asked.

"Which one?"

"Little Venice. You mean he's got more than one?"

"Sure. There's two that we know of. The one in Little Venice and one outside Arenys de Mar, in Spain."

"So where does his money come from?"

"He's a gangster."

"So I've heard. I didn't know they were back in fashion."

"They never really went away. They just adapted, changed names, switched rackets."

"What sort of a gangster is Clough, then?"

Burgess lit one of his small cigars before answering. "First off," he said, "he's got a legitimate front. He owns a very successful bar in Clerkenwell. Popular with the City Boys. Gets some good bands, serves first-class food and booze. You know the type of place: 'How about a little coke and crème caramel to end the perfect evening, darling?' Then they go off home for the perfect shag. We know he's into all sorts of things, but we've never been able to get him on anything. He runs things, delegates, doesn't get his hands dirty. Basically, he bankrolls dodgy or downright criminal operations and rakes in a big cut. As far as we know, he made a pile of money managing and promoting bands in the music business years ago and invested it in a life of crime."

"Bootlegging."

"What?"

"That's how he made his pile," Banks explained. "Making bootleg recordings of live concerts, getting them pressed and selling them."

Burgess narrowed his eyes. "You seem to know a lot about him. Sure you want me to go on?"

Banks smiled. "It's a matter of making a little go a long way. That's *all* I know. Anyway, it looks as if it paid off."

"Big-time."

"What kinds of things is he interested in now, if it's not drugs?"

"All sorts. I'll give him his due; he's innovative. Prefers newer, safer rackets to the old true, tested and tried. That's why I don't see him dealing drugs. Taking them, yes, but not dealing them. Not his style. You won't find him running girls or protection rackets, either. Not Barry Clough. Guns, though, now there's another matter. Remember that business with the reactivated firearms a year or so back? Up around your neck of the woods, wasn't it?"

"Thirsk," said Banks. "Yes, I remember." Undercover policemen posing as London gangsters had arrested four men on charges of conspiracy to transfer firearms and ammunition, and for selling prohibited weapons. Since stricter gun laws were introduced after the Dunblane school massacre, firearms became harder to get because the risk attached to possessing or selling them was far greater. That also put their price up. To fill the gap, workshops like the one near Thirsk sprang up. It took about two hours to reactivate an Uzi that had been disabled for legal sale to a collector, and you could sell it for about £1,250. Tanfoglio pistols went for about a grand apiece. Discount for bulk. Needless to say, the weapons were especially popular with drug gangs.

"We thought we had Clough on that but we couldn't prove he was involved."

"What made you think he was?"

"Circumstantial evidence. Tidbits from informers. He'd made a couple of trips to the area shortly prior to the arrests. One of the men arrested had been observed visiting Clough's house. He was a collector of disabled firearms himself. He had connections in both the drugs and firearms worlds. That sort of thing."

Banks nodded. He knew what Burgess meant. You could know it in your bones that a man was guilty of something, but if you couldn't get enough evidence to interest the Crown Prosecution Service, then you might as well forget it. And the CPS was notoriously difficult to interest in anything other than a dead cert. He also remembered the guns in the case on Clough's wall. Still, not evidence.

"What happened?"

"We leaned on him a bit. Not me personally, you understand, but we leaned. I think he shied away from that line of business, at least for a while. Besides, I think he found out that it's not as lucrative as he'd hoped. Reactivating guns is more trouble than it's worth, when you get right down to it. And it's not as if they aren't still being smuggled in by the cartload. Christ, I know where you could buy an Uzi for fifty quid not twenty minutes from here."

"And after that?"

"We suspect, and you know what I mean when I stress that it's just a suspicion, don't you?" Burgess flicked some ash and winked at Banks. "We *suspect* that, for one thing, he's behind one of the big smuggling operations. Booze and fags. High profit, low risk. You might not know this, Banks, but I've done some work with Customs and Excise, and about eight percent of cigarettes and five percent of beer consumed in this country are smuggled. Have you any idea what sort of profits we're talking about here?"

"Given the amount people smoke and drink, I should imagine it's pretty huge."

"Understatement." Burgess pointed his cigar at Banks. "A player like Clough might employ fifty people to get the stuff from warehouses in Europe to his retail outlets over here. Once they get it through customs at Dover, they go to distribution centers—industrial estates, business parks and the like—then their fleet of salesmen pick up their supplies and sell to the retailers. Shops, pubs, clubs, factories. Even schools. Christ, we've even got fucking pet shops and ice cream vans selling smuggled booze."

"And Clough's in it that big?"

"So we *suspect*. I mean, it's not as if he drives any of the freighters himself, or drops off a carton or two at the local chippie. Whenever Clough comes back from a month at his villa in Spain you can be damn certain he's clean as a surgeon's scalpel. It really pisses me off, Banks, that when a law-abiding citizen such as me drinks his smuggled French lager, there's probably a share of the profits going to a gangster like Clough."

"So what have you got on him?"

"Precious little, again. Mostly circumstantial. Earlier this year customs stopped a lorry at Dover and found seven million cigarettes. Seven fucking million. Would've netted a profit of about half a million quid on the black market—and don't ask me how much that is in Euros. Clough's name came up in the investigation."

"And what else is he into?"

Burgess flicked some more ash on the floor. "Like I said, we don't know the full extent of his operations. He's cagey.

Has a knack of staying one step ahead, partly because he contracts out and partly because he operates outside London, setting up little workshops like that one near Thirsk and then moving on before anyone's figured out what he's doing. He uses phony companies, gets others to front for him, so his name never appears on any of the paperwork."

Something in what Burgess had said rang a bell for Banks. It was a very faint one, a very poor connection, but it wasn't an impossible one. "Ever heard of PKF Computer Systems?" he asked.

Burgess shook his head.

"Bloke called Courage? Charlie Courage?"

"No."

"Jonathan Fearn?"

"Nope. I can look them up if you like."

"Doesn't matter," said Banks. "One's dead and the other's in a coma. Would murder be Clough's style at all?"

"I'd say a man who does as high a volume of crime as he does has to maintain a certain level of threat, wouldn't you? And if he does that, he has to make good on it once in a while or nobody's intimidated. He has to keep his workers in line. Nothing like a nice little murder for keeping the lads focused." He slurped down some lager and lime. "Two weeks after Clough's name came up in connection with that seized shipment, two known baddies got shot in Dover city center. No connection proven, of course, but they were business rivals. It's a fucking war zone down there."

Banks pushed aside the rest of his chicken, which was too dry, and lit a cigarette. He fancied a pint but held off. If he was going to see Barry Clough tonight, as he planned, then he'd need to be sharp, especially after what Burgess had said. "What about women?" he asked.

Burgess frowned. "What do you mean?"

"From what I can gather, Clough's a bit of a ladies' man."

"So I've heard. And apparently he likes them young."

"Has he ever been under suspicion of hurting or killing a woman?"

"Nope. Doesn't mean he hasn't done it and got away with it, though. Like I said, Clough's good at staying ahead of the game. The thing is, with someone like him, people don't like to come forward and make themselves known, if you catch my drift."

"Right." Banks sipped some black coffee. It tasted bitter, as if it had been left on the burner too long. Still, it beat instant. "Heard of Andrew Handley?"

"Andy Pandy? Sure. He's one of Clough's chief gofers."

"Dangerous?"

"Could be."

"Anything on him hurting women?"

"Not that I know of. Is this about Jimmy Riddle's daughter?"

"Yes," said Banks. Emily Riddle's murder was all over the newspapers that morning. As Banks had guessed, it hadn't taken the press long to ferret out that she had died of cocaine laced with strychnine, and that was far bigger news than another boring drug overdose.

"You're SIO on that?"

"Yes."

Burgess clapped his hands together and showered ash on the remains of his steak. "Well, bugger me!"

"No, thanks. Not right after lunch," said Banks. "What's so strange about that?"

"Last I heard, Jimmy Riddle had you suspended. I had to pull your chestnuts out of the fire."

"It was you who put them in there in the first place with all that cloak-and-dagger bollocks," said Banks. "But thanks all the same."

"Ungrateful cunt. Think nothing of it. Now he's got you working on his daughter's case. What's the connection? Why you?"

Banks told him about finding Emily in London.

"Why d'you do that? To get Riddle off your back?"

"Partly, I suppose. At least in the first place. But most of all I think it was the challenge. I'd been on desk duties again for a couple of months after the Hobb's End fiasco, and it was real work again. It was also a bit of a rush going off alone, working outside the rules."

Burgess grinned. "Ah, Banks, you're just like me when you get right down to it, aren't you? Crack a few skulls?"

"I didn't need to."

"Did you fuck her? The kid?"

"For Christ's sake," said Banks, his teeth clenching. "She was sixteen years old."

"So. What's wrong with that? It's legal. Tasty, too, I'll bet."

It was at times like this Banks wanted to throttle Burgess. Instead, he just shook his head and ignored the comment.

Burgess laughed. "Typical. Knight in bloody shining armor, aren't you, Banks?"

That was what Emily had called him in the Black Bull, Banks remembered. "Not a very successful one," he said.

Burgess took a long drag on his cigar. He inhaled, Banks noticed. "She was sixteen going on thirty, from what I've heard on the grapevine."

"What have you heard?"

"Just that she was a crazy kid, bit of an embarrassment to the old man."

"That's true enough."

"So he wanted you to head off any trouble at the pass?"

"Something like that."

"Any ideas?"

"I'd have to put Barry Clough very high on my list."

"That why you're here? To rattle his cage?"

"It *had* crossed my mind. I'm thinking of paying him a visit tonight."

Burgess stubbed out his cigar and raised his eyebrows. "Are you indeed? Fancy some company?"

It was a different bridge, but almost a repeat of his previous trip, Banks thought, as he walked across Vauxhall Bridge on his way to visit Kennington. He looked at his watch: almost three. Ruth had been at home last time; he just hoped she had a Saturday routine she stuck to.

As it turned out, he needn't have worried. Ruth answered the intercom at the first press of the button and buzzed him up.

"You again," she said, after letting him into the room. "What is it this time?"

Banks showed her his warrant card. "I've come about Emily."

A look of triumph shone in her eyes. "I knew there was something fishy about you! I told you, didn't I, last time you were here. A copper."

"Ruth, I was here unofficially last time. I apologize for pretending to be Emily's father—not that you believed me anyway—but it seemed to be the best way to get the job done."

"End justifies the means? Typical police mentality, that is."

"So you knew her real name?"

"What?"

"You didn't seem at all surprised when I called her Emily just now."

"Well, that's the name they used in the papers yesterday."

"But you already knew that, didn't you?"

"Yeah, I knew her real name. She told me. So what? I respected her right not to want to use it. If she wanted to call herself Louisa Gamine, it was fine with me."

"Can I sit down?"

"Go ahead."

Banks sat. Ruth didn't offer him tea this time. She didn't sit down herself, but lit a cigarette and paced. She seemed edgy, nervous. Banks noticed that she had changed her hair color; instead of black it was blond, still cropped to within half an inch of her skull. It didn't look a hell of a lot better and only served to highlight the pastiness of her features. She was wearing baggy jeans with a hole in one knee and a sort of shapeless blue thing, like an artist's smock: the kind of thing you wear when you're by yourself around the house and you think nobody's going to see you. Ruth didn't seem unduly concerned about her appearance, though; she didn't excuse herself to change or apply makeup. Banks gave her credit for that. The music was playing just a little too loud: Lauryn Hill, by the sound of it, singing about her latest misadventures.

"Why don't you sit down and talk to me?" Banks asked.

Ruth glared at him. "I don't like being lied to. I told you

last time. People always seem to think they can just walk right over me."

"Once again, I apologize."

Ruth stood a moment glaring at him through narrowed eyes, then she turned the music down, sat opposite him and crossed her legs. "All right. I'm sitting. Happy now?"

"It's a start. You know what happened?"

"I told you. I read about it in the paper, and saw it on telly." Then her hard edges seemed to soften for a moment. "It's terrible. Poor Emily. I couldn't believe it."

"I'm sorry. I know you were a friend of hers."

"Was it . . . I mean . . . were you there? Did you see her?"

"I was at the scene," said Banks, "and yes, I saw her."

"What did she look like? I don't know much about strychnine, but . . . was it, you know, really horrible?"

"I really don't think that's a good idea—"

"Was it quick?"

"Not quick enough."

"So she suffered?"

"She suffered."

Ruth looked away, sniffled and reached for a tissue from the low table beside her. "Sorry," she said. "It's not like me."

"I just want to ask you a few questions, Ruth, then I'll go. Okay?"

Ruth blew her nose, then nodded. "I don't see how I can help you, though."

"You'd be surprised. Have you spoken with Emily since she left London?"

"Only on the phone a couple of times. I think when she split up with this Barry she felt a bit guilty about neglecting me. Not that I cared, mind you. It was *her* life. And people always do. Neglect me, that is."

"When was the last time you talked?"

"A week, maybe two weeks before . . . you know."

"Was there anything on her mind?"

"What do you mean?"

"Did she confide any of her fears in you?"

"Only about that psycho she'd been living with."

"Barry Clough?"

"Yeah, him."

"What did she say about him?"

"She didn't give me any gory details, but she said he'd turned out to be a real waste of space, and she sounded worried he was going to come after her. Did she steal some money from him?"

"Why do you ask that?"

Ruth shrugged. "Dunno. He's rich. It's the sort of thing she'd do."

"Did she ever steal from you?"

"Not that I know of." Ruth managed a quick smile. "Mind you, I can't say I've much worth stealing. Someone ripped the silver spoon out of my mouth at a pretty early age. I've always had to work hard just to make ends meet."

"When did you miss your driving license, Ruth?"

"My license? How did you know about that? It was ages ago."

"How long?"

"Five, six months?"

"While Emily was here?"

"Yes, just after, but . . . you don't mean . . . ? Emily?"

"When the report came to me over the phone, the first officer on the scene told me the victim was Ruth Walker. He'd read the name off her driving license."

"Bloody hell. So that's what happened. I just thought I'd lost it. I do lose things. Especially bits of paper."

"What did you do?"

"Applied for a new one. The new kind with the photo on it. But what possible use could the old one be to Emily?"

"I think she used it to help her get one of those proof-of-age cards the clubs give out. She wouldn't have had much difficulty from what I've heard. They practically give them to pretty young girls, whether they've got any proof in the first place or not. The card has her photo on it, but your name and, I assume, your date of birth. Twenty-third of February, 1977."

"Bloody hell." Ruth shook her head. "I knew nothing about it."

"And maybe she also wanted to drive a car."

"She was too young to learn."

"That doesn't always stop people."

"I suppose not."

"Some of the most skilled car thieves I've met have been between ten and thirteen."

"You'd know about that."

"What did she say about Barry Clough?"

"Just that she thought she'd pissed him off big-time when she left without saying good-bye, and he wasn't the kind of man just to let it go by."

"Did she sound scared?"

"Not really scared. Bit nervous, maybe, in a giggly sort of way. She could put a brave face on things, could Louisa. Emily."

"When did she tell you her real name?"

"Shortly after she came to stay with me. She asked me not to tell anyone, that she wanted to be called Louisa, so I respected her wishes."

"Did you tell Clough what her real name was?"

Ruth jerked forward. "Give me a break! Why would I do something like that?"

"Only asking. So you didn't?"

"No fucking way."

"Has he been in touch with you at all, asking about her?"

"No. I haven't seen anything of him at all."

"What about Craig? Did you tell him?"

"No, but he might have known. She might have told him herself."

"But you didn't?"

"I didn't tell anyone. I can keep a secret."

Banks lit a cigarette and leaned back in the armchair. "How have you been, Ruth?"

She frowned. "What do you mean?"

"Just a simple question. Healthy? Happy?"

"I'm doing all right. As well as can be expected. Why do you want to know?"

"How's work?"

"Fine."

"What exactly is it that you do?"

"Computers. It's pretty boring stuff."

"But steady? Well-paid?"

"It's steady. That's about the best you can say."

"Do you own a car?"

Ruth got up and Banks followed her to the window. "There," she said pointing, "that clapped-out cream Fiesta down there."

Banks smiled. "I had one like that a few years back," he said. "Cortina, actually. Nobody believed I could possibly be driving such a thing. They'd stopped making them years ago. But it was a good car, while it lasted."

"Well," said Ruth, folding her arms at the window. "It'll have to last me a few years longer, that's for sure."

They sat down again. "Been on any trips lately?" Banks asked.

"Nope."

"Seeing anyone?"

"What's it to you?"

"Just being friendly."

"Well, you don't have to be. Remember, you're a copper and I'm a suspect."

"Suspect? What makes you think that?"

A nasty smile twisted Ruth's features. "Because I know you coppers. You wouldn't be here otherwise, asking all sorts of questions. No matter. I didn't do it. You can't blame me."

"I'm not trying to. How do you know coppers, Ruth? Ever been arrested?"

"No. I read the papers, though, watch the news. I know what racist, sexist bastards you are."

Banks laughed. "You must be thinking of Dirty Dick."

"What?"

"Never mind. Seeing as how you think you're a suspect, though, you might as well tell me where you were on Thursday."

"I was here. At home."

"Not at work?"

"I had a cold. Still have. I was off Thursday and Friday. Does that mean I've got no alibi?"

"You haven't been on any trips recently?"

"No. I told you. I haven't been anywhere. And for your information, no, I'm not screwing anyone, either. You've got to be careful these days. It's a lot different from when you were young, you know. We've got AIDS to think about. The worst you had to worry about was crabs or a dose of clap. Either way, it wasn't going to kill you."

Banks smiled. "I suppose you're right. Did you ever go up to visit Emily in Yorkshire over the past month?"

"No."

"Why not?"

"Too busy at work. Besides, she never asked me." Ruth snorted. "I can see why now."

"Why?"

"It said in the paper that her father's a chief constable and her mother's a solicitor. They don't sound exactly the sort of people she'd want to introduce someone like me to."

"Oh, I don't know," said Banks. "You shouldn't be too hard on yourself."

Ruth flushed. "I know what I am."

"Do you know Emily's mother at all? Rosalind?"

"No. Why should I?"

"Just wondering."

"Like I said, she'd hardly take me home to meet her mum and dad."

"I suppose not. So you never spoke with her?"

"She answered the phone a couple of times when I called."

"So the two of you *have* spoken?"

"Only to say hello, like, and ask for Emily."

"Rosalind didn't ask you any questions?"

"No. Just my name, that's all."

"And you told her?"

"Why wouldn't I? What is this? Are you trying to make out her mother killed her now?"

"I hardly think so. Just trying to get things clear, that's all. Have you seen anything of Craig?"

Ruth made herself more comfortable in the armchair, sitting with her legs curled under. "As a matter of fact, he

phoned me after he heard about Emily on the news yesterday morning. We had lunch together. He had to come into
town."

"What for? To pay a call at GlamourPuss?"

"How would I know? He didn't say."

"How did he seem?"

"Fine, I guess. I mean, we were both upset. Emily
breezed in and out of both our lives. But if you've met her,
then you'd know she certainly leaves an impression. The
thought of somebody doing that to her . . . it's too much to
bear. You *are* certain it wasn't just an accident, aren't you?
An overdose?"

"We're certain."

"Like I said, we were . . . you know, we couldn't believe
it. What about her father?"

"What about him?"

"Do you think he might have done it? I mean, she used to
go on about how horrible he was, and if anyone can get hold
of drugs and poisons, it's the police."

"Remember, he's the one who wanted her back."

"Yes," said Ruth, leaning forward and lowering her voice
to a whisper. "You told me that. But *why* did he want her
back? Have you ever thought about that?"

Though it was Saturday, there was no time off for Eastvale
CID that weekend. It would cost a fortune in overtime, but
ACC McLaughlin and Superintendent Gristhorpe would
hardly hesitate to approve the budget; there would be no stint-
ing on this case. If Annie hadn't seen the body for herself, she
might have felt a little uncomfortable about the favoritism of
it all, but having seen it, she knew that even if the victim had
been a pox-ridden whore she would have been working on the
case today, and working for nothing if she had to.

And Banks, the SIO, was down in London. Which left
Annie in charge. She understood that he had to go and follow the leads he already knew about, but it left her with an
unbearably heavy load, especially after so little sleep, and
she couldn't help but still feel irritated with him. After their
little talk the previous day, she had softened toward him, but

she still felt that he was holding something back. She didn't know why or what it was about—something to do with Emily's sojourn in London, she suspected—but it gave her the feeling that he knew something she didn't. And she didn't like that.

Already that morning she had called in at the incident room and found it the usual hive of activity. Winsome was sitting at the computer looking flustered as the pile of green sheets for entry into HOLMES rose quickly beside her, and Gavin Rickerd looked as if he had found his true calling in life making sure every scrap of information was neatly logged and numbered. He also looked as if he hadn't slept since the murder.

After that, Annie had organized the investigation into Emily's whereabouts between three and seven. She had ordered the posters the previous day and they were waiting when she got in. Banks had given her the photo he wanted used, and Annie thought it made Emily look a bit slutty. He said that was how people would remember her, and there was no point asking her parents for the sort of sanitized school photo or studio portrait they were likely to have. He also insisted that her description stressed that she looked older than her sixteen years.

The photo came above the question, "HAVE YOU SEEN THIS GIRL?" and that in turn was followed by the description, the hours they were interested in, and a telephone number to contact. She had sent out half a dozen uniformed officers to fix them to hoardings and telegraph poles along all the main streets and in as many shop windows as they could manage. After that, the officers were engaged in conducting a house-to-house in central Eastvale and the area around the Black Bull. Despite the stolen driving license, Emily didn't drive or have access to a car, as far as anyone knew, so the odds were that she had stayed in town. She could have taken a bus or a train, of course, so both stations were being thoroughly covered. There was every chance that a bus driver, fellow passenger, or ticket vendor would remember her if she had traveled anywhere in the missing four hours.

Annie herself was set to go on the evening news program,

she remembered, with a little twinge of fear. She didn't like television, wasn't comfortable with it at all, the way that, no matter how serious and public-spirited your appearance was, you knew you were only there to make the presenter look good. But that was one little prejudice she would have to swallow if she was to get the appeal for information across.

It was close to lunchtime, Annie's first real chance that day to sit down at her own desk and do a bit of detective work, with Kevin Templeton making phone calls in the background. Though it was a long shot, she thought she should check and see if there were any other crimes with similar MOs, using cocaine laced with strychnine as a murder weapon. The PHOENIX system, set up by the National Criminal Records Office, offered her nothing. But then there was every chance this killer hadn't ever been convicted.

CATCHEM offered a few more options. Essentially, you could enter the victim details, stressing the salient features of the crime, and the system presented you with a potential scale of probability in several categories. After a little tinkering, Annie discovered that it was not necessarily likely that Emily knew her killer and that the killer might well be someone who felt slighted by society and had sadistic tendencies.

So much for computers.

She was just about to go to lunch when DS Hatchley came in. Annie was one of the few women in Eastvale Divisional Headquarters, or Western Divisional Headquarters, as it was now officially known, who didn't particularly mind Sergeant Hatchley. She thought he was all show, all Yorkshire bluff. She knew he wasn't soft underneath it all—Hatchley could be a hard man—but she didn't think he was as daft as he painted himself, either, or as prejudiced as he pretended to be. Some men, she had come to realize over the years, act the way they think they're supposed to act, especially in institutions such as the police and armed forces, while inside they might be desperate to be someone different, to be what they really *feel* they are. But they deny it. It was a kind of protective coloration. Hatchley was no pussycat, but she thought he had a depth of understanding and sympathy that he didn't know quite what to do with. Marriage and fatherhood, too, had knocked off a few of the rough edges, or so she had heard.

Of course, despite Banks's little crack the previous day, Annie *hadn't* tracked down Dalton at the Fox and Hounds, and she felt a little guilty about palming Hatchley off on him. But not that guilty. Hatchley's eyes had certainly lit up at the prospect of a pint. Annie knew that if Dalton stayed around much longer, it was only a matter of time before they bumped into each other. He might even walk into the detectives' office this very moment, and then there would be no avoiding him. She didn't want to meet him, didn't want to talk to him, but she wasn't scared of him, and she was damned if she was going to go around the place trying to avoid him anymore.

Hatchley said hello and grumbled about his aching feet.

"Where've you been?" Annie asked, feeling conciliatory after asking the favor of him. "Not another alien abduction?"

"No such luck. Charlie bloody Courage. You know, some people just don't seem to care how much inconvenience they cause by getting themselves murdered."

Annie smiled. "Daleview again?"

"Aye. And about as much use as the time you were there."

"Nobody saw the van?"

"On a Sunday night about ten o'clock? Nobody there."

"Except Charlie."

"Except the PKF people, who we're trying to find, Charlie himself, and Jonathan Fearn, the van driver, who's still languishing in a coma in Newcastle."

"Best way to be, in Newcastle," said Annie.

"Nay, lass, it's not such a bad place. Some grand pubs there. Anyway, according to my sources, Charlie *did* know Jonathan Fearn, so we've got a connection there, however tenuous. Peas in a pod."

"Maybe Courage lined up the job for him, thought he was doing him a favor?"

"Could be."

"What did you find out from this DI . . . what's his name?"

"Dalton. DI Wayne Dalton. Seems a nice-enough sort of bloke. You ask me, though, he's down on a weekend break."

"In December?"

"Why not? The weather's not so bad. He's a bit of a rambler, apparently. Talking about going walking up Reeth way on Sunday morning. Says if he gets a nine-o'clock start, he'll just about be ready to enjoy a pint and roast beef dinner at The Bridge in Grinton by twelve. The Bridge does a lovely roast beef and Yorkshire pud. Nice pint, too. Not that you'd catch me walking, mind you."

Looking at him, Annie could believe it. Hatchley was about six feet two, with fine fair hair starting to thin a bit on top, the "roast beef" complexion of someone with blood-pressure problems and about thirty or forty pounds excess baggage, to be generous.

Her thoughts drifted off at what he said. Maybe that was the answer. If Dalton was indeed planning a walk on Sunday, the odds were that there wouldn't be many people around. The middle of nowhere might be the best place to confront him. The idea excited her. It would mean making herself scarce on Sunday morning, but she thought she could probably manage that if she had everything in order by then. After all, with Banks away, she was in charge, so nobody was going to question her if she was out of the station for a few hours.

Dare she do it? What would she say if she stepped out in front of him on a deserted footpath? What would he do? Would he get physical, perhaps even try to get rid of her permanently? Having seen him again, Annie didn't think she need worry on that score.

But perhaps, when it came down to it, what worried her more than what he might do to her in a lonely place was what *she* might do to *him*.

The lights were blazing in Barry Clough's Little Venice villa when Banks and Burgess arrived shortly after eight that Saturday evening. Someone had even rigged up some Christmas lights on the facade of the house and put up a big tree in the garden.

"Bit early for a party, isn't it?" said Burgess, glancing at his watch.

"It's never too early for this lot," said Banks.. "Their whole life is one long party."

"Now, now, Banks. Isn't envy one of the seven deadly sins? Thou must not covet thy neighbor's arse, and all that."

The iron gates were open, but a minder stood at the front door asking for invitations. He wasn't one of the two Banks had seen on his previous visit. Maybe Clough went through minders the way some people went through chauffeurs or maids. Hard to get good help these days. Banks and Burgess showed him their warrant cards, but he clearly wasn't programmed to deal with anything like that. The way he screwed up his face in concentration as he looked at them, Banks wondered if he even got past the photographs.

"These mean we get in free," said Burgess.

"I'll have to check with the boss. Wait here."

The minder opened the door to go inside, and before he could close it, Burgess had followed him, with Banks not far behind. Banks realized he had to remember whom he was with, what a loose cannon Burgess could be, and how he'd have to be on his toes. Still, he had invited the bastard, and it was good to have company you could depend on if the shit hit the fan. Burgess wasn't one to shirk trouble, no matter what form it came in.

There were people all over the place. All sorts of people. Young, old, tough-looking, artsy-fartsy, well-dressed, scruffy, black, white—you name it. Music blasted through speakers that seemed to be positioned, discreetly out of sight, just about everywhere. Cream's "Tales of Brave Ulysses," Banks noticed. How retro. Still, Clough would have been in his mid-twenties when he was a roadie for the punk band, which meant he had been in his teens when Cream came along, pretty much the same age as Banks. The air reeked of marijuana smoke.

The minder, who had noticed his mistake, elbowed his way roughly through the crowds in the hallway, upsetting one or two less-than-sober guests, whose drinks he spilled, and returned before the song finished with Barry Clough in tow.

The man himself.

"Did we come at a bad time, Barry?" Burgess asked.

After the initial cold anger had fleeted across his chiseled features, Clough smiled with all the warmth of a piranha, clapped his hands and rubbed them together. "Not at all. Not at all." The black T-shirt he was wearing stretched tight over his biceps, and other muscles bulged at the chest and shoulders. All he needed for the complete rebel look was a cigarette packet shoved up the sleeve. He wore no jewelry this time, and he was wearing his graying hair loose, tucked behind his ears on each side and hanging down to his shoulders. Banks was glad of that; he didn't think he could handle matching ponytails. The loose hair made Clough look younger and softened his appearance a little, but there was still no mistaking the icy menace in his eyes and the feral threat in his sharply angled features.

"Tales of Brave Ulysses" segued into "swlabr." Someone bumped into Banks from behind and muttered an apology. He turned and saw it was an attractive young girl, not much older than Emily had been. He vaguely recognized her from somewhere, but before he could remember where, she had disappeared into the crowd.

"Is there somewhere quiet we can talk?" Banks asked Clough.

Clough appeared to consider the question for a moment, head cocked to one side, as if it were *his* decision, a not-so-subtle way of gaining a psychological edge in an interview. It was wasted on Banks. He jerked his head toward the stairs. "Up there, for example," he said.

Finally, Clough gave a minuscule nod and led them up the stairs. The first room they went into turned out to be occupied by a couple squirming and moaning on a pile of the guests' coats.

"It's unhygienic, that," said Burgess. "I go to a party, you know, I don't expect to go home with my raincoat covered in other people's love juices."

Clough twisted one corner of his tight lips into what passed for a smile. "They'll be too fucking stoned to notice," he said, then he turned to Banks. "You're not drugs squad, are you?"

Banks shook his head.

"It's just that there are a lot of important people here. Even a few coppers. Anything like that would be terribly messy. It would make the Stones drugs bust look like a vicarage tea party."

"I remember that one," said Burgess. "I wasn't there, but I always wanted to meet the young lady with the Mars bar." A skinny young girl with a joint in her hand walked past them in the hallway. "In fact," Burgess went on, grabbing the joint from her, "some of us coppers quite enjoy a little recreational marijuana every now and then." He took a deep toke, held the smoke awhile, then let it out slowly. "Paki black? Not bad." Then he dropped the joint on the carpet and trod on it. "Sorry, Banks," he said when he'd done. "Forgot you might have wanted a toke. On the other hand, you don't strike me as the toking type."

"That's all right," said Banks, who actually wouldn't have minded trying the stuff again on another occasion. But he was keeping his mind clear for Emily. Instead, he lit a cigarette.

"I see," said Clough, staring down at the burned spot on the carpet. He looked at Burgess. "You're the bad cop and he's the good cop, right?"

"You don't know the half of it."

A muscular young man with bleached-blond hair came up to them as they walked down the upstairs hall. "Everything all right?" he asked Clough. "Only I didn't think Mr. Burgess here was on the invitation list."

"Yeah, everything's fine and dandy. Maybe we should remember to add him in the future. Seems like the life and soul of the party type to me."

"Who's that?" Banks asked Burgess.

"Jamie Gilbert. Nasty little psycho. He's Barry's chief enforcer."

Gilbert walked away laughing and Clough turned to them. "Jamie's my *administrative assistant*," he said.

"Well, that covers a multitude of sins," Burgess shot back.

They finally found an empty room on the top floor. Completely empty. No furniture. White walls. White floorboards.

"Is this the best you can do?" said Banks.

Clough shrugged. "Take it or leave it."

At least it was protected for the most part from the music downstairs, and there was a light. Trying to conduct an interview while sitting on the floor wouldn't be very dignified, so they all chose to stand and lean against walls. It gave a strange sort of three-sided edge to the conversation.

Clough folded his arms and leaned back. "So, what's it all about, then?"

"Don't tell me you don't know," said Banks.

"Humor me. Last time I saw you, you were a friend of Emily's father."

"I thought she was called Louisa?"

"No, you didn't. You knew what her name was. I only found out from the papers."

"So you do know what happened?"

"I know she's dead, yes. Nothing to do with me."

"Well, excuse us for thinking you're a good bet," Burgess cut in. He had agreed to let Banks do most of the interviewing, but Banks knew he would be impossible to shut up completely. Clough stared at Burgess as if he were a piece of dog shit on his shoe. He didn't know that Burgess thrived on looks like that; they only made him better at his job.

Banks could make out the faint sounds of "White Room" coming from downstairs. A "best of" album, then, and not *Disraeli Gears,* as he had originally thought. The song was strangely appropriate, Banks thought, looking around the white room they were in. He wasn't sure what he expected from this interview. Certainly not for Clough to confess. If anything, he wanted to go away with the certainty that he had the right man in his sights, a gut feeling, if that was the best he could come up with, then begin the slow painstaking grind toward finding enough evidence to prove it, knowing that was only the beginning of the struggle.

Between the Crown Prosecution Service's reluctance to

prosecute anyone, and the expensive barristers to whom Clough no doubt had access, there was every possibility that the man could get away with murder. Then what? Private vengeance? Would Riddle do it himself or try to hire Banks to kill Clough the way he had used him to find Emily? Christ, though, you had to draw the line somewhere, and Banks thought he drew his at murder, no matter how despicable the victim. He wasn't too sure about Burgess, though; sometimes his cynical gray eyes took on the look of a stone-killer.

"What we'd expect you to say," Banks went on, "but let's back up a little, first. How did you feel when Emily left you?"

"What do you mean, left me? I threw her out."

"Not what I heard."

"You heard wrong."

"Okay." Banks held his hand up. "I can tell you're sensitive about it, so let's carry on. That final night, at the party, you pushed her into a room with Andrew Handley, right?"

"I pushed her nowhere. She was so stoned she could hardly walk. She stumbled in there herself."

"But you don't deny she ended up in a room with Handley?"

"Why should I?"

"And that he tried to rape her?"

"Rape's a bit strong for what happened there."

"*Attempted* rape, then? I don't think so."

"Call it what you will. It was nothing to do with me. If Andy wanted to try it on with the little slut, that was his business."

"And Emily escaped, ran away?"

"When did she tell you all . . . wait a minute." Clough put one hand to the side of his head and made an expression of mock thinking. "Wait a minute. I get it. After she left the party, she ran to you. Right? She knew where you were staying. She spent the night with you. That's why you're so upset. Tell me, Chief Inspector Banks, did you like it? Did you like that wet, scaly little tongue of hers licking your—"

Clough didn't finish the sentence because as Banks struggled with the desire to lash out, Burgess beat him to it and gave Clough a backhander that sent him staggering toward the other wall. Typical Burgess, that; it was all right for him to tease Banks about sleeping with Emily, but not anyone else. Clough looked ready to fight back, muscles twitching, wiping a little thread of blood from the side of his mouth and giving Burgess one of those looks. But he regained his composure. And to give him his due, Banks thought, he didn't make any noise about lawsuits or revenge.

He stuck his tongue out and licked the blood from the corner of his mouth. "Sorry," he said, taking up his position against the wall again. "I got a little carried away then. Very rude of me to speak ill of the dead like that. I apologize."

Banks relaxed and offered him a cigarette. "Apology accepted."

Clough took it, and lit it with his own lighter. "Thanks. Forgot mine downstairs. I was in the kitchen enjoying a nice glass of Château Margaux when you two arrived."

"We'll make sure you get back to your wine before it turns to vinegar, Mr. Clough," said Banks. "But no more flights of fancy, okay? Just answer the questions."

"Yes, officer." Clough smiled and cracked the crust of blood, sending another thin stream down his chin. He wiped it off with the back of his hand and went on smoking, blood staining the filter of his cigarette.

"After Emily left, did you check up on her, find out who she was, where she lived?"

"Why would I do that? I'd finished with her. She wasn't worth the effort."

"So you didn't?"

"No."

"Did you know who she was?"

"Not until I read it in the papers. Sleeping with a chief constable's daughter, eh?" He laughed. "Wonder what my associates would say."

"Your associates being criminals?"

"Now that's close to slander, that is."

"Sue me."

"Not worth the effort."

"Not much is worth the effort with you, is it, Barry?"

"What can I say? Life goes on. Seize the moment. Live for the now."

Banks looked at Burgess. "And I never used to believe it when they said drugs could do you permanent damage."

Burgess laughed.

"Where'd you get the strychnine, Barry?" Banks asked.

"The what?"

"You heard."

"Never touch the stuff. I've heard it's bad for your health."

Banks sighed. "Is Andrew Handley here tonight? I wouldn't mind a word with him."

"I'll bet you wouldn't. Unfortunately, no, he's not. In fact, he's no longer in my employ."

"You fired him?"

"Let's say we came to a parting of the ways."

"Have you got his address?"

"We weren't that close. It was only business."

"Ever heard of PKF Computer Systems?"

"What?"

Was there just a slight flicker of recognition there? Clough off-guard for a moment, letting it through? Banks knew he could easily be imagining it, but he thought his internal antennae had detected something. It wasn't as far-fetched as he had originally thought when Burgess told him about Clough's business practices. Move into a business park, do whatever crooked little thing it is you do and then, before anyone twigs on to it, move somewhere else. Which is where the white van rented by PKF, which didn't exist, was going when it was hijacked. The driver still in a coma. There were plenty of business parks and trading estates in the country, most of them fairly remote. They were good places to operate from. And Emily had said something about Clough visiting Eastvale. She had also thought she saw Jamie Gilbert there. Could there be a motive for killing her in that? Something she knew about Clough's business operations? She had a photographic memory, like her mother, Banks remembered.

"PKF," Banks repeated.

"No, never heard of it. Why, should I have?"

"Charlie Courage?"

"I'm sure I'd remember someone with a name like that."

"But you don't."

"No."

Banks could sense Burgess getting impatient across from him. Maybe he had a point; they seemed to be getting nowhere fast. "Where were you last Thursday afternoon?" he asked.

"Why? Is that when it happened?"

"Just answer the fucking question." Burgess did his world-weary voice.

Clough didn't even look at him. "I was out of the country."

"All day?"

"All week, actually. In Spain."

"Nice for you. Sure you didn't nip up to Yorkshire for an hour or two?"

"Why would I want to do something like that? The weather's far better in Spain."

"Weekend in the country, perhaps? Get your own back on Emily? After all, you don't like losing your prized possessions, do you?"

Clough laughed. "If she told you that, then she's got a pretty inflated opinion of herself."

"A little overproof coke, Barry? Make her suffer?"

"You're mad." Clough pushed himself away from the wall. "Look, I've been patient with you, but this is absurd. Time for you to go wherever coppers crawl after dark and time for me to get back to my fun and games. Any more talking and my lawyer will be present."

"Here, is he?"

Clough grinned. "As a matter of fact, he is." Then he opened the door and gestured for them to leave. They stood their ground a moment, then, there being no point staying any longer, Banks gave Burgess the nod, and they left. As Burgess was passing Clough on the way out, Banks heard Clough whisper, "And don't think I'll forget what you did back there. I'll crush you for that, little man. I own people more important than you."

Burgess gave a mock shudder. "Ooh! I'm quaking in my boots."

Then they pushed their way through the stream of people coming up and down the stairs, edged through the hall and said good night to the minder, who grunted. While they were still in his earshot, Banks said, "Maybe we *should* call in the drugs squad, after all?"

The bouncer disappeared inside the house like a shot.

"Party pooper," said Burgess. "Besides, they're probably already in there."

They walked out of the gates and headed toward the canal. "It was an interesting evening, though," said Burgess. "Very interesting indeed. Thanks for inviting me. I enjoyed myself."

"My pleasure."

"And, I must say, Banks. You surprise me."

"What are you talking about?"

"Oh, listen to him. So modest. So naive. The girl, Banks. The girl in the hotel room. You're the quiet one, aren't you? But you've got hidden depths. My admiration for you has just grown by leaps and bounds. I didn't realize how close to the mark I was."

Banks gritted his teeth. They were near the Regent's Canal now, which gave Little Venice its name. For Banks, at that moment, it evoked fond memories not of Venice but of Amsterdam, and of Burgess flailing around cursing in the filthy water. Down the steps, a little push, a tiny trip. But no. That would be just *too* childish.

"Nothing happened," Banks said.

"Like I said, leaps and bounds," Burgess repeated, clapping his arm around Banks's shoulder. "And, now, my old cock sparrow, the night is still young, I suggest we head for the nearest pub and get shitfaced. What do you say, Banks?"

11

Annie didn't stop to consider the folly of her actions—or their possible consequences—until she was following Wayne Dalton up Skelgate Lane, a narrow, walled path to the north just before Reeth School.

An hour or so earlier, after asking Winsome Jackman and Kevin Templeton to cover for her, she had parked across North Market Street from the Fox and Hounds, then followed Dalton down to the market square, where he had parked his car. After that she followed him to Reeth about a half hour drive away, and the rest was easy.

Though it was a perfect day for walking, there were few other cars parked on the cobbles outside the shops and none on the green itself. Annie saw a number of people who looked as if they were dressed for rambling. A few clouds marred the blue winter sky, blocking the sun occasionally as they floated by, but the temperature was about ten degrees and there was very little wind.

Skelgate Lane was overgrown, stony and muddy in places after the recent rains. While Annie had put on suitable walking shoes, there were times, as she squelched through the unavoidable mud, when she thought her red wellies would have been more appropriate.

What the hell did she think she was doing anyway? she asked herself after the first half mile. The investigation into Emily Riddle's murder, of which she was DIO, was going full steam, still in its crucial early stages, and here she was leaving two DCs in charge while she took time out to settle old scores, or tilt at windmills. Her behavior offended even her own sense of professionalism, but when it came right down to it, her profession was the reason she was doing it. The situation with Dalton was something she had to get resolved quickly, because it had become too much of a distraction.

She had dressed like an anonymous rambler, in a charcoal anorak, black jeans tucked into her gray woollen socks, sturdy walking shoes, hat and an ash stick. She wasn't carrying a rucksack, nor did a plastic folder of Ordnance Survey maps hang around her neck. Instead, she carried a small book of local walks, and when she stopped for a moment to refer to it, she saw where Dalton was likely to be going. It was five and a half miles of relatively easy walking, taking them along the daleside above the River Swale, then down and back along the river to Grinton, arriving there around lunchtime. She looked for a good vantage point where she might confront him and decided that it would be best to wait until they had doubled back over the swing bridge near Reeth. Then they would be near the old Corpse Way to Grinton.

She had two choices: either walk down to the swing bridge and wait a couple of hours for him to come by, or follow him at a safe distance. She decided on the latter course, partly because there were a number of possible diversions from the route. The Dales were crisscrossed by hundreds of footpaths, signposted or not, going off in every direction, not all of them listed in guidebooks. He could, for example, turn off by Calver Hill into Arkengarthdale for a different walk, or continue along the high dale to Gunnerside, though then it would take him much longer to get back to Grinton—more like for dinnertime rather than lunch.

Besides, even if she were only ten yards from him, he would never recognize her, not with the hat and the anorak, and not when he wasn't expecting to see her.

Annie had always marveled at how, even in summer, you could walk for miles in the Dales and hardly see another

soul. In winter you were far less likely to bump into someone. Along the tops, after emerging from Skelgate Lane into
open moorland, she passed a small group of ramblers, probably a club, going the other way. Everyone politely said
good morning as they passed by. After that, she couldn't see
a soul except Dalton, a good half mile or more ahead, wearing a distinctive red anorak. It certainly made him easy to
keep in her sights.

The guidebook advised her to pause and enjoy views of
Fremington Edge back in the east and Harkerside on the opposite side of the valley, but though she glanced occasionally at the cloud shadows drifting over the greenish-brown
hillsides, with their distinctive patterns of drystone walls—
one field shaped like a milk jug, another like a teacup—
Annie was in no mood for sightseeing.

Still, up here on the heights looking down on the valley
below reminded her of cliff walks around St. Ives with her
father when she was younger. How he used to point out ex-
amples of interesting perspectives, shapes, textures and colors in the landscape, how he was always stopping to sketch
frantically into the book he carried with him, eyes and brain
tuned to his fingers. In moments like that she might as well
not have been there; she didn't exist.

All that was missing today was the crashing of the waves
and the screeching of gulls. Instead, hares hopped through
the spent heather, and grouse broke cover. The weather
turned nasty for a few minutes along the daleside, with a
brisk west wind whipping up and at one point blowing a
brief hailstorm at her. She had had to lean forward into the
wind to make progress, looking up occasionally to see the
red anorak in the distance.

By the time she came to the steep descent into the village
of Healaugh, the wind and hail had all gone, and as she
walked through the quiet streets she could almost believe it
was summer. A man in a white coat stood selling meat and
vegetables to villagers from the back of a small van. Everyone paused and looked at her as she walked past. None of
them smiled or said anything; they just stared. It was an odd
feeling. They didn't exactly seem unfriendly, but aloof, a lit-

tle mournful even, as if they were telling her that their world was not hers and never would be, that she was merely passing through it and she should keep going.

She did.

Shortly beyond the village, which was the turning point in the walk, the path led her through a field down to the riverside. She could see Dalton's red anorak ahead every now and then appearing and disappearing between the bare alders that lined the Swale. Empty brown seed cones still clung to many of the branches, making the trees look chocolate brown.

The closer she got, the more nervous and confused Annie became. She still wasn't physically afraid of him, but Dalton's arrival in Eastvale, and the memories it stirred, had played havoc with her usually calm emotional center. For one thing, she didn't know what to say to him. What *did* you say to a man who had been a willing accessory to your rape, a man who would have raped you himself if you hadn't managed to wriggle free from his grasp and escape? How would he react? Perhaps, she began to think, this wasn't such a good idea after all. It would be easy enough just to turn left at the swing bridge and walk up to Reeth, where her car was parked on the cobbles by the green, and forget the whole thing, get back to work.

But she kept on going.

It was only a small bridge. At that point, the river meandered through meadowland where cows grazed. It was, however, a genuine swing bridge and Annie experienced a frisson of fear as she walked the wooden planks and felt it sway. While not exactly phobic, she had always been a little nervous of bridges, though she didn't know why.

Dalton had paused by the riverbank at the other side, about a hundred yards or so ahead, and he appeared to be watching her approach. Feeling a little dizzy, Annie stayed on the bridge and pretended to admire the view, waiting for him to carry on. But he didn't. He stayed where he was and kept on looking at her. Her heart was in her mouth. Did he recognize her? Had he known she was following him all along?

There was only one thing to do if she wasn't going to run. She walked through the gate at the far end of the bridge and along the grassy path to where he stood. All the way he kept looking at her, but she still didn't sense any recognition on his part. Her fear was quickly turning into anger. How *dare* he not recognize her after what he had done? She tried to take long deep breaths to keep herself calm and centered. They helped a little.

Finally, about five or six yards away from Dalton, she stopped and took off her hat, letting her wavy chestnut hair fall free to her shoulders. She saw the recognition now. He hadn't known who she was before, she could tell, but he did now. She even heard his sharp intake of his breath.

"You," he said.

"Hello, Wayne," she said. "Yes, it's me. Nice to see you again."

Banks awoke from a disturbing dream at about eight o'clock on Sunday morning. He had been walking in an unfamiliar landscape, which kept switching between rural and urban settings. There was a river somewhere, or perhaps a canal. Whatever it was, there was a sense in the dream that it was never far away. It was always raining and always twilight, no matter where he was or how long he seemed to walk. Other people drifted by like shadows, but nobody he knew. He had the feeling that he was supposed to be following someone, but he didn't know whom or why.

Suddenly he found himself on a green iron bridge, and a man was walking just in front of him. At that point, Banks felt panic gather, felt as if he couldn't breathe and wanted to wake up and break out of it. The man turned. He wasn't a monster, though, just a perfectly ordinary-looking man.

"I know you've been looking for me," he said to Banks, smiling. "My name's Graham Marshall. I was in the army. Then I had my hair cut. Now I'm in the rain. Emily's with me, too, but she can't appear to you right now." Then he went on to tell a garbled life story of which Banks could remember nothing when he woke in a cold sweat to church bells ringing in the distance.

It was still dark outside, so Banks turned on the bedside light. He was in a small hotel near King's Cross, not the place he had stayed with Annie and Emily. Somehow, going back there hadn't seemed like a good idea.

When he had taken stock of himself, he realized with relief that he felt only mildly hung over. That was, he remembered, because he had declined the invitation to repair to Burgess's flat and drink whiskey all night. Surely he wasn't getting wiser in his old age? Anyway, he was glad that all they'd done was visit a few pubs and down a few pints. It must have been a dull evening for Burgess, though; they hadn't got into any fights or picked up any women. Mostly, Burgess had talked about Clough, and Banks got the impression that even if he didn't manage to pin Emily's murder on Clough himself, the man's days of freedom were limited.

The only problem with Clough as a suspect, thought Banks, was that he stood to gain nothing by Emily's death. Still, there was always the chance that she had stolen from him, as Ruth Walker had suggested, or that she knew too much about his business activities, though Banks thought she would have told him if that were the case. It was also possible that Clough only *thought* she knew something she didn't. This was assuming, of course, that the whole matter was one of logic and profit. What if it wasn't? Clough was certainly capable of killing, and if Emily had humiliated him in any way, then he was probably capable of killing her out of sheer malice.

Banks got up and poured himself a glass of water. The dream and the drink had left him with a dry mouth. As he showered in the tiny stall, he put the Graham Marshall dream out of his mind and found himself thinking again of what Ruth had said, how her words had cast suspicion even on Riddle himself, someone Banks had completely overlooked as a suspect.

He found it hard to take it seriously that a man like Jimmy Riddle would deliberately give his daughter cocaine laced with strychnine, even if for some obscure reason he did want her dead. And her death had done nothing to free Riddle of the shame of her exploits; in fact, it had quite the opposite effect, and already the tabloids were raking up stories of the chief constable's daughter and her wild life. That wouldn't do his budding political career any good at all, or his standing in the force, either.

Then there was Rosalind Riddle. Banks had had a strange feeling about her right from the start, when Riddle first asked him to go to London and find Emily. Rosalind hadn't appeared to want Emily back home for some reason. More recently, Rosalind had denied ever hearing of Ruth Walker, yet Ruth said she had spoken to her on the telephone on several occasions. That probably meant nothing, Banks realized, merely a lapse of memory, a misheard name over a poor connection, but Rosalind's role in all this still nagged away at the back of his mind. She was holding something back; of that he was certain. Whether it was important to the investigation or not, he couldn't say. All families have secrets that can fester away behind their protective walls.

Banks decided for the moment to concentrate on the line of inquiry he was pursuing in London, where Emily had done most of her drug-taking and mixed with a rough crowd: primarily Clough, of course, who lied about everything; then Ruth Walker, who remained a bit of an enigma to him, yet seemed a woman embittered far beyond her years; and finally Craig Newton, hurt ex-boyfriend-turned-stalker, and onetime amateur porn photographer, whom Banks was going to visit again that day.

After a quick breakfast of coffee and toast and a short walk around St. Pancras Gardens to clear his head, Banks felt ready to face the day. He was only about half a mile away from Euston, so he walked through the quiet streets of Somers Town to Eversholt Street. The train service to Milton Keynes was frequent, even on Sunday, and he only had to wait twenty minutes for an InterCity.

Watching the urban sprawl of London give way to prime commuter territory set amid rolling fields and grazing cows, Banks wrote up his notes on the previous evening's talk with

Barry Clough. Sometimes he took notes at the time, especially of important details, but that hadn't seemed appropriate standing in the white room with Clough and Burgess. Fortunately, though his memory was average in most respects, he had excellent audio recall and could remember a conversation practically verbatim for at least a couple of days.

He also thought about the coming interview with Craig Newton and tried to come up with a strategy. It was official business this time, not private-eye work for Jimmy Riddle. Approaching Craig Newton and getting any sort of trust out of him would be a delicate and difficult matter after all the lies he had told on his last visit. It had been the same with Ruth Walker, and Craig Newton struck him as a far more sensitive person than Ruth. On the other hand, Craig had lied to Banks, too.

Though it was his first visit in daylight, he still saw nothing of Milton Keynes on the taxi ride to Craig's house, except a few glimpses of concrete and glass. Perhaps that was all there was to see.

Craig Newton was home, and though he seemed puzzled to see Banks again, he invited him into the house. It hadn't changed much since the last visit, still very much the bachelor's house, with little piles of newspapers and magazines here and there and coffee rings on the low table.

"I'm sorry," said Craig. "You know . . . about your daughter. I read about it in the newspaper."

Banks felt like an utter shit. Craig seemed the trusting sort, and here he was, letting him down. Still, a hard lesson in the reality of deception probably wouldn't do the kid any harm in the long run. Having been a policeman for years, Banks had long since stopped trying to make everybody *like* him. He still felt like an utter shit as he pulled out his warrant card, though.

Craig gaped at him. "But . . . you said . . . ? I don't understand."

"It's simple, Craig," said Banks, sitting down. "I lied. Emily's father wanted me to find her, and it seemed a good idea to pretend that I was him instead of trying to explain myself. You can understand that, can't you?"

"I suppose so, but . . ."

"It was a simple strategy. Anyone would have more sympathy for the girl's father than for a policeman."

"So you lied?"

"Yes."

He seemed to draw in on himself. "What do you want this time?"

"More information. I'm not the only one who lied, am I, Craig?"

"You talked to Louisa?"

"You must have known I would."

"What did she say about me?"

"That you were bothering her, following her, stalking her."

"I'd never have done her any harm. I was just . . . I . . ."

"What, Craig?"

"I loved her. Can't you understand that?"

"It didn't give you the right to follow her around and scare her when she didn't want to see you."

"*Scare* her? That's a laugh. She hardly noticed me."

"Clough did, though, didn't he?"

"Who?"

"Oh, come on, Craig. You knew his name, didn't you? You just didn't want me to talk to him about your stalking Emily."

Craig rubbed his nose. "The bastard."

"Never a truer word. Anyway, let's leave that behind us for the moment, shall we?"

"Fine with me. Her real name is Emily. Is that right?"

Banks nodded.

"And Gamine?"

"A joke. It's an anagram of enigma, which is a sort of riddle. Emily Louise Riddle was her real name, and her father's my boss."

"I see. You probably didn't have much choice, then. I suppose I shouldn't have believed you in the first place, should I? I feel like a real idiot now."

"No need to. What reason could you possibly have had to think I was lying?"

"None. But still . . . I had my suspicions. I told you. I

thought there was something funny about you, the way you kept asking questions."

Banks smiled. "Yes, I remember. So credit yourself with that and let's move on."

"I can't see there's anything I could possibly tell you that's of any use. The papers said she took some poisoned cocaine in a club, is that right?"

"That's right. Did you ever supply Emily with cocaine, Craig?"

"No. I'm not a dealer. I never have been."

"A user?"

"I've snorted it on occasion. Not for a long time, though."

"She must have got it from somewhere."

"Ask her new boyfriend."

"I doubt that was the first time she took it."

"Well, ask Ruth's friends, then. It certainly wasn't me."

"What do you mean, 'Ruth's friends'?"

"Just that they're more into drugs than I am, that's all."

"Selling?"

"No. Just recreational. The music scene. Clubbing. That sort of thing."

"What about strychnine?"

"What about it?"

"Ever have cause to use it in your line of work?"

"I'm not a bloody rat-catcher, you know."

"I mean photography."

"No."

"Where were you last Thursday?"

Craig frowned. "Thursday? I don't remember. I could check . . . just a minute. That might have been the day . . ." He got up and pulled a pocket diary from his jacket out in the hall. When he opened it to the right date, he looked relieved. "Yes, that was the day. I was in Buckingham doing some publicity shots for the university."

"Anyone see you?"

"The person who was putting the promotional brochure together. A lecturer from the law department. Canadian bloke. I can give you his name."

"Please."

Craig gave it.

"How long were you with him?"

"For an hour or so in the morning."

"And then?"

"Then I walked around and took the photos."

"So you were pretty much on your own the rest of the day?"

"Yes, but people must have seen me. Am I a suspect?"

"What do you think? Emily finished with you, and you stalked her. It wouldn't be the first time that sort of thing's led to murder. Obviously, if you've got an alibi I can cross you straight off my list. Makes life easier, that's all."

But Craig Newton didn't have an alibi. He could easily have driven from Buckingham to Eastvale in about three hours. Banks had thought about the timing and decided that, while there was no telling exactly *when* Emily had been given the poison that killed her, the odds were that she wouldn't have left a stash of coke sitting around for too long without snorting any. There was also the fact that she was back living at home, and she wouldn't dare do it around her parents. It wouldn't be much fun at home alone, anyway, even if they were out. Coke was a social drug, and most likely she would have saved it for a party, or a night out clubbing. It made most sense, then, that whoever had given her the stuff had given it to her on Thursday afternoon, after first giving her a sample of perfectly good, uncontaminated cocaine. That would explain why she turned up a bit high at the Cross Keys.

"I didn't kill her. I told you: I loved her."

"Craig, if you'd been in this business as long as I have, you'd realize that love is one of the strongest motives."

"It might be in the twisted world you live in, but pardon me if I haven't had the chance to become that cynical. I loved her. I wouldn't have harmed her."

"Probably not," said Banks. "What kind of car do you drive?"

"Nissan."

"Color?"

"White. I suppose you want the number too?"

"Please."

Craig told him. It meant nothing yet, but if they came across someone who had seen Emily getting into a car, then it could be of value. "You should be going after that boyfriend of hers, you know," he went on. "Instead of harassing innocent people like me."

"So you keep saying. Believe me, Craig, he's never far from my thoughts. And I'm not harassing you. You'd know it if I was."

"Why don't you arrest him?"

"No evidence. You overestimate our powers. We can't just go around arresting people without any evidence." Actually, he could, but Craig wasn't to know that, and he couldn't be bothered to explain the difference between "arrest" and "charge." "Look, Craig, I realize you're not enjoying this, but I didn't enjoy seeing Emily's body, either."

"Was it . . . ? I mean . . . I've heard about what strychnine does."

"Did you ever contact Emily after she'd gone home?"

"I didn't even know she'd gone home. You never told me whether you'd found her or not, or whether she'd agreed to go back. To be honest, if I didn't read the papers pretty thoroughly I wouldn't even have known she was dead. I recognized the photo, but not her name."

"I understand you were in London yesterday?"

"That's right."

"Any particular reason?"

"I don't see what it's got to do with you, but I had two business appointments—and they are listed here in my appointment book, so you can check them if you want—and I also wanted to have a look at some new photographic equipment. The High Street here may be quaint, but you must have noticed that it's hardly chocka-block with camera shops."

"And you had lunch with Ruth Walker?"

"Again, that's right."

"She had a cold, didn't she?"

"She was sniffling a bit, yeah. So what?"

"What did you talk about?"

"We were both stunned to hear of Louisa's death. I suppose we wanted to mourn her together for a while, toast our memories of her. She'd been important to both of us, after all."

"Could Ruth have been jealous of you and Emily?"

"I can't see why. It's not as if Ruth and me were ever lovers or anything."

"But she might have wanted it that way."

"She never said anything. Like I told you before, Ruth and me were just good friends. There was nothing . . . you know . . . like that between us."

"At least not in *your* mind."

"It's the only one I can speak for."

"Perhaps she wanted there to be something?"

Craig shrugged. "I didn't fancy her in that way, and I'm pretty sure she knew it. Besides, what you're suggesting is absurd. If Ruth had to be jealous of anyone, it should have been the new boyfriend. He took Emily completely away from both of us."

"Jealousy's rarely rational, Craig. Emily breezed in and out of your lives and tossed you both aside. At least that's how Ruth put it. How did you feel about that?"

"Ruth can be a bit melodramatic when the mood takes her. How did I feel? You know damn well how I felt. I told you last time you were here, when you were pretending to be her father. I was devastated. Hurt. Heartbroken. But I got over it."

"Only after you'd followed her around for a while."

"Yeah, well, I'm not proud of that. I wasn't thinking clearly."

"Maybe you weren't thinking clearly when you killed her?"

"That's absurd. No matter how cynical you are, I loved her and I would never have hurt her."

"So you said. Are you sure?"

"Of course I'm sure. Look, are you suggesting I killed her over three months after she dumped me?"

"People have been known to brood for longer. Especially stalkers."

"Well, I didn't. And I'm getting sick of this. I don't want to answer any more questions." He stood up. "And if you want anything more out of me, you'll have to arrest me."

Banks sighed. "I don't want to do that, Craig. Really, I don't. Too much paperwork."

"Then you'd better leave. I've had enough."

"I suppose I had," said Banks, who had asked almost all the questions he wanted. "But there is one small thing you might be able to help me with."

Craig looked at him through narrowed eyes. "Go on."

"Last time I came to see you, you told me that when you saw Emily with her boyfriend in London, you were taking candid pictures in the street, right?"

"Yes."

"Were you really taking pictures or just pretending for the sake of cover?"

"I took some candids. Yes."

"Do you still have the photos from that day?"

"Yes."

"Do you have one of Clough?"

"I think so, yes. Why?"

"I know you're pissed off at me, Craig, but would you do me a favor and make me a copy?"

"I could do that. Again, though, why? Oh, I see. You want to show it around up north, don't you? Find out if anyone saw him up there. I suppose he's got a watertight alibi, doesn't he?"

"Something like that," said Banks. "Believe me, it would be a great help."

"At least you're thinking in the right direction again," said Craig. "I can probably get some prints to you by to-morrow."

"What about now?"

"Now?"

"Sooner the better."

"But I'd have to get set up. I mean . . . it'd take a bit of time."

"I can come back." Banks looked at his watch. Lunchtime. "How about I pop down to the nearest pub and have some lunch while you do the prints, then I'll come back and pick them up."

Craig sighed. "Anything to get you off my back. Try The Plough, down by the roundabout, end of the High Street. And you don't need to come back. I'll drop them off there. Half an hour to an hour, say?"

"I'll be there," said Banks.

"Will you do me a favor in exchange?"

"Depends."

"When's the funeral going to be?"

"That depends on when the coroner releases the body."

"Will you let me know? Her parents don't know me, so they won't invite me, but I'd like . . . you know . . . at least to be there."

"Don't worry, Craig. I'll let you know."

"Thanks. Now, I suppose I'd better get up to the dark-room."

Of all the different ways that Annie had tried to imagine this moment turning out—confronting her rapist—the one thing that had never occurred to her was that it would end with a sense of anticlimax, of disappointment.

But disappointment was exactly what she felt as she stood in front of Wayne Dalton on the banks of the River Swale, with a pile of steaming cow-clap between them. Indifference, even.

Her heart was still pounding, but more from the anticipation and the long walk than from the actual encounter, and he looked like a guilty schoolboy caught masturbating in the toilets. But instead of the monster she had created in her mind, what stood before her was all too human. Dalton wasn't frightening; he was pathetic.

For a few moments they just stared at each other. Neither spoke. Annie felt herself calming down, becoming centered. Her heart returned to its normal rhythm; she was in control.

Finally, Dalton broke the silence. "What are you doing here?"

"I work here. Eastvale. I followed you."

"My God. I never knew . . . What do you want?"

"I don't know," Annie replied honestly. "I thought I wanted revenge, but now I'm here it doesn't seem important anymore."

"If it's any consolation," said Dalton, avoiding her eyes, "there's not a day gone by when I haven't regretted that night."

"Regretted that you didn't get to finish what you started?"

"That's not what I mean. We were insane, Annie. I don't know what happened. The drink. The herd mentality." He shook his head.

"I know. I was there." Calm as she was inside, Annie felt tears prickling her eyes and she hated the idea of crying in front of Dalton. "You know, I've dreamed of this moment, of meeting one of you alone like this, of crushing you. Now we're here, though, it really doesn't matter."

"It does matter, Annie. It matters to me."

"What do you mean? And don't you *dare* call me Annie."

"Sorry. The guilt. That's what I'm talking about. What I have to live with, day in, day out."

Annie couldn't stop herself from laughing. "Oh, Wayne," she said, "that's a good one. That's a *really* good one. Are you asking *me* for forgiveness?"

"I don't know what I'm asking for. Just for some . . . some sort of end, some resolution."

"I see. You want closure, is that it? Popular term, these days, especially with victims. Everyone wants the bad guys put away. Gives them a sense of closure. Are you a victim here, Wayne, is that it?" Annie felt herself getting angry as she spoke, the indifference resolving itself into something else, into something harder. Two ramblers approached slowly from the woods beyond the river meadows.

"That's not what I meant," said Dalton.

"Then tell me exactly what you did mean, Wayne, because from where I'm standing *you're* the bad guy."

"Look, I know what we did was wrong, and I know that being drunk, being part of a group is no excuse. But I'm not that kind of person. It's the first, the *only* time I've ever done anything like that."

"So you're telling me that because you're not a serial rapist you're really an okay guy when it comes right down to it? Is that it? You just made one silly little mistake one night when you and your pals had had a bit too much to drink and there was this young bird just *asking for it*." She could tell her voice was rising as she spoke but she couldn't help herself. She was losing it. She struggled for control again.

"Christ, that's not what I'm saying. You're twisting my words."

"Oh, *pardon me*," said Annie, shaking her head. "I don't know what's worse, a contrite rapist or an unrepentant one."

"Don't get it all out of proportion. *I* didn't rape you."

"No. You didn't get your chance, did you? But you held me, you helped rip off my panties, and you stood there and enjoyed it while your friend raped me. I saw your face, Wayne. Remember? I know how you felt. You were just waiting for your turn, weren't you, like a little kid waiting for his go on the swings. And you would have done it, if you'd got the chance. In my mind that doesn't make you any different from the others. You're just as bad as the others."

Dalton sighed and looked at the ground. Annie glared at him as the ramblers passed by. They said hello, but neither Annie nor Dalton answered.

"So what do you want from me?" he asked.

"What do I want? I'd like to see you off the job, for a start. In jail would be even better. But I don't suppose that's going to happen, is it? Would I settle for an apology instead? I don't think so."

"What more can I do?"

"You can admit what happened. You can go back down there, go see the chief super again and tell him you lied, tell him the three of you got carried away and you raped me. That I did nothing to lead you on or encourage you or make you think I was going to let the three of you fuck me senseless. That's what you can do."

Dalton shook his head. All the color had drained from his face. "I can't do that. You know I can't."

Annie looked at him. She felt her eyes burning again. "Then the only thing you can do is fuck off, fuck off right out of my life and don't ever come near me again."

Then she turned and crossed the swaying bridge back to Reeth, the tears like fire as they coursed down her cheeks, not turning to see Dalton staring pathetically after her.

12

Banks came out of the meeting early Monday afternoon with only a little more information than he went in with. A weekend of showing Emily's photograph around town and making house-to-house inquiries had turned up several people who thought they had seen her in various Eastvale shopping areas on Thursday afternoon, always alone, but only one witness who thought she had seen her with anyone else. Unfortunately, the witness was about as useful as most; all she had seen was Emily getting into a car outside the Red Lion Hotel at the big York Road roundabout. She thought the time was about three o'clock. None of the bar staff at the Red Lion had seen Emily, and Banks was certain they would remember if they had.

When it came to the make of car, they all looked the same to the witness. All she could say was that it was light in color. She also hadn't noticed anything in the least bit odd about what she saw; the girl had seemed to know the driver and smiled as she got in, as if, perhaps, she had been waiting for the lift. No, she hadn't really got a glimpse of the driver at all, except that maybe he or she was fair-haired.

So, if their witness was to be believed, Emily had got into a light-colored car with someone she probably knew and trusted around the time of the meeting she had mentioned at lunch. She had left the Black Bull shortly before half past two. DC Templeton had checked the bus timetable and discovered that she must have taken the quarter-to-three to get there on time.

If—and it was a big *if*—their witness was right, then the sighting raised several interesting points. Banks walked over to his office window and lit an illicit cigarette. The day was overcast but balmy for the time of year. A crew of borough workers were putting up the Christmas tree in the market square, watched by a group of children and their teacher. The high-pitched whine of some sort of electric drill came from the extension down the corridor. It reminded Banks of the dentist's, and he gave a little shudder.

In the first place, Banks thought, why was Emily meeting someone on the edge of town rather than in another pub or in the Swainsdale Centre? Especially if this someone had a car and could easily drive into the town center. Answer: Because she was meeting someone who intended to kill her and who had insisted on the arrangement because he or she didn't want to be seen with Emily. Any secrecy could easily be explained by the fact that drugs were being sold.

Objection: If this person wanted to kill Emily, why not drive her into the country and do it at leisure, then bury her body where it would never be found?

That raised the whole issue of the *way* she was killed. Poison, or so the cliché goes, is a woman's weapon. In this case, if Emily's killer hadn't been in the Bar None at the time of her death, then the murder had also occurred at some distance from the killer. That suggested someone who wanted to get rid of her but didn't have any particular *emotional* stake in seeing her die. On the other hand, the use of strychnine as a method implied someone who wanted Emily to suffer an agonizing and dramatic death. There are far easier and less painful ways of getting rid of a pest. The murder had elements of both calculation in its premeditation and extreme sadism in its method, a profile which might easily fit Barry Clough, the gangster who didn't like to lose his prized possessions. But would Clough drive all the way from London simply to give Emily some poisoned cocaine because she had insulted his macho vanity? He had said he was in Spain at the time, and Banks was having that checked. It wouldn't be easy, given how lax border crossings were these days, but they could tackle the airlines first, and then find out if any of his neighbors in Spain had seen him.

Also, while strychnine wasn't as difficult to get hold of as some poisons, it wasn't exactly on sale in the local chemist's shop. Banks had looked it up. Strychnine, derived originally from the seeds of the *nux vomica* tree, which grows mainly in India, was used mostly as a rodenticide. It had some medical uses—vets used it as a mild stimulant, for example, and it was sometimes used in research, to cause convulsions in experiments for anti-seizure drugs, and in the treatment of alcoholism. None of Banks's suspects was a doctor or a nurse, and strychnine wasn't issued on prescriptions, so the medical side could be ruled out. Craig Newton was a photographer, and they sometimes had access to unusual chemicals, though not, as far as Banks could remember, strychnine. Barry Clough could no doubt get hold of anything he wanted.

Then there was Andrew Handley to consider: "Andy Pandy," Clough's gofer, the one he had "given" Emily to the night she fled to Banks's hotel. Such rejection could have driven Handley to revenge, if he was that kind of person. Burgess had said he would put some men on trying to track down Handley, so maybe they would get a chance to ask him soon.

But would Emily have *smiled* as she got in his car with either Clough or Handley? Christ, why hadn't Emily told Banks whom she was going to meet? Why hadn't he asked her? He rested his forehead against the cool glass and felt the vein throb in his temple.

It was no good, Banks decided; he needed far more information before he could even speculate about what had happened. He had found nothing of use in the contents of her handbag, once they had been gathered up and bagged. Nothing but the usual: cigarettes, tampons, electronic organizer, keys, a purse with £16.53 in it, makeup, a crumpled film magazine, an old family photograph—probably the one Ruth Walker had mentioned—Ruth's driving license, which she hadn't even really needed anymore, and the fake proof-of-age card.

The SOCOs had turned up nothing of interest from the ladies' toilet in the Bar None, except for any number of unidentified pubic hairs, and there were no prints except Emily's on the glassine bag in which the cocaine and strychnine had been kept. There were hundreds of prints around the stall—which testified to the frequency with which the owners thought it necessary to clean the toilets—but Banks suspected they would come to nothing. He was convinced that the killer, whoever it was, hadn't been in the Bar None toilets either with or without Emily, and had not even been in the club at the time of her death—had probably never been there. This was murder from a distance, perhaps even death by proxy, which made it all the more bloody difficult to solve.

DC Templeton had come up with a lead on the couple seen leaving the Bar None at ten forty-seven. A bartender at the Jolly Roger pub, a popular place for the student crowd on Market Street, seemed to remember them being in the pub earlier that evening. She had seen them before, she said, but didn't know their names; she only recognized the way they were dressed and thought they were students at the college, like most of her customers.

Next, Banks turned his mind to Charlie Courage's murder and felt a singular lack of progress there, too. Charlie's murderer had been at the scene, of course, but Charlie himself had been far from home, in the middle of nowhere. The only solid piece of evidence was the tire track, and that would be no use at all unless a corresponding car could be found. He decided to phone DI Collaton later in the day and see if anything had turned up at the Market Harborough end. Maybe he could have a word with DI Dalton, too, see if he had come up with anything more on PKF Computer Systems.

Banks stubbed out his cigarette in his wastebin, making sure it was completely dead, and tried to clear the air as best he could by opening the window and waving a file folder about.

When someone knocked at the door and walked in, he felt guilty, like the time his mother noticed ash from his cigarette on the outside window ledge of his room and stopped his pocket money. But it was only Annie Cabbot. He had asked her to drop by his office as soon as she had finished handing out actions to the newly drafted DCs that Red Ron McLaughlin had promised.

She looked particularly good this morning, Banks thought, her shiny chestnut hair falling in waves over her shoulders, her almond eyes serious and alert, though showing just a hint of wariness. She was wearing a loose white shirt and black denim jeans, which tapered to an end just above her ankles, around one of which she wore a thin gold chain.

"Annie. Sit down."

Annie sat and crossed her legs. She twitched her nose. "You've been smoking in here again."

"Mea culpa."

She smiled. "What did you want to see me about?"

"In the first place, I'd like you to go over to the transportation office at the bus station, see if you can find out who was driving the quarter-to-three bus to York, the one that stops at the roundabout."

Annie made a note.

"Have a chat with him. See if he remembers Emily being on the bus and getting into a light-colored car near the Red Lion. You might also see if he can give you any leads as to his other passengers. Someone might have noticed something."

"Okay."

"And have a chat with that bartender at the Jolly Roger, see if she can come up with anyone who might know where this couple lives, who they are. It's probably a dead end, but we have to check it out."

Annie made a note. "Okay. Anything else?"

Banks paused. "This is a bit awkward, Annie. I don't want you to get the impression that this is in any way personal, but it's just that since we started this investigation, I don't feel I've had your full cooperation."

Annie's smile froze. "What do you mean?"

"I mean it feels like there's a part of you not here—you've been distracted—and I'd like to know why."

Annie shifted in her chair. "That's ridiculous."

"Not from where I'm sitting."

"Look, what is this? Am I on the carpet, or something? Are you going to give me a bollocking?"

"I just want to know what's going on, if there's something I can help with."

"Nothing's going on. At least not with me."

"What's that supposed to mean?"

"Do I have to spell it out for you?"

"Try."

"All right." Annie leaned forward. "You said this wasn't personal, but I think it is. I think you're behaving this way because of what happened with us, because I broke off our relationship. You can't handle working with me."

Banks sighed. "Annie, this is a murder case. A sixteen-year-old girl, who also happens to be our chief constable's daughter, was poisoned in a nightclub. I would have hoped I wouldn't have to remind you of that. Until we find out who did it, this is a twenty-four-hour-a-day, seven-day-a-week job for us, and if you're not up to it for one reason or another, I want to know now. Are you in or out?"

"You're blowing this out of all proportion. I'm on the job. I might not be obsessed with the case, but I'm on the job."

"Are you implying I *am* obsessed?"

"I'm not implying anything, but if the cap fits . . . What I *will* say is that it's a damn sight more personal for you than it is for me. I didn't go to London to track her down, or have lunch with her on the day she died. You did."

"That's neither here nor there. We're talking about your commitment to the case. What about Sunday?"

"What do you mean?"

"Sunday morning, when I called in for an update. You were out of contact all morning, and DC Jackman sounded decidedly cagey."

"I'm hardly responsible for DC Jackman's telephone manner." Annie stood up, flushed, put her palms on his desk and leaned forward, jutting her chin out. "Look, I took some personal time. All right? Are you going to put me on report? Because if you are, just do it and cut the fucking lecture, will you. I've had enough of this."

With anyone else, Banks would have hit the roof, but he was used to Annie's insubordinate manner. It was one of the things that had intrigued him about her in the first place, though he still couldn't be sure whether he liked it or not. At the moment, he didn't. "The last thing I want to do is put you on report," he said. "Not with your inspector's boards coming up. I would hope you'd know that. That's why I'm talking to you one on one. I don't want this to go any further. I'll tell you something, though: If you keep on behaving like this whenever anyone questions your actions, you'll never make inspector."

"Is that a threat?"

"Don't be absurd. Look, Annie, sit down. Please."

Annie held out for a while, glaring, then she sat.

"Can't you see I'm trying to help you out here?" said Banks. "If there's a problem, something personal, something to do with your family, I don't know, then maybe we can work it out. I'm not here to supervise you twenty-four hours a day."

"You could have fooled me."

"But I need to be able to trust you, to leave you alone to get on with the job."

"Then why don't you?"

"Because I don't think that's what you've been doing."

"I trusted you, and look what I found out."

Banks sighed. "I've explained that."

"And I've explained what I was doing."

"Not to my satisfaction, you haven't, and I don't have to remind you that I'm SIO on this one. It's my head on the block. So if there's a problem, if it's something I can help you with, then spit it out, tell me what it is, and I will. No matter what you believe, I'm not after doing you any harm because of what did or didn't happen between us. Not everything is as personal as you think it is. Credit me with a bit more professionalism than that."

"Professionalism? Is that what this is all about?"

"Annie, there's something wrong. Let me help you."

She gave a sharp jerk of her head and got to her feet again. "No."

At that moment, DI Dalton popped his head around the door.

"What is it?" Banks asked, annoyed at the interruption. Dalton looked at Banks, then at Annie, and an expression of panic crossed his features.

"What is it, DI Dalton?"

Dalton looked at them both again and seemed to compose himself. "I thought you might like to know that the van driver died early this morning. Jonathan Fearn. Never regained consciousness."

"Shit," said Banks, tapping his pen on the desk. "Okay, Wayne, thanks for letting me know."

Dalton glanced at his watch. "I'll be off back to Newcastle now."

"Keep in touch."

"Will do."

Dalton and Annie looked at one another for a split second before he left, and Banks saw right away that there was something between them, some spark, some secret. It hit him smack in the middle of the chest like a hammer blow. *Dalton?* So *that* was what she had been up to. It fit; her odd behavior coincided exactly with his arrival in Eastvale. Annie and Dalton had something going. Banks felt icy worms wriggle their way up inside his spine.

Annie stood for a few seconds, her eyes bright, glaring at Banks defiantly, then, with an expression of disgust, she turned on her heels, strode out of his office and slammed the door so hard that his filing cabinet rattled.

Sometimes trying to get a lead was like drawing teeth, Annie reflected. The bus driver had been easy enough to find—in fact, he had been eating a late breakfast in the station café before his first scheduled trip of the day—but he had been no help at all. All he'd been able to tell her was that he remembered Emily getting off at the roundabout, but there had been far too much traffic to deal with for him to notice anything more. The bus had been mostly empty, and he didn't

know who any of the other passengers were. He could, however, state with some certainty that Emily was the only person to get off at that stop.

Disappointed, Annie headed for the Jolly Roger, still
fuming from her run-in with Banks. After her confrontation
with Dalton, she had actually felt better, more confident,
ready to get on with the job without distractions. She might
even have told Banks *why* she had been distracted in the first
place if he hadn't taken such a high-handed attitude.

The bloody nerve of him, having her on the carpet like
that. He *knew* she hated that sort of thing. Annie had never
been able to handle authority well, which can be something
of a liability in the police force, but most of the time she
could pay lip service when required. Not with Banks,
though. This time, he had hit her where it really hurt: her
professionalism. And the fact that he was partly right hurt
even more. She would show him, though. She wasn't going
to wallow in self-pity; she was going to get back on the
damn horse and ride again.

Annie paused briefly at the market square to watch the
awestruck expressions on the children's faces as they gathered around the Christmas tree. It took her back to her own
childhood in St. Ives. There had been few, if any, practicing
Christians down at the commune where she had grown up.
Most of the people who passed through had no religion at
all, other than ART, and those who had tended toward the
more esoteric kinds, such as Zen Buddhism and Taoism, the
ones without God, where you could ponder the meaning of
nothingness and the sound of one hand clapping. Annie herself, with her meditation and yoga, came closer to Buddhism
than anything else, though she never professed to *be* a Bud-
dhist. She wasn't detached enough, for a start; she knew that
desire caused suffering, but still she desired.

Christian or not, every Christmas had been a festive time
for Annie and the other kids there. There were always some
other children around, though most of them never stayed
long, and she got used to her friends' moving away, being
dependent on herself, not on others. But at Christmas,
someone always came up with a tree, and someone else

scrounged around for some tinsel and decorations, and Annie always got Christmas presents from whoever was living there at the time, even if many of them were just sketches and small hand-carved sculptures; she still had most of them, and some were worth a bit now—not that she would ever sell them. Christmas was as much a tradition at the commune as anywhere else, and it always brought back memories of her mother. She still had a photograph of her mother holding her up to look closely at the tree decorations. She must have been two or three years old, and though she couldn't remember the moment itself, the photograph always brought back waves of nostalgia and loss.

Shrugging off the past, she walked on to the Jolly Roger.

Eastvale didn't have a large student population, and the college itself was an ugly mess of red brick and concrete boxes on the southern fringes of the town, surrounded by marshland and a couple of industrial estates. Nobody wanted to live out there, even if there had been anywhere to live. Most of the students lived closer to the town center, and there were enough of them to turn at least one pub into the typical student hangout, and "the Roger," as they called it, was the one.

On first impression, Annie thought, the Jolly Roger was no different from any other Victorian-style pub on Market Street, but when she looked around inside, she noticed it was more run-down, and there was an odd selection of music on the jukebox, including far more angry, alternative stuff than pleasant pop and big-name bands. The clientele at that time in the afternoon consisted mostly of students who had finished early or had been there since lunchtime. They sat in small groups, smoking, chatting and drinking. Some favored the scruffy, Marxist look of old, while others cultivated a more clean-cut Tony Blair style, but they all seemed to mix cheerfully together. One or two loners in thick glasses sat at tables reading as they slowly sipped their pints.

Annie went to the bar and pulled out the fuzzy image taken from the CCTV video.

"I've been told you might know this couple," she said to the young man behind the bar, who looked like a student himself. "One of our lads had a word yesterday."

"Not me, love," he said. "I wasn't on yesterday. That'll be Kath over there." He pointed to a petite blonde busy pulling a pint and chatting to another girl across the bar. Annie walked over and showed her the photo.

"Any more thoughts on who this might be?" she asked, after introducing herself.

"I've given it a bit of thought," said Kath, "but I can't say as I have. I know I've seen them here, but I just can't place them."

"Let's have a look, Kath," said the girl. She didn't look old enough to be drinking, but Annie wasn't there to enforce the licensing laws. She was dressed all in black, including her lace-trimmed gloves, with orange hair and a pale, pixieish face.

She looked at Annie. "If that's all right with you," she added.

"That's fine," said Annie. "We need all the help we can get."

"I'm Sam. Short for Samantha."

Annie didn't think it was short for Samuel, but you never knew. "Pleased to meet you, Sam."

"Lousy picture," Sam commented. "That from the Big Brother video?"

"Yes," said Annie, "it's from the CCTV cameras in the market square."

"Talk about an invasion of privacy," the girl began. "You know—"

"I'd like to spend some time arguing the pros and cons of city center CCTV with you, Sam," said Annie sweetly. "Really I would, but a young girl, probably no older than you, was murdered in the Bar None last week, and we're trying to find out who killed her."

"Yeah, I heard," said Sam, looking away. "It's a fucking shame a woman can't go anywhere by herself these days."

"Any idea who they are?"

"Course I do."

"Will you tell me?"

"Did they do it?"

"I very much doubt it. But they might have seen something."

"It's Alex and Carly. Alex Pender and Carly Grant. Carly and I do art together."

"Know where they live?"

"They've got a flat on Sebastopol Avenue, you know, one of those big old Victorian terraces. Landlords divide them up into poky flats and rent them out for a fortune. Talk about exploitation."

"Do you know the number?"

Sam told her.

Knowing now the reasons for Annie's erratic behavior didn't make Banks feel any better. In fact, as the afternoon wore on, it made him feel worse. When she had stormed out of his office, he had stood for a moment to let his realization sink in, then felt the bile rise and burn in his throat. He might not be sleeping with Annie anymore, but the thought of her being with Dalton hurt. He had been through the same thing with Sandra. For months after she left, when he knew she had moved in with Sean, the intolerable images crowded his mind, and during the long nights of drinking alone, with random phrases from bitter Bob Dylan love songs echoing around his mind, the jealousy burned like acid on his soul.

Perhaps it wasn't even jealousy, but envy: he couldn't have Annie, but he couldn't bear thinking about Dalton having her. Whatever it was, it hurt, and Banks had to make an effort to put it out of his mind for the time being and get on with the job.

First, he sent DC Templeton off to get copies made of the photo of Clough he had got from Craig Newton. It was a good shot, candid or not, and Craig had cropped it so that it showed only Clough in full, mean face. When that was done, he would send a team out to check every hotel and guest house in the area to see if Clough had been staying there recently. He would also have Jim Hatchley and Winsome Jackman show it around Daleview and Charlie Courage's neighborhood. In the meantime, information had started trickling in now the working week had begun again.

He didn't learn much from the Riddles' phone records. British Telecom's Investigations Department had furnished DC Templeton with a list of numbers called on the Riddles' house telephone for the last month, and a subscriber check had supplied the names and addresses. Most seemed to be political cronies of Jimmy Riddle, or calls to Rosalind's law office. Someone, Emily presumably, had phoned Ruth Walker's number twice, but not within ten days of her death. There were no calls to either Craig Newton, Andrew Handley or Barry Clough. The only other calls Emily seemed to have made had been to Darren Hirst and to a sixth-form college in Scarborough. Banks thought it might be a good idea to get hold of Craig's and Clough's records, and do a cross-reference. It would take time, but it might throw up a lead of some sort. Oddly enough, Banks couldn't find the call that Emily had made to him the day before she died. Then he remembered the background noise and realized she must have used a public telephone.

Now that Jonathan Fearn was dead, Banks also had another murder on his plate, or manslaughter at least. Strictly speaking, it was DI Dalton's case, the way Charlie Courage's murder was Collaton's, but there was a strong Eastvale connection, the Daleview Business Park and PKF Computer Systems being at the heart of both. Banks was just about to check if anything was happening in the incident room when his phone rang. It was Vic Manson, the fingerprints expert.

"It's about that CD case you had sent over," Manson said.

"Find anything?"

"Some very clear prints. I've checked the national index and, lo and behold, they belong to a bloke called Gregory Manners."

"Who the hell's he when he's at home?"

"You may well ask. He's been a naughty boy, though. Did six months a couple of years back for attempting to defraud Customs and Excise."

"What?"

"Smuggling, to you and me."

"Well, well, well."

"Ring any bells?"

"So loud they're deafening me. Thanks, Vic. Thanks a lot."

"No problem."

The minute Banks got off the phone with Manson he called Dirty Dick Burgess at the National Criminal Intelligence Service.

"Banks. Solved your murder yet?"

"Murders. And no, I haven't."

"How can I help?"

"I've got a few loose strands that seem to be coming together. Remember that PKF business I asked you about?"

"Something to do with computers, wasn't it?"

"That's right. Charlie Courage, night watchman and one-time con, gets murdered the day after a van clears out PKF's Daleview offices, heading for another business park up Tyneside way. Over the past four weeks he's made five two-hundred-pound cash deposits at his bank. With me so far?"

"Hanging on your every word."

"The van itself gets hijacked north of Newcastle and the entire contents disappear. The driver, Jonathan Fearn, who, by the way is a known associate of Courage's, has just died of injuries received."

"Another murder, then."

"Looks that way. But let me finish. PKF is a phony company and we can't trace anyone involved in it. The only bit of evidence we've got is a CD case."

"That's hardly evidence, is it?" Burgess commented. "Stands to reason there'll be cases around computer people."

"That's not all. I've just found out that the prints on this CD case are those of one Gregory Manners, late of Her Majesty's first-class hotel in Preston. Manners did six months for smuggling a lorryload of cigarettes through Dover. Or trying to. When questioned he said—"

"—he was working alone, and nobody was able to prove any different. All right, you've got a point. As a matter of fact, I do remember that one. It was one of Customs and Excise's few successes that year."

"Let me guess who was behind it: Barry Clough?"

"The man himself. Seems he's everywhere we look, isn't he?"

"He certainly is. This Manners connection links him directly to PKF, whatever it was up to, and by extension to the murders of Charlie Courage and Jonathan Fearn."

"Still like him for the girl's murder, too?"

"Very much. But we don't have enough to bring him in yet. You told me yourself how slippery he is."

"As a jellied eel. You know what I'm thinking, Banks?"

"What?"

"This hijack you told me about. It sounds very much as if someone ripped Barry Clough off."

"Indeed it does."

"And we know Barry doesn't like that. Barry throws tantrums when people upset him."

"Enough for two people to end up dead?"

"I'd say so."

"So maybe Courage was on Clough's payroll, then he decided to work his own scam, selling information about when PKF was moving and where they were going. He'd hardly have looked the other way during a robbery at Daleview because it would have seemed far too obvious."

"A hijacked van's pretty obvious, too, if you ask me," said Burgess.

"Charlie wasn't *that* bright."

"Obviously not. Anyway, it all sounds possible. It must have been valuable merchandise, though, to make it worth the risk."

"There wasn't much risk to speak of, believe me. Not on the road up there at that time on a Sunday night."

"Ah, the provinces. They never cease to amaze me. Ever wondered where the stuff's got to?"

"Yes," said Banks. "Whatever it was, I'm assuming it's either been sold or it's in someone's lockup waiting to cool down. I'm trying to run a check on other business parks around the country, see if there've been any more PKF-type scams lately, but that'll take forever."

"What do you want me to do?"

"Can you fax me what you've got on Gregory Manners, for a start?"

"Sure."

"And have you any photos of Andrew Handley and Jamie Gilbert on file?"

"Indeed we do."

"Could you fax them up here, too? It might not be a bad idea to have someone show them around Daleview and Charlie Courage's neighborhood along with Clough's."

"Okay."

"Thanks. And will you keep a close eye on Clough?"

"It's being done as we speak."

"Because I'll be wanting to talk to him again soon, if anything breaks, and this time I think we'll have him up here."

"Oh, he'll like that."

"I'll bet. Anyway, thanks. I'll be in touch."

"My pleasure. By the way, there's nothing on Andy Pandy yet. It seems that when he wants to hide, he stays hidden. The lads are still on it, though. I'll keep you informed."

"Thanks."

Banks hung up the phone and tried to piece together what he'd got. Not much, really, just a lot of vague suspicions as far as both cases were concerned. There was still something missing: the magnet, the one piece that would rearrange the chaotic jumble of iron filings into a discernible pattern. Until he had that, he would get nowhere. He had a feeling that part of the answer, at least, lay with PKF and whatever it had been doing. At least he could have Gregory Manners brought in and find out what he had to say about the operation.

Annie found a place to park outside number 37 Sebastopol Avenue, walked up the front steps and rang the doorbell to flat number 4.

Luck was still with her; they were in.

The flat was quite nicely done up, Annie thought, when they let her in and offered her a cup of tea. The furniture looked used, probably secondhand or parental donations, but it was serviceable and comfortable. The small living room was clean and uncluttered, and the only decoration was a poster of a Modigliani nude over the tiled mantelpiece. Annie recognized it from one of her father's books; he had always been a big fan of Modigliani, and of nudes. Under the window was a desk with a PC, and a mini stereo unit stood in a cabinet along with stacks of compact discs. There was no television.

"What are you studying?" Annie asked as Alex brought the tea.

"Physics."

"Beyond my ken, I'm afraid." She nodded toward the painting. "Someone likes art, though, I see."

"That's me," said Carly. "I'm studying art history." She was a slight girl with dyed black hair, a ring through the far edge of her left eyebrow and another through the center of her lower lip, which gave her voice a curious lisp.

They talked about art for a while, then, when they both seemed relaxed, Annie got down to business. It wasn't as if she was there to interrogate them, but people often got nervous around the police, the way Annie did around gynecologists.

"Have you any idea why I'm here?" she asked.

They shook their heads.

"I found someone in the Jolly Roger who told me where you lived. Why haven't you come forward before now? You must know of all the appeals for information we've had out."

"Information about what?" Alex asked, a puzzled expression on his face. He was good-looking enough, in a boyish sort of way, though his hair looked as if it needed a wash and he had an Adam's apple the size of a gob-stopper. Could do with a shave, too, Annie thought, or was she just getting conservative in her old age? There was a time, she reminded herself, when she hadn't minded a little stubble on a man. She had even worn a stud through her nose. It wasn't that long ago, either.

"About the murder," she went on. "Emily Riddle's murder. Surely you know it happened at the Bar None shortly after you left on Thursday night?"

Alex and Carly looked blank. "No."

"It was in all the papers. On telly. Everyone's talking about it."

"We don't have a TV set and, well, to be honest," Alex said, "we haven't looked at a paper in days. Too busy at college."

Seems like it, Annie thought. "But haven't you heard anyone talking about it?"

"I've heard people talking about a drug overdose," Carly said. "But I didn't make the connection. I didn't pay much attention. It's so negative. I never read about things like that. It upsets my balance. Why are you here?"

"Why did you leave the club so early?"

They looked at one another, then Carly lisped, "We didn't like the music."

"That's it?"

"It's enough, isn't it. I mean, you wouldn't like to have to listen to that crap all night, would you?"

Annie smiled. She certainly wouldn't. "So why go in the first place?"

"We didn't know what sort of music they played," Alex answered. "Someone at college said it was a pretty good place to have a few drinks and dance, and you know . . . unwind."

"And buy drugs?"

Carly reddened. "We don't do drugs."

"Is that why you went? To buy drugs? And when you'd bought them you left?"

"She said we don't do drugs and we don't," said Alex. "Why can't you just believe us? Not every young person's some sort of drug addict, you know. I knew the cops were prejudiced against blacks and gays, but I didn't think they were prejudiced against the young in general."

Annie sighed. She'd heard it all before. "I'd love to believe you, Alex," she said. "In a perfect world, maybe. But a girl died a very nasty death after taking some adulterated cocaine in the Bar None not more than half an hour after you left and, as yet, we don't know when she got it or where she got it from. If you can give me any help at all, then surely that gives me the right to come here and ask you a few simple questions, doesn't it?"

"It still doesn't give you the right to accuse us of being druggies," said Alex.

"Oh, for crying out loud! Grow up, Alex. If I were accusing the two of you of being junkies you'd be down in the cells now waiting for your legal aid solicitor."

"But you said—"

"Let's move on, shall we?"

They both sulked for a moment, then nodded.

"What kind of music do you like?"

Alex shrugged. "All sorts, really. Just not that techno-rave-disco crap they play at the Bar None. It gives me a headache."

Annie got up and wandered over to look at their CD collection to see for herself. Hole, Nirvana, the Dancing Pigs, even an old Van Morrison. There was quite a variety, but certainly no dance mix. One odd thing she noticed was that some of the CDs had no covers, only typed labels stuck on the cases identifying the contents. When she looked more closely, she also saw that the CDs themselves didn't all have record-company logos. She glanced at the desk and saw a couple of popular computer software programs and games there. Again, there was no form of official identification.

"Where did you get these?" she asked, noticing that Carly had reddened when she picked up one of the CD cases.

"Shop."

"What shop?"

"Computer shop."

"Come on, Carly. You think I'm stupid just because I'm an old fogy? Is that it? You didn't buy this in any legitimate computer shop. It's a knock-off, like the music CDs. Where did you buy them?"

"It's not illegal."

"We won't go into the ins and outs of breach of copyright just now. I just want to know where you bought them."

After letting the silence stretch for almost a minute, Alex answered. "Bloke in the used bookshop down by the castle sells them."

"Castle Hill Books?"

"That's the one."

Annie made a note. It probably wasn't important, and it wasn't her case, but she couldn't dismiss the connection she felt with the empty CD case she had found at PFK. She would pass the information on to Sergeant Hatchley.

"Are you going to arrest us?" Carly asked.

"No. I'm not going to arrest you. But I do want you to answer a few more questions. Okay?"

"Okay."

"While you were in the club, did you notice anyone selling drugs or behaving suspiciously?"

"There weren't many people in the place," Carly said. "Everyone was just getting in drinks or sitting down."

"A few people were dancing," Alex added. "But things hadn't really got going by then."

"Did you notice this girl?"

Annie showed them a picture of Emily.

"I think that's the girl who came in with some friends just after us," Carly said. "At least it looks like her."

"About five foot six, taller in her platforms. Flared jeans."

"That's the one," Carly said. "No, I didn't see her doing anything odd at all. They sat down. Someone went for drinks. I think she was dancing at one point. I don't know. I wasn't really paying attention. The music was already driving me crazy."

"You didn't notice her talk to anyone outside her immediate group?"

"No."

"Did you see her go to the toilet?"

"We weren't watching people coming and going from the toilets."

"So you didn't notice her go?"

"No."

"All right. Did you recognize her? Have you ever seen her before?"

"No," Alex answered, with a sly glance at Carly. "And I think I'd remember."

Carly threw a cushion at him. He laughed.

"She was too young for you, Alex," said Annie. "And by

all accounts you'd have been far too young for her." She thought again of Banks and his lunch with Emily the day she died. Was there any more to it than that? She still got the impression he was holding back, hiding something.

Things were going nowhere fast with Carly and Alex, so she decided to wrap up the interview and call it a day. "Okay," she said, standing up and stretching her back. "If either of you remembers anything about that evening, no matter how insignificant it might seem to you, give me a ring at this number." She handed her card to Carly, who put it on the computer desk, then left the flat, ready to head home. It had been a rough day. Maybe she could treat herself to a book and a long hot bath and put Banks and Dalton out of her mind.

13

The postman came before Banks set off for work on Wednesday morning, and in addition to the usual bills and another letter from Sandra's lawyer, which Banks put aside for later, he also brought with him a small oblong package. Noting the return address, Banks ripped open the padded envelope and held in his hand his son's first officially recorded compact disc, *Blue Rain,* along with a thank-you note for the three-hundred-pound check Banks had sent him, and which had cut severely into his Laphroaig budget.

There was a photograph of the band on the cover, Brian at the center in a practiced, cool sort of slouch, torn jeans, T-shirt, a lock of hair practically covering one eye. Andy, Jamisse and Ali flanked him. It was a poor-quality photograph, Banks noticed—Sandra certainly wouldn't approve—and looked more like a grainy black-and-white photocopy of a color original. Banks didn't much like the band's name, either; Jimson Weed sounded far too sixtyish and druggie, but what did he know?

The music was what counted, and Banks was pleased to see that they had recorded their cover version of Dylan's "Love Minus Zero / No Limit," a song he had been surprised to hear them play on the only occasion he had seen them perform live. The rest of the songs were all originals, with Brian and Jamisse sharing most of the writing credits, apart from an old Mississippi John Hurt number, "Avalon Blues."

They weren't a blues band, but blues was an underlying influence on their music, sometimes overlaid with rock, folk and hip-hop elements: The Grateful Dead meet Snoop Doggy Dogg. Banks was also absurdly pleased to see that in the liner notes Brian had credited him with nurturing an interest in music. Hadn't mentioned that his dad was a copper, though; that wouldn't go down too well in the music business.

He didn't have time to listen to the CD before heading to the office. If he expected his team to put in a full day on Emily's murder, then he had to set an example. Thoughts of work soon led into thoughts of Annie, who had contributed toward yet another sleepless night. He couldn't understand what she saw in Dalton, who seemed such a dull, unprepossessing type to Banks. Not particularly good-looking, either. But, as he well knew, there was neither rhyme nor reason in matters of sex and love.

He just wished he could get the images of them out of his mind. Last night he had tossed and turned, unable to stop himself from imagining them making love in all sorts of positions, Dalton pleasing her far more than he had ever done, making her cry out in ecstasy as she climaxed, riding him wildly. The morning, dark and wet as it was, brought a respite from the images, but not from the feelings that had generated them. Working with her was turning out to be far more difficult than he had imagined it would be. Maybe she was right, and he just couldn't hack it.

As he turned toward the town center and slowed in the knot of traffic on North Market Street, which was just opening up for the day, he wondered if everyone suffered from jealousy as much as he did. It had always been that way for him; jealousy had wrecked his relationship with the first girl he had ever slept with.

Her name was Kay Summerville, and she lived on the same Peterborough estate as he did. For weeks he had lusted after her as he watched her walk by in her jeans and yellow jacket, long blond hair trailing halfway down her back. She seemed unobtainable, ethereal, like most of the women he lusted after, but he was surprised when one day, walking back from the newsagent's over the road with her, he plucked up the courage to ask her out, and she said yes.

Everything went well until Kay left school and got an office job in town. She made new friends, started going for drinks with the crowd regularly after work on a Friday. Banks was still at school, having stayed on for his A-Levels, and a schoolboy had far less appeal than these slightly older, better dressed, more sophisticated men of the world at the office. They had more money to flash around and, even more important, some of them had cars. Kay insisted there was no hanky-panky going on, but Banks became tortured with jealousy, racked by imagined infidelities, and in the end, Kay walked away. She couldn't stand his constant harping on whom she was seeing and what she was doing, she said, and the way he got stroppy if she ever so much as *looked at* another man.

Shortly after, Banks moved to London and went to college there. A year or two after that, and several casual relationships later, he met Sandra. After a rocky few months at the start, when he realized he wanted her so much he couldn't bear the thought of anyone else being with her, he saw that if he played his cards right, nobody else but him was going to be, and for the next twenty years or so he had very few problems with jealousy. Then she left him and Sean came on the scene, or vice versa. Now this with Annie. He was beginning to feel like a sex-obsessed, acne-plagued teenager again, and he didn't like it at all.

Though he couldn't play it, Banks had Brian's CD on the passenger seat beside him, feeling pride every time he managed to break off his miserable thoughts and look down to see his son's face on the cover. The marriage might have ended badly, but at least it had produced Brian and Tracy, Banks told himself, and the world was a better place for having them in it. He picked up the CD and dashed through the rain with it into the station. Once in his office, he set it on his desk, hoping that anyone who dropped by would ask about it.

Because Tuesday had been a day of paperwork, phonework and legwork, Banks was hoping some of it would pay off today. Teams of uniformed and plainclothes officers had been sent out with photos of Gregory Manners, Andrew Handley, Jamie Gilbert and Barry Clough. If any of those four had been up to no good in the Eastvale area over the past month or so, then someone would recognize them. Also, as he had looked at the cover of the Jimson Weed CD and thought about some of the things he had discovered lately, a number of disparate strands had started to come together, and he made an appointment to have lunch at half past one in the Queen's Arms with Granville Baird, of North Yorkshire Trading Standards.

Annie was surprised to find herself feeling so good on Wednesday morning, the best she'd felt in a long time. She had awakened after a long, deep and dreamless sleep feeling that old calm, had done her meditation and yoga and seemed to be getting back in the groove. Agitated voices still muttered in the distance of her mind and talons raked at the raw edges of her emotions, but even so, she felt much better. All would be well.

She wondered if it was anything to do with Dalton's having gone back to Newcastle and decided that was only partly it. Certainly it was a blessing not to have him around the place, constantly reminding her, whether he intended to or not, of that terrible night two years ago. In a way, though, she had exorcised all that by confronting him by the swing bridge. Anyway, she didn't intend to dwell on why she was feeling so good. One thing she had learned from her meditation was that sometimes it's best to let go, simply to accept the feelings you have and ride with them.

Banks had been cool and distant toward her since their blowup on Monday afternoon, and, while a little warmth wouldn't go amiss, that suited her perfectly well at the moment, because all she wanted to do was get on with the job.

And early that Wednesday afternoon, she was doing exactly that, heading for Scarlea House. The desk clerk there had said he recognized Barry Clough's photograph when one of the DCs turned up on the doorstep showing it around.

It was a dull afternoon, and Annie needed to turn her headlights on. The heavy gray cloud was so low it seemed to rest on top of Fremlington Hill, a high limestone scar, or "edge," which curved like bared teeth around the junction of Swainsdale and the smaller Arkbeckdale, which ran northwest.

She drove through sleepy Lyndgarth, with its village green like a handkerchief flapping in the wind, its chapel, church and three pubs. Smoke drifted from the chimneys and lost itself in the clouds like her thoughts when she meditated. She passed through the remote hamlet of Longbridge, a name most found funny as it had the smallest, shortest bridge in the dale. She remembered it was supposed to be famous because someone drove over it in the opening credits of a television program, but that had been before her time up north. Not a soul stirred; the hamlet looked deserted, its shop closed, rough stone cottages shut up. Only a glimmer of light from the pub showed that anyone lived there at all. It was an eerie feeling, especially in the half-light. Annie felt that if she got out of her car and walked around she would find everything in order—meals on the table, today's newspapers lying open, kettles boiling on the cookers—and nobody there, like on the *Marie Celeste*.

Scarlea House loomed ahead, a huge, dark Gothic limestone pile. None of the windows seemed to have any curtains. It stood on a slight rise at the end of a broad gravel drive, and in the weak light, against the backdrop of the rising, dull-green daleside, it looked like a vampire's castle from an old horror film. All that was needed to complete the effect was a few flickers of lightning and the distant rumble of thunder. But when Annie pulled up outside and turned off her engine, everything was silent apart from the occasional bird call and the burbling of the River Arkbeck on its way to join the Swain along the valley bottom.

Christ, Annie, she thought, you're about to enter one of the most upmarket shooting lodges in the Dales and just look at you; you're a mess. She hadn't dressed for upmarket when she climbed into her jeans and flung on a red roll-neck jumper that morning. Even less so when she picked up her

denim jacket on her way out. They'll just have to take me as
they find me, she told herself, opening the heavy front door
and walking over to the reception area.

The ceiling in the hall was taller than her entire cottage,
and if it wasn't quite the Sistine Chapel it was certainly or-
nate, complete with gilded panels and a chandelier. The walls
were all dark wood wainscoting, and here and there hung
overlarge oil paintings of men with bulbous noses wearing
their collars too tight, faces the color and texture of rare roast
beef, like Jim Hatchley's—the kind of paintings that Ray, her
father, called "optical egotism." They paid the rent, though. If
a local artist got one of those self-styled bigwigs to commis-
sion such a portrait, it would probably keep him in paint and
canvas for a few years. Even Ray knew the value of that.

"Can I help you, miss?"

An elegant silver-haired man in a black suit came forward to greet her. Annie's first impression was that he
looked like a funeral-parlor worker.

"Actually," she said, feeling a bit snotty and more than a
trifle intimidated by her surroundings, "it's not Miss, it's
Detective Sergeant Cabbot."

"Ah, yes, Sergeant, we've been expecting you. My
name's Lacey. George Lacey. General Manager. Please,
come this way."

He gestured toward a door with his name on it, and when
they went inside Annie saw it was a modern office, complete
with fax machine, computer, laser printer, the works. She
would never have expected it from the old-fashioned decor,
but the paying guests would be well-off businessmen, and
they would demand all the modern conveniences of the electronic age as well as the primitive excitement of blood lust.
And why not? They could afford it all.

Annie sat in a swivel chair and took out her notebook. "I
don't know if I can tell you any more than I told the other
officer," Lacey said, making a steeple of his hands on the
desk. He had prissy sort of lips, Annie noticed, shaped in a
cupid's bow and far too red. They irritated her when he
talked. She tried to keep her eyes on the knot of his regi-
mental tie.

"I'm just here to confirm that it really was the man in the photograph who stayed here." She laid her copy of Clough's photo on the desk in front of him. "This man."

Lacey nodded. "Mr. Clough. Yes. That was, indeed, him."

"Has he been here before?"

"Mr. Clough is a frequent guest during the season."

"Can you tell me the dates he was here?"

"Just a moment." Lacey tapped a few keys on the computer and frowned at the screen. "He stayed here from Saturday, the fifth of December, until Thursday the tenth."

"It's a bit late in the year for a holiday in the Dales, isn't it?"

"This is a *shooting* lodge, Sergeant. People do not come here for holidays. They come here to shoot grouse. This was the last weekend of the season and we were full to capacity."

"What about now?"

"Not quite so busy. It comes and goes."

"But you stay open all winter, even though the grouse season is over?"

"Oh, yes. We're generally booked up over Christmas and New Year, of course. The rest of the time it's . . . well, quieter, though we get a number of foreign guests. Our restaurant has an international reputation. One often has to make dinner reservations weeks in advance."

"It must be an expensive operation to run."

"Quite." Lacey looked at her as if the mere mention of money were vulgar.

"Was Mr. Clough alone while he was here?"

"Mr. Clough, as usual, came with his personal assistant and a small group of colleagues. The season is very much a social event."

"His personal assistant?"

"A Mr. Gilbert. Jamie Gilbert."

"Ah, yes. Of course." Banks had told her, when she had forced his confession about the lunch with Emily, that Emily had imagined she saw Jamie Gilbert in Eastvale the Monday of the week she died. Maybe she hadn't imagined it after all. It was also interesting that Clough had arrived in Yorkshire only a day or two before Charlie Courage's murder and left the day of Emily's, which meant that he had certainly been in a position to supply her with the strychnine-laced cocaine.

"Do you know what time Mr. Clough left on the tenth?" she asked.

"Not exactly. Usually our guests depart after breakfast. I'd say between nine and ten o'clock, perhaps."

"Is there anything else you can tell me about his stay, his comings and goings?"

"I'm afraid not. I am not employed to spy on our guests."

"Is there anyone who might be able to tell me?"

Lacey looked at his watch and curled his lip. "Mr. Ferguson, perhaps. He's the bartender. As such, he spends far more time close to the guests in social situations. He might be able to tell you more."

"Okay," said Annie. "Where is he?"

"He won't be in until later this afternoon. Around five o'clock. If you'd care to come back then . . . ?"

"Fine." Annie thought of asking for Ferguson's home address and calling on him there, but decided she could wait. Banks was at lunch with someone from Trading Standards, and Annie knew that he would want to be here if she took this line of inquiry any further. She could phone him on her mobile and arrange to meet back at Scarlea at five. In the meantime she would head out to Barnard Castle and investigate a reported sighting of Emily Riddle there the afternoon before she died.

The news about Clough was exciting, though. It was the only positive lead they had on him since Gregory Manners's fingerprints on the CD case linked him to PKF, and it was the first real lead they'd had linking Clough with Yorkshire and catching him out in a lie. Yes, Banks would certainly want to be in on this.

Banks had first met Granville Baird two years ago, when North Yorkshire Trading Standards had asked for police assistance after one of their investigators had been threatened with violence. Since then, they had worked together when their duties overlapped and had even met socially now and then for a game of darts in the Queen's Arms. They weren't close friends, but they were about the same age, and Granville, like Banks, was a jazz fan and a keen operagoer.

They chatted about Opera North's season for a while, then, jumbo Yorkshire pudding on order and a pint of Theakston's bitter in front of him, the buzz of lunchtime conversation all around, Banks lit a cigarette and asked Granville, "Know anything about pirating compact discs?"

Granville raised an eyebrow. "Does that mean you're in the market for something? The 'Ring' cycle, perhaps?"

"No. Though now you come to mention it, I wouldn't mind the complete Duke Ellington centenary set, all twenty-four, if you can run some off for me."

"Wish I could afford it. Does this mean that the police are actually looking at doing something about pirating at last?"

"Apart from copyright infringement, which is hardly a police matter, I wasn't aware that any laws were being broken. If you expect us to come charging in to Bill Gates's rescue every time someone pirates a copy of Windows, then you've got a very funny idea of what our job really is."

Granville laughed. "You're behind the times, Alan. It's big business these days. If it were simply a matter of copying Windows or the latest Michael Jackson CD for a friend, nobody would bat an eyelid, but we're talking big operations here. Big money, too."

"That's exactly what I'm interested in," said Banks. "How big?"

"The last raid we carried out we netted about a quarter of a million quid's worth of stuff."

Banks whistled. "That big?"

"Tip of the iceberg."

"So it would be a lucrative business for organized crime, would it?"

"Especially as you lot don't even seem to think it's a crime."

"Point taken. Look, we've got a case on right now—it started with a murder—and I've been putting two and two together and coming up with a pirating business. I don't

know how big yet. In fact, we don't know much at all."
Brian's CD had been the final piece in the puzzle. Seeing
its amateurishly produced cover, Banks had thought of the
CD case Annie had found at PKF, the CDs she saw at Alex
and Carly's flat, about Gregory Manners's fingerprints,
Barry Clough's dismissal as a roadie for bootlegging live
recordings, and the van worth hijacking, the driver worth
killing. They still hadn't found the van's contents yet, but
Banks would bet a pound to a penny they consisted of
equipment for copying CDs, along with any stock and
blank discs that happened to have been there. What Banks
needed to know from Granville Baird was whether there
was enough profit in the pirating business to make it of interest to Clough, the way smuggling was.

"What *do* you know?" Granville asked.

"A phony company leases small units in rural business
parks, operates for a while, then moves on. Make any
sense?"

Granville nodded. "I've heard rumors of such a setup,
yes. And if you had two or three of these operations running
at once, around the country, you could be turning over a mill
or two a year or more, easy. If you had the proper equipment, of course."

"Definitely worth his while, then?"

"Whose while?"

"We're not sure yet. This is just speculation. What sort of
things would they pirate?"

"Everything they can get their dirty little hands on.
Music, software programs, games, you name it. For the moment, by far the biggest profits are in games. Sony PlayStation stuff, that sort of thing. Everyone's kid wants the latest
computer game, right? We've even found pirated stuff on
sale that isn't on the market yet. Some of the *Star Wars* tie-
in games came over from the States before the film even
came out here."

"What about pirated movies?"

"There's a lot of that, but most of it's done in the Far
East."

"How do they get the originals? Insiders?"

"Mostly, yes. As far as the movies are concerned, though, sometimes all they have for a master is a hand-held video of the film being shown at a theater full of people. I've seen some of the stuff and it's awful. When it comes to the computer programs and games, though, it's easy enough for some employee to sneak a disc out, and if he can make a couple of hundred quid from it, all the better. There even used to be a private Web site where, for a membership fee, you got offered a variety of pirated stuff to download, but that's defunct. Mind you, it's very much a matter of caveat emptor. Some of it's a rip-off. We found a lot of games among the last haul that couldn't be played without complicated bypasses of internal security systems."

"The manufacturers are wising up, then?"

"Slowly."

Their food came, and they paused awhile to eat. Banks took a bite of his Yorkshire pudding filled with roast beef and gravy and washed it down with some beer. He looked at Granville, who was drinking mineral water and nibbling at a salad. "What's up? On a diet?"

Granville frowned. "Annual checkup last month. Doc says my cholesterol's too high, so I've got to cut out booze and fatty foods."

Banks was surprised. Granville looked healthy enough, played squash and was hardly any heavier than Banks was. "Sorry to hear that."

"No sweat. You just go right on enjoying yourself until it's your turn."

Banks, who felt he had led a charmed life healthwise thus far, despite the bad diet, the cigarettes and the ale, nodded. "It'll be either that or the prostate, I know. What about distribution?"

"Wherever you can shift it. I've even heard stories of the local ice-cream van selling PlayStation games to kids. Gives a whole new meaning to Mr. Softee."

Banks laughed. That made a lot of sense, he thought as he ate. Clough could use the same distribution network he had set up for the smuggled cigarettes and alcohol—small shopkeepers like Castle Hill Books, to whom DC Winsome

Jackman should be talking this afternoon, market stallholders, pubs, clubs, factories. After all, the customers would often be the same people, none of whom thought they were really doing anything wrong in buying the odd packet of smuggled fags or a pirated computer game for their kid's birthday. Half the cops in the country were smoking contraband cigarettes and drinking smuggled lager. Banks even knew a DI with West Yorkshire who drove to Calais every few weeks and filled up his trunk with booze and cigarettes. He made enough selling them at the station to cover the expenses of his trip and keep himself in the necessities till the next time.

So, why not? people thought. Big deal. They were getting a bargain, Bill Gates already had too much money, and the tax on booze and fags was extortionate. Now the EC had also cut out duty-free purchases between its members. In a way, Banks agreed, the consumers had a point—except that people like Barry Clough were getting rich from them.

He tried to work out how events might have occurred. Clough's men pay off Charlie Courage, whose ability to sniff out wrongdoing and try for a slice of the pie was legendary, then Charlie sells them out to a rival, who hijacks the van and steals the equipment and stock of pirated CDs to set up somewhere on his own. Only it goes wrong. Clough's men torture Charlie. Does he give up the hijacker? You bet he does. And what happens to both of them?

"It makes sense," he said to Granville. "Especially if there's the kind of money in it you're saying there is."

"Take my word for it. There is. And if your man's really organized, he'll have multidisc copying writers so he can churn them out by the dozen."

"That'd be an expensive piece of equipment, I should imagine?"

"Indeed it would. An investment of thousands."

That answered one question that had been puzzling Banks. If the PKF van had been carrying a few pirated discs, it would have hardly been worth hijacking, not to mention killing Jonathan Fearn. But if it had been carrying industrial-standard multidisc copying equipment, that was another matter entirely. "A very healthy return, I'd imagine, though, if you've got the start-up capital," Banks said.

"Indeed."

And Clough certainly had the capital to invest. From his gun-restoring racket, the music business, his club, his smuggling operations and whatever other dirty little scams he was involved in, he had plenty of seed money. The problem was how to prove his involvement. It was as Burgess had said about Clough's smuggling activities: there was plenty of ground for suspicion, but scant evidence of actual guilt. Everything was done through minions and intermediaries, people like Gregory Manners, Jamie Gilbert and Andy Pandy; Clough never got his own hands dirty. His only contact with anything but the profits was entirely circumstantial.

Or was it? Had Emily Riddle posed some sort of threat to him? Did she have knowledge he considered dangerous? Clough didn't like to lose, didn't like people walking out on him, especially if they took something with them, be that something money or knowledge.

It was beginning to seem entirely possible to Banks that the two cases were connected, and that Emily Riddle might have been killed by the same person and for the same reason as Charlie Courage. But who was it? Which of his minions had Clough used? Andy Pandy, who already had a grudge against Emily, the kind of grudge you develop from a hard knee in the balls? Jamie Gilbert, to whom Burgess had referred as a psycho? Or someone else, someone they hadn't encountered yet? Gregory Manners might be able to help them, if they could find him.

Banks finished his Yorkshire and lit another cigarette. He had about a third of a pint left, and he decided not to have another one. "You said you'd heard rumors about a big local operation," he said. "Anything in them?"

"There's always something, don't you think? No smoke without fire, as they say. It's mostly a matter of finding a lot more pirated goods flooding the markets around North Yorkshire, which reeks of the kind of organization you've just been talking about. You say they've moved on?"

"Their van was heading for another business park near

Wooler, in Northumbria, when it was hijacked. Everything disappeared, and the driver was in a coma for a few days before he died. No prints at the scene. Nothing. All we have is a CD case from PKF's Daleview operation which bears the fingerprints of one Gregory Manners, convicted for smuggling, and a known associate of our Mr. Big."

"That's the thing," said Granville, leaning forward. "They're getting into these new areas, the big guys, like cigarette smuggling and pirating games. There's a pile of money to be made if you do it right, and the risks are far less than dealing in drugs. Besides, drugs are cheaper than they've ever been these days. With smuggling and pirating, you just sit back and rake in the profits. That's what we've been trying to tell you lot for ages. And the more you squeeze the drug dealers, the more they're likely to find more creative ways of making their fortunes."

Banks looked at his watch. Just gone half past two. Time to check on what was happening in the incident room, then ACC McLaughlin and Detective Superintendent Gristhorpe would be waiting for an update. "I've got to go now, Granville," he said, "but could you do me a favor and keep your eyes and ears open?" Banks asked.

"My pleasure." Granville paused, then said, "I heard about Jimmy Riddle's daughter. Terrible business."

"Yes, it is," Banks agreed.

"Your case?"

"For my sins."

"Anything in those rumors in the papers? Sex and drugs?"

"You know what it's like, Granville," said Banks, stubbing out his cigarette and getting up to leave. "There's always something in it, isn't there? No smoke without fire."

Annie's news about Clough's being seen in the area around the time of both murders gave Banks that tingle of excitement he hadn't felt in a while as he headed for Scarlea House late that afternoon, taking the unfenced high roads, where the only things that slowed him down were wandering sheep. He put

Richard and Linda Thompson's *Shoot Out the Lights* on the car stereo and turned it up a bit louder than usual.

Annie's purple Astra was parked outside Scarlea, and she was waiting in the lobby when Banks arrived. Gerald Ferguson had reported for work ten minutes ago, according to George Lacey. He pointed the way, and Banks and Annie walked down the gloomy hallway to the double doors at the far end.

"Anything on that sighting in Barnard Castle?" Banks asked.

Annie shook her head. "False alarm. Witness was an elderly woman and she admitted all teenagers looked alike to her. Soon as I showed her the photo again she began to have doubts."

Banks pushed open the heavy doors—it took more strength than he expected—and they entered the magnificently appointed dining room. Once a banquet hall, he guessed, it had a number of large windows looking out over the valley bottom to the steep dalesides crisscrossed with drystone walls. It was too dark to see anything now, of course, but breakfasting grouse shooters could no doubt look at the view and anticipate the joys of the coming day's slaughter as they ate their eggs Benedict or juice and cereal.

There would probably have been one large central banquet table before the place had been turned into an upmarket restaurant, Banks thought, but now there were a number of tables scattered about the room, each covered by a spotless heavy linen tablecloth. At the far end were more doors, probably to the kitchen, and a long bar took up one wall, all dark polished wood and brass, the rows of bottles gleaming on shelves in front of the mirror at the back. Banks had never seen so many single-malt whiskeys in one place before. Most of them he had never even heard of.

A man in a burgundy jacket stood with his back to them fiddling with the Optic on the gin bottle when Banks went over and introduced himself and Annie.

"Charmed to meet you," the man said, glancing back at them. "I'm Gerald Ferguson, and this bloody thing is a pain in the arse, excuse my French, love. I've told them to buy a new one but they're too bloody tight-fisted. The hell with it."

He left the Optic and leaned on the bar to face them. "What can I do for you?"

He was a round little man of about fifty, with a red face, muttonchops sideboards and a soup-strainer mustache. His jacket tugged a bit at the gold buttons around his chest and stomach, and Banks thought one deep breath would pop them. "We were hoping you might be able to help us with some information about a guest, Mr. Ferguson," he said.

"Gerald. Please." He looked around, then put his finger to the side of his nose. "Fancy a wee dram?"

Banks and Annie sat on the high barstools. "We wouldn't want to get you into any trouble," said Banks.

Gerald waved his hand and looked toward the door they had entered by. His fingers were surprisingly long and tapered, Banks thought, the nails neatly clipped and shiny. Perhaps he played piano as a hobby. "What he doesn't know won't harm him. What's your poison?"

It was an unfortunate turn of phrase, Banks thought, as he scanned the row of bottles and settled on the cask-strength Port Ellen.

"Detective Sergeant Cabbot?"

"Nothing for me, thank you."

"You certain?"

"Certain."

Gerald shrugged. "Up to you." He poured two glasses of Port Ellen, very generous measures, Banks thought, set one in front of himself and another in front of Banks. *"Slainte,"* he said, and knocked it back in one.

"Slainte," said Banks, and took a little sip. Heaven. He set the glass down. "It's a guest called Clough we're interested in. Barry Clough. Apparently he's a regular in grouse season."

"Aye, he's that, all right."

Banks caught the tone of disapproval in his voice. "You don't like him?"

"I didn't say that, did I?" said Ferguson, pouring himself another Port Ellen. Banks guessed it wasn't his first and wouldn't be his last one of the day, either. At least this time he sipped it slowly.

"Tell us what you do think of him, then."

"He's a thug in fancy dress. And as for that factotum of his—"

"Jamie Gilbert?"

"If that's his name. The one with the queer hair."

"That's him. Go on."

Ferguson took another sip of whiskey and lowered his voice. "This place used to have a bit of class, do you know that? I've worked here going on twenty-five years and I've seen them all come and go. We've had MPs—a prime minister and an American president once—judges, foreign dignitaries, businessmen from the City, and some of them might have been stingy bastards, but they all had one thing in common: they were gentlemen."

"And now?"

Ferguson snorted. "Now? I wouldn't give you twopence for the crowd we get these days." He glanced over at the doors again. "Not since he came."

"Mr. Lacey?"

"Mr. George bloody Lacey, General Manager. Him and his new ideas. Modernization, for crying out loud." He pointed toward the windows. "What do you need modernization for when you've got the best bloody view in the world and all nature on your doorstep? Tell me the answer to that, if you can."

Banks, who knew a rhetorical question when he heard one, gave a sympathetic nod.

"Since he came," Ferguson went on, "we've had nothing but bloody pop stars, actors, television personalities, whiz kids from the stock market. Christ, we've even had bloody women. Sorry love, no offense intended, but grouse shooting never used to be much of a woman's sport." He knocked back another mouthful of Port Ellen.

Annie smiled, but Banks had seen that one before; she didn't mean it. Ferguson had better watch out.

"Half of them don't even know one end of a shotgun from t'other," Ferguson went on. "It's a wonder we don't have more accidents, I tell you. But they've got plenty of money to throw about. Oh, aye. Take a bloke like that there

Clough. Thinks if he tosses you a few bob at the start of the evening you're at his beck and call for the rest of the night. Pillock. And Mary, she's one the lasses clean the rooms. Nice lass, but a couple of bob short of a pound, if you know what I mean, the stories she's told me about some of the things she's found."

"Like what?" Banks asked.

Ferguson thrust his face forward and whispered. "Syringes, for a start."

"In Clough's room?"

"No. That were one of the pop stars. Stayed here a week and never once came out of his room. I ask you. Money to throw away, that lot."

"Back to Barry Clough, Mr. Ferguson."

Ferguson laughed and scratched his head. "Aye. Sorry. I do run off at the mouth sometimes, don't I? You got me started on one of my little hobbyhorses."

"That's fine," said Banks, "but can you tell us any more about Barry Clough?"

"What sort of things would you be wanting to know?"

"Did you see much of him while he was here?"

"Aye. I was on the bar every night—I get help when we're busy, like. Mandy, one of the local girls from Longbridge—and Clough was always here for drinks before dinner, and most times he ate here, too." Ferguson looked around and leaned forward conspiratorially. "They say the food's spectacular here, but if you ask me there's nowt edible. Foreign muck, for the most part."

"But Mr. Clough enjoyed it?"

"He did. And he knew what wines to order with what courses—we've got a wine waiter, sommelier, as he likes to call himself, the stuck-up bugger—from his Château neuf du bloody Pape to his Sauternes and his vintage Port. See, he's got all the trappings, the expensive clothes—Armani, Paul Smith—all the top-quality shooting gear and what have you, and he thinks he's got style, but you can tell he's common as muck underneath it all. Must've read a bluffer's guide, but he couldn't fool me. There's one thing you can't fake: class. Like I said, a thug. Why? What's he done?"

"We don't know that he's done anything yet."

"I'll bet you suspect him of something, though, don't you? Stands to reason. You mark my words, bloke like him, he's bound to have done something. Bound to."

"Did you talk to him much?"

"Like I said, he came on like he thought he was a gentleman, but he couldn't pull it off. For a start, a real gentleman wouldn't pass the time of day talking to the likes of me. He might make a friendly comment on the weather or the quality of that day's shooting, but that's as far as he'd go. There are clear lines. This Clough, though, chatty as anything, propping up the bar, drinking his bloody Cosmopolitans and smoking his Cuban cigars. And that bloody ponytail."

"What did he talk about?"

"Nothing much, when all's said and done. Football. Seems he's an Arsenal supporter. I'm a Newcastle man, myself. Goes on about his villa in Spain, about going to parties with all these bloody celebrities. As if I give a toss."

"Did he ever talk about his business?"

"Not that I recall. What is it?"

"That's what we'd like to know."

"Well, I won't say some people don't sometimes let something slip, you know. Comes with the territory. I've actually managed one or two good investments over the years based on things I've heard on this job, but don't tell anyone that. I'm paid to stand behind this bar all bloody night and sometimes people, they look on you as a sort of father confessor, not that I'm Catholic or anything. Straight C of E."

"Not Clough, though?"

"No. That's why I can hardly remember a word he said."

"Was he with a party?"

"Yes. About five or six of them."

"Who?"

"They were a mixed bunch. There was that pretty young pop singer whose picture you see all over the place these days, the one where she's wearing hardly more than a pair of gold silk knickers. Amanda Khan, she's called. Touch of the tarbrush. Lovely skin, though."

Banks had seen the image in question; it was on the cover

of her new CD and also graced posters in HMV and Virgin Records. She looked about as old as Emily Riddle.

"Couldn't even *hold* a bloody gun, her, let alone shoot one. Still, I must say she seemed a nice-enough lass, especially for a pop singer. Polite. And far too nice, not to mention too *young,* for the likes of Clough."

"Was she with him?"

"What do you mean? Were they sleeping together?"

"Yes."

"I don't know. Whatever they get up to when the bar closes is none of my business."

"Did you get the impression that they were sleeping together?"

"Well, they did seem a bit close, and I did see him touch her every now and then. You know, put an arm around her, pat her bum, that sort of thing. More as if she were a possession he kept wanting to touch than anything else."

That sounded like Clough, Banks thought. It hadn't taken him long to get another girl. "Who else?"

Ferguson scratched his head again. Banks took another sip of the fiery malt. "I didn't recognize any of the others. I'm sure our Mr. Lacey will let you have a look at the registration book, or bloody diskette or whatever he calls it now. Used to have a nice big black leather-bound book. Must've been worth a bob or two. But now it's all bloody computer discs and Web sites. I ask you. *Web sites.*"

Banks slipped the photograph of Emily Riddle out of his briefcase. "Did he ever meet with this girl?"

Some of the color left Ferguson's face. "So that's what it's all about, is it? I know who she is, poor lass. I read about her in the papers. You think he did it? Clough?"

"We don't know," said Banks. "That's why we're asking these questions."

"I can't give him an alibi," said Ferguson. "Like I said, I saw him most evenings, but never during the day. He could have slipped out anytime, really."

"An alibi's not much use in a case like this," Banks said. "At the moment it's enough to know that he was in the area at the time."

"Oh, he was in the area, all right."

"Did you see him meet with anyone outside his party?"

"Only the once."

"When was this?"

"I can't recall if it was Sunday or Monday. I think it must have been Sunday. That was the day we had the saddle of lamb. Would have been nice, too, if it hadn't been for all them fancy herbs and sauces cook sloshes over everything he makes. Freshen your drink?"

"No, thanks."

"Sure you won't have a drop, miss?"

"No, thanks, Mr. Ferguson."

"Gerald. I told you, it's Gerald."

Annie smiled that non-smile again. "No, Gerald."

He beamed at her. "That's better."

"This person Clough met," Banks said. "Man or a woman?"

"Man. You know, there was something familiar about him, but I just can't put my finger on it right now."

"A media personality?"

"I don't think so. But I've seen him in the papers."

"What did he look like?"

"About six-foot-something. Bit dour-looking, as if he's just been sucking on a lemon. Didn't seem at all comfortable to be there. Only drank mineral water. Kept looking around."

"Could you tell if they'd met before?"

"Hard to say, really. If I had to guess, I'd say it was their first meeting. I don't know why, but there you are. What you lot would call a hunch."

"Did you hear any of what they said?"

"No. I was here, behind the bar, and they had a window table."

"Did they seem friendly?"

"As a matter of fact, no, they didn't. The bloke got up and left before his main course had even arrived."

"Were they arguing?"

"If they were, they were doing it quietly. He was certainly red in the face when he left, I can tell you that."

"Clough?"

"No, the other fellow. Clough were cool as a cucumber."

"Anything else you can tell me about this man?"

"Bald as a coot, heavy eyebrows. There was something else familiar about him, too, about his bearing, as if maybe he was a military man or something. No . . . there's still something missing."

"A uniform, perhaps?" Banks suggested, feeling the tingle at the bottom of his spine. "A police uniform?"

Ferguson's eyes opened wide. "By George, I think you've got it. He was wearing a suit that night, but if you picture him in a uniform . . . You're right. I've seen him on telly opening farm shows and spouting about crime figures being down. Mr. Riddle, that's who it was, now I think back. Your own chief constable. I wonder what all that was about."

Great, thought Banks, with that sinking feeling. Just what we need. He had sensed something odd about Riddle the night he went to break the news of Emily's murder. Riddle had mentioned Clough immediately, though Banks had never told him the man's name, and he was damn sure Emily hadn't.

"Thank you, Mr. Ferguson," he said, slugging back the last millimeter of Port Ellen. "Thank you very much. We might need to talk to you again, if that's all right?"

"You know where I am. We'll try the Caol Ila twenty-two-year-old next time you drop by. Lovely drop of malt. It'll knock your socks off."

Banks felt as if his socks had been knocked off already as he walked out into the evening darkness. Neither he nor Annie could think of anything to say. He felt tired. His brain couldn't even grapple with the consequences of what Gerald Ferguson had just told him about Chief Constable Riddle dining with Barry Clough. There was too much to take in. But he couldn't let it lie; he had to confront Riddle, and the sooner the better.

Banks still felt tired when he pulled up yet again in front of the Old Mill that night. Annie had seemed annoyed back at the station when he told her he wanted to confront Riddle alone with Ferguson's story, but she hadn't argued. Riddle *was* chief constable, after all, and Banks didn't want to give the appearance of a formal interrogation, the way it would appear if two detectives turned up on his doorstep. He wanted an honest explanation, though he had his own ideas about what had transpired, and he believed that Riddle would give him one. It was a job he would have gladly delegated if he thought that was at all possible, but it wasn't. He was still SIO, and if anyone was going to face Chief Constable Riddle with this new development, then it had to be Banks.

Riddle himself answered the door and invited Banks in.

"Ros is out, I'm afraid," he said. "She's visiting with Charlotte King, our neighbor. Benjamin's in bed."

They walked through to the large living room and sat down. Riddle didn't offer anything in the way of refreshments, which was fine; Banks didn't want anything. He blamed the small whiskey he'd had at Scarlea for his tiredness. "How's he taking everything?" he asked. "Benjamin."

"He doesn't know what's happened. He knows that his sister has gone to live with Jesus, and he misses her terribly. He keeps asking if it's something to do with the funny pictures of her in the computer."

"What do you tell him?"

"That it's not. To forget about that. But it seems he can't. We're going to send him to stay with his grandparents—Ros's mother and father down in Barnstaple—after the funeral. He's always got along well with them and we think a change of scene will do him good."

"When's the funeral?"

"Tomorrow morning. The coroner released the body as quickly as she could." He paused. "Will you be there?"

"If I wouldn't be intruding."

"For better or for worse, you're part of this."

Banks wished to hell he weren't, but Riddle was right. "I'll be there," he said.

"Good."

"And your wife? How's Mrs. Riddle doing?"

"She's bearing up. Ros is strong. She'll survive. Anyway, you're not here to make small talk about my family, Banks. What is it? Have there been any developments?"

Banks paused. "Yes," he said finally. "As a matter of fact, there have."

"Out with it, then."

"You're not going to like it."

"More bad news?" Banks noticed a quick flash of fear in Riddle's eyes, something he had never seen there before. Riddle averted his gaze. "Anyway, it doesn't matter whether I like it or not," he said. "Things have gone too far for that. Two months ago, I wouldn't have even imagined having you in my house, let alone inviting you to my daughter's funeral. It doesn't mean I've changed my mind about you, Banks, just that circumstances have changed."

"I've been useful to you."

"And haven't I fulfilled my part of the bargain?"

"What were you doing having dinner with Barry Clough at Scarlea House on Sunday, December the sixth?"

Riddle paused before answering. "I was hoping you wouldn't find out about that," he said. "Too much to hope for, I suppose."

"You should have known."

"Yes, well . . . Anyway, I didn't have dinner with him. I left before things went that far."

"Don't split hairs. You met with him. Why?"

"Because he asked me to."

"When?"

"Two days earlier."

"Friday?"

"Yes. He telephoned me at the station and said he was coming up to Yorkshire for the end of the grouse season the next day, that he'd like to meet me to talk about Emily. That's all he would tell me on the telephone."

"He called her Emily?"

"Yes."

"Not Louisa?"

"No."

"So he'd found out who she was?"

"Oh, he'd found out all right. Starting with her conversation with you in his living room."

"Bugged?"

"Of course. That's what he told me, anyway."

"What did he want with you?"

"What do you think?"

"Blackmail?"

"In a nutshell. I've come across his kind before, Banks. They collect people they think they might be able to use at some point."

"Tell me about your conversation."

Riddle scowled. "You're enjoying this, aren't you?"

"What do you mean?"

"Putting me on the receiving end. Isn't this what you've always dreamed about?"

"You overestimate your importance to me," said Banks, "and to be perfectly honest, the answer's no, I'm not enjoying it. I haven't enjoyed any of this. Not breaking the news to you about Emily's death, not questioning you and your wife about her movements, and certainly not this. I've had the feeling that one or both of you has been lying or concealing things right from the start, and now I have some concrete evidence of it. I still wish I could simply wash my hands of the lot of you, but I can't. I've got my job to do, and believe it or not, I feel that I owe your daughter something."

"Why? What did she ever do for you?"

"Nothing. That's not it at all."

"What is, then?"

"You wouldn't understand. Let's just get back to that Sunday dinner at Scarlea, shall we? What did Clough want to talk to you about?"

"What do you think? He'd discovered that I'm chief constable and that I was contemplating entering into politics. The idea of having such an influential person in his pocket appealed to him."

"What did he say?"

"He said that he knew Emily in London—as Louisa Gamine, of course—that they had lived together for two or three months and that he had compromising photographs and all sorts of interesting stories he could give to the newspapers about her, things that would spoil my chances of election, should I ever get that far, and things that would even call into doubt my fitness to stay on as chief constable, should I not. He made a few obscene comments about her, and he also indicated that he could probably persuade her to go back with him anytime he wanted. He seemed to believe that all he would have to do was whistle."

"What did you say to him?"

"I told him to sod off. What do you think?"

"What did he say to that?"

"He said he could perfectly understand my reaction and that he'd give me a couple of weeks to think it over, then get in touch again."

"Is that when you got up and walked away?"

"Yes."

"Did you ever hear anything else from him after that?"

"No. It's only been a week and a half."

"No threats or anything?"

"Nothing. And I don't expect to."

"Why not?"

"Well, he's hardly going to draw attention to himself by making good on his blackmail threat to me now, is he? Not after the murder."

"You don't think the murder was a sort of warning for you, a signal?"

"Don't be absurd. Things were in a delicate balance. Clough had everything to lose by harming Emily and everything to gain by keeping her alive. He's not a stupid man, Banks. What do you imagine he'd guess my reaction to be if I thought for a moment that he'd murdered my daughter? It just doesn't make sense."

"I wouldn't be too sure about that." Banks really wanted a cigarette but he knew he couldn't have one, not in Riddle's house. "You must have known we'd find out sooner or later," he said. "Why on earth didn't you tell me?"

"It was a calculated risk. Why should I tell you? It was my personal business. My problem. It's up to me to deal with it."

"This wasn't a personal problem. It stopped being that the minute someone *murdered* Emily, for Christ's sake. Maybe Clough. You were withholding evidence."

"What evidence?"

"That he was in the area around the time of her death, for a start. He could have easily given her the drugs."

"I've tried not to interfere with the investigation in any way. I would like to have steered you away from Clough as a suspect, but I obviously couldn't do that without raising suspicion." Riddle leaned forward and rested his hands on his knees. "Think about it for a minute, Banks, before you go off half-cocked on this. What possible reason could Clough have for wanting to kill Emily when she represented his hold over me?"

"She didn't need to be alive for him to make good on his threat."

"But it wasn't just the threat of revelations he made, remember. He also said he could take her back with him whenever he wanted. He knew I wouldn't be able to bear the thought of her being with him. You should have told me, Banks. When you brought her back. You should have told us the sort of trouble she'd been getting herself into. You blame me for withholding evidence, but neither of you said a word about what Emily had been up to in London."

Banks sighed. "What good would it have done?" Though maybe he should have, he thought miserably. He had believed that in keeping quiet he was saving the Riddles from unnecessary pain, and saving Emily perhaps from their disciplinarian backlash. But look what had happened. Emily was dead and Jimmy Riddle was in deep trouble himself. Trouble from which he might never fully recover. Banks remembered what Emily had told him about Riddle being a poor detective, always coming up with the wrong killer in the crime novels he read as an adolescent. He could believe it. "It's no use blaming me," he went on. "Believe me, there are times I wish I'd done things differently. But you. You're a professional copper. You're a bloody chief constable, for crying out loud. I can't believe you'd be so stupid and stubborn and proud not to tell me that a man I've been seriously suspecting as your daughter's killer actually approached you as a blackmail target only four days before she was murdered."

Riddle's expression hardened. "I told you. It was a private matter. It has nothing to do with Emily's death. He had no motive for killing her. Don't you think that if I really believed Clough had killed Emily I'd have throttled him with my bare hands by now? You might not understand this, Banks, but I loved my daughter."

"Who can really know with someone like Clough?" Banks argued. "Perhaps from a business standpoint he would be better off with Emily alive, but he's also a violent man, from what I've heard, and a possessive one. He doesn't like people walking out on him. Maybe that's why he killed her. Besides, I don't believe she would have gone back to him that easily. She was frightened of him."

"Well, that might be one good reason for going back to him, mightn't it? Men like him might have a certain fascination for girls like . . . like Emily."

"What do you mean?"

"Precocious, mischievous, rebellious. She's always been like that. You know that she and I didn't get on, no matter how much I cared about her. It always came out wrong. And Clough. He's about my age, but he's a criminal. Policeman—criminal. Don't you see that she was doing this to hurt me?"

"If she'd wanted to hurt you, she'd have made sure you knew about it."

Riddle just shook his head.

"Did Clough say anything about his business interests at this dinner?"

"No."

"Did he mention PKF Computer Systems?"

"No."

"Charlie Courage? Gregory Manners? Jamie Gilbert?"

"No. I've told you what he said. Don't you think that if he'd told me anything incriminating I would have passed it along to you?"

"After what I've just heard, I don't know about that."

"There was *nothing*, Banks. Just his not-so-subtle black-mail hints."

"But he was here, in the Eastvale area, when both Charlie Courage and your daughter were killed. Doesn't that make you stop and think?"

"The first thing it makes me think is that he can't have been responsible for the murders. He's not so stupid as to be on the doorstep when they went down."

"Stop defending him. For crying out loud, anyone would think you had . . ."

"What?"

"Never mind."

"What are you going to do about it?"

Banks shook his head. "I don't know."

"Whatever it is, please have the decency to wait until after the funeral, would you?"

Banks said he would, but his mind was elsewhere, with what he had left unsaid. He could think of only one good reason why Riddle would be so unprofessional as to conceal the details about his secret meeting with Clough: that he was at least considering capitulating to Clough's request. Which brought Banks to consider an even greater problem. With Emily's death, clearly a large part of Clough's hold over Riddle had been extinguished. If Clough hadn't killed her, then, who *did* want Emily Riddle dead, and why?

14

A lot of people, Banks mused, thought that the police attended the funerals of murder victims in the hope of finding the killer there. They didn't. That only happened in books and on television. On the other hand, given that a victim's close relatives were likely to be at the funeral, and given that by far the largest percentage of murders were committed by close family members, then the odds were pretty good that the murderer *would* be at the funeral.

Not this one, though. Barry Clough wasn't there, for a start, and he was the closest they had to a suspect so far, even though Riddle was probably right about Emily being of far more value to him alive. Was Banks wearing blinkers when it came to Clough, or was he going off half-cocked, as Gristhorpe had warned him against doing? He didn't think so. He knew it didn't make sense for Clough to kill Emily just after he had used her to attempt to blackmail her father, but he was sure there must be something he was missing, some angle he hadn't considered yet. The only thing he *had* thought of, but didn't really believe in, was that Clough was some sort of psychopath and simply hadn't been able to stop himself. If that had been the case, he would have made damn sure he was there to watch and participate in Emily's murder.

Craig Newton and Ruth Walker had traveled up together; they stood looking puzzled and miserable in the rain as the vicar intoned the Twenty-third Psalm. Banks caught their eyes; Craig gave him a curt nod and Ruth gave him a dirty look.

"The Lord is my shepherd; I shall not want. He maketh me to lie down in green pastures: he leadeth me beside the still waters." There was nothing green about the Dales pastures that morning—everything, from sky to houses to the unevenly shaped fields and drystone walls was a dull slate-gray or a mud-brown—nor was there anything still about the River Swain, which tumbled over a series of small waterfalls beside the graveyard and, along with the wind screaming through the gaps in the drystone wall like a Stockhausen composition, almost drowned out the vicar's words. The wind also drove the rain hard across the churchyard, and the mourners seemed to draw as deeply into their heavy overcoats, gloves and hats as they could.

At least the vicar was using the old version, Banks noticed. "The Lord is my shepherd; therefore can I lack nothing" had about as much resonance as "as in a mirror, dimly," he thought. Not that he went to church very often, but like many people, he remembered the powerful church language of his youth and anything less fell far short. He hadn't known what half of it meant, either then or now, but it never seemed to matter; religion, he thought, was mostly a matter of mumbo-jumbo, anyway. Chants, mantras, whatever. Comforting mumbo-jumbo, in this case, though nobody was fooled. Rosalind Riddle dabbed at her eyes with a white hanky every now and then, Benjamin stood next to her, looking confused, and her husband looked as if he had been up all night grappling with his conscience.

When Riddle caught Banks's eye briefly on the way out to the graveside, he looked away guiltily. And well he might, thought Banks, who still felt a residue of anger toward him for stalling the investigation. He had realized after his interview with Riddle the previous day, though, that he had also been guilty of hiding too many things; he hadn't told Annie about the lunch with Emily at first, and he still hadn't told her about the night in the hotel room. With any luck now, she wouldn't find out about that. Of course, he could rationalize his own shortcomings a lot more easily than he could Riddle's, but he could at least *understand* why Riddle might not like to admit to him that he had kept a dinner engagement with his daughter's lover, a man who also happened to have a criminal reputation. Would Riddle have capitulated with whatever Clough wanted from him in order to protect himself and Emily? What kind of man was he when it came to the crunch? He would never have the chance to find out now. Virtue can't prove itself until it's tested.

"Yea, though I walk through the valley of the shadow of death . . ." *The valley of the shadow of death* was a phrase that had always moved Banks, sent a shiver up his spine, though he would have been hard-pressed to explain what it meant to him. It was one phrase they hadn't got rid of in the new translation, too. He thought of poor Graham Marshall all those years ago, walking through the valley of the shadow of death. They had never found his body, so he never had a funeral like Emily. There had been some sort of memorial service at school, Banks remembered, or a remembrance service, he wasn't sure which. The headmaster had recited the Twenty-third Psalm. So much death. Sometimes his head seemed full of the voices of the dead.

Banks found himself wishing the funeral would soon be over. It wasn't only the weather, the rain dripping down the back of his neck and the wet, cold wind that cut right through three layers of clothing to the bone, but the sight of the coffin perched at the graveside ready to be lowered, knowing that Emily was in there, the once-vital, mischievous spirit who had curled up and slept like a little child with her thumb in her mouth in a hotel room once, with him sitting in the chair listening to Dawn Upshaw's song about sleep. *Cold, cold is the grave,* a line from an old folk ballad passed through his mind. The grave looked cold indeed, but the only one not feeling it now was Emily.

When it was over, the body lowered into its final resting place, people started drifting toward the car park. Ruth and Craig approached the Riddles. The chief constable seemed oblivious to them, and Craig hung back. Ruth said something to Rosalind, something that looked deeply earnest. Rosalind uttered a few words and touched her arm. Then

Rosalind saw Banks alone and walked over to him with an elderly couple in tow.

"My mother and father," she said, introducing them.

Banks shook their hands and offered his condolences.

"Are you coming to the house?" Rosalind asked.

"No," he said. "I'm afraid I can't. Too much work." He could probably have spared half an hour or so, but the truth was that he didn't fancy making small talk with the Riddle family. "What did Ruth want?" he asked.

"Oh, so that's who it is," said Rosalind. "I wondered. She said she was a friend of Emily's and wondered if she might have some sort of keepsake."

"And?"

"I suggested she drop by the house and I'd see what I could do. Why?"

"No reason. The boy with her's Craig Newton. Emily's ex-boyfriend."

"Is he a suspect?"

"Technically, yes. He pestered her after they split up, and he doesn't have an alibi."

"But realistically?"

Banks shook his head. "I don't think so."

Rosalind glanced over at the two of them. "Then I suppose I should invite them both back to the house, shouldn't I?"

"They've come a long way."

"How did they know it was today?"

"I phoned Craig last night. The last time I interviewed him he said he'd like to be there, and I could see no reason why not. He must have contacted Ruth."

Rosalind shook Banks's hand and walked over with her mother and father toward Ruth's car. Banks also saw Darren Hirst and the others who had been in the Bar None with Emily on the night of her death, Tina and Jackie. They all looked shell-shocked. Darren nodded and walked by. That reminded Banks of a glimmer of an idea he'd had, something he wanted to ask Darren. Not now, though; it would keep. Leave the poor lad to his grief for a while.

*   *   *

Back at the office, before Banks could even get his overcoat off and sit down, DS Hatchley knocked on his door and entered.

"How's it going, Jim?" Banks asked.

"Fine. The funeral?"

"What you'd expect."

Hatchley shut the door behind him and sat down opposite Banks. He was the opposite of Annie when it came to looking comfortable, always perched at the edge of the chair, squirming as if something sharp were digging into his arse. He took his cigarettes out and glanced at Banks for permission. Banks got up and opened the window, despite the cold, and both of them lit up.

"It's about Castle Hill Books," said Hatchley. "I sent young Lose-Some out there yesterday afternoon and she came back with an interesting haul."

"Go on."

"The owner's a slimy little sod called Stan Fish. He's been selling porn on the side for years. Anyway, it turns out he's got a whole cupboardful of pirated computer software, games and music CDs. He says he got them from a chap he knows only as Greg. This Greg comes around every couple of weeks in a white van with a selection. So Lose-Some whips out her picture of Gregory Manners, and bob's-your-uncle."

"Good," said Banks. "That'll give us a bit of extra ammunition." He looked at his watch. "Manners is on his way here as we speak."

"Lose-Some also brought in a few samples of the goods," Hatchley went on. "Vic Manson's checking them for prints now. I'll get him to put a rush on it. If he can match them with Manners's . . ."

"It still doesn't give us much, though," said Banks. "Even if we can do Manners for pirating and distributing copyrighted software, it's hardly a serious charge."

"It might give you a handle on this other villain you're after, though."

"Barry Clough?"

"Aye." Hatchley stubbed out his cigarette. "Yon Lose-

Some has also been showing Manners's picture around Daleview and a couple of people recognized him."

"Nobody's seen Clough, Andy Pandy or Jamie Gilbert around there, though?"

"Not yet, but we're still asking." Hatchley got up to leave. Before he could go, the door opened and Detective Superintendent Gristhorpe barged in brandishing one of the more notorious London tabloids. Gristhorpe sniffed the air, scowled at both of them, then said, "Seen the papers this morning, Alan?"

Banks looked at the newspaper. "Even if I'd had time," he said, "it wouldn't have been that one."

A smile split Gristhorpe's ruddy, pockmarked face. "Wouldn't be my first choice either," he said. "More the sort of thing you'd be reading, eh, Sergeant Hatchley?"

"If I'd time, sir," muttered Hatchley, edging his way out of the office, winking at Banks as he shut the door behind him.

Gristhorpe dropped the tabloid on Banks's desk. "You'd better have a gander, Alan," he said. "It looks as if I'm going to be on damage control for the rest of the day." Then he left as abruptly as he'd entered.

The color cover photo in itself was almost enough to give Banks a heart attack. There were two photos, actually, one of Barry Clough leaving a Soho restaurant, thrusting his palm toward the cameraman, and one of Jimmy Riddle leaving police headquarters. The way the photos were arranged together made it look as if the two men were meeting face-to-face. Centered below them was a photograph of Emily. It was a good one, professional, and it featured her "sophisticated" heroin-chic look. She had her blond hair piled up in an expensive mess and wore a strapless black evening gown. Not the same dress she'd been wearing the night of the hotel room, but a similar one. Banks had seen the picture before, or one very much like it, in Craig Newton's house. Could Craig have sold it to the newspapers? Was he still that bitter over his split-up with Emily? More likely, Banks thought, that Barry Clough had got hold of some copies when Emily was living with him and that this was his response to Emily's death and Riddle's silence.

The headline screamed up at him: "CHIEF CONSTABLE'S DAUGHTER MURDER CASE: WHAT ARE THEY HIDING?" The story went on to tell of Emily's association with "well-known club owner and man-about-town Barry Clough," a man "the same age as her senior policeman father." After a couple of not so subtle indications that "well-known club owner and man-about-town" was sort of shorthand for gangster, there were a couple of morally high-handed digressions of the "Do you know what your daughter's doing and who she's with tonight?" sort before the reporter got the real nitty-gritty: speculation about Clough's expanding his "business empire" up north, and about his and Riddle's being involved in some sort of crooked partnership. Emily's role in all this was left to the readers to guess.

The article had obviously been vetted by the paper's solicitors, and it stopped just short of libel. For example, never at any point did the reporter state that Riddle and Clough *had* met and talked, or that Riddle had known about Emily's relationship with Clough—the reporter clearly hadn't found out about Scarlea House yet—but the whole thing was a masterpiece of innuendo, and the implications in themselves were damaging enough. Banks could only imagine how Riddle's political cronies would react to it.

Banks also realized that the damage wouldn't stop with the political set either; this sort of thing could also easily make Riddle a pariah on the Job. Whether there was anything in them or not, such rumors could effectively end his police career. Already Banks suspected there were mutterings at high levels about a chief constable so careless as to let his own daughter get murdered while snorting cocaine in a nightclub. Not to mention the rumors of drugs and sex that went with it all. One way or another, as a politician or as a high-ranking copper, Banks imagined that Jimmy Riddle's tenuous reign had come to an end. Humpty-Dumpty.

What surprised Banks was that he felt sorry for the poor bastard.

And what about Rosalind and Benjamin? What would all this do to them?

Banks still remembered Ruth Walker's final question to him only last Saturday: *Why* did Emily's father want her back, when he hadn't appeared to care about her before? Banks had thought about that a lot since. At first he had suspected Riddle wanted her back to avoid more damage to his career and, to credit him with some fatherly feelings, because he was worried about her after he saw the photos on the porno Web site. Perhaps he was wrong about that. At some point in the investigation, the Riddles themselves had joined the group of suspects in Banks's mind.

The big problem with Jimmy Riddle as a suspect was that whichever way you looked at it, Emily's murder only made things *worse* for him. Sure, her continuing existence had always held out the risk of scandal, but her death *guaranteed* it. On the other hand, given the pressure that Riddle might have been under since Clough's approach at Scarlea, something could have snapped in him.

And what about Rosalind? She hadn't particularly wanted Emily back at home. She had made that clear from the start. What if she had a good reason for it, and Emily had become, somehow, a threat to her? But how? Why? It still didn't feel right, especially given the method, but perhaps it was time to start pushing the grieving parents a bit harder.

A knock at his door jolted him out of his musings. It was DC Templeton.

"Yes, Kev?"

"Thought you'd like to know, sir, uniformed just brought Gregory Manners in. He's waiting in interview room three."

"Thanks, I'll be right there. Ask DS Hatchley to sit in, too, will you?"

"Will do, sir."

"By the way, where'd they find him?"

"Strangest place you could imagine."

"Oh? And where's that?"

DC Templeton grinned. "At home, sir. Nice little flat out Thirsk way."

Banks grinned back. "Oh, and Kev, there's one more thing I'd like you to do."

Gregory Manners was a smoothie, right from his carefully combed, impossibly brown hair to the soles of his Italian loafers. He was good-looking in a way, and Banks could see that he might appeal to a certain kind of woman.

The interview room was a dingy, airless sort of place with whitewashed walls, a tiny wire-mesh window and metal table and chairs bolted to the floor. The old blue ashtray, stolen from the Queen's Arms, was gone now that smoking had been banned from the building, but the air still seemed to smell of stale smoke, sweat and fear. Manners sat there coolly, legs crossed, idly staring into space. When Banks and Hatchley entered he asked why he had been brought there.

Banks ignored him and checked the tapes in the recording machine. Hatchley sat impassive as Buddha, and almost as fat.

The tapes worked. Banks went through the time, date and place routine, naming those present in the room, then he turned to Manners and said, "You're here to help us with our inquiries, Mr. Manners."

"What inquiries?"

"Things will become clear as we move along."

Manners leaned forward and rested his arms on the table. "Should I have my lawyer present?"

"I understand you put in a call to your solicitor before you left home?"

"Before I was brought here, yes. And all I got was his answering machine."

"They're busy people. You left a message?"

"I told him to get up here sharpish."

"In the meantime, you've been offered the services of a duty solicitor?"

"Some wet-behind-the-ears little pillock who can't get a proper job?"

"And you've declined?"

"Yes."

"In that case, Mr. Manners, let's proceed with the interview. Just for the record, you haven't been charged with anything yet so there's no need to get overexcited. I'm sure your own solicitor will get here as soon as he possibly can, but in the meantime let's just have a little chat, all right?"

Manners narrowed his eyes but sat back in his chair and relaxed, crossing his legs again. "What do you want to know? I've done nothing wrong."

"I'm sure you haven't." Banks took the CD case that Annie had found at PKF out of its envelope and pushed it over the rickety metal table to Manners. "Know what this is?"

Manners looked at it. "It's a CD container."

"Good. Maybe you can tell me what your fingerprints are doing on this particular CD container?"

"I suppose I must have touched it."

"Yes," said Banks. "Indeed, you must have touched it. Can you tell me what you were doing at the Daleview Business Park?"

"Daleview? Working. Why?"

"I don't know, Gregory. That's why I'm asking you."

"Well, that's what I was doing. Working. I don't understand this. I haven't done anything illegal. Why are you questioning me?"

"We want to know about the operations of PKF Computer Systems."

"What about it?"

"Is that who you worked for at Daleview?"

"Yes. But I still don't understand what you're getting at."

"And what if I told you that it's a dummy company? That it doesn't exist?"

"Then I'd be very surprised indeed."

"Who set it up?"

"What?"

"PKF."

"I did, of course. The whole thing's me. Just me. Look, there must be some mistake."

"There's no mistake."

"A mistake with the paperwork. I was sure I did it right."

"There is no paperwork, Gregory. Bugger all. PKF doesn't exist."

"Well, if it doesn't exist, then I can hardly know anything about it, can I? So why don't I just leave now?"

"Sit down!" Hatchley slammed his ham-sized fist on the table and the noise made Manners jump.

"Hey," said Manners. "There's no need for that. That's intimidation."

"Any more of this bollocks, and I'll show you what intimidation is," growled Hatchley.

"I'm sure if you just answer my questions as clearly and fully as you can, DS Hatchley will listen as eagerly as I will, won't you, Sergeant?"

"Aye," said Hatchley, "soon as he stops trying to feed us this crap."

Manners swallowed. "Look, what do you want to know? I'm sorry if I ballsed up the paperwork. Is it a criminal offense?"

"Probably," said Banks, "but we'll worry about that later. What did you do at PKF?"

"Developed, produced and marketed a commercial database program."

"Called?"

"PKF."

"You invented this?"

"I did."

"You worked alone?"

"For the most part."

"It sounds like a lot of work for one person."

"I've never been afraid of hard work. On occasion, I hired casual labor to help with distribution and such things."

"People like Jonathan Fearn?"

Manners frowned. "The name doesn't ring a bell, but I might have, yes."

Banks took the photographs of Andrew Handley, Jamie Gilbert and Barry Clough out of his file folder and slid them across to Manners. "Ever seen any of *these* men?"

"No."

Banks tapped the picture of Clough. "This one in particular," he said. "Go on, have a good look. Think about it."

"I told you. No."

"Didn't you do six months for smuggling offenses down south not long ago?"

"I just happened to get caught doing something people get away with every day."

"You must be a heavy smoker and drinker, then."

"I don't smoke."

"So you were going to sell the goods you smuggled?"

"Of course I was going to sell them. People go over to Calais and load up their cars every bloody weekend, for crying out loud. What's this got to do with anything?"

Banks tapped Clough's photo again. "We have information that leads us to believe this man was behind both the smuggling operation *and* whatever PKF was up to."

"Then your information is wrong. I've never seen him in my life. Or the other two. I *imported* the stuff myself, and I also ran PKF. Which wasn't up to anything, by the way. Maybe I got the paperwork wrong, maybe I just forgot to make everything all official, but if that's why I'm here, just charge me and get it over with. You know I'll be walking out the minute my lawyer gets here."

"Who said anything about charging you?"

"I can't understand why else you had me brought here."

"What's happened to PKF?"

"I'm sure you know already," said Manners. "The van was hijacked on its way to our new business' premises in Northumbria and everything was stolen. There *is* no PKF anymore."

"And the driver was killed."

"Yes. Very unfortunate, that."

"A Mr. Fearn. Jonathan Fearn."

"Yes, well, as I said, I'm sorry, but I don't remember his name. I simply hired him to do the job."

"Where did you find him?"

"Mr. Courage, the night watchman at Daleview, recommended him."

"Ah, yes," said Banks, shuffling some papers in his folder. "Charlie Courage. Small-time villain. Must have got in over his head."

Manners frowned. "Come again?"

"Funny you should mention Mr. Courage, Greg. He also met with an unfortunate accident, shortly after Mr. Fearn. He found himself at the wrong end of a shotgun."

"Yes, I read about that in the paper," said Manners. "It was a terrible shock. He seemed a decent-enough bloke."

"He was a crook, but you know all about that. Let's move on."

"By all means." Manners shifted in his chair and re-arranged his legs.

"Do you believe in coincidences?"

"They happen all the time."

"And do you believe that the van getting hijacked, Jonathan Fearn dying of injuries received, and Charlie Courage being shot just happen to be coincidences?"

"They could be."

"Why were you leaving Daleview?"

"The rent was too expensive. This new place was cheaper, and the space was better. Bigger."

"Tell me again what PKF actually did."

"I manufactured and distributed a database system I invented."

"Background in computers? College?"

"Self-taught. A lot of people in the business are."

"To whom did you distribute this software?"

"Retailers."

"Names?"

"Look, I'm sure I have a list somewhere. What is this all about?"

The knock came at the door, as arranged, and it couldn't have been better timed. Banks announced DC Templeton's arrival and paused the tape. "What is it, Kev?"

"Thought you might be interested in this, sir," said Templeton, glancing at Manners as he spoke. "It's just come in from fingerprints. Those CD cases."

"Ah, yes," said Banks. "Let's have a look, shall we?" He opened the file. Templeton left the office. Banks pored over the file frowning for a while, showed the papers to Hatchley, then he set the tapes going again.

"This is interesting," he said to Manners.

"What is it?"

"Fingerprint results. Another CD case."

"But I don't understand. You've already found my prints on the CD case. I've explained that to you already."

"But this is different, see, Greg," said Banks. "This is another case entirely."

"Well, I'm sure I've touched more than one."

"Yes, but it's where we found it and what it contained that interests me."

Manners seemed to turn a little pale. "I don't . . . where *did* you find it?"

"Shop called Castle Hill Books. Run by a man called Stan Fish. Ring any bells?"

"He might have been one of my retailers."

"For your PKF database software?"

"Yes."

"Then how come this particular case contained a brand-new Sony PlayStation game?"

"I don't know. Maybe the owner of the shop switched them around."

"Could be," said Banks. "In fact, I'd be inclined to believe that would be exactly the case, except . . ."

"Except what?"

"Except we found your prints on six other cases containing the same game, and we have a lot more to test before we're finished. Some of them contain a brand-new music CD by REM. Hardly even in the shops yet. Then there are a few word-processing programs and so forth. Funny, though, Greg, no PKF database system."

Manners crossed his arms. "Right, that's it," he said. "I'm not saying another word until my lawyer gets here."

Two hours later, toward the end of the afternoon, Manners was still in custody waiting for his solicitor and Banks was in his office reading through witness statements when his telephone rang.

It was Dirty Dick Burgess calling from London. "Guess what, Banks."

"You've been made head of the Race Relations Board?"

"Very funny. No. But Andy Pandy's turned up at last."

"Has he, indeed?"

"Thought you'd be interested."

"Any chance of a chat with him in the near future?"

"Not unless you fancy holding a séance. He's dead. Dead as the proverbial doornail, though I never could see how a doornail could be dead as it was never alive in the first place. Anyway, enough philosophical speculation. He's dead."

"Where?"

"Pretty remote spot on the edge of Exmoor. I tell you, Banks, if it weren't for the anorak brigade and the dog-walkers, bless their souls, we'd never find half the corpses we do."

"The long ride?"

"Indeed so."

"Shotgun?"

"Wound to the upper body. Pretty close range. Not much left."

"Same as Charlie Courage. Any signs of torture?"

"Christ, Banks, there's hardly any signs of the poor bugger's *chest*. What do you expect? Miracles?"

"So what do you think?"

"Pretty obvious, isn't it?"

"Humor me."

"Andy Pandy's been a naughty boy. He's ripped off Mr. Clough. Mr. Clough doesn't like being ripped off, so he sends Andy on the long ride. Way I see it."

"And Charlie Courage?"

"Part of it. Hardly an innocent bystander, from what you told me."

"He was taking money from Clough, or from Clough's local oppo Gregory Manners, to make sure PKF operated without hassles. Then suddenly, PKF is moving and Charlie's bonuses are gone. I think Charlie knew where PKF was moving to, and when. And I think Andy Pandy came along with a better offer."

"Why would he do that?"

"Because he's pissed off with Clough for taking him for granted. He wants more respect." And he's also angry with Clough over the incident with Emily, when she kneed him in the balls, Banks thought.

"Maybe," said Burgess, sounding unconvinced.

"So he hijacks the van to set up his own business. The van's full of PKF stock, but more important than that, it's also carrying two or three multidisc copying machines, very valuable pieces of equipment. He thinks Clough will never guess in a million years that he did it. But Clough's no fool. He sends a couple of goons up to push Charlie around a bit. Now, Charlie might have been a crook, but no one ever said he was a brave man. Charlie rats Andy Pandy out under torture, and they're both history. I wondered why Gregory Manners is still alive."

"Come again?"

"Manners was in charge of PKF, so he must have been Clough's first suspect. Clough put the frighteners on him and Manners must have convinced him he had nothing to do with the hijack. Maybe Manners told him Andy Pandy had been hanging about asking questions. We'll probably never know for sure now."

"So what do we do next?"

"We'll keep showing the photographs around Daleview. I've also got Gregory Manners kicking his heels in the cells here waiting for his lawyer, so maybe I'll have another chat with him first."

"He won't tell you anything. Too shit-scared of Clough."

"Probably, but I can push him a bit harder. It'd be nice to threaten him with conspiracy to commit murder or something juicy like that. At the moment there's nothing much except pirating software to hold him on, and that'll probably never stick. Minute his lawyer gets here he'll be off."

"And what's the betting you'll never see him again?"

"I'd put money on it."

"So where do we go with Andy Pandy?"

"We'll have a hell of a job proving it's anything to do with Clough," Banks said. "Anything at the scene?"

"Tire track."

Banks thought for a moment, then said, "I think it's about time we brought Mr. Clough up north for a chat. But first, I've got an idea."

It was late, and Banks was listening to Anne-Sophie Mutter's interpretation of Beethoven's *Spring* violin sonata and reading a biography of Ian Fleming when he heard a car draw up outside. That was unusual in itself. The dirt lane that ran in front of his cottage ended at the woods about ten yards farther, where it became a narrow path between the trees and Gratly Beck. Occasionally, tourists would take the wrong road and have to back out, but not usually at that time of night, or that time of year.

Curious, Banks put down his book, walked over to the window and opened the curtains a few inches. A sporty-looking car, to judge from its shape, had pulled up in front of the cottage and a woman was getting out. He couldn't make out her features, as it was pitch-black outside, she was wearing a scarf, and there were no street lamps on the isolated lane. He would soon find out, though, he thought, as she walked up to his front door and knocked.

When he opened it and saw Rosalind Riddle take off her scarf, he must have looked surprised enough to embarrass her.

"I'm sorry," she said. "Have I come at a bad time?"

"No," said Banks. "No, not at all." He stood aside. "Come in."

As she passed close to him in the doorway he felt her breast brush lightly against his arm, and he thought he could smell juniper berries on her breath. Gin, most likely. He took her fur coat and hung it in the cupboard by the door. Underneath, she was wearing a simple blue pastel dress, more suitable, Banks thought, for summer, than for a miserable winter's night like this one. Still, with a mink on top, you didn't really need anything underneath. He stopped that line of thought before it went any further.

"This is nice," she said, standing and looking around the small room, with its blue walls and melting-Brie ceiling. Banks had hung a couple of watercolors he had picked up at auctions on the walls, and a blow-up of what he thought the best of Sandra's photographs took pride of place over the mantelpiece. It had been taken, coincidentally, not far away from the cottage where Banks now lived alone, and it showed the view down the daleside to Helmthorpe in late evening, with a red-and-orange sunset sprawled across the sky, smoke drifting from the chimneys, the church with its square tower and odd little turret attached to one corner, the dark graveyard where sheep grazed among the lichen-stained tombstones, and crooked rows of flagstone roofs. He and Sandra might no longer be together, but that didn't mean he rejected her talent. There wasn't much furniture in the room, just a sofa under the window and two matching armchairs arranged at angles to the fireplace, where a couple of lumps of peat burned and cast shadows on the walls.

"Do you live here alone?" she asked.

"There's hardly room enough for two."

"I shouldn't have asked. I'm sorry. Of course, I do know something of your circumstances. Your wife . . ."

"Cup of tea or something?"

"Or something. After a day like this one, I need something a bit stronger than tea. Gin and tonic, if you've got it."

"Coming up." Banks went into the kitchen and took the gin out of the cupboard where he kept his haphazard selection of spirits—some rum, a few ounces of vodka, half a bottle of cognac and the Laphroaig single malt, that smoky Islay, his favorite and a constant drain on his wallet.

"How strange."

"What?" Banks turned to see that Rosalind had followed him into the kitchen. She was standing at its center with an odd expression on her face, as if she were listening to a distant voice.

"It feels . . . I don't know . . . sort of haunted, but in a good way."

Banks was gob-smacked. One of the reasons he had bought the house in the first place was that he had dreamed of the kitchen before he knew it existed—a dream full of warmth and feelings of extreme well-being—so that when he saw it, he knew he had to have it. Luckily the old lady who was selling didn't want it to fall into the hands of an absentee landlord, so she let him have it for the ridiculously low price of £50,000—a gift when you considered that there were semis and terrace cottages smaller even than this one going for £70,000 and above in some of the more popular Dales villages.

All Banks sensed about the kitchen was that there was definitely some sort of presence, that it was benevolent, and—only God knew why—that it was feminine. He didn't really believe in gods and ghosts, had never thought much about them, being a more practical sort of man, but this was another change that had taken place since Sandra left. In the end, he accepted, even embraced, whatever the presence was, and came to believe it was some sort of spirit of the house, the way places are said to have spirits. He had read a little about the subject and named his spirit Haltia, after the Finnish, generally believed to be the spirit of the first person to lay claim to a site either by lighting a fire on it, by building a house on it, or even, in some cases, the first person to die there.

Rosalind was the first person other than Banks to feel it. Others had been there—Tracy, Brian, Sandra, Annie, Superintendent Gristhorpe, Jim Hatchley—but none of them had felt the preternatural appeal of the kitchen. Banks felt almost inclined to tell Rosalind about the dream, but he held back for some reason. He hadn't told anyone about it yet for fear of seeming foolish or mad, and there was no point starting now.

"It's a comfortable room to be in," he said, pouring the drink. "You should see it when the sun's shining through the windows. Glorious." That was his favorite time in the kitchen, when the morning sunlight came skipping over Low Fell and sliding down the green daleside, spilling into the kitchen like honey. That wouldn't happen again for a few more months.

"I'd like that," said Rosalind. Then she looked away and

blushed. She had dark semicircles under her eyes, Banks noticed, which made her look mysterious, tragic, even, which was hardly surprising given what she had been through this past while. Despite the poor first impression Rosalind had made on him, Banks found himself thinking that she was a woman he would like to have known, perhaps in another time, another life. Also, in another part of his mind, he suspected that she might have had something to do with her daughter's murder.

"Ice? Lemon?"

"Just the tonic water, please."

Banks handed her the gin and tonic and poured himself a couple of fingers of rapidly dwindling Laphroaig. They went back into the living room. The only light came from the fire and the reading lamp by his armchair. He wondered if he should turn on the overhead light and decided not to. By the look of her as she sat down wearily opposite him, Rosalind Riddle looked glad of the semidarkness. He turned down the music and lit a cigarette.

"How was the get-together?"

"What you'd expect. You were fortunate you had work to keep you away."

"I'm not good at those sorts of things. Did you get a chance at talk to Ruth and Craig?"

"A little. You know what these things are like."

"What was your impression?"

"He seemed a nice-enough boy."

"He probably is," Banks said. "And Ruth?"

"I didn't really get much chance to talk to her. I'm just glad that it's over, that's all."

"Why did you want to see me? Was there something you wanted to tell me?"

"Tell you? No. What makes you think that?"

"What is it, then?"

She swirled her drink in her glass before answering. "I'm worried about Jerry. He's taking this all very badly."

"It's hardly surprising. I mean, after all, your only daughter is dead, murdered. He's bound to take it badly. He's not made of stone. And now this thing in the newspaper."

"No, it's more than that."

"What do you mean?"

Rosalind sighed and stretched her legs out, crossing them at the ankles. It was a gesture that reminded Banks of Annie Cabbot.

"All his life," Rosalind began, "the only thing that's counted for Jerry was his work. The Job. You know what it's like, what the demands are. The sacrifices he's made . . . we've made . . ." She gave a quick shake of her head. "I'm not saying he doesn't love us, his family, but we've taken the backseat all along. *My* career's taken a backseat, too. We've always had to move where and when Jerry wanted, no matter what I was doing or how well the children were getting on at school. It's been hard, but I accept it. I don't mind. After all, I don't *have* to stay if I don't want to. But the rewards have made it worthwhile. I know you think he's a social climber and maybe he is, but his origins are pretty humble. Like yours, I should imagine."

Banks smoked and listened. He had never thought about Riddle's origins before but remembered he had vaguely heard something about his coming from a farmworker's family in Suffolk. He got the impression that Rosalind just wanted to talk, and he was quite happy to let her ramble on as long as she liked, though why she had chosen him to unburden herself on was a mystery. Still, it felt good to have an attractive woman in the house—and one who understood the spirit of the place, at that—even if she was Jimmy Riddle's wife, and for another, there was always the possibility that he might learn something relevant to Emily's murder.

"As I said, he's worked hard and we've made a lot of sacrifices. Jerry isn't . . . I mean, he's not the most demonstrative of men. Our marriage . . . he finds it difficult to show emotion." She smiled. "I know most men are the same, but he's more so. He loved Emily dearly but he's never been able to express it. He's come across as overprotective, a sort of tyrant who sets the rules and leaves them to me to enforce. Which made me a tyrant in my daughter's eyes, too. He was never there when she might have needed him; they never managed to form a strong bond of any kind."

"Yet he loved her?"

"Yes. Dearly. He doted on her and her achievements as much as he's capable of doting on anyone other than himself."

"Why are you telling me all this?"

She smiled. "I don't know. Maybe because you're a good listener."

"Go on."

"There's not much more to tell, really. Because of what's happened, because of the guilt over never having been able to show his feelings, of always trying to control her rather than showing affection, he's coming apart at the seams. He just sits there. Half the time he doesn't even answer when I talk to him. It's as if he's come adrift, got lost in some inner hell and he can't find his way out. After the funeral, it was even worse. I can't talk to him anymore, he's shutting me out. Fortunately Benjamin's gone down to Barnstaple with my parents, or I don't know what I'd do. I know I'm not explaining this very well. I'm not very good with words, but I'm worried about him."

"Is there anything else on his mind?"

"I don't know. Nothing he's told me about, anyway. Isn't it enough?"

"Maybe you should try to get him to seek help? Grief counseling. I'm sure your doctor could recommend the right sort of treatment."

"I've mentioned it, but it's no good, he won't go."

"Then I don't know what to suggest."

"Would *you* talk to him?"

"Me?" Banks almost laughed out loud. "I can't see that doing him any good. You know he can't stand the sight of me."

"You might find that he's softened his attitude toward you a bit lately."

"Since I got Emily to come home?" Banks shook his head. "I don't think so. He's just sticking to the bargain." Banks remembered what Emily had told him about Riddle's envy. Deep-rooted feelings like that didn't just disappear after you'd done someone a favor or two. In most cases they intensified because people who didn't like you to start with resented being beholden to you. Besides, Banks had caught Riddle in a lie, too, and that must rankle. He remembered the guilty expression at the funeral.

"But he wanted you in charge of the investigation."

"That was a purely professional decision."

"I still wish you'd talk to him."

"If he doesn't listen to you, he'd hardly listen to me."

"He might. At least you're a man. He doesn't have a lot of friends."

"What about his political colleagues? He must have friends there."

Rosalind sipped some more gin and tonic. "They're dropping him like a hot potato. It started with Emily's murder, but it's got worse ever since the newspaper article with all those innuendoes. Plenty of phone calls, lots of sympathy, then the old '. . . perhaps it would be best for all us if . . . for the good of the party.' Hypocrites!"

"I'm sorry to hear that."

"Yes, well, I'm sure it will only contribute more proof to your poor theory of human nature, especially the human nature of Conservatives."

Banks said nothing. He looked into the fire and watched the burning peat shift and sigh out a breath of sparks.

"I'm sorry. I shouldn't have said that." Rosalind laughed harshly. "I'm talking about me more than about you. I must admit my own view of human nature has taken a bit of a nosedive over the past few days."

The music ended and Banks let the silence stretch.

"If you want to put something else on, that's all right," said Rosalind. "I like classical music."

Banks went to the stereo and picked another Beethoven violin sonata, the *Kreutzer* this time.

"Mmm," said Rosalind. "Lovely."

Banks marveled at how much she resembled Emily, especially her lips; they were the same full but finely outlined shape and the same natural pinkish red color; they even moved in the same way when she spoke. "I still don't see that there's anything I can do," said Banks. "Even if I do talk to him. And I'm not saying I will."

"You can at least try. If it does no good . . ." Rosalind shrugged.

"What about you?"

"Me? What about me?"

"How are you doing?"

"I'm coping. Surviving. Sometimes I feel as if I'm being pulled apart by millions of little red-hot fishhooks, but other than that, I'm fine." She smiled. "Someone has to be. I went back to the office this afternoon, after everyone had gone. I know it sounds odd, but boring estate deals help keep my mind off more serious matters. But Jerry hasn't even got his work now. He's got nothing. He just sits at home all the time brooding. It's frightening watching someone like him un-ravel. He's always been so strong, so solid."

How the mighty are fallen, thought Banks, but he didn't voice it because it would have been cruel. Even so, he had thought it, and that made him bad; was he such a rotten person? He understood what Rosalind meant, of course; it is far more terrifying to see someone you have always depended on, your rock, crack apart than it is to watch someone who was fragile to start with have yet another breakdown. Banks had a distant aunt who kept having "funny turns," as his mother called them, but as she was mentally flimsy to begin with, no one was much surprised. It wasn't that people didn't sympathize or care, just that her "turns" lacked any sort of tragic dimension.

"All right," he said. "I'll try to make time to go over to-morrow and have a talk with him. I can't promise anything, mind you."

Her face lit up. "You will? But that's wonderful. That's all I ask."

How do I let myself get talked into these things? Banks wondered. Do I look like a sucker? First I give up a week-end in Paris with my daughter—abandoning her to the clutches of the monosyllabic Damon—and head off to Lon-don to look for Emily Riddle, now I'm playing visiting shrink to Jimmy Riddle, the man who's done about as much for my career as Margaret Thatcher did for the trade unions.

"While you're here, there are a couple of things I'd like to ask you, if I may."

"Really?" Rosalind looked away from him and started twisting the wedding ring on her finger. She had finished her drink and let the empty tumbler stand on the arm of the chair.

"Another g and t?"

"No, thanks. I have to drive." She glanced at her tiny gold wristwatch and sat forward. "Besides, I really *should* be getting back. I told Jerry I was going for a drive. I don't like to leave him alone for too long at night. It's a bad time for him."

"I understand," said Banks. "I promise I won't keep you more than a couple of minutes more."

She sat back in the chair but didn't relax. What was she so nervous about? Banks wondered. What was she holding back?

"Ruth Walker told me that you had answered when she phoned to talk to Emily, but you said you'd never heard of her. Why?"

"You surely can't expect me to remember the name of every single person who calls and asks for Emily, can you? Perhaps she never even said what her name was."

"People usually do, though, don't they. I mean, it's only polite to say who you are."

"You'd be surprised how many people lack basic politeness. Or maybe you wouldn't. What exactly are you getting at?"

"I don't know. I just get this funny feeling that there's something you're not telling me. Maybe it's to do with Ruth Walker and maybe it's not, but you get very vague every time her name comes up."

"It must be your imagination."

"Maybe. I've been told more than once that I've got too much of it for my own good. Your husband's told me often enough." Banks leaned forward. "Look, Mrs. Riddle, you probably don't think it's very relevant or important, but I've got to warn you that you're making a poor judgment here. The best course of action is to tell me everything you know and let me be the judge. That's my job."

Rosalind stood up. "Thanks for the advice. If I did know anything of relevance to your investigation, you can be sure I'd take it, but as I don't . . . Anyway, I really must be going now. Thank you very much for your hospitality. You will call in on Jerry tomorrow?"

"Barring any emergencies, yes, I'll call. Don't tell him, though; he might board up the doors and bar the windows." Rosalind smiled. It was a sad smile, Banks thought, but nice nonetheless. "And please think about what I said? If there's anything . . ."

Rosalind nodded quickly and left. Banks stood in the doorway and watched her drive back toward the Helmthorpe road, then he poured another Laphroaig and returned to Anne-Sophie Mutter's Beethoven.

15

Banks and Annie watched Barry Clough walking along the corridor toward them, his police escort following behind, along with another man. Banks noted the Paul Smith suit, the ponytail, the matching gold chain and bracelet, the cocky, confident strut, and thought: *pillock.*

"Sorry to get you out of bed so early, Barry," he said, opening the door to interview room 2, the smallest and smelliest interview room they had. It passed the PACE regulations about the same way Banks's old Cortina had passed its final MOT test: barely.

"You'd better have a damn good reason for dragging me halfway across the country," Clough said cheerfully. "One my lawyer will understand." He gave Annie an appraising look, which she ignored, then turned to the man who had followed him down the corridor.

"Simon Gallagher," the man said. "And I'm the lawyer in question."

And very questionable indeed you look, thought Banks. For once, the client looked better-dressed than the lawyer, but Banks was willing to bet that Gallagher's casual elegance cost every bit as much as Clough's Paul Smith, and that it had been thrown together at short notice. He was also willing to bet that, appearances aside, Gallagher was sharp as a tack and very well-versed in the intricacies of criminal law. He was in his late twenties, Banks guessed, with a heavy five o'clock shadow, and his dark hair hung in greasy strands over his collar. He also had that edgy, wasted look of someone who stays up too late at too many clubs and takes too many class-A drugs. He sniffed the stale air of the interview room and pulled a face.

Annie turned on the tape recorders and went through the preamble, then she sat beside Banks, a little out of Clough's line of vision. On the periphery, Banks had told her, she could remain unnoticed or distract him with a movement if she wished.

"Can we get on with it?" Gallagher said, glancing at his watch. "I've got an important appointment back in the City this evening."

Banks smiled. "We'll do our best to make sure you don't miss it, Mr. Gallagher." Then he turned to Clough. "Do you have any idea why we want to talk to you?"

Clough held out his hands, palm open. "None at all."

"Okay. Let's start with Emily Riddle. You do admit to knowing her?"

"I knew her as Louisa Gamine. You know that. You came to my house."

"But you now know that her real name was Emily Louise Riddle?"

"Yes."

"How did you find out?"

"I told you. I saw it in the papers."

"Are you sure you didn't know before that?"

"How could I?"

"Perhaps the room in your house, the room in which I talked to her, was wired for sound?"

Clough laughed and glanced over at Simon Gallagher. "Get that, Simon. That's a laugh, eh? My house bugged." He looked at Banks again, no longer laughing. "Now you tell me why I'd want to do something like that?"

"Information?"

"What sort of information?"

"Business information?"

"I don't eavesdrop electronically on my clients or my partners, Chief Inspector. Besides, it's my home we're talking about, not my office."

"Let's leave that for the moment, then, shall we?" Banks went on. "What was your relationship with Emily Riddle?"

"Relationship?"

"Yes. You know, the sort of thing human beings have with one another."

Clough shrugged. "I fucked her once in a while," he said. "She was okay in bed. A hell of a lot better than she was at giving blow jobs."

"Is that all?"

"What do you mean, is that all?"

"Did you ever do anything else together? Talk, for example?"

"I suppose we must have, though I can't say I remember a word she said."

"Did you ever tell her anything about your business interests?"

"Certainly not. If you think I'd go around telling some bimbo about my business, you must be crazy."

"Did she live with you?"

"She lived in the same house."

"In Little Venice?"

"Yes."

"Did she live *with* you?"

"We were together some of the time. It's a big house. Sometimes guests come and forget to leave for a long time. You can get lost in there. You should know. You've seen it. Twice."

"Is this what happened with Emily? She sort of got lost in your big house?"

"I suppose so. I don't remember how she got there."

"A party?"

"Probably."

"Did you sleep together?"

"We didn't do much sleeping."

"Look, Chief Inspector," Gallagher chipped in, "this all seems pretty innocuous, as the girl in question was of legal age, but I can't really see where it's getting us."

"Did Emily Riddle know anything at all about your business dealings, Barry?"

"No. Not unless she spied on me."

"Is that possible?"

"Anything's possible. I'm careful, but . . ."

"What exactly *is* your business?"

"Bit of this, bit of that."

"More specifically?"

Clough looked at Gallagher, who nodded.

"I manage a couple of fairly successful rock bands. I own a bar in Clerkenwell. I also promote concerts from time to time. I suppose you could call me a sort of impresario."

"An impresario." Banks savored the word. "If you say so, Barry."

"Has a sort of old-fashioned ring to it, don't you think? 'Sunday Night at the London Palladium' and all that."

"Were you worried that Emily Riddle might have known too much about this impresario business of yours?"

"No. Why would I?"

"You tell me."

"No."

"Did she ever indicate that she did? Did she ask you for money, for example?"

"You mean blackmail?"

"Did she?"

"Emily? No. I told you, she was just some young bimbo I used to fuck, that's all."

"And now she's dead."

"And now she's dead. Sad, isn't it?"

"Yes," said Banks, reining in his rising temper. "It is."

Clough got to his feet. "Is that it, then? Can we go now?"

"Sit down, Barry. You'll go when I tell you to go."

Clough looked at Gallagher, who nodded again.

"Did you see Emily at all after she left London?"

"No. Easy come, easy go."

"Were you at Scarlea House between December the fifth and December the tenth this year?"

"I can't remember."

"Oh, come on, Barry. You were there for the grouse shooting. You had your minder Jamie Gilbert with you and a young woman in tow. Amanda Khan. The pop singer."

"Oh, yes. I remember now."

"Last time I asked you, you said you were in Spain at that time."

"I get confused. I do a lot of traveling. What can I say? But I remember now."

"You didn't see Emily while you were staying in the area?"

"Why would I? Amanda gives far better head."

"For old time's sake?"

"Let go and move on. That's my motto."

"Perhaps to give her a glassine envelope of cocaine laced with strychnine?"

"Chief Inspector," said Gallagher, "you're treading in dangerous territory here. Be careful."

"Did you?" Banks asked Clough.

"Now where would I get hold of strychnine?"

"I daresay you'd have your sources. Cocaine wasn't much trouble, was it?"

"You know as well as I do, Chief Inspector, that there's probably enough of that stuff around at any given moment to pay off the national debt. *If* you like that sort of thing. Not for me, of course. But strychnine . . . I wouldn't know where to start."

"While you were at Scarlea, did you have dinner with Chief Constable Jeremiah Riddle?"

"What if I did?"

"How did you know him?"

"Mutual acquaintance."

"Bollocks, Barry. When Emily left, with the information you'd overheard from our conversation, you found out who she really was, where she lived. And when you found that her father was a senior-ranking policeman, you tried to move in and blackmail him."

"Chief Inspector," Simon Gallagher broke in, "I'm going to have to ask you to stop these absurd insinuations. If you want to question my client, go ahead and question him in the prescribed manner."

"I apologize," said Banks. "Why did you have dinner with Chief Constable Riddle?"

"Why don't you ask him?"

"I already have."

Clough seemed surprised at that, but he soon regained his composure. "We talked about his daughter. And if he told you anything different, then he's a liar."

"How did you feel when Emily left you?"

"Come again?"

"You heard what I said."

"Feel? I didn't feel anything, really. Why would I? I mean she was only—"

"Some bimbo you used to fuck? Yes, yes, so you said before. No need to keep on repeating yourself. But you don't like your bimbos to run out on you, do you? You prefer to give them the boot yourself."

"That's exactly what happened. She'd served her purpose. It was time to move on. She didn't get the message, so I had to help her along a bit."

"By trying to toss her into bed with Andrew Handley?"

"Andy Pandy? What's he got to do with this?"

"You do admit to knowing him, then?"

"He works for me from time to time."

"Not anymore, Barry. He's dead."

"What? Andy? Dead? I don't believe it."

"He was found shot to death near Exmoor. Know anything about that?"

"Of course I don't. It's . . ."

"Sad?"

"Yeah. Andy was all right."

"Is that why you pushed Emily into a room with him?"

"I did no such thing. I've told you before. If she went into a room with Andy, she went on her own accord."

"Sure he didn't get tired of taking your leftovers and decide to strike out for himself?"

"Look, Chief Inspector, my client has answered all these questions before. Unless there's anything new—"

"Gregory Manners," said Banks.

"Who?" said Clough.

"Gregory Manners. He ran the PKF operation for you at Daleview. Remember, I told you. Their van got hijacked on the way to a new location, and the night watchman at Daleview was murdered. Oddly enough, it was the same MO as the Andrew Handley murder."

"I vaguely remember you going on about that when you came to the house with that other copper. I didn't understand why then, and I don't now."

"Right. So what about it?"

"What do you mean?"

"Come on, Barry. We found Gregory Manners's fingerprints on a whole stack of bootlegged games and software. That's what you were doing at PKF. A big operation. You had multidisc copying machines, and they were in that van. Andy Pandy wanted to break away, didn't he, go into business by himself? So he hatched a plot with the night watchman at Daleview. Charlie Courage had already figured out there was something dodgy going on at PKF—Charlie had a nose for that sort of thing—and you were paying him off. Then Andy comes along with a better offer. They arrange it to look like a hijack, but your lads pick up Gregory Manners first, and he tells you he thought there was something fishy going on between Charlie and Andy Pandy. Then you pick up Charlie, and he tells all. So they kill Charlie, and then they kill Andy Pandy. Isn't that how it went?"

Clough turned his head slowly to Gallagher and raised his eyebrows. "Am I missing something, Simon?" he said. "I am Barry Clough, aren't I? Mr. Banks here seems to have me confused with some criminal named Gregory Manners."

Gallagher stood up. "Chief Inspector, you've got an active imagination, I'll say that. But you can't corroborate any of this. You haven't a single shred of evidence connecting my client to either of these men."

"Mr. Manners is still helping us with our inquiries," Banks lied. "We have every reason to believe he'll tell us what he knows when he realizes the full extent of the charges that might be brought against him."

Clough gave Banks a stony gaze. "So what?" he said.

"What about Andrew Handley?" Banks said to Gallagher. "Your client has already admitted to knowing him."

"But that doesn't mean he had anything to do with Mr. Handley's unfortunate demise."

" 'Unfortunate demise?' " Banks repeated. "Andrew Handley's upper body was shredded by a close-range shotgun wound. I'd hardly call that an unfortunate fucking demise."

"Unfortunate turn of phrase," muttered Gallagher. "And there's no need to swear at me."

"We're all adults here, aren't we? And I'm hardly the first."

"There's a lady present," said Clough, grinning at Annie.

"Fuck you," said Annie.

Gallagher waved his hands in the air. "All right, all right, ladies and gentlemen. Can we all just calm down a minute and get back on track? If there *is* a track."

"Thank you, Mr. Gallagher," said Banks. "I believe we were talking about Andrew Handley."

"All right," said Clough. "Yes. I knew him. He worked for me sometimes."

"Doing what?"

"Managing things. I delegate a lot."

Banks laughed out loud.

"Chief Inspector!"

"Sorry. Couldn't help it. Delegate. Right. Would you say the two of you were friends?"

"Not really. We might have a drink together every now and then, talk about business, but other than that, no. I don't know what he got up to."

"Nor he you?"

"Suppose not."

"Do you own a shotgun, Barry?"

"Do I look like a fucking farmer?"

"You certainly have plenty of guns at your London house."

"They're all deactivated and all legal. I'm a collector."

"So you don't own a shotgun?"

"I've already told you."

"No, you haven't. You didn't answer my question. Do you own a shotgun?"

"No."

Banks paused a moment. "Then what did you use for shooting grouse at Scarlea? A peashooter?"

Gallagher put his head in his hands.

"They have guns available to their guests. For rental."

"Oh, come off it, Barry. Do you expect me to believe that a keen regular grouse shooter like you doesn't own a shotgun? I find that difficult."

"Believe what you want."

"We can check."

"Okay, okay. So maybe I own a shotgun."

"Then why didn't you say so?"

"Because the way things are going it looks as if you're trying to pin a fucking murder on me and my fucking lawyer is—"

"Barry!" said Gallagher. "Shut up. Just shut up. Okay? Let me take care of it."

"Lying just makes it worse," said Banks. He tipped Annie the nod and she officially terminated the taped interview.

"What's going on?" Clough asked. "Can I go now?"

"Afraid not, Barry," said Banks. "We'll be issuing a warrant for your shotgun to be examined by forensic experts in the murders of Andrew Handley and Charles Courage."

Clough smiled. "Go ahead. If I did have anything to do with those murders, which I didn't, do you think I'd be stupid enough to use my own shotgun and leave it lying around the house?"

Banks smiled back. "Probably not," he said. "But it doesn't really matter. At least a forensic examination will settle things one way or another, won't it? We're also looking into some tire tracks found at the murder scenes. In the meantime you can sample some of our legendary northern hospitality."

"You mean I can't go?"

Banks shook his head.

"Simon?"

"Your lawyer will tell you we can detain you for twenty-four hours, Barry. Any period of time after that has to be okayed by a more senior officer than me. But if you think that's likely to be a problem, remember that Emily Riddle *was* our chief constable's daughter, you know."

"He can't do this, can he, Simon?"

"I'm afraid he can," said Gallagher, staring at Banks. "But any detention longer than twenty-four hours will come under very severe scrutiny, I can assure you. Now, if you'll excuse me, I'd better cancel my appointment."

Banks opened the door and asked the uniformed officers to escort Clough to the custody suite in the station's basement. "You'll be well taken care of, Barry," Banks said. "Soon be lunchtime. Beefburger and chips, I think it is today. Sorry there's no Château Margeaux to accompany it. You might be able to get a mug of tea. Careful you don't crease your Paul Smith."

While Banks went to pay another visit to the Riddle house, Annie wandered into the incident room to see what was going on. It was a hive of activity; most of the phone lines were busy and the fax machines were churning stuff out. DC Rickerd held sway over it all, a man who had truly found himself. He blushed when Annie gave him a wink.

Poor Winsome was back at the computer, a stack of green sheets for input and another stack she had already entered.

"How's it going?" Annie asked, picking up the entered stack and idly leafing through it. Just because everything went into HOLMES didn't mean any of it was ever seen again, not unless some sort of link or connection came up, and then you had to be looking for it.

Winsome smiled. "Okay, I suppose. Sometimes I wish I'd never done that damn course, though."

"I know what you mean," said Annie. "Still, it'll come in useful when you sit your boards."

"I suppose so."

Annie was hardly reading the information on the entered sheets, more just letting her gaze slip over them, but something she saw on one of them reached out and smacked her right between the eyes. "Winsome," she said, picking it out and putting it on the desk. "What happened with this?"

Winsome scrutinized the sheet. "DCI Banks signed off on it yesterday," she said. "No further action."

" 'No further action,' " Annie repeated under her breath.

"Something wrong?"

"No," said Annie quickly, replacing the sheet in the pile. "Nothing. Just curious, that's all. See you later."

Annie hurried back to her office, aware of Winsome's puzzled gaze, noticed she had it all to herself, picked up the telephone and dialed an outside line.

"Hotel Fifty-Five," the answering voice said. "Can I help you?"

"Mr. Poulson?"

"Oh, you want Roger. Just a minute."

Annie waited a minute and another voice came on the line. "Roger Poulson here. Can I help you?"

"Detective Sergeant Cabbot, Eastvale CID. I understand you phoned our incident room yesterday with information relating to the death of Emily Riddle?"

"I wouldn't go that far," Poulson said. "It was just an odd coincidence, that's all."

"Tell me about it anyway, Mr. Poulson."

"Well, as I said to the gentleman yesterday—"

"What gentleman?"

"The policeman who called me back yesterday. I didn't catch his name."

I'll bet you didn't, thought Annie, and we'd have heard no more about it if I hadn't come across the name and number by accident. *Hotel Fifty-Five.* It was where she had stayed with Banks when they visited London in connection with the Gloria Shackleton case. When they were lovers.

"What did he say?" Annie asked.

"He simply took the details and thanked me for calling. To be honest, I didn't expect to hear any more of it. He didn't sound very interested. Why? Has something turned up?"

Annie felt a tightness in her chest. "No," she said. "Nothing like that. It's just down to me to keep the paperwork up-to-date. You know what it's like."

"Tell me about it," said Poulson. "How can I help you?"

"If you'd just go over the information again briefly . . . ?"

"Of course. As I said, it's nothing, really. It was about a

month ago, when I was on night duty. I think I saw her, the girl who was killed."

"Go on."

"At least, she looked sort of like the girl in the newspaper photo yesterday, with her hair up, a nice evening gown. Mostly it's the eyes and lips, though. I'd almost swear it was her."

"You say you saw her at the hotel?"

"Yes."

"Was she a guest?"

"Not exactly."

"What do you mean?"

"Well, she walked in—I think she'd just got out of a taxi—and said she wanted to see her father."

"Her father?" Annie was confused. She didn't know that Jimmy Riddle had been down to London looking for his daughter, only Banks. She felt icy water rising fast around her ankles.

"That's right. She said he was staying here. I had no reason not to believe her."

"Of course not. What did you do?"

"I called his room and told him his daughter was in the lobby, wanting to see him, and she was in a bit of a state. Naturally, he told me to send her up. The thing was, you see, she looked very disheveled, as if she'd been attacked or involved in some rough stuff. Natural to come to Daddy under such circumstances, even if it was three o'clock in the morning."

"When you say rough stuff, what exactly do you mean?"

"Nothing really serious, but there was a tear in her dress and a little blood at the corner of her lip."

"What happened after she'd gone up?"

"Nothing. I mean, I didn't see anything. I was on duty until eight o'clock the next morning, and I didn't see either of them again."

"So she stayed in his room the rest of the night?"

"Yes."

The cold water was up to Annie's navel by now and she decided to plunge right in. Sometimes it was the best way. "What was her father's name?"

"Well, it wasn't Riddle, like it says in the paper. As I said to your colleague yesterday, that's why I thought it was funny. So I pulled the credit card slip. He's stayed with us here before, I remember. Once with a very attractive young lady. His name is Banks. Alan Banks."

The shock numbed Annie's blood, even though she had been half expecting it. She thanked Mr. Poulson, then hung up in a daze. *Banks*. In a hotel room with Emily Riddle half the night. The *same* hotel he'd taken Annie to. *And he hadn't told her.* This put a new complexion on things indeed.

Banks slipped the tape he had made of Brian's band's CD in the cassette player and reflected on his interview with Clough as he drove out to the Old Mill. Clough was still cooling his heels in the holding cells, but they wouldn't really be able to hold him much after the following morning. Gallagher was right about that. Any infringement of PACE because Clough was a suspect in the murder of the chief constable's daughter would go down very badly indeed and only increase his chances of getting off scot-free. That was how things were now. In the old days, they used to be different, of course, and Banks still wasn't certain which was best. He just hoped to hell that some of the information he was desperate for arrived before the deadline.

The question he always came back to, though, was that if Clough *had* killed Emily, what was his motive? Clough was an astute gangster, surely smart enough not to let an affair with a sixteen-year-old girl ruin the rest of what was clearly a charmed and profitable life. Still, Banks thought, remembering the famous gangsters of movieland—James Cagney, Edward G. Robinson—there were plenty of mob bosses who were also psychopaths and killed for reasons other than pure business. If Banks were Clough, though, when he found out that Emily had gone and then discovered she was a chief constable's daughter, he would have cut his losses and left well enough alone. But perhaps that was why Banks *wasn't* Clough.

Had Emily really been doing something foolish, like trying to blackmail Clough? Banks didn't think so. She was a mixed-up kid, but he didn't think she was a blackmailer. He had also got the feeling from talking to her that she was genuinely scared of Clough, and that the more permanent distance there was between them, the better. Besides, her family didn't lack for money, and as Riddle had pointed out at the start, they had spoiled her rotten. Even so, the idea of an undisclosed income of her very own might appeal. But would it overcome her fear?

Also, why would Clough wait so long to kill her if he was after revenge for her leaving? It was over a month since Banks had brought Emily back from London. Perhaps it had taken him that long to find out who and where she was. Or perhaps it had taken her that long to start blackmailing him. There had been no telephone calls to Clough on Riddle's phone records, but that didn't necessarily mean Emily hadn't called him from a public box. Something about the sparse phone records nagged at his mind, but he couldn't quite grasp it. Never mind. As his mother always said, if it was that important, it would come to the surface soon enough.

He showed his warrant card to the officers at the end of the lane, and they waved him through. A hundred yards farther on, he pulled up on the gravel drive outside the Old Mill and turned off the engine. The rain had stopped but it had swelled the millrace, which sounded even louder and faster than on his last visit.

This time, Riddle wasn't watching for his arrival. He wondered if Rosalind had told him Banks was coming. He hoped not. He knocked at the door and waited. Nothing. Surely Riddle couldn't have gone back to work already? He knocked again, harder, in case the noise from the stream was covering the sound. Still nothing.

Banks stepped back a few paces from the front door and looked at the front of the house. No windows open. It was a dull afternoon, and someone at home might have put a light or two on, but none showed. Perhaps Riddle had gone out, maybe for a long drive to think things over. Banks felt relief. He had come to fulfill his promise to Rosalind, but it wasn't *his* fault if Riddle wasn't home. What more could he do?

But surely, if Riddle had gone out, the duty officers would have told Banks?

It was then that he became aware of another faint noise beyond the sound of the rushing millrace. At first, it didn't mean much, then, when he realized what it was, it sent a chill through him.

It was coming from the converted barn, and it was the sound of a car engine idling.

Banks dashed toward the barn, doubting his own ears at first, but there was no mistaking the smooth purr of the German engineering. The garage door was closed but not locked. Banks bent and grasped the handle, pulling as he moved back, and the door slid up smoothly and silently on its overhead runners. The stink of exhaust fumes hit him immediately, and he staggered back, digging his hands in his raincoat pocket for a handkerchief. He couldn't find one, but he went in anyway with his forearm over his nose and mouth.

It was dark and smoky inside the garage, and Banks couldn't make out very much at first. His eyes adjusted as he moved inside, noticing that rolled-up cloths or towels had been placed against the gap between the floor and bottom of the garage door on the inside. He did the best he could to keep the fumes at bay, covering his mouth and nose with one hand, breathing only as little as necessary. At least now air from outside was displacing the carbon monoxide.

When Banks got to the car, he could see Riddle slumped across the two front seats. There was no way of knowing yet whether he was dead, so Banks first tried to open a door. They were all locked. He looked around and found a crowbar on one of the shelves. Standing back and swinging it hard, he broke open one of the back windows to avoid disturbing the front, reached inside and disengaged the lock mechanism. Then he opened the front door at the driver's side, reached across Riddle and turned off the engine. The fumes were dissipating slowly now the garage doors stood wide open, but Banks was beginning to feel nauseated and dizzy.

He felt for a pulse and found none. Riddle's whole face

was as red as his bald head got when he was angry. Cherry-red. The hosing he had rigged from the exhaust to the back window was still in place. He had opened the window a crack to admit it and stuffed the opening with oil-stained rags.

Riddle was wearing his uniform, everything polished, shiny in order, apart from the thin streak of yellowish vomit down his front. Above the dashboard was a sheet of paper with handwriting on it. Leaving it where it was, Banks leaned over and squinted. It was short and to the point:

> *The game's over. Please take care of Benjamin and try to ensure that he doesn't think too ill of his father. I'm sorry.*
>
>   JERRY.

Banks read it again, angry tears pricking at his stinging eyes. You bastard, he thought, *you selfish bastard.* As if his family hadn't suffered enough already.

Groggy and sick, Banks stumbled outside and made it to the millrace before he emptied out his lunch. He bent over and took handfuls of cold clear water and splashed it over his face, drinking down as much of it as he could manage. He knew that there were two officers only a hundred yards away, but he wasn't sure his legs would carry him that far, so he went back to his car, picked up his mobile and called the station, then he bent forward, put his hands on his knees and took deep breaths as he waited for the circus to begin.

16

Banks spent the evening at home trying to make sense of the day's events. He still felt weak and nauseated, but apart from that, there seemed no serious damage. The ambulance crew had insisted on giving him oxygen and taking him to Eastvale General for a checkup, but the doctor pronounced him fit to go home, with a warning to lay off the ciggies for a while.

From what he had been able to piece together so far, it appeared almost certain that Riddle had committed suicide. They wouldn't know for sure until Dr. Glendenning performed the postmortem, probably tomorrow, but there were no signs of external violence on Riddle's body, the note appeared to be in his handwriting, and the rags and towels used to keep the petrol fumes in the garage had been placed on the *inside* of the doors, after they had been closed. There were no windows or other means of exit.

Banks would never have pegged Riddle as the suicidal type, but he would be the first to admit that he had no idea if such a type existed. Certainly the murder of his daughter, the destruction of all his political and professional hopes, and the smear campaign started against him in the tabloid would be enough to drive anyone over the edge.

So suicide it may be, Banks thought, but Barry Clough still had a lot to answer for. Clough was enjoying the hospitality of the Eastvale cells that night, while the detectives and forensic experts mobilized by Burgess down south were working overtime following up all the leads they had on the Charlie Courage and Andy Pandy shootings. With any luck, by tomorrow Banks would have something more substantial to confront Clough with in the interview room.

It was nine o'clock when a car pulled up and someone knocked at the door. Puzzled, Banks went to see who it was.

Rosalind Riddle stood there in the cold night air, wearing only a long skirt and sweater. "Can I come in?" she said. "It's been a hell of a day."

Banks could think of no reply to that. He stood aside to let her in and shut the door behind her. She smoothed down her skirt and sat in the armchair by the fire, rubbing her hands together. "There's a chill in the air," she said. "We might get frost tonight."

"What are you doing here?" Banks asked.

"I've been going insane just sitting around the house. Charlotte came to stay with me for a while but I sent her away. She's nice, but you know, we're not *that* close. It's so empty, and there's nothing to do there. My mind has been running around in circles. I want to talk to you. It seemed . . . I don't know . . . I'm sorry. Perhaps I shouldn't have come." She moved to stand up.

"No. Sit down. You might as well stop. You're here now. Drink?"

Rosalind paused. "Are you sure?"

"Yes."

"All right." She sat down again. "Thank you. I wouldn't mind a glass of white wine, if you have any."

"I'm afraid I've only got red."

"Okay."

"It's nothing fancy."

She smiled. "Don't worry. I might be a snob about some things, but not about wine."

"Good." Banks headed into the kitchen to open the Marks and Sparks Bulgarian Merlot. He poured himself a glass, too. He had a feeling he would need it. After he had handed Rosalind her drink, Banks sat opposite her. She had clearly made an effort to look her best, wearing an expensive gray skirt and Fair Isle jumper, applying a little makeup to give some color to her pallid features, but there was no disguising the bruiselike circles under her eyes, or the rims pink from crying. This was a woman hanging on the edge by her fingernails.

"How are you?" he asked. It sounded like a stupid question after what had happened to her, but he couldn't think of anything else to say.

"I'm . . . I . . . I don't really know. I thought I was coping, but inside . . ." She tapped her chest. "It all feels so tight and hot inside here. I keep thinking I'm going to explode." Her eyes brimmed with tears. "It's quite a thing, you know, losing both your daughter and your husband within a week of one another." She gave a harsh laugh, then thumped the armrest of her chair. "How *dare* he do this? How *dare* he?"

"What do you mean?"

"He's run away from it all, hasn't he? And where does that leave me? A cold, heartless bitch because *I'm* still alive? Because I didn't care about my daughter's murder enough to kill myself over it?"

"Don't do this, Rosalind," said Banks, getting up and putting his hands on her shoulders. He could feel the little convulsions as grief and anger surged through her.

After a while, she reached up and gently disengaged his hands. "I'm all right," she said, wiping the tears out of her eyes. "I'm sorry for inflicting myself on you, but it's been on my mind all day. Going over and over it again. I can't understand my feelings. I should feel sorrow, loss . . . but all I feel is anger. I *hate* him. I hate him for doing this! And I hate myself for feeling like that."

Banks could do nothing but sit down helplessly and let her cry again. He remembered his own reaction to finding Riddle's body; there had been a lot of anger in that too, before it gave way to guilt. *The selfish bastard.*

When Rosalind had finished, he said, "Look, I can't pretend to know how you feel, but I feel terrible myself. If I'd gone out there sooner I might have saved him." It sounded even more pathetic than his opening gambit, but he felt he had to get it off his chest.

Rosalind gave him a sharp look. "You? Don't be silly. Jerry was a very determined man. If he wanted to kill himself, he'd damn well do it, one way or another. There was nothing you could have done except perhaps postpone the inevitable."

"Even so . . . I keep thinking if only I hadn't put off the visit. If only I hadn't . . . I don't know."

"Disliked him so much?"

Banks looked away. "I suppose that's a part of it."

"Don't worry. Jerry wasn't a very likable man. Even death won't change that. There's no sense in your feeling guilty."

"I've been thinking about what might have caused him to do it," Banks said after a short pause. "I know you said he was depressed over Emily's death and all the fallout that engendered, but somehow, even all that just didn't seem enough in itself."

"He was upset about those lies in the newspaper."

Banks paused. He knew he shouldn't be telling Rosalind about her husband's problems with Barry Clough, but he felt she deserved something from him; he also thought it might put Riddle's death in perspective for her a little more clearly. Call it guilt talking. He took a deep breath, then said, "I was out at a place called Scarlea House yesterday afternoon. Ever heard of it?"

"I've heard of it, yes. It's an upmarket shooting lodge, isn't it?"

"Yes. According to the bartender, your husband had dinner with Barry Clough there the Sunday before last."

Rosalind paled. "Barry Clough?"

"Yes. The man Emily lived with for a while in London."

"I remember the name. And you're telling me that Jerry had *dinner* with him?"

"Yes. Are you sure you didn't know?"

"No. Jerry never said anything to me about it. I knew he was out for dinner that night, yes, but I thought it was just one of his political things. I'd stopped asking him where he went a long time ago. How would a newspaper find out about that anyway, even if it is true?"

"They didn't have to know about that specific meeting,"

said Banks. "Remember, the article never made any direct assertions; it was all innuendo. It's even possible that someone on the staff at Scarlea House—one of the waiters, perhaps—talked to a reporter but refused to be quoted as a source. I don't know. These journalists have their tricks of the trade. The point is that it happened. Did you have any idea at all that your husband had talked to or met with Clough?"

"No. Absolutely none."

Banks believed her. For one thing, Riddle wasn't stupid enough to tell his wife he was having dinner with the man suspected of murdering their daughter. "Your husband told me that Clough was trying to blackmail him. Using Emily."

"But Jerry would never agree to anything like that."

"I think that was his dilemma. That was what tore him apart. Certainly Emily's murder hurt him deeply, but this was what finally pushed him over the edge. There he was, a man of honor, who has to decide whether he wants to fall into the hands of a gangster or have his daughter and, by extension, his entire family, vilified in public."

"Are you saying that he didn't know whether he would have done what Clough asked or not, and he couldn't face making the decision?"

"Possibly. But going by the tabloid article, it looks as if he had already turned Clough down, or that Clough had lost patience waiting."

"If Clough was behind it."

"Who else?"

"I don't know." Rosalind leaned forward. "But, if all you're saying is true, it doesn't make sense . . ."

"For Clough to kill Emily?"

"No."

"That's true. That's what your husband said, too, when I asked him about it. Clough had nothing to gain. I still think he's a strong candidate, but I must admit the whole thing's been puzzling me a lot."

"Who, then?"

"I don't know. I feel as far away from a solution as I ever have."

"What will you do about Clough?"

"Keep at him. There are other things we want to talk to him about, too. I've got to tell you, though, that I'm not at all hopeful about convicting Clough of anything, no matter what he's done."

"Why not?"

"A man like him? If he can blackmail a chief constable, imagine what else he's got going, who he might have in his pocket. Besides, he never does anything himself. He delegates, keeps his hands clean. Even if, for some reason we haven't considered, he was responsible for Emily's murder, he'd have got one of his minions like Andrew Handley or Jamie Gilbert to do the dirty work. And he's rich. That means he'll be able to afford the best defense."

"Sometimes I wish I was in criminal law," Rosalind said, her eyes burning. "I'd love to take on his prosecution."

Banks smiled. "First we'd have to persuade the CPS it was worth pursuing, and that's a Herculean effort in itself. In the meantime, we've still got a murderer to catch."

Rosalind sipped some wine. At least she didn't pull a face and spit it out. "You've probably deduced this already," she said, "but our marriage was very much a matter of convenience. He gave me the things I wanted and I didn't embarrass him in public. I like to think I might even have helped him advance. Other than that, we went our separate ways."

"Affairs?"

"Jerry? I don't think so. For one thing, he didn't have the time. He was married to his work and his political ambitions." She looked Banks straight in the eye. "Me? A few. Nothing important. All discreet. None recently."

They sat quietly for a few seconds. A gust of wind rattled the loose window upstairs. "You said you wanted to talk to me?" Banks said.

"Oh, it's nothing to do with the murder. I'm sorry. I didn't mean to mislead you in any way. It's just that, well, you give the impression you think I've been holding something back, not telling you everything."

Banks nodded. "Yes. I do think that. I have done from the start."

"You're right."

"And now you're going to tell me?"

"No reason not to, now. But first, do you think I might have another glass of wine?"

That evening at home, Annie reheated some vegetable curry in a bowl and sat in front of the television, hoping the flickering images would take her mind off her problem. No such luck. There seemed to be nothing on but nature programs, current events or sports, and nothing she watched had the power to absorb or distract her at all. She flipped through her meager collection and briefly entertained the idea of watching a comfort video, *Doctor Zhivago* or *The Wizard of Oz*, but she even felt too agitated to concentrate on a movie.

Damn Banks, she thought as she washed out her dish. How could he do this to her? Maybe she *had* let things cool between them romantically, but that gave him no right to treat her like some probationary DC who couldn't be trusted with the full story. She knew that his action hadn't been technically wrong in any way, but it *had* been dishonest and cowardly. As SIO, Banks was quite entitled to follow up a lead and decide whether it required action or not. Obviously, in the case of his night with Emily Riddle, he knew exactly what had occurred, so he knew that no further action was needed.

He must also have known that he was hiding the truth from Annie, though, or he would have told her about that night before, when he came clean about going to London to find Emily and having lunch with her the day she died. Annie remembered asking him then if that was all he had to tell, and he had said yes. That made him a liar.

So what to do about it? That was the question she agonized over. The way she saw it, she had two choices. She could, of course, simply do nothing, just put in for a transfer and leave the whole mess behind. That had its appeal, certainly, but it left too much up in the air. She had hidden from unpleasant things and turned her back for far too long. Now that her career had actually come to *mean* something to her again after the years of apathetic exile in Harkside, where she had conned herself into thinking everything was well with the world, Annie wanted to set things on the right track. And just how would an abrupt transfer look, with her inspector's boards coming up so soon?

On the other hand, she could confront Banks and find out what he had to say for himself. Maybe she should give him the benefit of the doubt, innocent until proven guilty and all that. After all, it wasn't as if she didn't still have feelings for the bastard.

But she already knew he wasn't innocent, that it was simply a matter of *what* he was guilty of. How much might a run-in with Banks upset her chances of making inspector? She didn't think he was vindictive, didn't think he would deliberately stand in her way, but everything has fallout, especially given the history Banks and Annie had between them.

Giving up on the television, Annie did what she usually did when she felt agitated and unable to find her calm center; she flung on her fleece-lined jacket and went for a drive. It didn't matter where.

It had turned into a cold night, and she got the heater going full-blast. Even so, the car took a while to warm up. The mist was crystallizing on the bare trees, sparkling as her headlights flicked across branches and twigs on her way out of Harkside. Ice-crusted puddles crackled under her wheels.

She crossed the narrow bridge over the River Rowan between the Harksmere and Linwood reservoirs. Harksmere stretched, cold and dark, to the west, and beyond it lay Thornfield Reservoir, where the remains of Hobb's End had once more been covered with water. That was where she had first met Banks, she remembered, toward the end of the hottest, driest summer in years. He had come scrambling down the steep rim looking like a sightseer, and she had stopped him at the bridge. She had been wearing her red wellies and must have looked a sight.

He still didn't know this, but Annie had known who he was the minute she saw him—she had been expecting him—but she wanted a little fun first, so she had challenged him on the packhorse bridge. She had liked his manner. He hadn't been stuffy or officious with her; he had simply made some reference to Robin Hood and Little John. After that, Annie had to admit that she hadn't resisted him very hard.

And now he was her senior officer, and he had been keeping things from her.

Past the old air base, Annie took the left fork and headed for the open moorland that stretched for miles on the tops between there and Swainsdale. Up on the unfenced road, the full moon came out from behind the thinning cloud cover, and she could see that the ground all around her was white with rime-frost. It had an eerie beauty that suited her mood well. She could drive for hours through this lunar landscape and her mind would empty of all her problems. She would become nothing but the driver floating through space—the wheel, the car merely extensions of her being, as if she were traveling the astral plane.

Except that Annie knew now where she was going, knew that the road she was on was the one that led over the moors and down through the village of Gratly, where Banks lived.

And she knew that when she got to his drive she would turn into it.

Banks refilled the wineglasses and sat down again. "Go on," he said.

Rosalind smiled. "You might find this hard to believe," she began, "but I haven't always been the dull, decent wife of the dull, decent chief constable."

Banks was startled by her smile. It had so much of Emily in it, that hint of mischief, of *Just watch me*. "That sounds like the beginning of a story," he said.

"It is."

"I'm all ears."

"First, we have to go back a while. Believe it or not, my father was a vicar. He's retired now, of course. I grew up in the vicarage in a small village in Kent, an only child, and my childhood was relatively uneventful. I don't mean that it was bad in any way. I did all the normal things kids do. I was happy. It was just unexceptional. Dull, even. Like the way Philip Larkin described his in that poem. Then, in the mid-seventies, when I was sixteen, we moved to a parish out Ealing way. Oh, it was a very nice area—none of that inner-city stuff—and the parishioners were for the most part law-abiding, reasonably affluent citizens."

"But?"

"But it was near the tube. You can't imagine what wonderful new worlds that opened up to an impressionable sixteen-year-old."

Banks thought he could. When he moved from Peterborough to Notting Hill at the age of eighteen, his life had changed in many ways. He had met Jem across the hall from his bed-sit, for a start, and had lurked at the fringes of the sixties scene—which stretched well into the early seventies—enjoying the music more than the drugs. There was an excitement and vibrancy about the capital that was missing from Peterborough, and would certainly have been missing from a vicarage in Kent.

"Let me guess: The vicar's daughter went a little wild?"

"I was born in 1959. It was November 1975, when we moved to Ealing. While everyone else was listening to Queen, Abba and Hot Chocolate, me and my friends were taking the tube into town to listen to The Sex Pistols. This was right at the start, before anyone really knew anything about them. They'd just played their first gig the day after Bonfire Night at Saint Martin's College of Art, and one of the girls at my new school was there. She couldn't talk about anything else for weeks. Next time they played, she took me with her. It was fantastic."

Punk. Banks remembered those days. He was older than Rosalind, though, and identified more closely with sixties music than that of the seventies. When he had lived in London his favorites had been Pink Floyd, Led Zeppelin and the various local blues bands that seemed to form and split up with amazing regularity. Still, he had responded to the angry energy of some of the punk music—especially The Clash, by far the best of the bunch in his opinion—but not enough to buy any of their records. Also, as he had been a probationary police constable back then, he had experienced the violence of punk first-hand, from the other side, and that, too, had put him off.

"Pretty soon," Rosalind went on, becoming more animated as she relived her memories, "it was in full swing. The look. The music. The attitude. Everything. My parents didn't know me anymore. We saw The Clash, The Damned, The Stranglers, The Jam. You name them. Mostly in small clubs. We Pogoed, we hurled ourselves into one another, and we spat at each other. We dyed our hair weird colors. We wore torn clothes, safety pins in our ears and . . ." She paused and pulled up the sleeve of her jumper. Banks could see a number of more or less round white marks, like old scars. "We stubbed cigarettes out on ourselves."

Banks raised an eyebrow. "How on earth did you explain all that to your husband?"

"He was never that curious. I just told him it was an old burn scar."

"Go on."

"You can't imagine how exhilarating it was after the stuffy and boring childhood in a village in Kent. We went *wild*. Anyway, to cut a long story short, I was just seventeen, and I got pregnant. It doesn't matter who the father was; his name was Mal, and he was long gone before I even knew myself. It happened in someone's poky bed-sit after The Pistols did one of their gigs at the 100 Club, the summer of 1976. This is what I could never tell Jerry. He was a terrible prude, as if you didn't know. I don't know if he actually believed I was a virgin when we married, but I'm certain *he* was. If he'd ever found out, well . . . who can say? I kept it from him."

Banks remembered the 100 Club well. On Oxford Street, it had been part of his patch, and he had been inside the cavernous cellar more than once trying to stop fights and help get rid of unruly customers. It turned into a jazz club some years later, he remembered. "I can understand why you might not have wanted him to know," he said. "Even in this day and age, some people are funny about that sort of thing, and it doesn't surprise me that Jimmy—I mean the chief constable, was. But why is that important now?"

"He knew you all called him Jimmy Riddle, you know."

"He did? He never said anything."

"He didn't care. Something like that, it didn't bother him, wasn't even of passing interest to him. He was strangely impervious to criticism or having the piss taken. He really didn't have much of a sense of humor, you know. Anyway, I haven't told you the full story yet. You'll see why it's important." She moved forward in her chair and clasped her hands on her knees. When she spoke, she almost whispered, as if she thought someone were eavesdropping on them. "My first thought was to have an abortion, but . . . I don't know . . . I didn't really know how to go about it, if you can believe that. A fully fledged punk, pregnant, but I was still a naive country girl in a lot of ways. Then there was my religious background. When it came down to it, I hadn't the nerve to face it all by myself, and the boy, well, as I said, he was long gone. My father's a good man. He had been preaching about grace, mercy and Christian charity all his life."

"So you went to your parents?"

"Yes."

"And?"

"They took it well, considering. They were upset, naturally, but they were good to me. They persuaded me to have the baby, of course, as I knew they would. Father doesn't believe in abortion. It's not only Catholics who don't, you know. Anyway, we did it the way they used to do it years ago. A spell with Aunt So-and-So in Tiverton for the last few months, when it started to show, a quick adoption, and it was as if nothing had ever happened. In the meantime, if I happened to get cured of punk, so much the better."

"Did you?"

"Get cured of punk?"

"Yes."

"By the time I'd had my baby I was about to sit my A-Levels. It was 1977. I don't know if you remember, but punk had become very popular and the big bands were all being signed up by major labels. The whole scene had got very commercial. Now it seemed that everybody was talking about it, adopting the look. Somehow, it just wasn't the same. They weren't *ours* any more. Besides, I was older and wiser. I was a mother, even if I wasn't a practicing one. Yes, I was cured. I spent the summer at home, and in October I went to the University of Bath to study English Literature, became an intellectual snob and switched to new wave, which I'd always secretly preferred, anyway. Elvis Costello, Talking Heads, Roxy Music, Television, Patti Smith. Art school music. I did one year of English, then changed to law."

"There's more, isn't there?"

"Yes."

"The child?"

"As you know, it's perfectly legal now for children to track down their birth parents. I can understand it, but I have to say that in many cases it's the cause of nothing but grief."

"In your case?"

"She found me easily enough. Last January, it was. The Children's Act came into effect in 1975, before she was born, as you probably know. That meant she didn't even have to go for counseling before the Registrar General gave her the information that led her to me. It was always on the cards. She just walked into my office one day. It didn't take her long to work out that I was terrified of her telling my husband. I don't know what would have happened. It was bad enough that he was so prudish and possessive, and that I'd kept it from him all those years, but this also happened just as his political ambitions were getting all stirred up, and I wanted to be on that ride, too. I wanted Westminster. Jerry was always big on family values, and any hint of a family scandal—*ex-punk wife of chief constable, love child tells all*—well, it would have ruined everything. At least, I believed it would."

"What did she do?"

"Asked for money."

"Your own daughter blackmailed you?"

"I wouldn't call it that. She just asked for help now and then."

"Financial help?"

"Yes. I mean, I *did* owe her, didn't I? Apparently, she hadn't had such a good life with her adoptive parents. They turned out to be unsuitable, she said, though she didn't explain why, and they didn't have much money. Then they died in a fire just after her second year of university, and she was left all alone. She was in her last year of university at the time she found me, so every little bit helped. I didn't really mind."

"Did she ever threaten to tell your husband the truth if you didn't pay up?"

"She . . . she hinted that she might."

"And you paid for her continuing silence?"

Rosalind averted her eyes. "Yes."

"Even after she left university?"

"Yes."

"That's blackmail," said Banks. "Are you going to tell me who she is?"

"Does it matter?"

"It might."

Rosalind drank some wine, then she said, "It's Ruth. Ruth Walker."

Banks almost choked on his drink. "Ruth Walker is your daughter? Emily's half-sister?"

Rosalind nodded.

"My God, why didn't you tell me this before?"

"I can't see how it could be relevant."

"That's for me to judge. Did Emily know this?"

"I didn't think so."

"What do you mean?"

"As far as I knew at the time, they met only once. Ruth used to come to my office in Eastvale. That's where we did all . . . all our business. Believe it or not, I didn't even know her address, where she lived, except she told me she'd grown up in Salford. Once—last Easter, I think it was—Emily was there. She'd come to borrow some money from me to go shopping. Ruth walked in. I introduced my daughter and told her Ruth was there about the new computer system we were thinking of installing. They chatted a bit, about music, what school Emily was at, that sort of thing. Just polite chitchat. That was all. Or so I thought."

"So Emily didn't know *who* Ruth really was?"

"That's what I believed at the time."

"What changed your mind?"

"After Emily came . . . after you brought Emily back home, the phone rang one day. It was Ruth. I thought she was calling for me. I was angry because I'd specifically told her never to phone the house, but she asked to speak to Emily."

"And?"

"Afterward, I asked Emily about it. Then she told me about how Ruth had phoned her a lot at school, how she'd even been down to London once for a weekend and stayed with her. How they were *friends*."

"So Emily knew that Ruth was her half-sister?"

"Yes."

"What was her reaction?"

"You knew Emily. She thought it was all rather cool, her mother having a secret past. She promised me not to say anything. She was well aware of how her father would react."

"Did you trust her?"

"For the most part. Emily wasn't malicious, though she could be unpredictable. You know, at her age, I wasn't much different. If we'd been contemporaries, who knows, we might have been friends."

"I can only imagine the havoc the two of you might have wreaked."

Rosalind smiled her Emily smile again. "Yes."

"Did she know about the blackmail?"

"Good Lord, no. At least, she never said anything about it. And I doubt that's something Ruth would have admitted to her half-sister. Emily was very headstrong and irresponsible, but she was honest at the bottom of it all. I can't see her condoning what Ruth was doing if she knew about it."

That made sense. But what if Emily had found out on her own? "Why tell me all this now?" he asked.

Rosalind shrugged. "A lot of reasons. Jerry's death. Your

finding him. Your bringing Emily back. You know, for better or for worse, you've become part of our lives this last while. I had to tell *someone* and I couldn't think of anyone else. Isn't that pathetic? Ever since Emily came home, I've been going crazy keeping it to myself, but I couldn't risk telling you then. Not while Jerry was alive. I know you didn't like him, but I know that you policemen stick together. And anything you discover often makes its way into the papers. I'm not saying *you* would have said anything, but . . ."

"The walls have ears?"

"Something like that."

"And now?"

"It doesn't matter now, does it? Nothing matters now. Apart from my anger, I just feel empty." She put her glass aside and stood up. "Now I really must go. I've said what I came to say. Thank you for listening."

As Annie was about to turn left into Banks's drive just before Gratly Bridge, a car shot out backward and swung toward her so fast she had to floor the brake pedal to avoid a collision. The other car then set off down the hill toward Helmthorpe.

Heart beating fast, Annie turned left and drove slowly up to Banks's cottage. She could see him silhouetted in the open door, wearing only a shirt and jeans despite the cold.

Annie pulled up in front and got out.

"What the hell are you doing here?" Banks said.

"That's a nice welcome. Can I come in?"

He stood aside. "You might as well. Everyone else does."

Annie had come prepared to launch right into him, having pumped herself up on the drive, but the adrenaline surge of her near accident and Banks's offhand manner took some of the wind out of her sails. Inside the cottage, she sat down in the armchair. It was still warm from whoever had just left it.

"And what can I do for you?" Banks said, shutting the door and going over to put more peat on the fire.

"First you can get me a drink." Annie nodded toward the low table. "That wine will do just fine."

Banks went into the kitchen, got another glass and poured her some wine.

"Who was that?" she asked, taking the glass.

"Who?"

"The person who just left like a bat out of hell. The person who damn near backed right into me."

"Oh, *that* person. Rosalind Riddle."

"Friend of yours?"

"Work."

"Work? Oh, well, I can see why you wouldn't want to tell *me* anything about it, then. After all, I'm only your DIO, aren't I?"

"Knock off the sarcasm, Annie. It doesn't suit you. Of course I was going to tell you."

"Like you tell me everything?"

"Come again?"

"Oh, you know what I mean."

"Humor me."

"Rosalind Riddle is work like her daughter was work, right?"

"I don't get it. What are you implying?"

"I'm not implying anything." Annie told him about leafing through the green sheets and finding the reference to the Hotel Fifty-Five. "No further action, or so Winsome told me. So I wondered why I hadn't heard anything about it. I phoned the hotel and, lo and behold, who spent most of a night there together a month ago?"

Banks said nothing; he just gazed sheepishly into the fire.

"What's the matter?" Annie went on. "Cat got your tongue?"

"I don't see why I should have to explain myself to you."

"Oh, you don't, don't you? I'll tell you why. Murder. That's why. Emily Riddle was murdered last week, or have you forgotten that?" As she spoke, Annie felt the embers of her anger start to rekindle again. "Now, after the things I've discovered, I don't think you're fit to be working the case, but I'm your DIO and you owe me at least the *fucking* courtesy of telling me the truth about your relationship with the victim."

"There *was* no relationship."

"Liar."

"Annie, there—"

"Liar."

"Will you let me talk?"

"If you tell the truth."

"I *am* telling the truth."

"Liar."

"All right. So I *liked* Emily. So what? I don't know why. She was a pain in the arse. But I liked her. That's all. More like a daughter than anything. That's as far as it went. It was my job to find her in London. She got herself into a bit of bother at a party and the only place she knew to come was to the hotel. I'd given her a card with the name written on, so she could contact me if she decided to come home. She was scared and alone and she came there. It's as simple as that."

"What bother?"

Banks told her about the incident with Andy Pandy at the party.

"And you didn't see fit to share this tidbit of information with me, your DIO?" Annie shook her head. "I can't believe it. What else have you been keeping me in the dark about?"

"Nothing, Annie. Look, I know it was wrong of me, but surely you can see why I was worried how it might appear?"

"How it might *appear*? Emily Riddle turns up at your room at three o'clock in the morning and stays there the rest of the night, and you're worried about how it might appear. Oh, yes, I think I can see why."

"Surely you can't think . . . ?"

"What else am I supposed to think? You tell me. You spend the night in a hotel room with a randy sixteen-year-old slut, and you want me to believe nothing happened? Do you think I was born yesterday?"

"Emily Riddle wasn't a slut."

"Oh, pardon me! Isn't that grand? Coming to the defense of your poor damsel in distress."

"Annie, the girl's dead. At least you could show—"

"Show what? Respect?"

"Yes."

"Were you showing her respect when you slept with her in that hotel room?"

"Annie, I've told you. I *didn't* sleep with her."

"And I don't believe you. Oh, maybe you only intended to comfort her, give her a little cuddle, tell her everything was all right now, but from what I've heard of her, and from what I know about *men,* I very much doubt it ended there."

"I never touched her."

"You should have got her a room of her own."

"I was going to, but she fell asleep on the bed."

"Oh, come on."

"She did. She was stoned. That's exactly what happened."

"And you? Where were you? I remember those rooms. They're not very big."

"In the armchair by the window. I sat up for a while listening to some music on the Walkman, then I spent the rest of the night listening to her snoring while I was trying to get to sleep, if you must know."

Annie said nothing. She was trying to work out whether he was telling the truth or not. She suspected that he probably was, but she was determined not to let him off the hook that easily. However much it hurt or upset Annie, whether Banks had slept with Emily Riddle or not wasn't the real issue, she told herself. He could sleep with whomever he damn well pleased, even if it happened to be a sixteen-year-old girl. Annie had no hold over him. What really mattered was that he had kept important information from her, as he had done before in this investigation, and she was beginning to find it harder and harder to trust him.

"Anyway," Banks went on, "you've got some bloody nerve accusing me of screwing up on the job."

Annie stiffened. "What do you mean?"

"What about you? Do you really think you've been pulling your weight lately?"

Annie flinched from the accusation. "I've had a few problems. That's all. I told you. Personal problems."

"A few problems? Is that what you call sneaking off to sleep with DI Dalton every minute my back was turned? Don't think I didn't notice. I'm not stupid."

Annie shot forward and slapped him hard across the face. She could tell it hurt him, and he drew back, his cheek reddening. Hot tears brimmed in her eyes.

"I'm sorry," he said. "I didn't mean it to sound so harsh. But you've got to admit you were pretty obvious. How do you think I felt?"

Annie could feel the blood roaring through her veins and her heart knocking against her ribs, even louder and faster than when the car almost hit her earlier. She paused for what felt like hours, taking slow, deliberate breaths, trying to calm herself, get rid of the panic and rage that seemed to possess her. When she finally spoke, it was in a voice barely above a whisper. "You bloody idiot. For your information, DI Dalton was one of the men who raped me. But don't let that bother you. I'll go now." She started to get up.

"Jesus Christ, Annie! No, don't go. Please don't go." Banks grasped her wrist. She looked at his hand for a moment, then she sat down again, all the fight gone out of her. Banks refilled her wineglass and his own. "I don't know what to say," he said. "I feel like a fool. Why didn't you *say* something?"

"Like what? Come crying to my boss the first week on the job?"

"Like 'This is the man who raped me.' Is he the one who actually—"

"One of the others. But it doesn't mean he wouldn't have done it, too, if I'd given him half a chance. As far as I'm concerned they're all three of them equally guilty."

"But you could have told *me*. You knew that I'd understand."

"And what would you have done? Gone flexing your macho muscles? Beat him up? Something like that? Had a pissing competition? No, thanks. It was *my* problem. I preferred to handle it myself."

"Looks like you did a good job."

"He's still alive, isn't he?"

Banks smiled. "Annie, you don't have to handle everything in life by yourself."

"Shows what you know about it. Wasn't anyone around to help when it happened, was there?"

"That doesn't mean there's no one now."

Annie looked at him and felt herself soften. "I can't handle this," she said, shaking her head.

"Annie, I'm sorry. What can I say?"

"It doesn't matter."

"Yes, it does. I saw the way you and Dalton tensed up when you met and I read it wrongly. I thought there was something between you."

"There was. Just not what you thought it was."

"I know that now. And I'm sorry. I should have trusted you."

Annie made a sound halfway between a sniff and a laugh. "Like I trusted you?"

"I was jealous. Besides, I didn't give you much reason to trust me, did I? I've handled this all wrong."

"You can say that again."

"Annie, I swear on my honor that nothing happened between me and Emily Riddle except she passed out in my room. What was I to do? The next day I bought her some new clothes on Oxford Street and we went home on the train."

"And you really sat in one of those horrible hotel armchairs listening to your Walkman?"

"Yes. And smoking."

"And smoking. Of course."

"Yes."

"Then you tried to sleep but her snoring kept you awake?"

"Yes. And the wind and rain."

"And the wind and rain." He looked so earnest that Annie couldn't help herself; she burst into laughter. The thing was, she could just picture him there doing exactly what he said. He looked hurt. "I'm sorry, Alan. Really, I am. Nobody could make up a story as silly as that if it didn't really happen."

Banks frowned. "So you believe me now?"

"I believe you. I just wish you'd told me earlier. All this deception . . ."

"On both sides."

"Oh, no. I didn't deceive you. You read the situation wrongly."

"But you kept something from me."

"That was private business. It wasn't to do with the case, not like your relationship with Emily Riddle. You really liked her?"

"I don't think I could have stood being around her for very long. She could be quite exhausting. Never stopped talking. And a hell of an attitude. But, yes, I did."

Annie tilted her head and gave him a crooked grin. "You're a funny one. You're so straight in some ways, but there's a definite bohemian edge to you."

"Is that good?"

"It'll do. But I want you to know that I'm still seriously pissed off at you for not treating me as a professional. You've got a lot of making up to do."

"Annie, I'm sorry. Really, I am. It's been difficult, given what we had, then me thinking you and Dalton . . . you know. I mean, it's not as if I don't still . . ."

Annie felt her heart give a little somersault. "Don't still what?"

"Fancy you." The fire was waning and the air becoming chilly. Banks looked at Annie and she felt the stirrings of her feelings for him that she'd been trying to ignore since they split up. He picked up a lump of peat. "Are you staying?" he asked. "Shall I put some more on? It's getting cold."

Annie gave him a serious look, then bit her lip, stretched out her hand, the same hand she had slapped him with, and said, "Okay, but we've got a lot of talking to do."

17

Annie pulled up in the staff car park of the red brick fire station in Salford just past eleven-thirty the next morning, after over an hour spent crawling along the M62 and getting lost in the center of Manchester. A lorry had overturned at one of the junctions near Huddersfield, and traffic was backed up as far as the intersection with the M1. The weather hadn't helped, either. After last night's deep freeze, the roads were icy despite the brilliant winter sunshine that glinted on windscreens and bonnet ornaments.

The fire station stood on an arterial road near the estate of shabby Georgian semis where Ruth Walker had grown up. Banks had told Annie about Ruth's being Rosalind Riddle's daughter. Ruth had told a lot of lies, he said, and he thought they should find out more about her background, including the fire in which both her parents were killed eighteen months ago. It had been easy to track down the address via the Salford Fire Department, which was Annie's first port of call. The fire-station captain, George Whitmore, said he would be pleased to talk to her.

The firemen were sitting around playing cards in a large upper room above the gleaming red engines. The place smelled of sweat, aftershave and oil. They were an odd lot, firemen, Annie had always thought. When everything was going well, they had no job to do at all, just the way the police would have nothing to do if people weren't committing crimes. Annie had known one of the local lads back in St. Ives who spent his time at work writing Westerns under a pseudonym, selling about one a month to an American publisher. She had also been out with a fireman who ran a carpet-cleaning business on the side, and one of his friends ran an airport taxi service. They all seemed to have three or four jobs on the go. Of course, fires are as inevitable as crime, and when it came to the crunch, nobody would deny the heroism of firemen if the occasion demanded it. And no matter how politically correct you tried to be about it, no matter how much people talked about recruiting more women to the job, whether you called them Combustion Control Engineers or Flame Suppressant Units, the truth about firemen was summed up in what they always had been and always would be called as far as Annie was concerned: *firemen.*

"Mr. Whitmore around?" she asked one of the card players.

He gave her the once-over, smiled as if he thought he was sexy and pointed with his thumb. "Office back there."

Annie felt his eyes on her behind as she walked away, heard a whisper, then men's laughter. She thought of turning and making some comment about how childish they were but decided they weren't worth the effort.

George Whitmore turned out to be a pleasant, good-natured man with cropped gray hair, not far from retirement age by the look of him. He had framed photos of his family, including grandchildren, on his desk.

"You're the lass who phoned earlier, are you?" he said, bidding Annie to sit down.

"Yes."

"Well, I should've told you you've probably made a long journey for nothing."

Annie smiled at him. "I don't mind. It's nice to get out of the office for a while." She took out her notebook. "You remember the Walker fire?"

"Yes. I was on the crew back then, before my bad back put me on office duties a year ago."

"You were at the scene?"

"Yes. It happened, oh, about three or four in the morning, or a bit after. I could look it up if you want the exact time."

"It doesn't matter for the moment. Just your impressions will do."

He paused and frowned. "If you don't mind me asking, love, why do the police want to know about the Walker fire now, after all this time?"

"It's just a background check," Annie said. "Routine."

"Because there was nothing funny about it."

"I understand there was no police investigation?"

"Not beyond what's required by law and the insurance company. No reason for one."

"What was the cause of the fire?"

"A smoldering cigarette end down the side of the sofa."

Another reason smoking's bad for your health, thought Annie. "And you ruled out arson?"

Whitmore nodded. "Early on. There were no signs of forced entry, of anything being disturbed, for a start. There was also no evidence of accelerants being used, and, quite honestly, nobody had any reason to harm the Walkers."

"You knew them?"

"Only in passing. To say hello to. They were active in chapel. Everyone knew that. I'm not a particularly religious sort myself. Nice, God-fearing couple, though, by all accounts. Nice daughter they had, too. Poor lass barely escaped with her life."

"That'd be Ruth?"

"Aye. They only had the one."

"So what happened from the moment the alarm went off?"

"They didn't have a smoke detector. If they'd had one, it's likely they wouldn't have died. A neighbor saw the smoke and flames and phoned us. By the time we got there, most of the neighbors were already out in the street. See, a cigarette can smolder for hours and generate a lot of heat. When it takes hold, it really goes. The fire had taken hold by then, and it took us a good hour or so to put it out completely. At least we managed to stop it spreading."

"Where was Ruth at this time?"

"They'd taken her to hospital. She jumped out of her bedroom window in the nick of time. Broke her ankle and dislocated her shoulder."

"Nasty."

"The ankle was the worst. Bad fracture, apparently. Took her weeks before she could walk again without crutches or a stick. Anyway, it wasn't nearly as nasty as what happened to her mum and dad. She was the lucky one. There'd been a shower earlier in the evening, and the ground was soft, or she might have broken more bones."

"How did her parents die?"

"Smoke inhalation. That's what the postmortem showed. Never even had time to get out of bed. Ruth had inhaled some smoke, too, before she jumped, but not enough to do her much harm. A whiff of oxygen and she was right as rain."

"Why did she have time to escape and her parents didn't?"

Whitmore shrugged. "Younger, stronger, quicker reflexes. Also, her room was at the front, and the fire was worse further back. Her parents were probably dead when she jumped."

"Can you tell me anything else?"

"That's about it, really, love. Told you you'd probably had a wasted journey."

"Well, you know what it's like," said Annie. "Was the house completely destroyed?"

"Pretty much. Inside, at any rate."

"And now?"

"Oh, someone bought it and had it renovated. To look at it now you'd never know such tragedy happened there."

Annie stood up. "Where is it from here, exactly?"

"Carry on along the main road, go left at the next lights and it's the second street on the right."

"Thanks very much." Annie left Whitmore's tiny office and walked back past the card players. This time one of them whistled at her. She smiled to herself. It felt quite nice, actually. Thirty-something and she still got whistled at. She'd have to tell Alan about that.

Alan. They had talked most of the night while the peat fire blazed in the hearth and soft jazz played in the background. He told her about Rosalind's visit, about Emily and Ruth, about the guilt he felt on finding Riddle dead in his garage, and she told him about how Dalton's appearance had knocked her out of kilter, brought back feelings she didn't know she still harbored, and how she had confronted him on Sunday morning.

Had it been summer, they would have been up talking until dawn, but because it was December, the only light that shone through the windows at four o'clock in the morning came from a full moon as white as frost. Even then they continued to talk, and the way Annie remembered it she thought she had probably fallen asleep in mid-sentence.

It wasn't until both had slept for about three hours that they made love—tentatively and tenderly—and in the morning they had to scrape the ice off their car windows and drive like hell to get to work on time.

Now, it seemed to Annie as if there were no more secrets, as if nothing stood between them. She still worried about their working together, especially now that she was stationed at Western Divisional HQ, too, and she could never quite get over her fear of commitment, of rejection. But Banks hadn't asked her for commitment, and if anything, it was *she* who had rejected *him* last time, out of fear of his past impinging on her life.

All she really knew, she decided, was that whatever it was they had, she wanted it. It was time again to take her lesson from Eastern philosophy—go with the flow.

Annie smiled as she touched up her makeup, using the rear-view, then she headed off to see if she could discover anything from the Walkers's neighbors.

The atmosphere that had hung over the death scene at Riddle's garage the previous day seemed to have permeated the entire station, Banks thought as he looked out of his window at the market square. The place had all the atmosphere of a funeral parlor. While Riddle might not have been the most loved or admired chief constable they had ever had, he *had* been one of them, and he was dead. It was like losing a member of the family. A distant and austere uncle perhaps, but still a family member. Even Banks felt heavy-hearted as he sipped his bitter black coffee.

The dark mood reminded him of the days after Graham Marshall's disappearance, when everyone in the school seemed to be going around walking on eggs, in a daze, and conversations all seemed to be carried out in whispers. Those days had given Banks his first real taste of guilt, a sense of being responsible for people that was one of the things that spurred him on now in his job. He knew deep down that he was no more responsible for Graham Marshall's disappearance than he was for Phil Simpkins's bleeding to death on the railings, or Jem's overdose of heroin, but he seemed to attract the guilt, draw it to him and wrap it around himself like a comforting mantle.

When he thought of Annie, though, he felt his spirits rise. He knew not to expect too much—she had made that quite clear—but at least they had got beyond the rumors and fears they had been bogged down in the past week. Banks sensed the possibility of a new, deeper trust. It would have to develop naturally, though; there could be no pushing, not with someone as scared of intimacy as Annie was, or someone as recently battle-scarred as himself. Sandra's asking for a divorce and telling him she wanted to marry Sean might have given him a sense of finality, of liberation, but the old wounds were still there. Which reminded him: he ought to respond to the second solicitor's letter, or Sandra would think he had changed his mind.

Banks could see a knot of reporters outside the station. He looked at his watch: almost opening time. Pretty soon they'd all be ensconced in the Queen's Arms padding out each other's expense accounts. Riddle's suicide was the kind of thing that got the London dailies this far up north. No official statements had been issued yet, and the Riddle house was still under secure guard. Of course, they could have a field day with this one: CHIEF CONSTABLE COMMITS SUICIDE WITH POLICE GUARD ONLY YARDS AWAY. They could spin that to read whatever way they wanted.

Rosalind was going down to stay with her parents in Barnstaple when she had made the funeral arrangements.

Then, she had told Banks just before she left the previous evening, she would sell the house and decide what to do next. There was no hurry—she would be well provided for—but she would move as far away from Yorkshire as possible. Banks felt for her; he had absolutely no conception of how awful it must feel to lose a daughter and a spouse in the space of only a few days. He couldn't even imagine how terrible it would be to lose Brian or Tracy.

Banks's ancient heater hissed and sputtered as he sat down and thought over the previous evening's conversation with Rosalind. One obvious point was that, by telling him what she had, she had inadvertently supplied him with a motive for getting rid of Emily. Or was it inadvertent? He had no doubt that Rosalind could be devious when she wanted to—after all, she *was* a lawyer—but he had no idea as to why she would want to incriminate herself that way. Put simply, though, if Rosalind wanted to keep Ruth's existence from her husband, and if Emily was a loose cannon on the deck, then Rosalind had a motive for getting Emily out of the way.

And, by extension, she had an even better motive for wanting Ruth Walker out of the way permanently.

Since Riddle's suicide, though, it was all academic. The money, the status, the celebrity, the possibility of political life—they had all vanished into thin air. Nothing remained for Rosalind except Benjamin and Ruth, and Banks doubted she would have anything more to do with Ruth after all that had happened. It was enough to prove the writer of Ecclesiastes right when he wrote that all is vanity.

Banks couldn't bring himself to believe that Rosalind had actually given her own daughter cocaine laced with strychnine, or that she was right now plotting the demise of her other daughter, but at the same time he had to bear in mind that there was no love lost between any of them and that, once, Rosalind had given her child away to strangers and moved on to the wealth and power and their trappings she seemed to need so much. And when it came right down to it, no matter what Banks's gut instinct told him, we are all capable of murder given the right incentive.

Whichever way he looked at it, Ruth Walker's sudden

prominence in the case was a complication he could do without. While Annie dug up information on Ruth's background in Salford, Banks was trying to find out as much as he could about her present life in Kennington while he waited for a call from Burgess. He had already made several phone calls and had two pages of notes.

When his telephone rang, he thought it was Ruth's boss calling him back, but it was the other phone call he'd been waiting for, Burgess's, the one that gave a green light for the second interview with Barry Clough. And not before time, too; they could only hang on to him for another couple of hours at most.

It seemed a pleasant enough neighborhood, Annie thought, standing by the side of the road looking at the houses. Not at all the sort of place you would expect in Salford, though if she was honest she would have to admit she had never been to Salford before and had no idea what to expect. Semi-detached houses lined both sides of the quiet road, each with a fair-sized front lawn tucked away behind a privet hedge. The cars parked in the street were not ostentatious, but they weren't rusted and clapped-out ten-year-old Fiestas, either. Most of them were imported Japanese or Korean models, and Annie's Astra didn't look too out of place. Crime-wise, she guessed, the biggest problems would be the occasional break-in and car theft.

Number 39 was much like the other houses. As Whitmore had said, there was no indication whatsoever of the tragedy that had taken place there. Annie tried to imagine the flames, the smoke, the screams and neighbors standing out in their slippers and dressing gowns watching, helpless, as Ruth jumped from the upstairs window and her parents suffocated, unable even to get out of their beds.

"Help you, dearie?"

Annie turned and saw an elderly woman clutching a shopping bag with arthritis-crippled fingers.

"Only you look like you're lost or something."

"No," said Annie, smiling to reassure the woman she wasn't crazy or anything. "Just lost in thought, maybe."

"Did you know the Walkers?"

"No."

"Only you were looking at their house."

"Yes. I'm a policewoman." Annie introduced herself.

"Tattersall. Gladys Tattersall," the woman said. "Pleased to meet you, I'm sure. Don't tell me you're opening an investigation into the fire after all this time?"

"No. Do you think we should be?"

"Why don't you come inside. I'll put the kettle on. I'm at number thirty-seven here."

It was the semi adjoining the Walker house. "It must have been frightening for you," Annie said as she followed Mrs. Tattersall down the path and into the hall.

"I was more frightened during the bombing in the war. Mind you, I was just a lass then. Come in. Sit down."

Annie entered the living room and sat on a plum velour armchair. A gilt-framed mirror hung over the fireplace and the inevitable television set sat on its stand in the corner. At the far end of the room was a dining table with four chairs arranged around it. Mrs. Tattersall went into the kitchen and came back. "Won't be long," she said, sitting on the sofa. "You're right, though. It was a frightening night."

"Was it you who called the fire brigade?"

"No. That was the Hennessy lad over the road. He was coming home late from a club and he saw the flames and smoke. It was him came knocking on our door and told us to get out fast. That's me and my husband, Bernard. He passed away last winter. *Cancer.*"

"I'm sorry to hear it."

"Oh, it's all right, lass. It was a blessing, really. It was in his lungs, though he was never a smoker. The painkillers weren't doing him much good toward the end."

Annie paused for a moment. It seemed appropriate after the mention of the late Mr. Tattersall. "Was your house damaged?"

Mrs. Tattersall shook her head. "We were lucky. The walls got a bit warm, I can tell you, but the fire brigade sprayed the exterior with enough water to start a swimming pool. It was August, you see, warm weather, and we'd left a window open, so a bit of it got inside and did some damage to the walls—peeling paper, stains, that sort of thing. But nothing serious. The insurance paid for it. Perhaps the worst that came out of it for us was having to live here while the people that bought the house after the fire hammered and banged away all hours of the day and night."

"The renovators?"

"Yes." The kettle boiled. Mrs. Tattersall disappeared for a few minutes and returned with the tea service on a tray, which she set down on the low table in front of the electric fire. "You haven't told me why you're asking," she said.

"It's just a routine check. Nothing to do with the fire, really. It just seemed like an easy place to start."

"Routine? That's what you always say on telly."

Annie laughed. "It's probably about the only realistic thing about TV coppers, then. It's Ruth we're interested in. The daughter."

"Is she in any trouble?"

"Not as far as I know. Why do you ask?"

Mrs. Tattersall leaned forward and poured. "Milk and sugar?"

"Just milk, please."

"You wouldn't be asking about her for the good of your health, would you?"

"It's to do with a friend of hers," Annie said. Like most police, she was loath to give away the slightest scrap of information.

"I suppose that'll have to do, then," said Mrs. Tattersall, handing Annie the cup and saucer.

"Thank you. Did you know the Walkers well?"

"Pretty well. I mean, as well as you could do."

"What do you mean?"

"They weren't the most sociable types, weren't the Walkers."

"Standoffish? Snobbish?"

"No, not really. I mean, they were polite enough. Polite to a tee. And helpful if you needed anything. Lord knows they didn't have much themselves, but they'd give you the shirt off their backs. They just didn't mix." She paused, then whispered, *"Religious,"* the same way she had whispered *cancer.*

"More than most?"

"I'd say so. Oh, it was nothing strange. None of those weird cults or churches where you can't have blood transfusions or anything. Straight Methodist. But strict observers. Against Sunday shopping, drinking, pop music, that sort of thing."

"What was Mr. Walker's occupation?"

"Wages clerk."

"Did his wife work?"

"Pauline? Good heavens, no. They were as traditional as you get. She was a housewife."

"You don't get many of those in this day and age."

Mrs. Tattersall laughed. "You're telling me you don't, lass. Me, half the time I couldn't wait to get out of the house and to work. Not that I had such a wonderful job, myself, I was only a receptionist at the medical center down the road. But you get to meet people, chat, find out what's going on in the world. I'd go barmy if I was stuck between four walls day in, day out. Wouldn't you?"

"I would," said Annie. "But Mrs. Walker didn't seem to mind?"

"She never complained. But it's against their religion, isn't it, complaining?"

"I didn't know that." Annie would have been the first to admit that she didn't know much about religion except what she had read, and she had read mostly about Buddhism and Taoism. Her father was an atheist, so he hadn't subjected her to Sunday school or any of the usual childhood indoctrination, and the people who came and went in the commune carried with them a variety of ideas about religion and philosophy. Everything was always up for debate, up in the air.

"I mean, if whatever happens to you is God's will, good or bad, then you've no call to be complaining to God about God, if you see what I mean."

"I think I do."

"They were just a bit old-fashioned, that's all. People used to laugh behind their backs. Oh, nothing vicious or anything. It was mostly good-humored. Not that they'd have noticed. That was another thing that wasn't in their religion. Humor. I *did* feel a bit sorry for young Ruth sometimes."

"Why?"

"Well, there wasn't much *fun* in her life. And young people need fun. Even us old 'uns need a bit of fun from time to time, but when you're young . . ." She sighed. "Anyway, the Walkers' values were different from other folks'. And they didn't have much money, with only him working."

"How did they get by?"

"Parsimony. She were a good housekeeper, Pauline, I'll give her that. Good budgeter. But it meant that young Ruth could hardly stay up-to-date with fashions and whatnot. You'd see her in the same outfit year after year. A nip here and a tuck there. And shoes. Good Lord, she'd be clomping around in the most ugly things you could imagine. Pauline bought her them because they were durable, you see. Sturdy, sensible things with thick soles so they'd last a long time. None of these Nike trainers or Reeboks, like the other kids were wearing. Like it or not, love, fashions are so important to children, especially in their teens." She laughed. "I should know; I've brought up two of them."

"What happened?"

"The usual. The other girls at school laughed at her, called her names, tormented her. Children can be so cruel. And they'd no time for music or telly, either—wouldn't have a record player or a television set in the house—so poor Ruth couldn't join in the conversations with the rest. She didn't know all about the latest hits and the popular television programs. She was always a bit of a loner. It wasn't as if she was a great beauty, either. She was always a rather pasty-faced, dumpy sort of lass, and that kind are easy to pick on."

It was starting to sound like a pretty miserable household to grow up in, Annie thought. The artists' colony where she had grown up herself didn't have a television, either, but there was always music—often live—and all sorts of interesting people around. Some nights they would sing songs and recite poems. She could hear them from her bedroom. It was all mumbo-jumbo to her then, of course, none of it rhymed or anything, but they seemed to enjoy themselves. Sometimes, they let her sing for them, too, and if she said so herself, she didn't have a bad voice for traditional folk music.

Still, she thought she could relate to Ruth's feeling of being an outsider. If you're different in any way—no matter whether your family's too strict or too liberal—you get picked on, especially if you aren't up on the latest styles, too. Children *are* cruel; Mrs. Tattersall was right about that. Annie could remember some of their cruelties of her own childhood very well indeed.

Once, when she was about thirteen, a gang of classmates had waylaid her in the lane on her way home from school, dragged her into the trees, stripped her and painted flowers all over her body while they made remarks about filthy, drug-taking hippies and flower power. They had then run off with her clothes and left her to make the rest of her way home naked. *Cruel*. You could say that again. She had found her clothes hanging on a tree by the side of the lane going to school the next day. And that was in 1980, when hippies were history and the sixties was something her classmates could only have read about in books or seen on television documentaries. The people who lived at the commune were artists and writers, free thinkers, yes, but *hippies?* No. Annie's only sin was to be different, to wear the kind of clothes she wanted to wear (and that her father could afford, artists never having been among the richest members of society). Yes, in an odd way, she could sympathize very easily with Ruth Walker: two sides of the same coin.

"Ruth went off to university, didn't she?"

"Yes. That's what changed everything."

"What do you mean?"

"Well, they wanted her to go to Manchester, like, and keep on living at home so they could keep an eye on her, but she went to London. They thought university was a den of iniquity, you see, full of sex and drugs, but they also knew you don't get very far in this day and age without a good education. It was a bit of a dilemma for them. Anyway, she got her student grant or loan or whatever they get, so she had a bit of money of her own for the first time, and in the holidays she usually got a job. It gave her her first taste of independence."

"What did she do with her money?"

"Bought clothes, mostly. You should have seen her when she came back after her first year. Had all the latest styles. Whatever they were wearing at the moment. It all changes far too quickly for me to keep up with it. Anyway, she looked like any other rebellious young lass her age. Had her hair dyed all the colors of the rainbow, rings through her ears and eyebrows. Looked awfully painful. She'd found her brave new world, all right."

"How did her parents react?"

"I don't know. They never said anything in public. I can't imagine they were pleased, though. I got the feeling they were ashamed of her."

"Did you hear any rows? Through the walls."

"They never got angry. Against their religion. I think they pleaded with her and tried to get her to switch to a course at Manchester and come back home, but she'd changed too much by then. It was too late. She'd had her taste of freedom and she wasn't about to give it up. I can't say I blame her."

"So the matter went unresolved?"

"I suppose so. She spent that summer working at the local supermarket, general floor washer and shelf stacker, that sort of thing. She was a bright lass and a hard worker, and to do her justice, even when she looked like a tearaway she didn't cause any trouble. She was always polite."

"So she just looked strange?"

"That's about all. I think she'd reacted against the religion, too. At least she didn't go to chapel with them anymore. But kids do that, don't they?"

"They do," Annie agreed. "I was talking to one of the firemen, Mr. Whitmore, earlier."

"I know George Whitmore. He was a friend of my Bernard's. They used to enjoy a game of darts down at the King Billy on a Friday night."

"He said they didn't see any need to investigate the fire."

"That's right. I can't see why they would. That's why I was wondering what on earth you were doing here. Nobody would want to hurt the Walkers."

"Mr. Whitmore said it was probably started by a cigarette left smoldering down the side of the sofa."

"Well, that *was* a bit odd," said Mrs. Tattersall slowly. "Being religious and all, the way they were, you see, the Walkers didn't smoke or drink."

"But I'll bet Ruth did," said Annie.

Clough looked a little the worse for wear after his night in the cell, though the kind of suit he wore hardly showed a wrinkle. He had chosen not to shave, and the stubble, along with the tan, the gold and the elegant dress, made him look slightly unreal, like some sort of aging pop star. His lawyer, Simon Gallagher, however, who had no doubt spent the night in Burgundy House, Eastvale's poshest and priciest hotel, had taken the opportunity to clean himself up a bit, and now he looked every inch the high-priced solicitor. He still had the twitchy, perky manner of a habitual cokehead, though, and Banks wondered if he'd snorted up a couple of lines before the interview. He didn't say a lot, but he just couldn't sit still.

With Annie in Salford and Winsome back inputting data into HOLMES, Banks got Kevin Templeton to attend the interview with him. After the usual preliminaries, Banks began.

"Hope you had a comfortable night, Barry."

"You don't give a rat's arse what kind of night I had, so why don't you cut the crap and get to the point." Clough looked at his watch. "According to this, my twenty-four hours are up in about one hour and forty-five minutes. That right, Simon?"

Simon Gallagher nodded. Or twitched.

"We aim to please," said Banks. "Anyway, I don't know if you've heard, but since we last talked, Chief Constable Riddle committed suicide."

"Well, at least that's one thing you can't bang me up for, then, isn't it?"

"Is that all you've got to say about it?"

"What do you expect? I didn't know the man."

Even people who did know Riddle, Banks thought, might show as little concern as Clough. Banks himself hadn't liked the man, and he didn't intend to be hypocritical about it now, but the tragedy and despair of the act pierced his dislike to some extent. Nobody should be reduced to that. "Were you putting pressure on him, Barry?"

"What do you mean?"

"I think you know what I mean. Putting pressure on him to become your man, to do you the odd favor or two, make sure we looked the other way when you set up your little scams in North Yorkshire."

"Why would I want to do that?"

"You tell me."

"I wouldn't."

"But that's what your meeting was about, wasn't it? That's why he walked out before you really got started, isn't it? What were you using, Barry? Was it Emily? Do you have photographs? Did you threaten him that you could take her back anytime you wanted?"

Clough sighed and rolled his eyes at Gallagher.

"I think you've already exhausted this line of questioning," Gallagher said. "As you are well aware, my client could have had nothing to do with Mr. Riddle's unfortunate death, even if it hadn't been suicide. He has the best of all alibis: he was in your cells."

"Your client might have been one of the chief factors that drove the chief constable over the edge."

"You can't prove that," said Gallagher. "And even if you could, it hardly constitutes an indictable offense. Stick to the facts, Chief Inspector. Move on."

Banks was loath to give up and move on, but Gallagher was probably right. It would take a hell of a lot more than he had to persuade the CPS to even look at the possibility of prosecuting someone for complicity in the suicide of another. If Banks remembered his criminal law correctly, complicity could mean aiding, abetting, counseling or procuring another's suicide, and there was no evidence that Clough, even though he might have been trying to blackmail Riddle, had done any of those things. He was simply the straw that broke the camel's back.

Banks moved on. "Remember we were talking yesterday about Charlie Courage and Andrew Handley?"

"Vaguely."

"That both were killed by shotgun blasts, and both were found in rural areas some distance from their homes."

"I believe I asked what that had to do with me at the time, and now I'm asking again."

"Just this," said Banks, pausing and opening the file folder he had brought in with him. "While you've been enjoying our hospitality downstairs, we've been very busy indeed, and our forensics men have been able to match the tire tracks at the two scenes."

"I'm impressed," said Clough, raising an eyebrow. "The wonders of modern science."

"There's even better to come. On further investigation, they were able to match the tracks found at the scene of the two murders to a cream Citroën owned by a Mr. Jamie Gilbert. One of your employees, yes?"

"Jamie? You already know that."

"And it also turns out that one of Charlie Courage's neighbors recognized the photograph of Jamie Gilbert our officer showed her. Jamie was *seen* getting into a car with Charlie Courage around the time he disappeared. Anything to say?"

"They must be mistaken."

"Who?"

"Your scientists. This witness."

Banks shook his head. "Afraid not. Not only do the tires match, but we were also able to find hair samples and minute traces of blood we believe belong to either Charlie Courage or Andrew Handley in the car. Jamie was careless. He didn't clean it out thoroughly enough. The samples are being checked for DNA now."

"I don't know what to say," said Clough. "I'm shocked. Stunned, even. And I thought I knew Jamie."

"Evidently not. Anyway, Mr. Gilbert is in custody back in London at the moment. He'll no doubt be telling the interviewing officers down there exactly what happened."

"Jamie won't . . ."

"Jamie won't *what*, Barry?"

Clough smiled. "I was just about to say that Jamie won't be saying anything. You don't know him as well as I do. He's not the type."

"But you said just now that you only *thought* you knew him, that you're surprised he's a murderer."

"An alleged murderer," Simon Gallagher chipped in.

"My apologies," Banks went on. "An alleged murderer."

"You know what I mean."

"Do you have any idea *why* Jamie Gilbert would want to kill Charlie Courage and Andrew Handley?"

"None at all."

"Did he even know Charlie Courage?"

"I don't know who he hangs about with in his spare time."

"But he works for you."

"*Worked.* If you think I'm going to keep a murderer in my employ you must think I'm crazy. He's fired as of now."

"He worked for you at the time of the murders. He was your chief enforcer. And he *did* know Andrew Handley."

"Jamie was my administrative assistant. I already told you that."

"What did he administer for you? Punishment?"

"He handled my business affairs."

"Just exactly what might those be?"

"For crying out loud!" Clough looked at Gallagher. "Can't you get him to stop this? It's like an old LP with the bloody needle stuck."

"Legitimate questions, Barry. Legitimate questions."

Clough glared at Gallagher, who turned to Banks. "Get to the point quickly, Chief Inspector. We're all running out of time and patience here."

"Not me," said Banks. "Barry, is it true you were fired as a roadie for bootlegging the band's live performances?"

Clough faltered, clearly not expecting the question. "What the hell has that got to do with anything?"

"Just answer my question, please."

"It was years ago. There were no charges or anything."

"But you do have a history in bootlegging?"

"It was a mistake."

"Well, pirating is big business these days. Movies, computer software, games. Big business. Maybe not as big here as it is in the Far East or eastern Europe, but big enough to provide maximum profits for minimum risks. Just the kind of business venture that interests you, isn't it, Barry?"

"Chief Inspector!"

"Sorry, Mr. Gallagher. Slip of the tongue." Banks could see Kevin Templeton trying to stifle his grin. "You've already admitted you know Gregory Manners, haven't you?" Banks pressed on.

"I've admitted no such thing."

"Mr. Manners has a conviction for smuggling. Customs and Excise had their eyes on him for a while."

"What's that got to do with me?"

"They had their eyes on you, too."

"Well, if they'd seen anything they'd have arrested me, wouldn't they?"

"You're obviously a very careful man. It's odd, though, isn't it?"

"What is?"

"So many of your friends and employees being criminals. Jamie Gilbert. Andrew Handley. Gregory Manners. Charlie Courage."

"I told you, I've never heard of a Gregory Manners or a Charlie Courage."

"Of course not. My mistake. The others, though."

"Like I said, it's hardly my responsibility what my employees get up to in their own time. Maybe criminals have more fun."

"One might be forgiven for assuming that they were merely carrying out your orders."

"Assume what you want. You can't *prove* anything."

"I'd say if a man has one criminal employee, that might be carelessness, but two . . . ?"

"Are we going anywhere with this, Chief Inspector?"

Gallagher chipped in. "Because if we're not, we can stop right here. As they say in the vernacular, either shit or get off the pot."

"And you a well-educated man, Mr. Gallagher. Tut-tut. I'm appalled. Wash your mouth out, as my mother would say."

Clough stood up. "I've had enough of this."

"Sit down, Barry," said Banks.

"You can't make me. I'm free to go whenever—"

"Sit down!"

Clough was so taken aback by Banks's harsh tone that he subsided slowly into his chair again. Gallagher said nothing. He looked as if he badly needed another couple of lines. Banks leaned forward and rested his arms on the table. "Now, let me tell you what I think happened, Barry. You had a nice little earner going, pirating software and games. You'd rent units in business parks all over the country for a while under phony company names, flood the local markets, using the same distribution setup you'd organized for your smuggling business; then you'd move on, like playing hopscotch, always one step ahead of Trading Standards. Gregory Manners ran the operation in the Daleview Business Park and Andrew Handley oversaw the regional operation. Just my guess, of course, but Andy wasn't seen around the place as much as Mr. Manners was. Andy Pandy got very pissed off at you, perhaps because of the way you treated him like shit, pushing Emily into the room with him, passing on your left-overs. He decided, in revenge, to rip off the operation. To do this, he enlisted Charlie Courage, night watchman and petty criminal. Charlie probably arranged for the move to Northumbria and passed the details on to Andy Pandy, who arranged a hijack, killing the driver, Jonathan Fearn, a local wide-boy recruited by Charlie. How am I doing so far?"

Clough sat with his arms folded, a supercilious grin on his face. "It's fascinating. You should write detective fiction."

"But you suspect a double cross. You don't trust what you hear about Charlie Courage. Maybe you don't like strangers being brought in on things. Whatever. You lean on Gregory Manners enough to know it's not him. Which leaves Andy Pandy. Then you have Jamie Gilbert and another minder pick up Charlie and ask him a few questions. The hard way. Charlie never did have much of a stomach for violence, and it doesn't take long before he spills the whole scam. They take him for the long ride and blow him away, then they do the same with Andy Pandy, after they've beaten the whereabouts of the stolen stock and multidisc copying machines from him."

"And where are these machines, then, seeing as you're so clever?"

"Barry," Gallagher cut in, "I'd strongly advise—"

Banks waved him down. "It's all right, Mr. Gallagher. I'll answer Barry's question. Andy Pandy had a lockup in Golders Green, and it was broken into shortly after he disappeared. I think your lads also did that, took back the stolen equipment. My guess is that you've sold it by now and moved on to something else. How am I doing so far?"

Clough contemplated his fingernails. "Like I said, it's a fascinating story. You've missed your vocation. See, Simon, they've got nothing?"

"Remember, Chief Inspector," said Gallagher, "time's running out. Shit or get off the pot."

Banks paused, scribbled a couple of meaningless notes in his file, then got up and said to Kevin Templeton, "Take Mr. Clough downstairs to the custody sergeant, Kevin, and have him charged with conspiracy to commit murder. I'm sure Mr. Gallagher will make sure everything's done according to PACE regulations."

Clough flushed. "You can't do this. Tell them, Simon. Tell them they can't do this!"

"I'll deal with it, Barry," said Gallagher. "Don't worry, I'll have you out in no time."

"What do you mean, you'll have me out in no time? Out of where?"

"He means out of prison, Barry," said Banks. "And if you ask me, I think he's being overly optimistic."

"If truth be told," said Banks to Annie over an after-work pint in the Queen's Arms that evening, "I think it was me being overly optimistic in thinking we can make any charges stick against Clough."

Annie sipped her pint and settled into her chair. She looked around. The pub was pretty quiet at that time in the evening; most people were at home having dinner and watching the news. Occasionally, a Christmas shopper or two would come in with carrier bags from Marks & Spencer's, Tandy's or W.H. Smith's in the Swainsdale Centre across the square, knock back a quick whiskey to warm the cockles and head out again. Christmas decorations hung across the ceiling. The pub's dim light glowed in the polished wood and brass, the dimpled, copper-topped tables, the sparkling glasses and the bottles arranged behind the bar. Cyril, the landlord, stood chatting to a regular. The jukebox was mercifully silent and Annie could hear the church choir collecting for a refugee relief fund, singing "Away in a Manger" under the giant Christmas tree outside. Poor kids, she thought. It was real brass-monkey weather out there; they must be freezing.

"You don't think there's much hope, then?" she asked.

Banks shrugged. "We'll set up a meeting with Stafford Oakes in the CPS office, but let's just say it's pretty flimsy evidence so far."

"What about the forensics?"

"I've never put much faith in tire tracks. Most people don't know Goodyear from Michelin."

"But the blood?"

"Might be something there, if the lab doesn't 'lose' the evidence."

"What do you mean?"

"Remember that fire at the Wetherby lab a few years ago?"

"Yes."

"That was started to destroy evidence being kept there. Don't you think someone like Clough is capable of something similar?"

"I hadn't thought of that. What about the witness who saw Jamie Gilbert with Courage?"

"Easy meat."

"Oh, dear."

"Indeed. I have a terrible feeling that they'll both walk. Conspiracy's always a bugger to prove. And as for implicating him in Riddle's suicide . . . that was pissing against the wind."

"It *was* suicide, then?"

"Not much doubt about it. I had a brief word with Dr. Glendenning after he did the postmortem this afternoon. No signs of a struggle, no signs of restraint or drugs in the system. He'll run a full tox check, of course, just to be certain. And the note's been checked by an expert. It's Riddle's handwriting. No, I think we can be pretty certain that Jimmy Riddle voluntarily sat in his car with the engine running. We can also be damn certain that the business with Emily and the pressure Clough was putting on him were a big part of what drove him to it, but we can't touch Clough for that."

"He's a slippery bastard, all right."

"Anyway, I'm getting more and more interested in Ruth Walker."

"You think she killed Emily?"

"I think she might have. It never really made any sense to me that Clough would have done it, especially after he tried to blackmail Riddle, much as I'd have loved to put him away for it."

"But Ruth?"

"She certainly had the opportunity, for a start. She was off work, poorly, at the time Emily was killed, or so she says. She could have driven up and back easily."

"And the means?"

"She said she had a cold, but I think her sniffle might have been caused by something else."

"Coke?"

"At a guess."

"What about the strychnine, though?"

"One of the leads I'm following up. As far as I can piece it together, her degree's in computers and information technology. She's very bright, got first-class honors and walked straight from university into a good job. She works for a computer software company. One of the employees told me that they custom-design specific software systems for specific business applications."

"You think she could be connected with Clough's pirating racket?"

"It is a connection that springs immediately to mind, I'll admit, but no. That's not it. This isn't the sort of thing you could profitably pirate. It's tailor-made for very specific business functions."

"So where does it lead us?"

"This employee I talked to, she thinks that Ruth's working on an inventory-control system for a large pharmaceutical company."

Annie whistled. "I see."

"What I'm trying to find out, if I can get hold of the boss there, is whether the job could possibly have given her access to controlled drugs such as strychnine."

"And if there's any missing?"

"Yes. But it could have been such a small quantity it wouldn't be missed. I don't know how tightly they control these things."

"Pretty tightly, I'd say. But if Ruth really was working on inventory control . . ."

"She might have access to the inventory. Yes. And she might also have been in a position to falsify data about quantities. We'll just have to wait and see. In the meantime there's another couple of things we need to follow up on." Banks lit a cigarette. "Want something to eat?"

Annie shook her head. "I've got some leftover pasta at home. Pub food's not very appetizing to a vegetarian."

"They do a nice salad sandwich, I'm told."

"I know. I've had one. A strip of wilted lettuce and a couple of slices of green tomato. What next?"

"First off, I want you to ask Darren Hirst, the boy who was with Emily the night she died, for access to his cellphone records. I just realized last night what was bothering me about the Riddles's phone records."

"What?"

"Emily's call to me the day before she died. It wasn't listed."

"She could have used a public box."

"That's what I thought at first, with the background noise

and all. But Darren has a cell phone and she was out with him and the gang that night. It's my bet she used his phone, and that she also used it to talk to whoever she set up the drug buy with. It's hardly likely she'd risk using her home phone for something like that. What I'd like to know is whether she used Darren's phone to call Ruth close to the time of her murder."

"That should be easy enough to find out."

"There's another thing. I also phoned Craig Newton, Emily's ex-boyfriend down in Stony Stratford."

"And?"

"When I went to talk to him, I remember noticing some photographs of Emily that bore a strong resemblance to the one that appeared in the newspaper yesterday."

"You think he was behind the story?"

"Craig? No. But he confirmed that Ruth also had prints of the photos because they'd been taken at a party they'd all attended."

"One of Clough's parties?"

"Not this time, no. Before Clough. The point is, though, that Ruth could have supplied the newspaper with the photograph and the hints about Clough and Jimmy Riddle."

"But how could she know?"

"I've no idea. It's all speculation so far. She obviously knew about Emily and Clough, probably knew Clough was a bit of a gangster. If she had discovered that Rosalind Riddle was her birth mother and was blackmailing her over it, it's no great leap of imagination to assume that she knew Jimmy Riddle was chief constable."

"I suppose not. But *why*?"

"To cause trouble for the Riddles. She was already blackmailing Rosalind, remember. Perhaps after Emily's murder Rosalind refused to pay up any more."

"Are we going to talk to Ruth again soon?"

"Definitely. Up here this time. I'll have her brought up tomorrow. I hope we'll have answers to some of our questions before she arrives. There's one other thing."

"What's that?"

"We need to talk to the person who saw Emily get into

the car at the Red Lion. So far I've been thinking that a light-colored car driven by someone with short blond hair probably meant Jamie Gilbert."

"And now?"

"Ruth Walker. She drives a cream car—I've seen it—and she'd bleached her hair blond the second time I saw her. Another drink?"

"Better not," Annie said. "I've got a long drive home. You should be careful, too."

"You're going home?"

"Don't look so disappointed. We've got a busy day tomorrow."

"You're right. But you can't blame me for showing a little disappointment."

Annie smiled. "I'd be pissed off if you hadn't. Anyway, after last night I'm worn out. I'm surprised you're not tired, too."

"It's been a long day. That's true." Banks swirled the last quarter of his pint around the bottom of his glass. "Do you think Ruth killed her adoptive parents?"

"Very unlikely. Mind you, I think she was definitely responsible for the cigarette end that started the fire. Her parents didn't smoke or drink. They were good Methodists. Ruth went a bit wild when she got to university. Maybe she'd had a few drinks and didn't put it out properly."

"It doesn't sound as if she made any attempt to save them."

"Who knows what happened in there, what she could or couldn't have done? She hurt herself badly getting out."

"Yes, but she lived. Were postmortems performed on the parents?"

Annie nodded. "I checked. No cause for suspicion. In both cases death was due to smoke inhalation. Just as with Chief Constable Riddle, there were no signs that they were restrained in any way, or drugged, and no indication that any obstacles had been placed in the way of their getting out. They were old and slow. That's all there is to it."

"Makes you wonder, though, doesn't it?"

"About what?"

"Oh, life, the universe, everything."

Annie slapped his arm, laughed and stood up. "I'm off before you start getting *really* philosophical. What about you?"

"One more cigarette, then I've got a couple more things to do back at the office."

"See you tomorrow, then."

"See you."

Annie walked out into the cold night air and paused for a while, listening to the choir singing "Silent Night" through chattering teeth. Then she dropped a few coins in the collection box and hurried off to her car before she changed her mind about Banks's offer.

18

Ruth Walker arrived with her police escort shortly after lunch the following day. Wearing baggy jeans and a shapeless mauve sweatshirt with sleeves that fell long past her hands, she looked both nervous and defiant as she took her seat in the gloomy interview room. She held her head high, but her eyes were all over the place, everywhere but on the person speaking to her. A sprinkling of acne lay over her pale cheeks, and her skin looked pasty and dry.

Unlike Barry Clough, who was now back at his Little Venice villa, Ruth didn't have an expensive lawyer in tow. They had offered to bring in a duty solicitor for her, but she said she didn't need anyone. Banks set the tape recorders going, gave details of the session and began. Annie sat beside him. He had the answers to most of his previous day's questions—including two calls from Darren's mobile, only one of which had been to Banks—in a buff folder on the desk in front of him, and he didn't like the story they told one bit.

"I suppose you know why you're here, don't you, Ruth?" Banks began.

Ruth stared at a squashed fly high on the opposite wall.

"We've been doing a bit of digging."

"Not really the season for that, is it?" Ruth said.

"This isn't a joking matter," Banks said. "So drop it, Ruth. It doesn't suit you."

"Whatever."

"You've told me a lot of lies."

"Lies? Pork pies. They're what I've been living. What else have I got to tell you?"

"It's my job to try and sort out a few truths. Let's start with the fire."

"What's that got to do with it?"

"With what?"

"With why I'm here."

"I told you, I'm trying to get at some truths."

"There was a fire. I woke up and my room was full of smoke. I had to jump out of the window. I broke my ankle really badly. You might have noticed I've still got a limp."

"What else can you tell us about the fire?"

"What's to tell? It was an accident. I couldn't walk for weeks."

"What caused the fire?"

"They said it was a cigarette. It can't have been mine. I put it out. I remember."

"Whose was it then?"

Ruth shrugged. "Dunno. It wasn't mine."

"Ruth, it *must* have been your cigarette. Your parents *died* in that fire, and all you can think about is your broken ankle. What's wrong with this picture?"

"You tell me. And they *weren't* my parents. Everyone says I was the lucky one, so I suppose they must be right."

"Did you *feel* lucky?"

" 'Do you feel lucky today, punk?' Sorry. Bad joke again. Blame it on being deprived of humor throughout my childhood and adolescence."

"Were you deprived of humor?"

"It wasn't part of the deal."

"What deal?"

"You know. The one where you're not supposed to dance, sing, laugh, cry, love, fuck. The religious deal. I sometimes think the reason they had to adopt a child was that they thought it was a sin to do what they had to do to produce one naturally."

"How did you feel toward your parents?"

"I told you, they *weren't* my parents. They were my *adoptive* parents. Believe me, it *does* make a difference. Do you know, they never even told me I was adopted?"

"How did you find out?"

"The papers."

"But surely they must have been destroyed by the fire?"

"They were kept in a safety deposit box at the bank. I only found out after they died and I had to open it. That's where they kept *me*. In a box."

"But they *were* the only parents who brought you up."

"Oh, yes. Everyone says they were decent, honest, God-fearing folk. Salt of the earth."

"What do you say?"

"They were stupid imbeciles, too brainwashed to make their own decisions about anything. They were scared of everything except the chapel. Their bodies. The world beyond the street. Their lives. They inflicted all that on me. And more. They made my life miserable, made me a laughingstock at school. I had no friends. I had no one to talk to. They didn't like me hanging around with the other kids. They said God ought to be enough of a friend for anyone. What do you expect me to say about them?"

"Were you glad they died?"

"Yes." Ruth's left hand shot out of the end of her sleeve and scratched the side of her nose. Her grubby fingernails were bitten to the quick.

"What about your birth mother?"

"Ros? I call her that, you know. It's a bit late to be calling her 'Mother,' don't you think? And Mrs. Riddle seems just a wee bit too formal."

"How did you find her?"

The edges of Ruth's lips curled in an ugly smirk. "You ought to know that, if you've done so much digging. My degree's in information technology. You can find out anything these days if you know where to look. The telephone directory is usually pretty reliable, you know. A good place to start. But there's the Internet, too. Lots of information out on that superhighway."

"Where did you begin?"

"With the Registrar General's office. They'll let you see your original birth certificate if you ask them nicely. From there it's pretty easy."

"What did the birth certificate tell you?"

"That I was born at seventy-three Launceston Terrace, Tiverton, on the twenty-third of February, 1977."

"What else?"

Ruth stared at the walls again, looking bored. "That my mother was Rosalind Gorwyn and that there was a blank space where my father's name was supposed to be."

"What did you do next?"

"I went to seventy-three Launceston Terrace, Tiverton, and found an elderly couple by the name of Gorwyn living there. It's not a very common name, even in Devon. I knew they couldn't be my real parents—they were too old—so I pushed them a bit and found out they were her aunt and uncle and that she had stayed with them while she had the baby. *Me*. Hid away from the world while she gave birth to me."

"What else did they tell you?"

"That my mother had married a man called Jeremiah Archibald Riddle, an important policeman, that she was a solicitor now, and they lived in North Yorkshire. By then they'd have told me anything to get rid of me. After that it was really easy. A child could have found them."

"Did you speak to Rosalind's parents at all?"

"Not right at first. But I found out that they'd retired to Barnstaple. He was a vicar. Which probably explains why my mother let me live."

"What do you mean?" Annie asked.

Ruth looked at her as if seeing her for the first time. She didn't seem to mind what she saw. "Well, either way I didn't have much of a chance, did I?" she said. "She could've just got rid of me, had an abortion. That's what I'd have done in her place. Then I would never have existed at all and none of this would have happened."

"Or?"

"She could have kept me. Then I'd have been an un-wanted baby with a single mother and your chief constable would never have married her. I'd probably have been brought up in some sort of punk commune or something, with people shooting heroin all around my cot, getting high and forgetting me, so I'd have crawled to the edge of the stairs and fallen over and died anyway. So I imagine she thought putting me up for adoption was a better choice for her. Pity it didn't turn out that way for me. I've been told the adoption people are pretty good, very strict in their standards, but some of us slip through the cracks. Like I said, everyone thought the Walkers were the salt of the earth, that they would make wonderful parents, but the Lord hadn't seen fit to bless them with issue. You'd think they'd take that as a sign, wouldn't you?"

Banks and Annie paused to take in what she said, then Banks picked up the questioning again. "You went to Rosalind's law office?"

"Yes. I thought it would be best that way. Turned out I was right." Ruth gave a mean little giggle. "She was scared shitless I'd say something to her husband. Thought he'd turf her out on her arse if he found out."

"So you blackmailed her."

Ruth slammed her fist onto the desk. "It was only my due! I only asked for my due. I'd had nothing from her in all those years. *Nothing*. And I'd had fat little but misery from the bloody Walkers. Do you know they once made me wear an old pair of shoes that were so small and tight that my toenails came off and my shoes were full of blood when I got home from school? That was what your bloody salt-of-the-earth Walkers were like. I had a *right* to something from Ros. She *owed* me. Why should *she* get it all just because she was born a few years later than me, on the right side of the blanket? Answer me that one. It should all have been mine, but she tossed me away. It was only my due."

The interview room was starting to feel very claustrophobic. Banks couldn't quite sort out the *she*'s; half the time it seemed as if Ruth was referring to Rosalind, the rest to Emily. "Were you abused by your adoptive parents, Ruth?"

Ruth gave a harsh laugh. "Abused? That's a good one. You at least have to *care* about someone to abuse them. No,

I wasn't abused, not in the way you mean it. I suppose there's more than one kind of abuse, though. I mean, I'd call being made to wear those shoes until my toes bled abuse. Wouldn't you? Mostly, they were just cold. Ironic they should die by fire, isn't it?"

Again, Banks felt that shiver creep up his spine. He saw Annie frowning. Ruth paid them no attention. "Did you see Rosalind often?" Banks asked.

"Not that often."

"When you needed something?"

"I only wanted my due."

"What about Emily? How did you feel toward her?"

"I'd be a liar if I said I liked her."

"But you befriended her, took her in. At least I assume that's how it happened and you didn't just meet her by accident near the station. Is that right?"

Ruth nodded. "When I met her the once in Ros's office, I made a point of finding out where she went to school. She was a boarding student, so I phoned her there, and visited her. When she started to trust me, when we began to be friends, she used to call me a lot from school, too. She'd complain about her parents, how strict they were. I had to laugh. I mean, she'd complain to *me* about that. I told her that after she was sixteen she could do what she wanted. It was near the end of the school year and she'd had her birthday, so I said why didn't she come and stay with me in London for a while if she wanted."

"You mean you lured her to London? You encouraged her to leave home?"

"I think *lured* is too strong a word. I had no trouble getting her there. She was only too pleased to come."

"But you didn't tell her parents where she was?"

"Why should I? It was her business, and she didn't want them to know."

"Do you think Rosalind knew?"

"I doubt it. She didn't know how close me and Emily had become. I don't think she even knew where I lived. Didn't bother to ask. That's how interested in me she was after all those years."

"Did you introduce Emily to Craig Newton?" Banks asked.

Ruth's face clouded. "I thought he was my friend. I thought he loved me. But he was just like all the rest."

"Did it hurt you when she took up with Craig?"

Ruth shot him a tortured glance. "What do you think?"

"Is that why you killed her?"

"I didn't kill her."

"Come on, Ruth. We've got the evidence. We know. You might as well tell us how it happened. I'm sure there were extenuating circumstances. What about Barry Clough? What part did he play in all this, for example?"

Ruth's eyes narrowed. "I wondered when you'd get around to him."

"What do you know about him?"

"Plenty."

"Like what?"

Ruth paused a minute and rubbed her fist over the top of her thigh as if she had an itch. "I bet it's something *you* don't know, clever clogs."

"Maybe it is. Why don't you tell me?"

"They didn't name my father on the birth certificate, as I told you. But I found out. That's who it was. Barry Clough. My *father*." Ruth flopped back in her chair and stared at the ceiling. "I'm tired and I want something to eat. You have to give me something to eat, don't you?"

"I don't know about you, Annie," Banks said when Ruth was back in her cell eating her canteen beefburger and chips, "but I could do with a breath of fresh air."

"My feelings exactly."

They left the station and walked across the market square, then they took the narrow, cobbled Castle Wynde past the bare formal gardens down to the riverside. It was a crisp, cold winter day, and their breaths plumed as they walked, crunching over puddles. The hill went down to the river steeply, with small limestone cottages lining both sides, and the cobbles were slippery. Banks could feel the icy wind blowing up from the river. It was just what he needed to get the smell of the interview room out of his system.

"What do you make of all that, then?" Annie asked when they were halfway down.

Banks didn't know what to make of Ruth's bombshell. He didn't even know if it was true; after all, she had told plenty of lies already. But why lie about something like that? "It raises more questions than it answers," he said.

"Such as: Did anyone else know, and did it have anything to do with Emily's murder?"

"For a start. If Rosalind Riddle knew, she kept it well hidden. I hadn't thought her *that* good an actress."

"Do you think Ruth killed Emily?"

"If she didn't, she knows what happened, she knows who did. She's a part of it, I'm certain of that."

They arrived at the river and paused for a while by the waist-high stone wall that ran along its bank. The falls rushed and foamed along the shallows, huge moss-covered slabs of ancient rock jutting out here and there, the result of a geological fault millions of years ago. Banks could feel the icy spray on his cheeks and in his hair. If the cold spell continued for much longer, even the falls would freeze. Above them, the dark mass of the ruined castle keep and towers lay heavy against a pewter sky; it was a black-and-white world, or like the world of a black-and-white photograph with all its subtle variations of gray. Annie slipped her arm in his. It was a good feeling, the only good feeling he'd had that morning.

They walked along the riverside path, past the terraced gardens, no more than a small park dotted with trees, to their left. There weren't many people around, just a young couple walking their Airedale and an old age pensioner in a flat cap taking his daily constitutional. Banks had often considered buying a flat cap himself. All these years in Yorkshire and he still didn't have one. But he didn't like wearing hats, even in winter.

Across the river, to the right, bare trees lined the opposite bank. Beyond them, Banks could make out the shapes of the large houses facing The Green, beyond which lay the notorious East Side Estate, which pretty much kept the Eastvale police in business year-round.

In one of those big houses lived Jenny Fuller, a psychologist Banks had worked with on a number of cases. A friend, too, and a one-time potential lover. Jenny had been polite but cool toward him ever since he stood her up on a date three months ago through no fault of his own. It was more than just that, though; it was as if Jenny had put too much of herself on the line, exposed her feelings for him, and the seeming rejection had grazed a raw nerve, made her curl in on herself. She was on the rebound from a sour relationship with an American professor at the time, Banks already knew, so she was hurting to start with. He wished he could do something to bridge the distance, rekindle the friendship. It had been important to him over the years.

But there was Annie, too. Banks was no expert, but he knew enough of women to realize that Annie wouldn't appreciate his spending time with someone other than her now that he felt free from his marriage.

"Sandra wants a divorce," he suddenly said to Annie. He felt her arm stiffen in his, but she didn't remove it. First good sign. This was one thing he hadn't told her the other night, one thing he had found too difficult to put into words. It still was, but he knew he would have to try if he and Annie were to go any further. It might put her more at ease or it might scare her off; that was the risk he would have to take.

"I'm sorry," she said, without looking at him.

"No, I didn't mean it like that. I mean, I'm glad."

Annie slowed down and turned slowly to face him. "You're what?"

They started walking again, and he tried to explain to her what he had felt in London, after he first heard the news. He wasn't sure whether he did a good job or not, but Annie nodded here and there and seemed to contemplate what he'd said after he'd finished. Finally, she said, "That's all right, then."

"It is?"

"Time to let go."

Second good sign. "I suppose so."

"Does it hurt?"

"Not anymore. Oh, there are memories, always will be,

and some residual feelings—anger, disappointment, whatever. But no, it doesn't hurt. In fact, I feel better than I have in years."

"Good."

"Look, do you fancy coming over to the cottage for Christmas dinner? Tracy will be there. Just the three of us."

"I can't. Really, I'm sorry, Alan, but I *always* go home for Christmas. Ray would never forgive me if I missed it."

"I understand."

Annie gave his arm a little squeeze. "I mean it, Alan. It's not an excuse. I'd love to meet Tracy. Maybe some other time?"

Banks knew she was telling the truth. Annie wasn't a very good liar, as he had discovered. Lying made her all grumpy and withdrawn. "We'll have a drink together sometime, then," he said.

"Do you think she'll hate me?"

"Why should she?"

Annie smiled. "Sometimes you can be pretty damn thick when it comes to women, Alan Banks."

"I'm not being thick," Banks said. "Mothers, daughters, fathers, it can all get pretty complicated. I know that. But Tracy's not a hater. I know my daughter. I wouldn't expect her to rush up to you and hug you—no doubt she'll be a little hesitant, checking you out, as they say—but she's not a hater, and she doesn't see me as the villain in all this. She's got a good head on her shoulders."

"Unlike Ruth Walker."

"Indeed. Did you feel the atmosphere in that room?"

Annie nodded.

"I felt something like it before, the times I talked to her in London," Banks said, "but it wasn't as powerful. I think it's because she senses she's near the end. She's given up. She's unraveling."

"You think so?"

"Yes. I think she wants us to know it all now, so we can see her point of view. So we can understand her. Forgive her."

Annie shook her head. "I don't think she wants forgiveness, Alan. At least, not the way I'm reading her. I don't think she sees there's anything to forgive."

"Perhaps not. I should have known."

"Should have known what?"

"That something was wrong there."

"But you've only just found out Ruth was Emily's half-sister. How could you have known that?"

"I don't know. I should have dug deeper sooner."

"Why do you have to take the burden on yourself like this? Why is everything your fault? Why do you think if you only acted differently you could prevent people being killed?"

Banks stopped and looked out over the swirling river; it was the color of a pint of bitter, an intruder in the black-and-white world. "Do I?"

"You know you do."

Banks lit a cigarette. "It must be something to do with Graham Marshall."

"Graham Marshall? Who's he?"

"A boy at school. I won't say a friend because I didn't know him very well. He was a quiet kid, bright, shy."

"What happened?"

"One day he simply disappeared."

"What happened?"

"Nobody knows. He was never found. Dead or alive."

"What did the police think?"

"The general consensus was that he'd been abducted by a child molester who'd murdered him after he'd had his way. This would probably have been around the time of the Moors Murders, though in a different part of the country, so people were especially sensitive to the disappearance of children."

"That's sad." Annie rested her elbows on the wall beside Banks. "But I still don't see what it's got to do with you."

"About three or four months before Graham Marshall's disappearance I was playing with some friends down by the river. We were throwing stones in, just having a bit of harmless fun, the way kids do. . . ."

As he spoke, Banks remembered the day vividly. It was

spitting and the raindrops pitted the murky water. A man approached along the riverbank. All Banks could remember now was that he was tall—but then every adult was tall to him then—and thin, with greasy dark hair and a rough, pockmarked complexion. Banks smiled and politely paused before dropping in a large stone, one he had to hold in both hands, to let the stranger pass by without splashing him.

The next thing he knew, the man had grabbed him by the arms and was pushing him toward the river, the stone forgotten at their feet. He could smell beer on the man's breath, the same smell he remembered from his father, and something else—sweat, a wet-dog smell, body odor, like the smell of his socks after a long rugby game, as he struggled for his life. He called out and looked around for his friends, but they were running down to the gap in the fence where they had got in.

The struggle seemed to go on forever. Banks managed to wedge his heels at the edge of the riverbank and push back with all his might, but the grass was wet, and the soil under it was fast turning to mud. He didn't think he could keep his grip much longer.

His smallness and wiriness were his only advantages, he knew, and he wriggled as hard as an eel to slip out of the man's strong grasp. He knew that if he didn't escape he would drown. He tried to bite the man's arm, but all he got was a mouthful of vile-tasting cloth, so he gave up.

The man was breathing hard now, as if the effort was becoming too much for him. Banks drew on his last reserves of energy and wriggled as hard and fast as he could. He managed to get one arm free. The man held him by the other arm and punched him at the side of his right eye. He felt something sharp, like a ring, cut his skin. He flinched with pain and pulled away, succeeding in freeing his other arm. He didn't wait to see if he was being pursued, but ran like the clappers to the hole in the fence.

Only when he caught up with his friends at the edge of the park did he dare risk looking back. Nobody in sight. His friends seemed sheepish as they asked him how he was, but he toughed it out. No problem. Inside, though, he was terribly shaken. They made a pact not to say anything. None of them was supposed to be playing down by the river in the first place. Their parents said it was dangerous. Banks didn't dare tell his parents what had happened, explaining the cut by his eye by saying he had fallen and cut it on a piece of glass, and he had never relied on anyone to help him out of trouble again in his life.

"I was wrong. I *should* have told my parents, Annie. They would have made me report it to the police, and they might have caught him before he did any more harm. There was a dangerous man out there, and my fear and shame left him free to do as he pleased."

"You blamed yourself for what happened to Graham Marshall? For the acts of a child molester?"

Banks turned away from the beer-colored water to face Annie. "When he went missing, all I could think of was the tall man with the greasy dark hair and the body odor." Banks shivered. Sometimes he still woke in the night gagging on the taste of the dirty cloth of the man's sleeve, and in the dream, when he looked at the river, it was full of dead boys all floating in the same direction, in perfectly matched rows, and Graham Marshall was the only one he recognized. So much guilt.

"But you don't *know* that it was the same man."

"Doesn't matter. I still took the guilt on myself. I'd been attacked by an older man, possibly a pervert, and I didn't report it. Then a boy was abducted, possibly by a pervert. Of course I blamed myself. And I certainly couldn't say anything about it later."

Annie put her hand on his arm. "So you made a mistake. So you *should* have reported it. You can't spend your life sulking over all the mistakes you've made. You'd never bother getting out of bed in the morning."

Banks smiled. "You're right. I try not to let it get me down too much. It's only when something like this happens, something I think I could have prevented."

Annie started walking again. "You're not God," she said over her shoulder. "You can't change the way things are."

Banks flicked his cigarette in the river and followed her.

Annie was right, he knew; he only wished he could *feel* better about it.

They turned left at the main road by the pre-Roman site, a sort of barrow where ancient graves had been discovered, and then left again, back toward the station, toward whatever other horrors Ruth Walker had in store for them.

Banks started the tape recorders again. "All right, Ruth," he said, "you've had some food and rest. Ready to talk to us again?"

Ruth nodded and retracted her hands deep into the sleeves of her sweatshirt.

"For the record," Banks said, "Ms. Walker nodded to indicate that she is ready to resume the interview."

Ruth stared down at her lap.

"Before the break, Ruth, you told us that Barry Clough is your father. I'm sure you know that gives rise to a lot more questions."

"Go ahead."

"First of all, is it true?"

"Of course it is. Why should I lie about it?"

"You've lied before. Remember, right at the beginning you told me your life has been a lie?"

"This is true. He's my father. You can check."

"How did you find out about this if it wasn't on the birth certificate?"

"I talked to Ros's parents."

"And they told you, just like that?"

"It wasn't as easy as that."

"How easy was it, then?"

"It was a matter of finding out what name he was using now."

"What do you mean?"

"All they could tell me was that Ros got herself made pregnant by some punk. He hung around with bands, worked as a roadie, played bass a bit, something like that. Ros had told them his name, but he was long gone by the time she even found out she was pregnant. He was in America, they told me. And she didn't want anything to do with him anyway. Neither did her parents. Everybody just did their best to forget him, and it seems as if that was pretty easy."

"What was his name?"

Ruth laughed. "You know what they were like back then, all using silly names, thinking they sounded tough? Rat Scabies. Sid Vicious. Johnny Rotten."

"I remember," said Banks.

"Well, this bloke was going by the name of Mal Licious. I ask you. *Mal Licious*."

What an apt name for Barry Clough, Banks thought. "So nobody knew his real name?"

"Ros's parents and uncle and aunt didn't."

"Did you ask Rosalind herself?"

"Yes."

"And?"

"She didn't know, either. Mal Licious was all he went by. She just called him Mal. Seems she hadn't known him that well. I think it was a one-night stand. She didn't really want to talk about it."

"How *did* you find out, then?"

Ruth shifted in her chair. "Easy. Information technology. I know a bit about the music scene, I've been to a lot of clubs and raves and stuff, and Craig had a few contacts, he'd taken band photos, that sort of thing. I asked around. It seemed a logical way to start. There was always a chance that this Mal Licious was still on the scene somewhere. A lot of these people never grow up. Look at Rod Stewart, for Christ's sake. Clough was a pretty well-known name on the scene, partly because of his trendy bar and partly because of the bands he promoted. There were still people around who'd known him way back, and someone told me he used to be called Mal Licious. Thought it was a bit of a laugh. Well, there can't have been two of them, can there? Stands to reason."

Indeed it did, thought Banks. Bright girl. Or woman. A lot of things were starting to make sense now. "So none of what happened since Emily went to London was coincidence, then?" he said.

"What do you mean?"

"Emily shacking up with Barry Clough, Clough finding out about Riddle, the article in the newspaper linking them together."

A look of triumph filled Ruth's eyes. "No," she said. "None of it was coincidence. It was all *me*. I set things in motion. Beyond that, they took on a life of their own. I soon found out that Clough liked young girls, and it wasn't hard to get an invitation to one of his parties. What happened next was up to nature, not me. It really pissed off Craig."

"Did you ever approach Clough? He's a wealthy man. Wealthier than Rosalind, I should imagine."

Ruth frowned at him. "It's not *all* about money, you know. No, I didn't approach him. What was he going to say? Probably didn't even remember Ros's name, let alone that he'd shagged her. They were probably stoned out of their minds."

"Did you tell Rosalind about Emily and Clough?"

"No."

"Why on earth not? He was her . . ." Banks had to pause and think for a moment. No matter how terrible it seemed for Rosalind's daughter to be sleeping with a man her mother had slept with, and whose child she had given birth to, Emily wasn't any relation to Clough whatsoever. "Emily was your half-sister," was all he could manage.

Ruth smiled. "Information management. Knowledge is power, as I'm sure you know. If you use it only a little at a time, it can go a long way. I might have had a use for that information eventually. But I was enjoying myself plenty with what I already had. I think if I'd told Ros about them, everything would have come tumbling down, and it wasn't time for that yet."

You're damn right the whole house of cards would have come tumbling down, Banks thought. Before he could respond, Annie eased in. "You said you were enjoying yourself, Ruth. In what way?"

Ruth faced her for a moment before her eyes went off in another direction. "Why shouldn't I enjoy myself? I've had little enough fun in my life. Why not have a bit for a change?"

"Fun?" repeated Annie. "Ruth, two people have died because of all this. Emily and her father. A family's been torn apart. And you think it's fun?"

"I didn't mean to kill her."

Annie glanced at Banks and indicated he should pick up the thread. It was the first hint of a confession they'd heard from Ruth so far. Banks didn't want to lose her now, but at the same time he wanted no problems over PACE. "We're heading into dangerous ground, Ruth," he said. "I'm telling you again that you're entitled to have a solicitor present, and I'm asking you if you want us to provide one for you."

"I've told you before," Ruth shouted directly into the microphone. "I don't want any fucking solicitor. Is that clear enough for you?"

"It'll do," said Banks. "Let me get this straight, then. You discovered that Barry Clough was your father and you didn't tell either him or Rosalind this. Am I right?"

"Yes."

"Did you tell Emily?"

"Of course not."

"But you introduced them at a party."

"That was all I needed to do." Ruth's eyes shone. "That was the beauty of it, you see. I knew Clough liked young girls, and you didn't have to talk to Emily for long before you found out what a twisted little Electra complex she had. She wanted to fuck her daddy. Well, I couldn't arrange that, but at least I could give her a chance to fuck mine. It was perfect."

"Why?"

"Because *I was the only one who knew the truth.* The joke was on them, on someone else, for a change, not on me."

"What about Barry Clough and Emily's father?"

"That was just a bonus. I know a young reporter. It was a big story, probably made his career. I just gave him one of those photos of Emily all dressed up for a party and I told him that she was fucking Barry Clough and her father was a chief constable. He was off to Yorkshire like a shot. Did the rest of the footwork himself."

"What about Barry Clough, after Emily had left? Did you tell him who she was, where she lived, who her father was?"

"Yes. I thought it would probably interest him. He struck me as the kind of man who liked to own others. I just thought it would be interesting to put the two of them together when neither of them knew how close they really were."

"So he doesn't know that you're his daughter or that Emily's your half-sister?"

"Of course not. It wasn't time to go *that* far yet."

"Again, why?"

"They all thought they were so cool, so beautiful, so powerful, so in control. But all the time it was me pulling the strings. *Me*. They were just running around like headless chickens."

"And this amused you?"

"Yes. I'm not mad, if that's what you're thinking. I'm not looking to get off on some insanity plea or anything like that. I *would* like a little recognition for all the work I put in, though."

"What about Emily? You told her she was your half-sister, didn't you?"

"I had to, otherwise she would never have trusted me or come to live with me. She'd have thought I was after her or something. This way it made more sense. It was our little secret."

Banks paused before going on, knowing he had reached a crucial stage. "Ruth, we know you were working for a pharmaceutical company and had access to strychnine. Cocaine's easy enough to get. Did you give Emily the lethal mixture?"

"It wasn't meant to be lethal."

"What did you intend it to do to her?"

"Give her a scare. Give her the jitters. I didn't mean for it to kill her. Honest. I'm not a murderer."

"What are you, then?"

Ruth tugged at a frayed edge on her sweatshirt. "Maybe I've got some problems. People don't like me. But I'm not a murderer." There were tears in her eyes.

"All right, Ruth. What happened?"

"We'd talked on the telephone a few times and she kept

saying she was off the stuff. First, I just wanted to see if I could get her back on again. I mean, people say all sorts of things, don't they, like they've given up smoking, but if you offer them a cigarette, if you put just a little temptation their way . . ."

"And that's what you did?"

"Yes. Dangled a carrot. Well, a gram of coke, actually. She could probably have scored some up north if she'd asked around, but that was a bit too close to her father's territory. I mean, you never know if your dealer is an undercover cop, do you? I even offered to deliver it. Said I had to visit some relatives in Durham and I'd stop by on the way."

"What did she say?"

"She said she'd ring me back. I knew she was thinking seriously about it. Anyway, the day before, I was working late . . . she phoned me at work on some lad's mobile and said she was getting bored and she wouldn't mind some for the next day. She was going clubbing with some mates. I knew I could get a couple of days off, say I had a cold or something. Anyway, just after I talked to her and said I'd see her the next day, I had to go into the controlled area to do some product coding, and that's when I got the idea of the strychnine. I didn't know how much to put in. I'd heard they sometimes used it as a base in some street drugs and it makes your jaw and your neck stiff. I just wanted to give her a scare, that's all. It was only a little bit. I didn't think it was enough to kill her, but it might make her twitch a bit in public, maybe even puke and piss herself."

"That was what you wanted to do to her? Humiliate her in public?"

"It was a start."

"Even though you wouldn't be there to witness it?"

"But I'd *know,* wouldn't I? Being there would be too dangerous. Don't you see the point? I mean, I didn't actually see her doing it, but I knew she was fucking my father. If you have a bit of imagination you can amuse yourself easily enough."

"It has to be more than that, Ruth," Annie chipped in.

Ruth looked away. "Why?"

"It just does. Why did you hate Emily so much? What did she ever do to you?"

"She had my life, didn't she? What should have been mine."

"Why did you want her to suffer?"

"Because she had it all. She took Craig from me."

"Craig was never with you that way," Banks said, picking up on Annie's rhythm. "He was never your lover."

Ruth jutted her chin out. "That's what *he* says now."

"Why should he lie?"

"He's against me. She poisoned him against me."

"That's not enough, Ruth," Annie chimed in again.

Ruth gave her a sharp glance. "What do you want? Blood?"

"No. That seems to be what *you* wanted. We want some answers."

"It was all so bloody easy for her. Everything just fell into her lap. Craig. Barry Clough. My own father, for Christ's sake, was running his hands over her thighs ten minutes after they met."

"But that was part of your plan, you said," Annie went on.

"You can't always arrange things so they don't hurt you at least just a little bit. She got everything she wanted, just like that."

"Then why did she want to run away from home, Ruth?"

"Uh? What do you mean?"

"If everything was so perfect in Emily's life, why did she want to run away from her parents?"

"They wouldn't let her do what she wanted. They were strict."

"Like yours?"

"Nowhere near as bad as mine. You don't know the half of it."

"Then why didn't you sympathize with her?"

"I did. At first. Then she just . . . she got everything she wanted. Craig started ignoring me. Even Emily deserted me."

Banks took over again. "Why did you kill her, Ruth?"

Ruth didn't know whom to look at. She looked at the squashed fly again. "I didn't. I didn't mean to kill her."

"But you did kill her," Banks pressed on. "Why?"

Ruth paused and her face seemed to go through the kind of contortions as Emily's must have when the strychnine hit.

"Why did you kill her, Ruth?" Banks persisted, his voice hardly above a whisper. "Why?"

"Because they took her back!" Ruth blurted out. "After all that happened. After everything she did to them. She broke their hearts and they took her back. She threw me out, but she took her back. They took her back! They took her back!" Ruth started crying, fat tears rolling down her acned cheeks.

There was nothing more to say. Banks called in the uniformed officers to take Ruth back to her cell. Now it was time to charge her and bring on the lawyers.

Banks drove out to the Old Mill that night with a heavy heart. He knew he had to be the one to tell Rosalind what had happened, what Ruth had done, just as he had had to break the news about Emily's murder, but it wasn't a task he cherished.

The lights were on in the front room. He parked out front, glancing toward the garage as he pulled up his collar against the wind and rain, and rang the doorbell.

Rosalind answered and invited him in. She was wearing a short skirt and a cashmere jumper. He followed her into the living room. Her legs looked good, and it didn't seem as if she was wearing any tights. He thought he noticed something different about the smell of the place, but he dismissed it; there were far more serious matters on his mind.

"Drink?" Rosalind asked.

"Small whiskey, please."

"You might as well have a large one. I don't like the stuff, and there's no one else to drink it."

"I have to drive."

She raised her eyebrow as she poured. "Really?"

"Really." Christ, Banks thought, she was flirting. He would have to tread carefully. He accepted the crystal glass and sat down in the only uncovered armchair. The room was as sterile as ever, and a couple of packing crates sat on the floor. The baby grand was covered by a white sheet, as was most of the other furniture. He took a sip of whiskey. It was Glenfiddich, not one of his favorites. At the moment, though, anything would do.

"I was just doing some packing," Rosalind said. "Do you know how remarkably little I have to show for all these years?" She poured herself a large gin and tonic, clearly not her first of the evening, pulled a sheet off one of the armchairs and sat down opposite Banks. As she did so, he caught a glimpse of black silk between her legs. He looked away.

"Where are you going?" he asked.

"First?"

"That's a start."

"I'm going down to Barnstaple after the funeral to be with Benjamin. We'll be staying with my parents for a while. I can't stand hanging about up here any longer. I feel like some crazy old woman all alone in a Gothic mansion. It's too big to be here alone in. I've even started talking to the furniture and the creaks in the woodwork."

Banks smiled. "And then, after Barnstaple?"

"I don't know. I'll have to reinvent myself, won't I? I rather fancy the coast. A little Devon fishing village, for example. I can become the mysterious woman who paces the widow's walk in a long black cloak."

"That was Lyme Regis," Banks said. *"The French Lieutenant's Woman."*

"I know. I saw the film. But this is my version."

"What about your job?"

"That's not important. It never has been. Jerry's was the only important career in the family, and now that's gone, none of it really matters."

"And Benjamin?"

"He can walk with me. It would make me more mysterious. I'm sorry, I don't mean to be flippant. It's just . . ." She ran her hand across her brow. "I've probably had too much to drink." She frowned. "Why are you here?"

"I've got something to tell you."

Her eyes widened. "Have you caught him? Emily's killer?"

Banks swallowed. This was going to be harder than he had imagined. "Yes," he said. "We've got a confession."

"Clough?"

That was another bridge he'd have to cross: *Mal Licious.* "No. Not Clough." He leaned forward and cupped his drink in both hands, staring into the pale liquid and catching a whiff of it. "Look, there's no easy way to say this."

"What?"

"It was Ruth."

"Ruth? But . . . she can't . . . I mean . . ."

"She confessed. She said she didn't mean to kill Emily, just to give her a scare."

"Is that true?"

"I honestly don't know. She's contradicted herself quite a bit."

"Ruth." Rosalind fell silent and Banks let it stretch. Wind lashed the rain against the windowpanes the way it had the first night he came to the Riddle house. It seemed like years ago.

"Do you want to hear what happened?" Banks asked.

Rosalind looked at him. There was fear in her large blue eyes. "I suppose I'd better," she said. "Look, do smoke if you want to. I know you're a smoker."

"It's all right."

"Suit yourself." Rosalind got up a little unsteadily and pulled a packet of Dunhills and a box of matches from her handbag. She lit up, refreshed her gin and tonic and sat down again.

"I didn't know you smoked," said Banks.

"I didn't. Not for twenty years. But I've started again."

"Why?"

"Why not?"

Banks lit up too. "It's bad for you."

"So's life."

There was no answer to that. Slowly, Banks told her the whole story about Ruth Walker's twisted, private campaign of hatred and revenge against the Riddle family. First he told her about Ruth's less-than-perfect life with the overzealous Walkers and about the fire that killed them. Then he told her how Ruth had discovered that Barry Clough was her father and had hooked him up with Emily out of spite, then put the tabloid on the scent of a scandal, and he told her how Ruth arranged to meet Emily and give her the poisoned cocaine, how she didn't even need to be there, that it was enough for her simply to imagine Emily's pain and shame as she humiliated herself. As he spoke, what little color there had been left Rosalind Riddle's face and her eyes filled with tears. They didn't fall, just gathered there at the rims, waiting, magnifying her despair. Rosalind left her drink and her cigarette untouched as she listened. A long column of ash gathered and fell onto the hardwood floor when a slight tremor passed through her fingers.

When Banks had finished, Rosalind sat in silence for a while, taking it all in, digesting it as best she could, shaking her head slowly as if disagreeing with some inner voice. Then she knocked back the rest of her drink and whispered, "But why? Why did she do it? Can you answer me that one?"

"She's ill."

"That's no reason. Why? Why did she do it? Why did she hate us so much? Didn't I do my best for her? I didn't have an abortion. I gave her life. How the hell was I to know her adoptive parents would turn out to be religious fanatics?"

"You weren't."

"So why does she blame me?"

Ruth's last words still echoed in Banks's mind from that afternoon: *Because they took her back. She broke their hearts and they took her back.* "Because Ruth sees everything from her own point of view, and only that," he said. "All she knows is how things affect *her,* how things hurt *her,* how *she* was deprived. In her way of looking at the world, everything was either done for her or against her. Mostly it was *against* her. She doesn't know any different, doesn't recognize people's normal feelings."

Rosalind laughed harshly. "My daughter the psychopath?"

"No. No, I don't think so. Not as simple as that. She enjoyed exercising power over people, inflicting pain, yes, but she didn't have the detachment of a psychopath. She was obsessed, yes, but not psychopathic. And she knows the difference between right and wrong. You'd have to ask a psychiatrist, of course, but that's my opinion."

Rosalind got up and fixed herself another drink. She offered Banks one, but he refused. He still had a quarter inch in the bottom of his glass, and that would do him nicely.

"Will she be put in a mental hospital?" Rosalind asked.

"She'll be sent for psychiatric evaluation, for what it's worth. They'll determine what's best done with her."

"There'll be a trial? Prison?"

"I'm afraid so."

Rosalind shook her head. "Emily's dead. Jerry's dead. Ruth's a murderer. Before Emily died she lived with the man who left me pregnant with Ruth more than twenty years ago. Then I find out that my daughter, my abandoned daughter Ruth, led her into it on purpose, just to humiliate us all in her eyes, so that she could be the only one to know we were all living a lie. Then she killed her. I had two daughters, and one murdered the other. How do you expect me to put all that together? How can I possibly make sense of it all?" She took a long sip of gin and tonic.

Banks shook his head. "I don't know. In time, perhaps."

"Remember the first time we met," Rosalind said, crossing her long legs and leaning back in her chair so that a smooth white stretch of thigh showed. Her voice was a little slurred.

"Yes."

"I was obnoxious, wasn't I?"

"You were upset."

"No, that's not it at all. I was obnoxious. Jerry was upset. If anything, I was annoyed, irritated by Emily's irresponsible behavior, worried what impact it might have on Jerry's political ambitions, on *my* future. I didn't want Emily back. I couldn't handle her."

"You wanted to protect the world you'd made."

"And what a world that was. All style and no substance.

All glitter and no gold." She waved her arm in a gesture at the room and spilled some gin and tonic on her jumper. She didn't bother to wipe it off. "All this. It's strange, but I was thinking about it when you arrived, while I was packing. Funny, it doesn't mean very much now. None of it does. You were right to despise me."

"I didn't despise you."

"Yes, you did. Admit it."

"Maybe I resented you a little."

"And now?"

"Now?"

"Do you despise me now? Resent me?"

"No."

"Why not? I'm the same person."

"No, you're not."

"How profound. But you're right. I'm not. All the money, the status, the power, the thrill of political ambition, the whiff of Westminster . . . it all used to mean so much. It means nothing now. Less than nothing. Dust."

"What does have meaning for you now?"

Rosalind paused, sipped some more gin and tonic and stared at him, her eyes slightly unfocused. Outside, the wind continued to howl and rain lashed against the windowpanes. "Nothing," she whispered. "Not yet. I have to find out. But I won't give up until I do. I'm not like Jerry." She got unsteadily to her feet. "Stay and have another drink with me?"

"No. Really. I must be going."

"Please. Where do you have to go to that's so important? Who do you have to go to?"

She had a point. There was Annie, of course, but he wouldn't be going to Annie so late. Another *small* drink couldn't do any harm. "All right."

The drink, when it came, wasn't small, but he didn't have to drink all of it, he told himself.

"I'm sorry there's no music," Rosalind said. "We never did have music in the house. I remember your little cottage, how cozy it is with the fire, the music playing. Maybe I'll find somewhere like that." She looked around bleakly. "There was nothing like that here."

Banks wanted to point out the grand piano, but he had a feeling it was just for show. Emily had been forced to take piano lessons, he remembered, because it was part and parcel of the Riddle lifestyle, along with the pony, the proper schools and the rest. Some people managed to be happy with those things for their entire lives, then there were people like Rosalind, who caught Tragedy's wandering eye and got to watch it all come toppling down around them.

"I should never have put her up for adoption."

"What else could you do?"

"I could have had an abortion, and then Emily's killer would never have been born."

"If we all knew the consequences of every decision we made, we'd probably never make any," said Banks. "Besides, it wasn't your fault that you had to give Ruth up for adoption. Your parents played a part in that. Does that make them responsible for Emily's death, too?" He shook his head. "It doesn't make any sense, Rosalind. You were young. You couldn't have cared for a child properly, especially without the father's help. You thought she would have a better life. It wasn't your fault that the adoption agency thought they had found Ruth a home with decent people who turned out to be strict religious types. And it wasn't even the Walkers's fault that Ruth turned out the way she did. I'm sure they did their best in many ways. From what I've gathered, they weren't intentionally cruel, just thoughtless and strict and cold. No. You can keep on assigning blame here, there and everywhere, but when it comes right down to it, we're responsible for what we do ourselves."

Rosalind stubbed out her cigarette and tossed back the rest of her drink. "Oh, you're right. I know. It'll pass. Everything's just too overwhelming at the moment. I can't seem to take it all in." She went to refill her glass and bumped her hip against the corner of the cocktail cabinet. Glasses and bottles rattled.

"I'd really better be going," Banks said. "It's getting late."

Rosalind turned and walked toward him, swaying a little. "No, you can't go yet. I don't want to be alone."

"I can't help you anymore," said Banks.

Rosalind pouted. "Please?"

"There's nothing more I can do."

"There must be. You're a nice man. You've been good to me. You're the only person who has."

Banks walked toward the front door and opened it. He felt the cold wind around his hands and bare head. Rosalind leaned against the wall, drink in her hand, tears in her eyes.

"I'm sorry," said Banks, then he pulled the door shut behind him and dashed toward his car. Sorry as he felt for Rosalind Riddle, he didn't want to be part of her life any longer. He wanted to put as much distance between them as possible. Gratly would do for a start, and Barnstaple would be even better.

Before he could get into his car, he heard the crystal tumbler shatter against the door behind him.

EPILOGUE:
CHRISTMAS DAY

B anks woke up early on Christmas morning, and after sitting quietly in the kitchen for a while drinking his tea and enjoying the peace he always felt there, he went into the living room, turned the tree lights on, slipped his *Buena Vista Social Club* CD in the stereo and went back to the kitchen, humming along with "Chan Chan" as he stood over the large free-range chicken that lay splayed on the chopping block, a copy of *Delia Smith's Christmas* open flat beside it.

He was going to make the traditional pork, sage and onion stuffing, for which he had purchased all the ingredients yesterday. He was shocked to read that Delia Smith said you should make your stuffing on Christmas Eve, but he decided that was perhaps because the enormous turkey she was cooking would probably take all day. He'd be fine. He looked at his watch. Plenty of time.

His back ached because he had had to sleep on the small sofa downstairs. It was a small price to pay for having *both* of his kids with him for Christmas, though.

A couple of days ago, Brian had phoned to say that he had bought the car he'd been after and he had a few days free. He offered to pick up Tracy in Leeds on his way to Gratly if Banks had room for them both. Banks was overjoyed. Of course he had room. He immediately went out and bought more presents: a three-CD history of the Blue Horizon label for Brian, and some of the finest, most-expensive makeup brushes he could find for Tracy, along with a few odds and ends to fill out their stockings.

They were both staying until Boxing Day, when Brian would drive Tracy down to London to see her mother and Sean, who were spending Christmas in Dublin. Annie was with her father and the rest of his colony of oddballs in Cornwall, but that was all right. She would be back soon, and they had a date for New Year's Eve.

So this was his imperfect Christmas with his imperfect family, but at least, he reminded himself, he still had a family, despite the damage done over the last year. All Rosalind Riddle had was a young son who would be forever asking where his daddy and his big sister had gone, and a long-abandoned daughter facing charges for murdering her half-sister; though Banks had a feeling that Ruth Walker would probably be committed to a mental hospital rather than sent to prison.

Many times over the past week or so Banks had remembered that expression of despair on Rosalind's face as she sat amid the packing crates and sheeted furniture listening to him tell her the full story of Ruth's obsession. He also remembered the sound of the crystal glass shattering against the door as he left. It had worried him so much that he had called on Rosalind's closest neighbor, Charlotte King, on his way home, and asked her to keep an eye on Rosalind.

He had also attended Jimmy Riddle's funeral, with full police honors, a week before Christmas. Rosalind had been there, along with Benjamin and her parents, but she had ignored him. Another person who had opened up to him too much, like Jenny Fuller, and revealed far too much of the raw, naked self below the surface, then regretted it and turned away.

Afterward, he heard, they had all gone down to Barnstaple, and the Old Mill was on the market. He wished Rosalind well; God knew, she had suffered enough.

Banks peered at the recipe. He had just mixed the bread crumbs, sage and onion with the boiling water when his telephone rang. Who the hell could that be at nine o'clock on

Christmas morning? he wondered, as he put the bowl aside and went into the living room.

"Merry Crimble, Banks."

Bloody hell! It was Dirty Dick Burgess. "Merry Christmas," Banks said. "To what do I owe the honor?"

"Got a Christmas present for you."

"You shouldn't have."

"*I* didn't."

"Okay, I give up. What the hell are you talking about?"

"I thought it would come better from me, rather than you reading about it when it's all over the papers or watching it on television."

"What would?"

"Barry Clough."

"Barry Clough? What about him?"

"He's dead."

"Dead?"

"Stop talking like a bloody parrot, Banks. Yes. Dead. DEAD *Dead*."

Banks gripped the handset tighter and sat down. "Tell me what happened."

As far as Banks knew, after he and Annie had gone to see Stafford Oakes at the CPS Office a week or so ago, all charges against Clough had been dropped. It turned out that the tire match probably wouldn't withstand a close cross-examination, and someone had cocked up on the warrant for the search of Jamie Gilbert's car, rendering all evidence found therein inadmissible. British justice. To add to their troubles, the witness who said she had seen Jamie Gilbert with Charlie Courage had begun having mysterious lapses of memory.

"In the early hours of the morning," Burgess said, "Clough was coming out of a nightclub in Arenys de Mar, just up the coast from Barcelona, and somebody shot him. Dead."

"Who?"

"Girl named Amanda Khan. Supposed to be some kind of pop star—that's why it's going to be a *big* story—but I can't say as I've ever heard of her. Sounds like an A-rab to me."

"She's half Pakistani," said Banks. *Amanda Khan.* Clough's new girlfriend. Emily's replacement.

"Whatever. Anyway, it sounds like the classic love triangle from what I've managed to pick up so far. Seems that Clough jilted her for some dago bimbo, and this Amanda was a few stops closer to Barking than he realized. Funny old world, innit?"

"You can say that again." Banks didn't usually smoke in the mornings, but he reached for his cigarettes.

"What makes it even funnier," Burgess went on, "is that she used one of Clough's own guns. Fine irony, that. She was staying at his villa, and apparently he was carrying on with this Dolores Somebody-or-other right under her eyes and trying to palm Amanda off on one of the servants. She picked up one of Clough's guns and waited for them until they came out of the club. Shades of Ruth Ellis."

"Indeed." Ruth Ellis was the last woman to be hanged in England; she had shot her lover outside a London pub. "Was the girl hurt?"

"Winged. One bullet in her upper arm. Flesh wound. Nothing serious. According to my Spanish sources, the Khan woman fired six shots. Two of them hit Clough: one in his ugly mug and one in his miserable bloody heart. Wonder it didn't just bounce off, but he was dead before he hit the ground. Two hit Jamie Gilbert: one in the chest and one in the groin. He's not dead, but they say he'll never be quite the same again and his voice has gone up a few octaves. One shot hit the girl, and the last hit an innocent bystander in the hand, a local teenager. He lost two fingers."

"So," said Banks, "justice of a kind."

"Best we'll get."

"Thanks for calling. The girl, how is she?"

"Amanda Khan? Why? Don't tell me you know her, too?"

"No. I was just wondering."

"As well as anyone in the custody of the Spanish police can expect to be. Bye-bye, Banks. Have a good Christmas."

"You, too."

Banks put the phone down slowly. Clough dead. He could only feel a sense of relief that something had finally gone wrong for the bastard. For a while, Clough had seemed able to get away with anything and everything and thumb his nose at the rest of the world while he was doing it. No more. It probably wasn't very Christian to celebrate another man's death, especially on Christmas Day, but Banks would have been a hypocrite if he hadn't admitted to himself that he was glad Clough wouldn't be around to wreak his peculiar brand of havoc on the world anymore.

He also imagined the pain and confusion that must have driven Amanda Khan to such an extreme act, how those six shots had probably destroyed her life, too: her future, her career. But if any death was worth celebrating, it was Barry Clough's.

Banks stubbed out the half cigarette that remained, then went back into the kitchen and washed his hands before he started working the sausage meat into the sage-and-onion mixture. He looked at the chicken, not entirely certain which end was which.

Rubén González's delicate, joyous piano playing on "Pueblos Nuevo" drifted through from the living room. A little sunlight spilled over the long anvil-shaped top of Low Fell into the kitchen and glinted on the copper bottoms of the pans hanging from the wall. Banks heard stirrings from upstairs, old floorboards creaking. Probably Tracy. Brian liked to sleep all morning.

Banks remembered how, when they were kids, they got up before dawn to open their presents. Once, as he had been creeping around their rooms at one o'clock in the morning filling pillowcases with presents, he was certain he had felt Brian's eyes on him, awake to see if there really was a Santa Claus. Neither of them had ever referred to the incident, and Brian had acted as he always did when he opened his presents, but Banks suspected that from that Christmas on, his son had lost a little of his innocence.

That was probably how it happened, he mused—innocence was something you lost a bit at a time, over the years; it didn't just happen overnight. But there *were* intense experiences, epiphanies of a kind, that brought about quantum leaps.

Banks remembered standing by the riverbank that day, rain pitting the water, smiling like an idiot, being polite, clutching the big stone to his chest so as not to wet the gentleman passing by. Then the struggle, the hot beery breath, his heels slipping on the muddy bank, the terror, the punch. The world had changed for him that day, and even now he could still taste the dirty, sweaty cloth of the man's sleeve as he leaned against the kitchen counter.

He thought of Emily Riddle, of Rosalind, of Ruth Walker and Amanda Khan. When he heard Tracy's footsteps on the staircase, he had a sudden image of Dr. Glendenning's scalpel bisecting the spider tattoo on Emily's midriff, and he realized with a shock that the loss of innocence *never* stopped happening, that he was still losing it, that it was like a wound that never healed, and he would probably go on losing it, drop by drop, until the day he died.

Maggie Forrest wasn't sleeping well, so it didn't surprise her when the voices woke her shortly before four o'clock one morning in early May, even though she had made sure before she went to bed that all the windows in the house were shut fast.

If it hadn't been the voices, it would have been something else: a car door slamming as someone set off for an early shift; the first train rattling across the bridge; the neighbor's dog; old wood creaking somewhere in the house; the fridge clicking on and off; a pan or a glass shifting on the draining-board. Or perhaps one of the noises of the night, the kind that made her wake in a cold sweat with a thudding heart and gasp for breath as if she were drowning, not sleeping: the man she called Mr. Bones clicking up and down The Hill with his cane; the scratching at the front door; the tortured child screaming in the distance.

Or a nightmare.

She was just too jumpy these days, she told herself, trying to laugh it off. But there they were again. Definitely voices. One loud and masculine.

Maggie got out of bed and padded over to the window. The street called The Hill ran up the northern slope of the broad valley, and where Maggie lived, about halfway up, just above the railway bridge, the houses on the eastern side of the street stood atop a twenty-foot rise that sloped down to the pavement in a profusion of shrubs and small trees. Sometimes the undergrowth and foliage seemed so thick she could hardly find her way along the path to the pavement.

Maggie's bedroom window looked over the houses on the western side of The Hill and beyond, a patchwork landscape of housing estates, arterial roads, warehouses, factory chimneys and fields stretching through Bradford and Halifax all the way to the Pennines. Some days, Maggie would sit for hours and look at the view, thinking about the odd chain of events that had brought her here. Now, though, in the pre-dawn light, the distant necklaces and clusters of amber street lights took on a ghostly aspect, as if the city weren't quite real yet.

Maggie stood at her window and looked across the street. She could swear there was a hall-light on directly opposite, in Lucy's house, and when she heard the voice again she suddenly felt all her premonitions had been true.

It was Terry's voice, and he was shouting at Lucy. She couldn't hear what he was saying. Then she heard a scream, the sound of glass breaking and a thud.

Lucy.

Maggie dragged herself out of her paralysis, and with trembling hands she picked up the bedside telephone and dialed 999.

Probationary Police Constable Janet Taylor stood by her patrol car and watched the silver BMW burn, shielding her eyes from its glare, standing upwind of the foul-smelling smoke. Her partner, PC Dennis Morrisey stood beside her. One or two spectators were peeping out of their bedroom windows, but nobody else seemed very interested. Burning cars weren't exactly a novelty on this estate. Even at four o'clock in the morning.

Orange and red flames, with deep inner hues of blue and green and occasional tentacles of violet, twisted into the darkness, sending up palls of thick black smoke. Even upwind, Janet could smell the burning rubber and plastic. It was giving her a headache, and she knew her uniform and her hair would reek of it for days.

The leading fire-fighter, Gary Cullen, walked over to join them. It was Dennis he spoke to, of course; he always did. They were mates.

"What do you think?"

"Joy-riders." Dennis nodded towards the car. "We checked the number-plate. Stolen from a nice middle-class residential street in Heaton Moor, Manchester, earlier this evening."

"Why here, then?"

"Dunno. Could be a connection, a grudge or something. Someone giving a little demonstration of his feelings. Drugs, even. But that's for the lads upstairs to work out. They're the ones paid to have brains. We're done for now. Everything safe?"

"Under control. What if there's a body in the boot?"

Dennis laughed. "It'll be well-done by now, won't it? Hang on a minute, that's our radio, isn't it?"

Janet walked over to the car. "I'll get it," she said over her shoulder.

"Control to 354. Come in please, 354. Over."

Janet picked up the radio. "354 to Control. Over."

"Domestic dispute reported taking place at number thirty-five, The Hill. Repeat. Three-five. The Hill. Can you respond? Over."

Christ, thought Janet, a bloody domestic. No copper in her right mind liked domestics, especially at this time in the morning. "Will do," she sighed, looking at her watch. "ETA three minutes."

She called over to Dennis, who held up his hand and spoke a few more words to Gary Cullen before responding. They were both laughing when Dennis returned to the car.

"Tell him that joke, did you?" Janet asked, settling behind the wheel.

"Which one's that?" Dennis asked, all innocence.

Janet started the car and sped to the main road. "You know, the one about the blonde giving her first blow job."

"I don't know what you're talking about."

"Only I heard you telling it to that new PC back at the station, the lad who hadn't started shaving yet. You ought to give the poor lad a chance to make his own mind up about women, Den, instead of poisoning his mind right off the bat."

The centrifugal force almost threw them off the road as Janet took the roundabout at the top of The Hill too fast.

Dennis grasped the dashboard and hung on for dear life. "Jesus Christ. Women drivers. It's only a joke. Have you got no sense of humor?"

Janet smiled to herself as she slowed and curb-crawled down The Hill looking for number thirty-five.

"Anyway, I'm getting sick of this," Dennis said.

"Sick of what? My driving?"

"That, too. Mostly, though it's your constant bitching. It's got so a bloke can't say what's on his mind these days."

"Not if he's got a mind like a sewer. That's pollution. Anyway, it's changing times, Den. And we have to change with them or we'll end up like the dinosaurs. By the way, about that mole."

"What mole?"

"You know, the one on your cheek. Next to your nose. The one with all the hairs growing out of it."

Dennis put his hand up to his cheek. "What about it?"

"I'd get it seen to quick, if I were you. It looks cancerous to me. Ah, number thirty-five. Here we are."

She pulled over to the right side of the road and came to a halt a few yards past the house. It was a small detached residence built of redbrick and sandstone, between a plot of allotments and a row of shops. It wasn't much bigger than a cottage, with a slate roof, low-walled garden and a modern garage attached at the right. At the moment, all was quiet.

"There's a light on in the hall," Janet said. "Shall we have a dekko?"

Still fingering his mole, Dennis sighed and muttered something she took to be assent. Janet got out of the car first and walked up the path, aware of him dragging his feet behind her. The garden was overgrown and she had to push twigs and shrubbery aside as she walked. A little adrenalin had leaked into her system, put her on super alert, as it always did with domestics. The reason most cops hated them was that you never knew what was going to happen. As likely as not you'd pull the husband off the wife and then the wife would take his side and start bashing you with a rolling pin.

Janet paused by the door. Still all quiet, apart from Dennis's stertorous breathing behind her. It was too early yet for people to be going to work, and most of the late night revellers had passed out by now. Somewhere in the distance the first birds began to chatter. Sparrows, most likely, Janet thought. Mice with wings.

Seeing no doorbell, Janet knocked on the door.

No response came from inside.

She knocked harder. The hammering seemed to echo up and down the street. Still no response.

Next, Janet went down on her knees and looked through the letterbox. She could just make out a figure sprawled on the floor at the bottom of the stairs. A woman's figure. That was probable cause enough for forced entry.

"Let's go in," she said.

Dennis tried the handle. Locked. Then, gesturing for Janet to stand out of the way, he charged it with his shoulder.

Poor technique, she thought. She'd have reared back and used her foot. But Dennis was a second row rugby forward, she reminded herself, and his shoulders had been pushed up against so many arseholes in their time that they had to be strong.

The door crashed open on first contact and Dennis cannonballed into the hallway, grabbing hold of the bottom of the banister to stop himself from tripping over the still figure that lay there.

Janet was right behind him, but she had the advantage of walking in at a more dignified pace. She knelt beside the woman on the floor and felt for a pulse. Weak, but steady. One side of her face was bathed in blood.

"My God," Janet muttered. "Den? You okay?"

"Fine. You take care of her. I'll have a look around." Dennis headed upstairs.

For once, Janet didn't mind being told what to do. Nor did she mind that Dennis automatically assumed it was a woman's work to tend to the injured while the man went in search of heroic glory. Well, she *minded,* but she felt a real concern for the victim here, so she didn't want to make an issue of it.

Bastard, she thought. Whoever did this. "It's okay, love," she said, even though she suspected the woman couldn't hear her. "We'll get you an ambulance. Just hold on."

Most of the blood seemed to be coming from one deep cut just above her left ear, Janet noticed, though there was also a little smeared around the nose and lips. Punches, by the looks of it. There were also broken glass and daffodils scattered all around her, along with a damp patch on the carpet. Janet took her personal radio from her belt-hook and called for an ambulance. She was lucky it worked on The Hill; personal UHF radios had much less range than the VHF models fitted in cars, and were notoriously subject to black spots of patchy reception.

Dennis came downstairs shaking his head. "Bastard's not hiding up there," he said. He handed Janet a blanket, pillow and towel, nodding to the woman. "For her."

Janet eased the pillow under the woman's head, covered her gently with the blanket and applied the towel to the seeping wound on her temple. Well, I never, she thought, full of surprises, our Den. "Think he's done a runner?" she asked.

"Dunno. I'll have a look in the back. You stay with her till the ambulance arrives."

Before Janet could say anything, Dennis headed off towards the back of the house. He hadn't been gone more than a minute or so when she heard him call out, "Janet, come here and have a look at this. Hurry up. It could be important."

Curious, Janet looked at the injured woman. The bleeding had stopped and there was nothing else she could do. Even so, she was reluctant to leave the poor woman alone.

"Come on," Dennis called again. "Hurry up."

Janet took one last look at the prone figure and walked towards the back of the house. The kitchen was in darkness.

"Down here."

She couldn't see Dennis, but she knew that his voice came from downstairs. Through an open door to her right, three steps led down to a landing lit by a bare bulb. There was another door, most likely to the garage she thought, and around the corner were the steps down to the cellar.

Dennis was standing there, near the bottom, in front of a third door. On it was pinned a poster of a naked woman. She lay back on a brass bed with her legs wide open, fingers tugging at the edges of her vagina, smiling down at her large breasts at the viewer, inviting, beckoning him inside. Dennis stood before it, grinning.

"Bastard," Janet hissed.

"Where's your sense of humor?"

"It's *not* funny."

"What do you think it means?"

"I don't know." Janet could see light under the door, faint and flickering, as if from a faulty bulb. She also noticed a peculiar odour. "What's that smell?" she asked.

"How should I know? Rising damp? Drains?"

But it smelled like decay to Janet. Decay and sandalwood incense. She gave a little shudder.

"Shall we go in?" She was whispering without knowing why.

"I think we'd better."

Janet walked ahead of him, almost on tiptoe, down the final few steps. The adrenalin was really pumping in her veins now. Slowly, she reached out and tried the door. Locked. She moved aside, and Dennis used his foot this time. The lock splintered, and the door swung open. Dennis stood aside, bowed from the waist in a parody of gentlemanly courtesy, and said, "Ladies first."

With Dennis only inches behind her, Janet stepped into the cellar.

She barely had time to register her first impression of the small room—-mirrors, dozens of lit candles surrounding a mattress on the floor, a girl on the mattress, naked and bound, something yellow around her neck, the terrible smell stronger, despite the incense, like blocked drains and rotten meat, crude charcoal drawings on the whitewashed walls—before it happened.

He came from somewhere behind them, from one of the cellar's dark corners. Dennis turned to meet him, reaching for his baton, but he was too slow. The machete slashed first across his cheek, slicing it open from the eye to the lips. Before Dennis had time to put his hand up to staunch the blood or register the pain, the man slashed again, this time across the side of his throat. Dennis made a gurgling sound and went to his knees, eyes wide open. Warm blood gushed across Janet's face and sprayed onto the whitewashed walls in swirling abstract patterns. The hot stink of it made her gag.

She had no time to think. You never did when it really happened. All she knew was that she couldn't do anything for Dennis. Not yet. There was still the man with the knife to deal with. Hang on, Dennis, she pleaded silently. *Hang on.*

The man still seemed intent on hacking at Dennis, not finished yet, and that gave Janet enough time to slip out her side-handled baton. She had just managed to grip the handle so that the baton ran protectively along the outside of her arm, when he made his first lunge at her. He seemed shocked and surprised when his blade didn't sink into flesh and bone but was instead deflected by the hard baton.

That gave Janet the opening she needed. Bugger technique and training. She swung out and caught him on the temple. His eyes rolled back and he slumped against the wall, but he didn't go down. She moved in closer and cracked down on the wrist of his knife-hand. She heard something break. He cried out and the machete fell to the floor. Janet kicked it away into a far corner when she took the fully-extended baton with both hands, swung and caught him on the side of the head again. He tried to go after his machete, but she hit him again as hard as she could on the back of his head and then again on his cheek and once more at the base of his skull. He reared up, still on his knees, spouting obscenities at her, and she lashed out one more time, cracking his temple. He fell against the wall, where the back of his head left a long dark smear on the whitewash as he slid down, and rested there, legs extended. Pink foam bubbled at the side of his mouth, then stopped. Janet hit him once more, a two-handed blow on the top of his skull, then she took out her handcuffs and secured him to one of the pipes running along the bottom of the wall. He groaned and stirred, so she hit him once more, two-handed, on the top of the skull. When he fell silent, she went over to Dennis.

He was still twitching, but the spurts of blood from his wound were getting weaker. Janet struggled to remember her first aid training. She made a compress from her hand-

kerchief and pressed it tight against the severed artery, trying to nip the ends together. Next she tried to make the 10-9
call on her personal radio—officer in urgent need of assistance. But it was no good. All she got was static. A *black
spot*. Nothing to do now but sit and wait for the ambulance
to arrive. She could hardly move, go outside, not with Dennis like this. She couldn't leave him.

So Janet sat cross-legged and rested Dennis's head on her
lap, cradling and muttering nonsense in his ear. The ambulance would come soon, she told him. He would be fine, just
wait and see. But it seemed that no matter how tightly she
held the compress, blood leaked through to her uniform. She
could feel its warmth on her fingers, her belly and thighs.
Please, Dennis, she prayed, *please* hang on.

Above Lucy's house, Maggie could see the crescent sliver of
a new moon and the faint silver thread it drew around the old
moon's darkness. *The old moon in the new moon's arms.* An
ill-omen. Sailors believed that the sight of it, especially
through glass, presaged a storm and much loss of life. Maggie shivered. She wasn't superstitious, but there was something chilling about the sight, something that reached out
and touched her from way back in time when people paid
more attention to cosmic events such as the cycles of the
moon.

She looked back down at the house and saw the police car
arrive, heard the woman officer knock and call out, then saw
her male partner charge the door.

After that, Maggie heard nothing for a while—perhaps
five or ten minutes—until she fancied she heard a heart-
tending, keening wail from deep inside the bowels of house.
But it could have been her imagination. The sky was a
lighter blue now and the dawn chorus had struck up. Maybe
it was a bird? But she knew that no bird sounded so desolate
or godforsaken as that cry, not even the loon on a lake or the
curlew up on the moors.

Maggie rubbed the back of her neck and kept watching.

Seconds later, an ambulance pulled up. Then another police car. Then paramedics. The ambulance attendants left the front door open, and Maggie could see them kneeling by someone in the hall. Someone covered with a fawn blanket. They lifted the figure onto a wheeled stretcher and pushed her down the path to the ambulance, back doors open and waiting. It all happened so quickly that Maggie couldn't see clearly who it was, but she thought she could glimpse Lucy's jet-black hair spread out against a white pillow.

So it was as she has thought. She gnawed at her thumbnail. Should she have done something sooner? She had certainly had her suspicions, but could she somehow have prevented this? What could she have done?

Next to arrive looked like a plainclothes police officer. He was soon followed by five or six men who put on disposable white overalls before they went inside the house. Someone also put up white and blue tape across the front gate and blocked off a long stretch of the pavement, including the nearest bus-stop, and the entire side of the road number thirty-five stood on, reducing The Hill to one lane of traffic in order to make room for police vehicles and ambulances.

Maggie wondered what was going on. Surely they wouldn't go to all this trouble unless it was something really serious? Was Lucy dead? Had Terry finally killed her? Perhaps that was it; that would make them pay attention.

As the daylight grew, the scene became even stranger. More police cars arrived, and another ambulance. As the attendants wheeled a second stretcher out, the first morning bus went down The Hill and obscured Maggie's view. She could see the passengers turn their heads, the ones on her side of the road standing up to get a look at what was happening, but she couldn't see who lay on the stretcher. Only that two policemen got in after it.

Next, a hunched figure shrouded in a blanket stumbled down the path, supported on each side by uniformed policemen. At first Maggie had no idea at first who it was. A woman, she thought from her general outline and the cut of her dark hair. Then she thought she glimpsed the dark blue uniform. *The policewoman.* Breath caught in her throat. What could have happened to change her so much so fast?

By now there was far more activity than Maggie had ever thought the scene of a domestic argument could engender. At least half a dozen police cars had arrived, some of them unmarked. A wiry man with closely-cropped dark hair got out of a blue Renault and walked into the house as if he owned the place. Another man who went in looked like a doctor. At least he carried a black bag and had that self-important air about him. People up and down The Hill were going to work now, driving their cars out of their garages or waiting for the bus at the temporary bus-stop someone from the depot had put up. Little knots of them gathered by the house, watching, but the police came over and moved them on.

Maggie looked at her watch. Half past six. She had been kneeling at the window for two and a half hours, yet she felt as if she had been watching a quick succession of events, as if it had been done by time-lapse photography. When she got to her feet she heard her knees crack, and the broadloom carpet had made deep red criss-cross marks on her skin.

There was far less activity outside the house now, just the police guards and the detectives coming and going, standing on the pavement to smoke, shake their heads and talk in low voices. The knot of haphazardly-parked cars outside Lucy's house caused traffic back-ups.

Weary and confused, Maggie threw on jeans and a T-shirt and went downstairs to make a cup of tea and some toast. As she filled the kettle, she noticed that her hand was shaking. They would want to talk to her, no doubt about that. And when they did, what would she tell them?

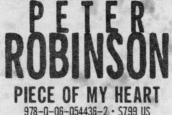